For the First Time in Her Life,
She Felt Like the Woman
She Was Born to Be. . . .

His lips ground into hers fiercely, hungrily, parting them, and his tongue raked her mouth, luxuriating in its sweetness. Alexis clung to him as he began to explore her neck. His breath against her skin seared like flames while his lips and teeth and tongue evoked little whimpers of pleasure from her throat. Her name sounded like a groan upon his lips, and he kissed her again, dizzyingly. Alexis dug her fingers into his hair as if to hold him there forever, her breath rasping and quick. The world was suddenly a hot, wild kaleidoscope of emotion, and for the first time she felt that her senses were really alive.

Suddenly Brant released her and stepped back. She could hear his breath struggling in his throat. "I want you," he said.

Also published by POCKET BOOKS/RICHARD GALLEN

The Velvet Promise
  by Jude Deveraux

Some Distant Shore
  by Margaret Pemberton

The Sun Dancers
  by Barbara Faith

The Golden Sky

KRISTIN JAMES

PUBLISHED BY RICHARD GALLEN BOOKS
Distributed by POCKET BOOKS

Ⓡ A RICHARD GALLEN BOOKS *Original* publication
Distributed by
POCKET BOOKS, a Simon & Schuster division of
GULF & WESTERN CORPORATION
1230 Avenue of the Americas, New York, N.Y. 10020

ISBN: 0-671-42773-3

First Pocket Books printing April, 1981

10 9 8 7 6 5 4 3 2 1

RICHARD GALLEN and colophon are trademarks of
Simon & Schuster and Richard Gallen & Co., Inc.

Printed in the U.S.A.

To
Pete Hopcus,
for his love and persistence

The Golden Sky

Chapter 1

The phone shrilled, startling Alexis, who had been bent over the *Southwest 2d Reporter*, her forehead creased in concentration. With a sigh, she stretched and looked at her watch. As usual, she had let time slip away from her, and if she did not hurry, she would be late for her date tonight. The phone buzzed persistently, and she picked it up.

"Alexis Stone," she said crisply as she marked her place in the book and sat it atop a stack of similar tomes.

"Sorry to bother you," her secretary said, "but it's Mr. Stone."

"All right, put him on," Alexis replied, and smiled. No secretarial wall of silence had ever withstood Alec Stone.

"Alexis?" His voice was deep and impatient. "I need to see you up here right away."

She felt a spurt of disappointment that his call was not a friendly chat, but a quick business summons. Quickly she dismissed the feeling. Its occurrence was much too common to let it get to her.

"Okay, be right up." She matched him terseness for terseness. It would be useless to point out to him that it was six-thirty on a Friday afternoon and that she had a date with Darrell at eight. He would simply dismiss those points as immaterial and would then have an opportunity to accuse her of thinking like a female. She had spent far too much time and effort trying to convince her father that she didn't have a speck of feminine weakness to be lost on someone like Darrell Ingram. Truth be known, she couldn't have cared less if she had to cancel the date entirely.

Grabbing a yellow legal pad and pen on her way out, Alexis strode briskly to the elevator. "Up here," where she had been commanded to appear, was the top floor of the twenty-story, blue-glassed Stone Building, a familiar landmark to those who traveled the Central Expressway daily. The top floor was the home of the executive offices, the largest and most beautiful of which belonged to the chairman of the board and president of Stone Oil Company, Inc.: Mr. Alec Stone.

With a *whoosh*, the elevator doors opened onto a waiting room containing heavy Spanish-style furniture and plush, rust-colored carpeting. Alexis waved to Mrs. Jenkins, her father's long-suffering secretary, as she pushed through the swinging glass door and crossed the outer office to the massive wooden door that closed it off from the president's. She gave Mrs. Jenkins a questioning raise of the eyebrows before she pulled the handle. The executive secretary nodded.

"Alexis!" her father boomed as she came in. "Good to see you. Sit down."

"Hello, Daddy," she replied, and sank into the cushy velvet chair closest to his desk. It was too tall and straight against her back and too deep a seat for a woman, even one as long-legged as she. However, she knew her father's psychology, and this was the seat he expected her to take. Elegant and nearest to him, it was the chair of power and intimacy. The more comfortable one farther away indicated fear.

"Alexis, I have a problem I want you to solve," he said, settling himself on a corner of his desk, his fingers tapping restlessly against a file folder lying there.

Alexis allowed a brief smile to touch her lips and

spread her hands in a palms-up gesture. "That's what I went to law school for."

"Well, it'll take more than law school to handle this one. That's why I want a member of the family to do it. There's a lease I want in Barrett. I'm positive there's a good natural gas deposit on the land. I always had a hunch about it, ever since I was there in the late fifties with the Thompson Number One, and now our geologists' latest findings confirm it. I'm going to drill there, but that damn fool Brant McClure is standing in my way."

"He owns the property?"

"Yes, and he refuses to lease it to me for love or money. I've had my best men up there bargaining with him, and he won't budge an inch. Stubborn as a mule." He sighed and handed her the folder. "Here is everything I have on him. Not much leverage for us, I'm afraid."

Alexis took the file and flipped it open, casually scanning the statistics: thirty-four, single, parents divorced, father dead, one sister, one illegitimate son; hair brown, eyes hazel, height six foot three, weight two hundred pounds, one identifiable scar on upper right arm.

"His father was Judson McClure, a stiff-necked, stubborn man if I ever saw one," Stone continued, running a hand through his dark, thick hair. "He had a real thing about oil. I wanted to drill on his land when I was there on the Thompson well, but he refused, and . . . well, I never followed up on it."

"Is Brant's mother still living?"

"Yes. I think she is in New Mexico, married to a pharmacist or some such. The report says that she never comes to visit her children. I think there's some bad feeling there. Her name is Selena—beautiful woman."

"You knew her?"

"Yes, when I was in Barrett on the Thompson Number One. I was there on and off for the better part of the year. It was a very important well to me . . . I was taking a big risk on it. Anyway, I met quite a few people in Barrett—not that anyone there is very interesting."

He paused and Alexis turned the page to skim over the report. Brant McClure sounded ordinary enough. He had played football in high school and at Texas Tech, although he had left college after two and a half years. Then he had gone into the army for three years, one of them in Vietnam.

"Apparently he's never had any serious romantic entanglements," her father said with a tone of regret. "No scandals or broken marriages. He seems to date casually and offer no expectations. About the only thing we have on him is the kid."

Alexis smiled ruefully. Alec Stone had little compunction about using blackmail to get what he wanted, and it always disappointed him when he was unable to find such a toehold.

"Well, there it is. Do with it what you can. I want you to go up there tomorrow and talk to him. I'll call Rusty Thompson and see if you can use his landing strip. Funny thing, McClure's sister, Elizabeth, is married to Rusty Thompson, one of the biggest gas and oil leasers in the Panhandle! I bet old Judson had apoplexy over that!"

Alexis suppressed a sigh. Her father had never heard of weekends. It would be pointless to ask to wait until Monday. Usually she paid no more attention to days off than he did, but this week she had been looking forward to a little rest. For some reason, she had been feeling tired and dissatisfied of late.

Alec jabbed at a button and spoke into his intercom. "Mrs. Jenkins, get Rusty Thompson in Barrett on the phone for me." He looked back at his daughter. "Better take your own plane. Wertz has the company plane up in Canada right now."

"Tell me something," Alexis began. "Why do you

think I can do better with this McClure fellow than your other people?"

"Because you are *my* daughter, that's why," Stone replied firmly. "You have proved who you are, Alexis. I know you are as stubborn as I am, and you won't give up until you come back with lease in hand. You are hard and smart and persistent and ruthless, just like me. And that is what I need. Besides, I thought maybe a woman could get to him."

A despairing giggle burst from Alexis's throat. "Oh, Daddy . . . it says here that he's thirty-four years old, still single, and has never had a serious relationship! He probably *can't* be lured by a woman!"

Alec gave a short grunt of laughter. "Well, he left a bastard in Vietnam, so he must have some liking for women. In fact, that's about the only thing we have on him. He fathered a kid by a Saigon girl and left the boy behind when he was shipped back to the States in 1971. Ever since 1972, he's been trying to get the kid out of Saigon, but with no success."

"First he abandoned the boy, then he wants him back. Sounds like a strange sort. What is the child's name?"

"Paul . . . Huang Li, over there."

"I take it you think you can get Paul out of Vietnam if McClure will sign the lease."

"Exactly." Her father smiled, a faint trace of pride on his face. "I am not without influence with our government . . . and with some others as well. Oil calls the tune now. Don't forget that."

Alexis stirred uncomfortably. Maybe it wasn't as bad as blackmail, merely a little bribery, but she didn't want to use it. Alec wouldn't have a qualm about exploiting that weakness of fatherly feeling, but his daughter felt a sting of dislike and guilt at the idea.

"Don't you think using his child against him is a little cruel?" she asked, keeping her tone cool and slightly sardonic. She didn't want to lower herself in Alec's estimation by displaying either emotion or moral rebuke.

Alec shrugged away her question. "Why? He can't do it by himself, and I can get the child for him. He gets the kid, we get the lease, and everybody benefits. Where's the harm in that?"

"Well, let's just hope your methods never get investigated," Alexis said lightly, dismissing the subject. She was not about to tell her father that she doubted she could use the boy to obtain the lease. She could not bear to feed on another person's anxiety or love, to hold a man's son out as a reward or punishment.

"He has enough money, so he can afford to turn down my lease, though why any reasonable business-man would do that, I can't imagine. His main assets, of course, are the ranch—about ten thousand acres—and his cattle. The land is estimated at about three or four million dollars. Not that much liquidity, but he isn't a pauper. He doesn't need the money, and apparently he doesn't want it. The kid is the only thing we've got . . . unless, of course, you can use your feminine wiles to persuade him."

"So you are going to throw your virgin daughter into the volcano," Alexis remarked in an amused but brittle tone.

Stone frowned, his blue eyes darkening. He had never liked her levity. "Don't be an idiot, Al—as if any twenty-six-year-old woman were a virgin these days! Anyway, I'm not saying you have to sleep with him. All I'm saying is, get that lease for me. I don't care if you bribe him, blackmail him, seduce him, or what. Just come back with that lease."

Alexis stirred and sighed. Her shoulders were aching now from an afternoon spent hunched over the law books. "Okay, will do."

"Good." Alec rose on the word and moved behind his desk, satisfied. His intercom buzzed, and he said, "That must be Rusty on the line. Have a good trip, and come up here as soon as you get back." He pushed in a button on the intercom. "Yes?"

Alexis stood up, put the folder beneath her arm, and started for the door. She knew she had been dismissed. That was Alec Stone for you, and it was foolish of her to feel this hot pricking behind her eyes or to wish that he had said a few personal words to her. But that was not the way of a man who, after twenty-odd years, still did not call his secretary by her first name. Alexis knew she ought to be pleased that he had entrusted this matter to her, that he had told her she was just like him. After all, wasn't that what she had been working for all her life? It was for his approval, even if that were only tacit.

Although the Central Expressway could never be called uncrowded, the worst traffic was over as Alexis made her way to her North Dallas condominium. The quiet hum of her elegant silver-green Mercedes did not soothe her jangled nerves, and she began to go over her father's words. He had said that she was hard, persistent, smart, and ruthless, but she knew he wasn't entirely accurate in his assessment of her. She wasn't ruthless; sometimes she thought she wasn't even very hard. Unlike Alec, who would use any means, fair or foul, to get what he wanted, she would not. She had little taste for bullying or blackmailing or bribing.

Apparently she had given a good imitation of hardness. God knows, she had tried, for in the legal jungle a woman who showed any weakness would be driven to her knees by male lawyers. In negotiations, she had been as tough as or tougher than the men, knowing that any other behavior on her part would be taken advantage of. At least she had fooled her father and, she supposed, the others, even if after every confrontation her stomach was a bundle of nerves and her knees went weak.

Alexis wished, suddenly, that she had someone to talk to. It was at times like this, when she felt the ambivalence of trying to follow her father's demands

despite her weaknesses, or of struggling with her own
morals against her love for her father and the desire to
please him, that she wished she could pour out all her
mixed-up feelings into a sympathetic ear. But to whom
could she turn? Certainly not to her mother, who was
violently opposed to any sort of conflict or problem;
she would just dither and worry and leave Alexis more
confused than ever. And not to Darrell Ingram, either;
Alexis did not feel close enough to him to reveal
anything of herself or her family. To her sister Morgan,
maybe; Alexis felt closest to her. But Morgan would
probably be out on a date. Anyway, Morgan had never
had to strive to please their father; she had simply been
loved for her beauty. After the Stones' divorce,
Morgan had always been on their mother's side; more
than once she had engaged their father in stormy
argument. Alexis doubted that Morgan would have any
trouble deciding between Alec and her own conscience.

Alexis signaled for her exit and crossed under the
expressway. Fifteen minutes later she entered the stone
and iron gates of the condominium complex. The
security guard waved to her from his little sentry box.
She smiled back at him, then drove past the tennis
courts, clubhouse, pool, and along the golf course,
turning at last into her street and pulling into her
garage.

She hurried inside and up the stairs to her bedroom,
hardly noticing her elegant surroundings. Her mother
and Morgan had decorated the place for her; Alexis
had never had the time or the desire to do it herself.
Shades of blue and gray and white lent a tranquil look
to her home. The furniture was plain, almost stark: the
chairs and couch a pale blue and white print, the tables
chrome and glass. But the delicate silk prints and ink
sketches that adorned the walls softened the effect of
the severe furnishings.

Upstairs, in Alexis's bedroom, guest room, and
study, the modernistic chrome and glass gave way to
the muted tones of ash and fruitwood. Here the plush

carpet was deep blue, perfectly coordinated with each room's accessories. Morgan's decorating efforts had suited Alexis's personality very well, even down to the surprising luxury of the sunken marble bath.

As she mounted the stairs, Alexis decided that she simply did not have the energy to see Darrell tonight. All she wanted was to eat a light supper, relax a little, and go to bed early in preparation for flying to Barrett the next day. Alexis knew she could call Darrell and cancel the date; he would not mind. Her father's plans would come first with him. She suspected that it was Alec Stone's wealth on which Darrell Ingram had his eyes set, not on Alexis Stone's allurements.

Quickly, Alexis shrugged out of her gray jacket and kicked off her shoes, then peeled herself out of skirt, blouse, and hose to stand in blessed freedom in only her slip and underwear. She stretched, rolled her head to release the built-up tension in her neck, then strode to the phone and punched out Darrell's number.

"Hello?" he answered in a deep baritone.

"Hello, Darrell, this is Alexis."

"Yes!" His reply was heartily cheerful. "I was just getting ready to pick you up."

"Well, there has been a snag. Daddy called me up to his office before I left, and I just got home. So it'll be at least another hour before I'm ready. I'm afraid that will spoil our going to the play, won't it?"

"That's all right. I can get the tickets changed to another night, and we can go to a movie or something instead." His voice was concerned, and Alexis wondered why she always suspected his motives and why she never felt much warmth in return.

"If you don't mind," she said, "I think I'd rather call it off for tonight. Daddy is sending me to the Panhandle tomorrow, and I should get to bed early tonight. Besides, I'm dead tired, and I still have some work to do."

"Sure, I understand," Darrell replied evenly, his voice sympathetic but coolly logical. "We'll make it some other time, maybe next weekend. Will you be back by then?"

"I hope so."

"Well, we can set it up tentatively for next Saturday, and I'll try to get the tickets changed for then. How does that sound?"

"Great. I really appreciate it, Darrell."

"Don't give it another thought. Have a good time on your trip."

Alexis laughed shortly. "I'm afraid this is shaping up as anything but a pleasure trip."

He joined in her laughter. "Good luck, then. That may be more appropriate. Call me when you get back."

"Okay, I will. Good-bye, Darrell."

"Bye."

Alexis hung up the phone with a vague feeling of dissatisfaction. She had gotten out of the date, just as she had wanted, and Darrell had been very pleasant about it. But, unreasonably, she wished he had displayed a little temper or disappointment or had tried to argue her out of not going. Surely, if he had any feeling for her, he would have been more anxious to see her.

She went into the bathroom, turned on the water in the tub, and swiftly removed the pins that held her thick red-gold hair in a soft bun on the crown of her head. Luxuriating in the release that taking down her hair always brought, she pushed her hands into the mass of curls and gently massaged her scalp. A long, warm bath would complete the relaxation process, she thought, and then perhaps she would be rested enough to tackle packing and another look at that file.

Studying her reflection in the mirror over the bathroom sink, Alexis picked up her brush and began to pull it rhythmically through her hair. She was not unattractive, she thought. Oh, not a beauty like Morgan or her mother, but still, more than passable. The thick, lush hair that tumbled to her shoulders was an unusual color, neither red nor blonde, but a shade somewhere in between. The face it framed was thin, with high, angular cheekbones and a firm chin that bespoke determination. Straight, narrow, red-brown brows slashed across her forehead in perfect opposition to the straight, vertical line of her nose. Beneath her brows, clear, dark blue eyes stared gravely back at her, framed in lashes so long and thick that their shadow turned her eyes almost violet. Her figure was tall and leggy, and her breasts, though not large, were high and firm.

Alexis bit her lip thoughtfully as she stripped off her remaining clothes and stepped into the tub. It was not like her to assess her looks, any more than it was like her to feel this strange disquiet and fatigue that she had been experiencing the past few weeks. Whatever was the matter with her?

For a long time she remained in the bath while the heat pulled the tension from her muscles. Her mind was at rest, merely floating lazily along. Finally, feeling much better, she got out and wrapped herself in a thick towel.

The phone rang just as she had finished drying off. Quickly, she fastened the towel around her and dashed to the bedroom. "Hello?" she said breathlessly.

"Hello, darling," a laughing male voice responded. "You must have known it was me—sounds like you ran to answer."

Alexis giggled. "Oh, Nick!"

"What are you doing home on a Friday night? Not that I'm not glad to catch you, of course, but a lovely thing like yourself shouldn't be sitting around dateless."

"Nick, you're hopeless," Alexis said, smiling. Nick Fletcher had lived in the dark Tudor home next to her father's spacious Colonial in Highland Park when she was a girl. Ever since she could remember, Nick had been her friend, even though he was two years older than she and possessed of a happy-go-lucky personality she had never been able to understand. Nick was a wealthy playboy, a country-club type who was more

interested in cars and tennis and raising hell than in any
profession or business. Fortunately for him, his father
had made more than enough money in real estate
investments to support Nick in the lifestyle he chose.
He did not understand Alexis's seriousness and ambition, and she did not understand his frivolity, but she
could not help liking him. He was one person she could
always feel comfortable with.

"Since I was lucky enough to catch you," he went on,
"how about going out with me? I was thinking of going
dancing."

"Where?"

"Élan?" he suggested, naming an elegant nightclub.
"Whiskey River?"

"Tell me, what is a handsome man like you doing
without a date on a Friday night?"

Alexis could picture his cheerful shrug and dancing
grin as he replied, "I was stood up. Sad but true."

"Oh, so I'm second choice, huh?" Alexis bantered
playfully.

"But always first in my heart," he countered, and she
laughed.

Lately, there had been times when Nick seemed
more serious in his joking offers of romance, and this
disturbed Alexis. She told herself that she was imagin-
ing things, that no one like Nick would ever have any
interest in a drone like her, that surely he must realize
how little they had in common. He was a pleasant
companion for now and then, but Alexis knew he
would never be anything more to her. Nick couldn't
really believe that she could be anything more to him.

"Well, I hate to turn down an offer like that," Alexis
said, "but I have to fly to the Panhandle early tomorrow."

"I see the hand of Alec Stone in this," he mocked.

"Too true. It's business, as usual."

"Haven't you given up enough of your life for your
father?" Nick asked, his voice turning suddenly grim.

"What are you talking about!" Alexis retorted, shocked that his question hurt.

"Don't pull that innocent act with me, Alexis. Remember, this is Nick talking, the one who's known you since you were nine."

"Just because you've known me so long doesn't mean you know what you're talking about," Alexis replied hotly. "I haven't given up my life for my father!"

"No?" he said coolly. "Then who is it you've been driving yourself for all these years, if not for Alec Stone? Do you know that this Darrell character is the first guy you've ever dated for any length of time, and he's a real zero?"

"You don't even know him."

"Oh, I've met him, honey, and that's all it took. He's got about as much real emotion as a dead fish."

Alexis could not restrain the giggle that bubbled up at this description. "Nick, that's unkind . . . True, I'm afraid, but unkind. Still, that doesn't have anything to do with Daddy. I was just never very interested in anyone. I had too much work to do."

"I know. You had to finish high school a year early and then college a year early. Why, you were only twenty-three when you graduated from law school. And you had to make the highest grades—Dean's list, Phi Beta Kappa, Honors, and all that—not to mention the *Law Review* and the Order of the Coif when you got to law school. Next it was the bar you had to study for, and not just pass, which is all that's necessary, but get a high mark as well. Then, for the past three years, you've devoted yourself to the legal department of Stone Oil. Others might take off evenings and week-ends, but not Alexis Stone, no, sir. *She* has to work every night till eight or nine, and every Saturday, too."

"I always have work to do."

"If there was that much extra work to do, they ought to hire another lawyer. You know as well as I do that you've been trying to get your hard-working, flint-hearted daddy to notice you, to say, 'Good girl.'"

"Nick, that's not true!" Alexis cried angrily. "Daddy's not hardhearted. He's just wrapped up in his company. Besides, he always wanted a son."

"Uh-huh." Nick paused pointedly. "I remember, even if you don't, Alexis Stone, your saying when you were thirteen years old, 'I have to be the best, Nicky, because Daddy never got a boy. Sometime I'm going to do something wonderful, and then he'll say that I'm better than any old boy.'"

Alexis sighed and shifted uneasily. She could remember the incident as well as Nick, and she had to admit it was true. "Oh, all right, I guess I have always been overly ambitious, and I did always want Daddy to notice me. But is it so wrong to be hard-working?"

"I wouldn't know about that." Nick's voice had regained some of its former lightness. "I've never done a lick of work myself. It seems a little silly to me, when you've got all that lovely money sitting there, wanting to be spent."

Alexis laughed. "You ought to be Morgan's friend, not mine. You two would get along perfectly."

He joined in her laughter. "No, we'd be broke within a year."

"Anyway, I've started dating some now. Witness Darrell Ingram."

Nick snorted. "He's no competition for anybody, let alone your father! What you need is somebody who knows how to laugh and have a good time, a skilled lover and a born entertainer, somebody strong enough to knock all that nonsense out of your stubborn, beautiful head."

"And I presume you are applying for said position?" Alexis returned sarcastically.

"Who better? I have a terrific idea, Alexis. Instead of going to the Panhandle this weekend on business, come to Las Vegas with me. We can wallow in all kinds of sinful, sybaritic, completely unproductive delights. How does that sound?"

"Nick, you are a dear person, and a very good friend. But you'll just have to accept me the way I am. I doubt if I'll ever change very much. Frankly, I can't see why you're interested in me at all."

"Well, number one, we were two lonely little rich kids growing up together. Number two, you are very attractive and quite pleasurable to be with, when you let yourself relax. Number three, my father always said you might make a man out of me if anybody could, which he doubted. And, number four, I happen to have been in love with you for some time now."

Alexis drew in her breath, taken aback by his last statement. He had to be teasing. Nick Fletcher could not possibly be in love with her. On the heels of that thought came another—poor Nick. She knew she was not in the slightest in love with him. "Nick, I—" She stopped awkwardly.

"Oh, don't worry, it's nothing new. Everyone else has known it for years. You're just slow on the uptake. I'm not going to plague you with it." His voice sounded as it always did. "Well, if you're still going to be cruel and stuck-up and to deny me my fun, I guess I'll just have to find a more willing girl."

Alexis smiled faintly. "I'm sorry, Nick, but I can't go. I really have to fly to Barrett tomorrow."

"I know. I know. I've always heard the Stones had oil in their veins instead of blood."

Alexis laughed. "Nick, you are my dearest friend—"

"I hope so. Be careful, now. I'll see you when you get back."

"Okay. Bye, Nick."

"Good-bye."

Abstractedly, Alexis rose and tossed her towel into the bathroom, then pulled on a loose robe. Nick had left her confused and a little sad. Had he really meant that about loving her? He couldn't have; he couldn't have loved her for years without her having noticed. Or had she always been so wrapped up in her career and herself that she hadn't seen what was plain to others? She sighed. One more thing to add to the confusion and disturbance she had been feeling lately.

After she had dressed, she went downstairs to whip up a light dinner, ate it with dispatch, and returned to her room to pack. Alexis believed in traveling light and abhorred taking more than one suitcase, but it was difficult to know what to take to a place with such uncertain weather as the Panhandle of Texas, and for an indefinite period of time. Anyway, what were the best outfits to impress and persuade a stubborn young rancher?

She pulled out a light coat from her closet. Although the late-October days in Dallas were still quite warm, she knew that in the arid Panhandle, which lay much farther north, the weather was likely to be chilly, especially in the evenings and mornings. She had known it to freeze and even snow there at this time of year. Jeans and boots and comfortable tops were a must, too, she imagined; she might have to follow Brant McClure into the pastures to get him to listen to her. And, of course, the tailored, dressy sort of suits that she favored for business wear. Two or three should do it, and shoes to go with them. She pondered her wardrobe thoughtfully, her eyes narrowing. Perhaps she also ought to take a fancier, more feminine kind of dress, something suitable for the evening, just in case. She had found in the past that it was better to be prepared for all contingencies.

Once she had finished packing, Alexis washed her face, brushed her teeth, and slipped into her night-gown. She set her alarm for early the next morning. She wanted to be in her plane and on the way by nine o'clock. Taking a pad, she jotted down her flight plan for tomorrow, then picked up the phone and dialed the flight weather service to check on the conditions along her route.

These details finished, she settled down in bed to read Brant McClure's folder before she went to sleep. This time she studied it slowly, but came up with little that was new. She put it aside and picked up the picture that lay on the bottom. It was an enlarged, glossy photograph that looked to be a candid shot, probably from a newspaper, its lines somewhat blurred by the blowup. In the photo, McClure's head was turned toward someone to the side, his eyes intent. She saw a firm, square jaw and stern mouth, hair that was neither long nor short, and a nose that was unremarkable except for a slight irregularity near the top. There was no particular feature that stood out, but Alexis had the impression of implacable strength and leashed power. No smile touched him anywhere.

She stared at the picture for several minutes, as though she could find the man's soul hidden on his face. This man had abandoned his son, had carelessly fathered a mixed-blood child and left him in the less-than-kindly hands of the Communists. This man seemingly had no commitments to anyone, floating as he had through years of casual relationships with women. Looking at his hard jaw and chin, his compressed lips, Alexis could believe it; no emotion showed on his face. And yet he had also searched for and located that son and had tried for eight years to bring the boy to the States. She could see that, too: the stubbornness, the will, the power that did not count the odds. Was there love there as well?

With a snap, she closed the file. Now she was getting downright fanciful about the whole thing. She would be better off planning how she was going to get him to sign the lease. It seemed like a hopeless situation. Why was her father so insistent on this piece of land? And why did he think she would have any influence with Brant McClure?

He's a cowboy, she told herself scornfully, and no doubt he'll resent a woman lawyer. She would probably be lucky if he didn't tell her she ought to be at home in the kitchen, where she belonged. He certainly didn't look like the easy kind who would succumb to the use of soft, feminine wiles, which she had never had any skill with anyway. If that would be the thing to convince him, her father should have sent Morgan instead.

Certainly there was no reason to think McClure would accept rational arguments from Alexis when he had obviously accepted them from no one else. She knew she couldn't use the tactics her father had recommended, and with both reason and force gone, what was left? It looked as though she was setting an impossible task for herself . . . or, rather, Alec was.

Yet she knew she could not bear to come home without the lease, as a failure in her father's eyes, just when he was beginning to think she was a success.

The phone rang harshly, interrupting Alexis's thoughts, and she sighed with exasperation. She would not be able to get anything done, or even get to sleep early, if these calls continued.

The soft, breathy voice of her mother sounded in her ear. "This is Ginny. How are you?"

"Fine," Alexis replied, resigning herself to a wasted half hour. It was hard to get her mother off the phone in anything less.

Ten years ago, when Alexis was still in high school, her newly divorced mother had decreed that her daughters stop calling her "Mama" and call her by her first name, Ginny, instead. She wanted to be their friend, Ginny said, although Alexis suspected that she didn't want any of her new dates to hear an almost grown girl call her Mother. Morgan was so much like their mother in looks and interests that she truly was a friend to her, and she had no trouble calling her mother Ginny. Nor had the youngest girl, Cara, who now at nineteen had known her as Ginny as long as she had known her as Mama. But for Alexis, the habit had been hard to break, and she still felt a twinge of discomfort saying "Ginny," which resulted in her avoiding as often as possible the use of any name at all.

"I just called to see how you were, dear. What have you been up to lately?"

Alexis knew that the business matters which occupied the majority of her time were not things that counted in her mother's perception of "being up" to something. So she searched her mind for the more social things she had done recently. "Well, I was going with Darrell Ingram to the Theater Center tonight, but I left work too late, so we decided not to go."

"Oh, you must!" Ginny bubbled excitedly. She was on her own ground here, something that did not often occur with her eldest daughter. "Morgan saw the play on Wednesday and said it was marvelous. An old play, of course, but she said they had staged it well and revamped it quite a bit without spoiling it."

"Oh, we'll go next Saturday, I'm sure. Darrell said he would exchange the tickets."

"I'm sorry you didn't go out with him tonight," her mother remarked politely. "He seems like a nice young man."

Alexis laughed and said teasingly, "Now, don't try to con me, Ma—Ginny. I know that your heart is set on my marrying Nick Fletcher, and has been ever since I was ten."

"Well, he is such a handsome man, and so witty. I think he is exactly what you need to spark you up."

"Mama, I have no desire to marry a playboy, even if I loved Nick, which I don't. He has no purpose in life. He is never serious about anything. He goes through women the way he goes through cars. He drinks too much. And, he is unbearably lazy."

"Well, he does play the field a lot now, but that doesn't mean he would after you got married. Besides, serious men can be just as unfaithful as fun-loving ones, you know. Sometimes I think the ambitious ones are the worst."

Alexis frowned. It was not like Ginny to be so cynical or blunt. "Anyway"—she took up the argument—"what makes you think Nick wants to marry *me*? He certainly has never given me that impression." She was not about to get into the subject of Nick's feelings with her mother.

"That is because you ignore him. Everyone else knows the poor boy has been crazy about you for years."

"Ginny, you are exaggerating," Alexis demurred, but faintly, remembering Nick's words of a few hours ago.

"No, I'm not," Ginny contended stoutly. "But I know it doesn't help for me to champion him, so I am going to shut up about it. Have you heard from Morgan since she got back?"

"No, and I didn't know she had gone anywhere."

Her mother clucked in despairing tones. "Alexis, you never pay any attention to anything but your job. She told you she was going to Puerto Vallarta last week with Cindy Dennheim."

"Who?"

"Some girl from Houston. She was in Pi Phi with Morgan."

"Oh, yes." Alexis quickly slipped away from that subject. Her refusal to join a sorority, in particular her mother's own Pi Phi, had been a sore point between them when Alexis went to The University of Texas. "So how did she like it?"

"Loved it! She came back with the most beautiful tan and brought this absolutely devastating German man with her. He is from Stuttgart and has the most divine accent. He sounds just like Maximilian Schell, and even looks like him a little, too."

"Who is Maximilian Schell?"

"I swear, Alexis, you can be so exasperating . . . He is an actor! Anyway, Helmut was in Puerto Vallarta on vacation and was so taken with Morgan that he followed her back when she came home, and is spending the rest of his vacation here so he can be around her. Isn't that exciting?"

"He's probably a gigolo," Alexis said dryly.

"Alexis! How can you say that? As if only a gigolo would be interested in Morgan!"

"Oh, I'm not saying Morgan isn't pretty enough to attract almost anybody. I'm just saying that smooth foreigners who are so smitten with American heiresses that they follow them home sound fishy to me."

Ginny sighed and then laughed reluctantly. "That's what Morgan said, too. I guess you two must be more alike than I thought."

Alexis chuckled. "Good for her. Morgan, at least, never gets carried away by her own looks. Listen, Ginny, I'm sorry, but I really have to hang up now. I have some more work to do, and I must get to sleep early. I'm flying up to Barrett tomorrow on business."

There was a moment's pause on the other end. Then Ginny said, her voice dropping in disappointment, "Oh. Will you be gone all next week? I was hoping we might get together for lunch one day."

Alexis felt a lurch of pity and remorse. She really neglected her mother, and though they had little in common, it was not fair of her. She rationalized that Morgan was much better with Ginny, but she knew that even Morgan would not make up for the lack of interest of Ginny's oldest child. Alexis knew, guiltily, that she probably spent as much time with Daddy's new wife as she did with her own mother.

"Well, I won't be there all week," Alexis reassured her. "Tell you what—as soon as I get back, I'll give you a call, and we can go out to dinner some evening. How does that sound?"

"Wonderful!" Ginny cried, her voice once again girlishly happy, and Alexis reflected that the nice thing about her mother was that it took very little to restore her spirits. "Maybe we can go to a show afterward."

"Sounds great," Alexis said firmly. "But I really have to go now."

After she replaced the receiver in its cradle, Alexis sighed and ran a hand through her loose-flowing hair, then picked up the folder again. She turned back to the picture and stared at it for a moment. McClure was good-looking in a rugged sort of way, she decided, but hard; he would hide all weak spots.

She closed the file and tossed it onto the floor, then reached to turn off the lamp beside her bed. She snuggled into her pillows, enjoying the pleasant feeling of release throughout her tired body. Slowly, sleep drifted over her, and as she sank into unconsciousness, she saw again, quite clearly in her mind's eye, the picture of Brant McClure. Her last thought was, strangely enough, what color are his eyes?

Chapter 2

The Cessna glided down smoothly, settled onto the asphalt runway, then taxied to the end of the strip, where a blue Piper already sat. The door of the Cessna opened and Alexis emerged, to jump lithely down and fasten the nose and wings with heavy nylon rope to the tie rings sunk in the asphalt. She straightened and glanced around her. Everywhere the Panhandle stretched tan and flat, dotted irregularly with gray-green mesquite bushes and yucca plants. Overhead, the sky was bright blue and immense, without a cloud in sight. Alexis shivered slightly as a chill wind seeped through her blouse. Reaching into the plane, she pulled out the jacket of her crisp, cream-colored pants suit. Then she removed her suitcase and briefcase and closed the door. Thank heavens she wouldn't have to be here long, she told herself; this monotonous emptiness was not her idea of beauty.

Briskly, she started toward an old car parked to one side of the runway. Her father had told her that the Thompsons usually kept a car there for the trip back to their house. Alexis thought with amusement that only in the Texas countryside would people take out across the fields in a car, just as if it were a truck or a jeep. She could remember the horrified words of a visitor from

23

North Carolina: "The two things I remember most about my visit to Texas were that everybody drove a hundred miles an hour, and that they would just drive off the road in their fancy cars all over the fields!"

As Alexis was about to put her luggage in the back seat of the battered blue Chevy, a horn sounded, and she looked up to see a red pickup truck bearing down on her. She wondered if some ranch hand was coming to tell her that this was a private landing strip and not for public use. The truck stopped beside her, and a small woman with close-cropped light brown hair jumped down. She wore jeans and boots and a casual pullover sweater, but it was obvious at a glance that none of her apparel was inexpensive. She smiled at Alexis and raised a hand in greeting, her hazel eyes alight with curiosity. Her whole face glowed with vitality, giving the impression of great energy and enthusiasm.

"Hi! I'm Beth Thompson," she said cheerfully, and came around the hood of the truck to shake hands. "I saw you fly over and land, and I thought I would come pick you up. I was wanting to meet you."

Alexis smiled at the woman's frank manner. It would be difficult to dislike her, she thought. "Why, thank you. I am Alexis Stone, but then I guess you know that."

"Oh, sure," Beth said, and easily lifted Alexis's suitcase into the bed of the truck. "Alec called Rusty—my husband—and said you were coming and asked if you could use the landing strip." She laughed. "As if Rusty would deny Alec Stone anything."

Alexis was not exactly sure how to respond to that remark, and so said nothing as she climbed onto the passenger's seat inside the high cab. Beth, swinging in on the other side, didn't notice her silence and went blithely on. "Rusty told me you're here to try to convince Brant to lease his mineral interest to you." She jerked the truck into gear and set off across the rough terrain at a speed that jarred Alexis, but she never paused in her conversation. "Well, I wish you luck with Brant. If you can persuade *him* to do something, you'll be the first person who ever did."

Alexis was a little taken aback by the woman's candid remark, but then she remembered that Rusty Thompson's wife was also Brant McClure's sister and could speak about him with easy familiarity. Interesting, now that Alexis thought about it, that this vibrant woman could be the sister of that stern-faced man in the photograph.

Beth cast a considering look in her direction. "Of course, if anybody could do it, you look like you could."

Alexis was unsure what she meant by that, and said noncommittally, "Mr. McClure is your brother, isn't he?"

"Oh, sure, but we don't share the same views on oil. Well, you know about the leases Rusty has with Stone Oil. I can tell you, my daddy about came unglued when I married Rusty. You would have thought he was the devil incarnate just because he was old H. R.'s son, and H. R. was the one who opened this place up to the oil and gas men. Do you know, those two old guys wouldn't even speak to each other? Their *fathers* played dominoes together at the domino parlor in town, and their *children* married each other, but *they* never said a word to each other after 1959. Not even at our wedding! Can you imagine?"

"It is a little strange," Alexis admitted. "Oil has a weird effect on some people."

Beth shrugged. "Well, it sure did on my father, and Brant is almost as bad. That's why I don't hold out much hope for you. I know for a fact that Stone has had four different men up here trying to convince him." She shot Alexis another speculative look, and Alexis had the sudden suspicion that something was brewing in Beth Thompson's mind. Her chatter was disarming, but Alexis felt it was a cover for an intense appraisal of herself.

"Now, I want you to come stay with us," Beth said, cutting into her thoughts. "We have plenty of room, and I would just love to have you."

"Oh, no," Alexis demurred automatically. "I couldn't impose on you like that."

"No imposition!" Beth exclaimed earnestly. "Rusty's dad built the most monstrously huge house you ever saw when the oil and gas money first started coming in. We're living there now that old H. R. is in a fancy nursing home because he had a stroke last year. Anyway, the house has five bedrooms, and we only use three. It wouldn't be a bother, believe me. It's so isolated out here that I could just scream sometimes. We lived in Amarillo most of the time since we've been married, until H. R. had that stroke, and I'm used to having neighbors, which is impossible out here. I would honestly love the company."

Alexis could hear the sincerity in her voice. Even if there was some scheming going on in Beth's head, her desire for companionship was patently real. Alexis smiled a little, feeling herself yielding. She didn't relish spending her time alone in a motel in Barrett.

"Well . . ."

Beth heard the hesitation and pressed her point. "Please, you must stay. The motel here isn't exactly the Hyatt, and there's nobody there but the men working on the rigs. You wouldn't enjoy it, believe me. Besides, when Rusty told me you were coming, I decided it was a good time for a little party. I invited some of the people here, and my big brother, too. I thought it might help you with him if you could meet him socially at my house first."

Alexis agreed readily; the advantages were clear. "But why are you so eager to help me convince your brother?"

Beth sighed. "Oh, a lot of reasons. I love him very much, and I would like to see him get something out of life. Money, for one thing. I have to admit that I'm sold on those royalty checks. He could do a lot of things with the ranch that he's always wanted to do and that cost too much to be profitable. But more than that, I think he's trying to live up to something our father imposed on him, some image of how he and the world should be. He's shut himself off from everyone, pretending he can be a rancher and live all alone, like some modern pioneer. It's unrealistic. He ignores the present and the way things really are. I don't know . . . It's so vague that it's hard for me to explain. I would just like to see him sign the lease."

"You don't have any interest in those mineral rights, do you?" Alexis asked. She had read that in the report last night, and it had struck her as odd.

"No. Daddy left the land to Brant, all of it, and all the mineral rights, too. He left me money and stocks. He wasn't about to let those mineral interests get into my hands. He was sure Rusty and I would go contrary to his wishes, but he knew Brant wouldn't. Daddy never trusted women very much. I don't know why, except that my mother left him. So that, coupled with my having married an oil man's son . . ." Beth's voice trailed off.

"Well, we are not so different, then," Alexis said spontaneously. "Both our fathers preferred sons."

"Oh, do you have a brother, too?"

"No, much to my father's disappointment. He just *wanted* a son and got three girls instead." Alexis was somewhat surprised at her own openness. Usually she would never have said anything like that to a stranger, but Beth Thompson had immediately struck a responsive chord. She remembered wishing last night that she had someone to talk to about her confusion regarding this project. She thought that Beth was the sort of person in whom she would have been able to confide.

"There's the house," Beth said, her voice bubbling with amusement. "A real monster, isn't it?"

Alexis had to admit that it looked like the prototype

of a newly rich oil man's house. Sprawling starkly
against the uncluttered horizon, the one-story modern
ranch dwelling spread out into three wings. As they
drew closer, she could see the glint of sunlight on the
pristine aqua surface of a swimming pool. The truck
racketed around to the side and stopped, and Beth
leaped down from the cab.

"Let Rusty get your suitcase," she said. "Come on in
and meet the family." She went through the garage
door into a spacious kitchen, calling, "I'm home!"

Alexis trailed Beth through the house as she searched
out the members of her family. Rusty was in the den,
watching a college football pre-game show on television.

"Rusty, this is Alexis Stone," Beth said.

Her husband unfolded himself from his seat and
smiled. "Pleased to meet you." He was a lanky, quiet
man, the very antithesis of his wife. His face was that of
a weather-beaten man who has spent his life outdoors,
and squint lines sprayed out from his sherry-brown
eyes. It was easy to see the origin of his nickname: the
thinning crop of hair on his head was a deep auburn.

"How about lunch? Where are the girls?" Beth
rattled on.

"In the playroom."

"Alexis's suitcase is in the back of the truck. Would
you get it, honey? Come on, Alexis, I'll give you the
grand tour, and we'll get the girls."

They traveled through a sunken living room, a dining
room, a library, and then down a long hall flanked by
bedrooms. Beth paused at one and gestured inside.

"I thought I would put you in here, if that's all right.
It's the only one besides the master bedroom that has
its own bath. All the others have connecting baths."

"Oh, it looks fine," Alexis said, glancing around the
large, pale sea-green room. A silvery sheen emanated
from the light green carpet. Beth, or someone, had
decorated very simply, but tastefully, with cherry wood

furniture, which gave the room a gracious, warm, slightly old-fashioned look.

"I think I hear the kids yelling." Beth started down the hall again. She pointed out her daughters' frilly bedrooms and finally stopped at the door of a huge playroom, where two little girls were romping about on roller skates.

"Girls!" Beth raised her voice to be heard above the din. "Time for lunch. Get off those skates. We have a visitor, Alexis Stone. She's come to see Brant."

The children flopped down on the floor and began to remove their skates, all the while eyeing Alexis curiously. They looked to be about nine and seven, bright-eyed, pretty little carbon copies of their mother, except for the shock of carrot-colored hair that covered their heads. Once their skates were off, they trooped forward to be introduced.

"Alexis, this is Jennifer, the oldest. She is nine years old. And this is Stephanie, who's six."

"I'll be seven in December," the child volunteered, and Alexis smiled.

"Hello, Jennifer, Stephanie. I am very pleased to meet you."

"Are you going to go look at Uncle Brant's cows?" Jennifer questioned. "Can I go, too?"

Beth laughed. "Not this time, sweetheart. They're going to talk business, not visit the cows."

"Oh." Jennifer's expression revealed her puzzlement that anyone would pass up visiting the cattle, but she accepted the vagaries of adults.

"I'm hungry," Stephanie announced loudly.

"Then I guess we'll just have to stir up something to eat, huh?"

They made the trek back to the kitchen, where Beth began piling sandwich meats, cheese, potato chips, and bread on plates that she brought to the table. "Hope you don't mind a casual lunch," she told Alexis. "I never fix anything on Saturdays."

The simple meal was enlivened by the chatter of the little girls, who seemed determined to inform Alexis of every detail of their lives. After they had eaten, Beth shooed them into their playroom and put the remaining food back in the refrigerator.

"Rusty," she said to her husband, who still sat at the table, working on his second sandwich, "I think I'll go into town and do my grocery shopping. If you want to come along, Alexis, I'll show you the sights of Barrett, such as they are. Or you can stay here and get some rest."

"I think I'll come." Alexis enjoyed Beth's company, and she didn't expect to get much rest if she remained at home with the children.

"Great. I love company."

"Beth, while you're there, would you stop by the feed store?" Rusty asked. "Sloan's has that new feed I want to try."

"Okay." Beth made a slight grimace toward Alexis. "That means we'll have to take the pickup again."

The road to the highway was far smoother than the trackless way they had come from the airstrip, a caliche and sand section road that, happily, had no rocks or deep holes. Within a few minutes they were on an asphalt highway and humming the fifteen miles into town.

"That's Brant's land," Beth said once, waving toward some land on the left that Alexis found indistinguishable from the rest of the country. "But the entrance is on the north side, off 412. This is just the back of it. See that shack on the other side of the road? Would you believe that man has four active gas wells? He has plenty of money, but he was poor before they discovered gas on his farm, and I guess he's afraid he'll be poor again. He's never moved out of that house and still drives the sorriest 1958 pickup you ever saw."

They entered the outskirts of town and made their way to the grocery store, with Beth offering a nonstop commentary on the history, spicy and otherwise, of the families whose houses they passed. She seemed to know everyone and everything.

"It's growing up in a tiny town," she explained with a grin. "There is nothing else to do, so you spend all your time talking about everybody else. If it weren't for gossip, we would all have died of boredom long ago."

Despite the slightly scatterbrained appearance Beth cultivated, she was quick and efficient while shopping, and Alexis was surprised at the ease with which they finished.

"I hope you haven't been too bored," Beth said as they left the store.

"No, honestly, I haven't. I really enjoy listening to you. It's fun." Alexis shook her head. "You know, it just occurred to me while you were talking that I never had any close friends when I was growing up. Female friends, I mean, to go shopping with and listen to records together and giggle. I never did any of that."

"Why?" Beth glanced at her, surprised.

Alexis shrugged. "I was always studying or reading. Nobody else seemed to share any of my interests."

"Oh, it probably doesn't matter. Most people I know hated their adolescence, anyway. It was the most awful, awkward, embarrassing time. Maybe it was easier lived through if you read and studied and didn't really get into it."

Alexis sighed. "Maybe, I don't know. While I was studying, girls like you were dating and flirting, giggling and having fun, seeing shows and going shopping together, gossiping and daydreaming, being their age. Being what they were, not what they thought someone else wanted them to be."

Beth cast her a sideways glance. "I knew there was some reason I thought you and Brant would hit it off. He was always just as serious and just as anxious to live up to our father. Somehow, he felt that he had to make it up to Daddy because Mama left him. The way I saw it, I figured it was more likely Daddy's fault that Mama left *us*, not the other way around. Brant was older than

I, about twelve when Mama left, and it hit him a lot harder. I don't think he ever really got over it. Maybe that's why he's never let a woman get really close to him."

Beth's usually merry face saddened as she spoke about her brother, and Alexis realized that she worried about him and even ached for his hurt. Morgan was like that about Ginny. With a pang, Alexis wondered if *she* was incapable of feeling that way for someone. Was she really a cold, hardhearted business machine? Or was it just that her father, on whom she pinned her love, never allowed anyone to become close?

"I wish," Beth continued in a soft voice, "that Brant would find somebody good, someone really right for him. He needs someone to break him out of his shell."

"Do you think another person can make someone change?" Alexis asked.

"I don't know. I think it would take someone very special, someone just as tough and stubborn as Brant himself, so that he couldn't keep his distance and couldn't simply forget her."

Alexis looked at the other woman with a dawning awareness of the ulterior plan that she had suspected Beth of concocting from the moment she had met her. Beth was trying to work up a romance between Alexis and Brant! Alexis had to stifle a giggle at the thought. Everyone seemed to want to make a match between her and Brant McClure—first Alec, because he wanted the lease, and now Beth, because she wanted her brother to be happy. The only people apparently disinterested in the whole affair were McClure and Alexis.

They pulled up in front of the feed store. "I'll run in and tell Sloan to load the feed in the back," Beth said. "You can stay here if you'd like."

"Yes, I think I will." Alexis wanted a few minutes alone to think about the implications of Beth's intentions for her and McClure.

The October sun was warm through the glass, and soon Alexis rolled down the window to let in a little cool air. For the first time, she glanced toward the feed store and saw that it looked like something straight out of a Western movie: an old, weather-beaten, peeling frame structure with a covered front porch and a faded sign hanging above. There were even three men in jeans, work shirts, and boots lounging by the steps.

As she watched them, a jeep pulled into the parking lot a few feet away from her, and a broad-shouldered man swung out and started toward the steps. Alexis straightened up and stared at him . . . Why, that was the man in the picture, Brant McClure! There·was no mistaking the big-boned frame, the firm jawline and the hard-set mouth. The only difference was the thick brown mustache that now outlined his upper lip and gave him a rather piratical look.

He stopped to talk to the men on the porch, and Alexis took the opportunity to study him further. He was tall and tanned, his height increased by the scuffed, brown cowboy boots he wore. His faded blue jeans fitted him like a glove, emphasizing his flat stomach and the long, clean line of his legs. Years in the sun had bleached his brown hair to a lighter color and added streaks of blazing gold. Deep lines ran out from his eyes and were etched into the taut skin around his mouth. He looked very much like his picture, yet there was a tough vibrancy about him that no photograph could capture.

As the men talked, one of them made a gesture toward the truck in which Alexis sat, and McClure turned to look at her. For a moment their eyes met and held. A strange jolt went through Alexis, like that from an electric shock. Then she glanced away, chagrined having been caught staring at him. When she looked up again, he had disappeared, and she felt a peculiar pang of disappointment.

Moments later, Beth emerged, her face suffused with

excitement and a triumphant smile on her lips. Following her was her brother. The pair came straight for the truck, and Alexis was conscious of a sudden, intense desire to run. There was something about McClure that was frightening . . . overpowering. And the last thing Alexis wanted to be was overpowered.

"Alexis," Beth said gaily, stopping beside her door, "this is my brother, Brant. He came into the store asking who on earth that lovely girl in our pickup was, so I was kind enough to say I would introduce you. Alexis, this is Brant. Brant, this is Alexis."

Looking out the window at them, Alexis felt trapped. "How do you do?" she said stiffly.

"Ma'am," Brant replied, with that brief incline of the head that seemed to pass for a greeting in the Panhandle. He looked straight at her, and Alexis saw, with a pleasurable little shiver, that his eyes were a pale golden brown, the color of amber. Tawny eyes, she thought, like a lion's. She wet her lips nervously.

"Now, Brant, I have to run back in and sign the bill. You stay here and keep Alexis entertained for me," Beth said, breaking the awkward silence, and hurried away.

McClure leaned casually against the truck, one foot resting on the running board. "Soon as I saw the truck, I knew Beth or Rusty was here, so I stopped to talk. I wasn't expecting to see someone like you sitting in it, though."

Alexis laughed a little breathlessly and said, "I hope that is a compliment."

For the first time, a smile creased his stern face, lighting his eyes. "I think you can safely say that it is. I take it you're a friend of Beth's?"

Alexis nodded. She had noticed that Beth had not mentioned her last name, and Alexis wondered if she had done that on purpose. Did she think it would be better for Alexis to get to know her brother before he found out what Alexis was here for? He might be more receptive if they established a friendly social ground first. Alexis decided she would play along for a moment, until she was more certain of him.

"From Amarillo?"

"No, I live in Dallas, actually."

"Oh, then you're in pretty foreign territory here."

Alexis smiled. "It is rather different from Dallas, I'll admit."

"It takes a while to get used to it," he acceded, "but once you do, you can see its unique beauty."

Alexis's look must have betrayed her disbelief, for he quickly protested, "No, I'm not crazy. It's different, I know, but there's a grandeur and a wild sort of beauty to it. There isn't any place where the sky is so clear and blue, or where you have the same muted greens and tans and browns of the landscape, slashed now and then by that red clay."

"You sound like an artist." This man was not fitting her preconceived notion of a bull-headed, insular cowboy.

"Oh, I don't paint, if that's what you mean. But I do appreciate beauty." His golden eyes bored into her blue ones. "In land . . . and in women."

His words, even in the broad light of day, had a sensual suggestiveness to them, and Alexis found her glance drawn to his lips, hard and firm beneath the curve of his mustache. She wondered if they ever softened and how they would feel against her own. At the realization of what she was thinking, a flush rose in her cheeks. Had her face betrayed her thoughts?

"Are you going to be at Beth's party tonight?" he asked.

She nodded. "Yes. Are you?"

"I am now," he replied, his voice touching her like a caress.

Alexis shifted a little in her seat and changed the subject. "You are a rancher, aren't you?"

"Yes, ma'am, I have a ranch out on 412. Would you

like to come out and see it sometime while you're here? We could ride a couple of my horses, see it up close."

"Why, yes, I would like that. Thank you." Alexis suppressed a niggling guilty feeling that he would not have been so anxious to invite her to his ranch if she had revealed who she was. It was only a slight deception, she told herself, and perfectly necessary when dealing with a man like him.

"Good. You going to be here long?"

"I—I'm not sure, exactly . . ." Alexis fumbled, and breathed a sigh of relief when she saw Beth emerging from the store.

Beth reminded Brant about the party, then stepped into the truck and, with a wave, backed out. "Well," she said as soon as they were on the road, "what did you think?"

"He is a very attractive man," Alexis replied slowly.

"You think so? I'm glad. I've always thought he was devastating myself, but then, I'm a little prejudiced. That's the way baby sisters are, I'm afraid."

"Did you leave out my last name on purpose?"

"Well, yes . . . You see, Brant has got such a thing about Stone Oil, and I was afraid he might make the connection. I was hoping you two could get to know each other a little before that comes up to cloud everything. I thought maybe if he liked you, he would at least listen to you."

"I see. But how long can I go on pretending I'm not who I am?" Alexis countered.

Beth shrugged. "As long as it's feasible, I guess. I mean, you'll have to talk to him about the oil and gas lease sometime, but maybe tonight a time will come up when you can ease into it."

Alexis bit her underlip thoughtfully. She had her doubts about this idea. If he was attracted to her, as his comments seemed to suggest, then it certainly would not please him to make a pass at her and then discover who she really was. She imagined that the smartest thing to do would be to make the situation clear right from the start. That way, at least he couldn't hold a grudge against her for deceiving him.

When they reached the Thompson house, Alexis was ready for the brief nap that Beth suggested. The plane trip had tired her, and she felt strangely drained after her meeting with Brant McClure.

She awoke feeling refreshed and eager to meet the challenge of the evening. Humming to herself, she took a leisurely bath in the luxurious marble bathtub, then washed and dried her hair. Since it was a party occasion, she put on light makeup and mascaraed her long sandy lashes, something which was not part of her busy daily routine. Next she pulled her burnished hair straight back from her face, fastened it on either side with a pair of tortoiseshell combs, and with a curling iron quickly turned her hair into a glowing mass of curls. The severe front and the soft pouf behind created a lovely frame for her fine-boned face and made her blue-violet eyes look enormous.

Alexis was glad that she had remembered to bring her pearl earrings, which accented the soft sheen of her hair.

The silk dress she wore was pale peach, with a mandarin collar and a straight skirt. A belt set off her slender waist, and the severity of the skirt was negated by a long slit on the right side that revealed a good deal of her shapely leg. The peach color was a perfect foil for her white skin, and highlighted the coppery shine of her red-blond hair.

Looking at herself in the mirror, Alexis decided that she would do. She was glad Morgan had insisted on dragging her into that store in North Park where she had found this dress. It really was a jewel. It gave her the confidence she needed for her meeting with Brant McClure.

Alexis could feel the pulse pounding in her throat, and her stomach was jumping at the thought of seeing him again tonight. It was the excitement of battle, she told herself, that heightened awareness and pump of adrenalin she felt whenever she faced a challenge. Something important would happen this evening. Before it was through, either she would have won him over or they would be at daggers-point.

There was a knock on the door, and then Beth sailed in. "You ready? It's almost time. Oh, Alexis, you look gorgeous. Wherever did you find that dress? I must get to Dallas sometime to go shopping. That dress just *oozes* sophistication. I feel like a nun next to you."

Alexis laughed. Beth looked quite smart in her neat black dress, and she had the sparkle of a woman who knows without a doubt that she is attractive.

"Well, shall we brave it?" Beth asked, and gestured toward the door. Alexis nodded and went out. "I hope you don't starve. We're having the barbecue catered at nine, with drinks first. But I'm beginning to discover that our light lunch isn't going to stick with me clear till then. I may devour the hors d'oeuvre tray."

"I'm too nervous to be hungry," Alexis admitted.

"You? Why? At meeting Brant?"

"Anything important, any kind of confrontation, I always feel this way. I would be a lousy courtroom attorney."

"Well, don't let Brant frighten you. Just remember, he's soft as a lamb under all that gruff exterior."

"Hmmph," Alexis grunted in disbelief. "Spoken with all the impartiality of a little sister."

Beth laughed. "Well, maybe I exaggerated a little. But not to worry—he likes you. I could tell. When he came into the feed store this afternoon, he was bursting at the seams, trying to find out who you were!"

Rusty's chuckle sounded from the sunken living room, followed by the fainter, tinkling giggle of a woman. "Oh, Lord, Eileen Bittinger is already here. I'd recognize that giggle anywhere. Why am I always late to my own parties?"

They paused briefly just outside the closed living-room door. Alexis smoothed the front of her dress in a habitual gesture, just as she smoothed all trace of anxiety from her face. Beth winked at her and made a thumbs-up sign.

"Here goes."

Alexis raised her chin a trifle, fixed a firm smile on her face, and followed Beth into the room.

Chapter 3

It was rather disconcerting to sweep into the party, all primed for battle, and find that her adversary was not there to appreciate her entrance. A quick glance was enough to tell Alexis that the tall, striking-looking subject of her file folder was absent.

About five people were already there. Beth took Alexis around and introduced her, then hustled her off to the refreshment table. "Not the most exciting group, but they'll look better after you've had a Scotch," Beth whispered. "Why is it that the dull ones always show up first and leave last?"

Smiling, Alexis accepted a drink from Rusty while Beth prowled around the canapés, gathering a collection on her cocktail napkin. "Don't these look delicious? Brant's late, of course. He always is. He hates these things. In fact, he told me today that he hadn't planned to come until he met you."

More guests arrived, and Beth sighed and went forward to greet them. Alexis took desultory sips from her drink, which was altogether too strong, and waited for Brant to come, her stomach churning with anticipation. One of the new arrivals joined her and determinedly kept up a conversation for ten minutes, but Alexis did little more than smile or nod at what seemed

appropriate times. Afterward, she had no recollection
of what the woman had said, or even who she was.

At last she heard the lilt of Beth's voice as she cried,
"Brant! I was about to give up on you!"

Alexis cast a quick glance at the front door, where
Beth was enthusiastically hugging her brother. She saw
that Brant's eyes were raking the room, and with a
feminine instinct she had not known she possessed, she
turned back to her companion and nodded her approval of whatever the woman had said. She certainly
did not want Brant to catch her waiting for him.

She was concentrating so hard on not looking at him
that she jumped when a work-roughened hand touched
her arm. "Sorry, didn't mean to scare you," said a
drawling masculine voice that she immediately recognized as McClure's.

She turned to him, smiling, unaware of the radiance
that lit her face. "Hello. Nice to see you again."

"Brant, how *are* you?" the other woman gushed.
"It's been ages since I saw you last! Where have you
been keeping yourself?"

"Oh, just working, Mrs. Collins."

"You shouldn't work so hard," Mrs. Collins said
playfully, and Alexis racked her brain for a way to ease
out of the woman's tenacious social grasp.

"Here, let me refill your drink," Brant offered,
quickly taking the glass from Alexis's hands even
though it was still half full, and carrying it to the bar,
where Rusty was mixing drinks.

Beth descended on them, smiling falsely from ear to
ear, and proceeded to engage Mrs. Collins in a steady
stream of words. Alexis smiled her thanks at her friend
and eased herself out of the trio, murmuring softly,
"Excuse me."

She turned toward the bar and saw Brant lounging
there, talking to Rusty. Alexis took a longer look at
Brant now that his attention was not focused on her,
and decided that he was even more attractive than he

had seemed this afternoon. He wore light brown slacks and a soft, golden-brown turtleneck sweater that heightened the color of his eyes. Tonight his feet were encased in brown leather shoes, not boots.

As Alexis approached, Brant turned and smiled, the weathered lines at the corners of his eyes crinkling up. "I knew Beth would come to our rescue."

Rusty laughed and handed Alexis her drink. "I've always liked Bill Collins, but that wife of his is enough to make you crazy. Beth nearly killed me when I told her I invited them tonight."

Alexis sipped at her drink, suddenly unsure of herself. What could she say to this handsome stranger who stood so close to her and made her breath come hard and fast in her throat?

"What are you up to these days?" Rusty asked Brant, to fill in the dead silence that had descended on them.

"Not much," Brant replied, his gaze going briefly to Rusty, then back to Alexis. "Checking the fences for winter, selling off some cattle so I won't have so many to feed. I'm shipping a bunch of them up to the auction next week."

"Is that what you do primarily?" Alexis asked, to join the conversation. "Raise cattle?"

"That's it." Brant grinned. "Unlike Rusty here, who is an oil baron."

Rusty snorted impolitely at that comment and glanced at the rest of the party. "Uh-oh, Jane Collins is once again alone and pursuing."

"Let's go outside," Brant suggested in an undertone, and put his hand under Alexis's arm to guide her toward the French doors that led onto the patio. Her skin tingled where his fingers touched her bare flesh, and she was aware of a hard constriction in her throat.

On the patio, he released her arm, saying, "I hate crowds. It's too hard to talk."

Alexis pulled a little away from him, fighting the

crazy confusion of her senses. Why did this man, of all men, have such a bizarre effect on her?

"Beautiful, isn't it?" Brant said, tilting back his head to gaze at the vast night sky.

Alexis looked up and nodded mutely. It *was* lovely. The moon floated high in the blue-black sky, a perfect circle that illuminated the night with its radiance. All around, scattered like diamonds on a velvet cloth, the stars glowed whitely.

"I've never been a particularly intellectual or spiritual person," Brant remarked, "but there is something about a sky like this that always makes me feel as though something is welling up inside me, grand and joyful." He looked at her ruefully. "I am probably making you think I'm crazy."

"No, not at all," Alexis denied truthfully. She had been touched by his words, moved by a feeling she had never known before and had no words for.

"Would you like to go for a ride?" he asked suddenly. "There is a place with a fantastic view I love to go to."

Alexis hesitated. "What about the others? Won't everyone wonder what happened to us?"

Brant laughed, the rich sound rolling across the vacant lawn. "They won't wonder about me. People are used to my leaving a party early. I am known as antisocial. Now, they may look around for you." He paused, then murmured, "Would that bother you?"

Alexis flushed, her heart tripping. "No. Let's go."

It seemed perfectly natural when Brant put his hand on her arm to lead her to his car, yet at the same time intoxicating and almost frightening. There was something about the touch of hands, hard from physical labor, that sent a thrill through her, some magnetism about him that drew her. She could not remember ever having such feelings about any other man. Though Alexis told herself that it was only lightheadedness from a strong drink on an empty stomach, her reason and control seemed to slip away from her, streaking out behind her as did the stars above, as she and Brant sped down the empty road in his burgundy Ford.

She smiled for no reason at all and said breathlessly, "I could go on like this forever. There is nothing like driving at night in Texas. It's so peaceful—no trees looming up at you, no clouds to hide the moon and stars, nothing but emptiness and quiet for miles and miles around. And the road running up at you."

They drove to town, turned left at the first street, and traveled down it to another paved road that led out of town. The car slowed and then turned into a dirt road with a black iron fence running beside it. Alexis sat up straighter and stared at the fence, beyond which lay row after row of markers and monuments, clear in the moonlight.

"A cemetery?" she squeaked. "We're going to look at the view in a cemetery?"

He chuckled. "No, it just happens to be on the same road."

A few moments later he pulled off the road and stopped the car. "Here it is. You want to get out? It's easier to see."

Alexis nodded and opened her door. They were on one of the few rises in Barrett County. The land sloped gently away from them in a wide, grassy pasture. Beyond the pasture were breaks: gullies and gaps, small cliffs and mesas, etched into the earth by ancient waters. The moonlight washed the vista with a pale light, turning the long, waving grasses beige and fading the bright red clay of the breaks. The clumps of mesquite and yucca and grass that dotted the land were black shadows.

"It's lovely," Alexis breathed. "I can see why you like it."

"After my father died, I would come out here and sit and think. I had never paid any attention to it before, but when I really stopped and looked at it, I realized how serene it is."

They stood together, looking out over the landscape,

and he laid his arm lightly around her shoulders. Unconsciously, Alexis leaned against him. She felt lazy, relaxed, very much at peace with the world.

She moved her gaze from the view before them and looked up at Brant. He loomed above her, his eyes glittering in the pale light, his mouth sensual, and Alexis's heart began to thud in wild, irregular leaps. She hardly knew McClure, had come prepared to dislike him and dismiss him as a thickheaded cowboy. Yet here she was, alone with him in the vacant Texas night, uncomfortably aware of his power, his elemental magnetism, the peculiar effect he had on her insides. And here he was, with a certain cynical shrewdness in his eyes, extolling the beauty of the land and the night. He did not fit. It was not right . . . and it was dangerously exciting.

"Brant," she breathed, and then his lips swooped down on hers, obliterating all words, all thoughts.

Instinctively she responded, pressing herself up against his rock-hard chest, her arms curling and clasping about his neck. She felt the shudder that ran down ' him, and he wrapped his arms around her, crushing her body into his. His mouth was hot and insistent on hers, soft, and yet as hard as his need for her. Finally Brant lifted his head and looked down at her, but did not release his hold. His eyes were dark gold with passion; they roamed her face as though to memorize every curve, every line.

"God, you are beautiful," he said huskily. "I wanted to do that the moment I saw you sitting in the pickup."

She smiled. "That might have startled the people on the porch."

For a long time he held her against him, and she could feel the heavy thudding of his heart under her head. A long, shuddering sigh escaped him, the only break in the deep silence.

Then Brant said, "Are you hungry? I guess we missed the meal at Beth's. Let's go down to the cafe."

"All right." She stepped back, out of his arms, aware

of an acute disappointment. Why had he stopped with one kiss? Was she too inexpert? Too dull?

They drove into town and stopped before a small white stucco building whose neon sign across the front wall read "Nora's Cafe." Inside, it was as plain as the outside, aluminum and vinyl chairs and formica-topped tables, with a green-flecked linoleum floor. A row of red booth seats and tables lined the wall. It was to one of these that Brant guided her.

"This place is the quintessence of a truck stop," Alexis murmured as they seated themselves.

Brant laughed shortly. "Small-town cafe. Not very fancy, but no other place serves as good a hamburger or chicken-fried steak."

"Hi, Brant, how's it going?" A middle-aged red-haired woman dressed in a white uniform came to their table.

"Fine, Nora. How are you? Jimmy still in the hospital?"

"No, he got out two days ago. I went up to Pampa to get him. He's doing real well, if I can just keep him in bed and off that leg. That kid doesn't know the meaning of the word 'rest.'"

"Nora, this is Alexis . . ." Brant stared at her in consternation.

Alexis felt her stomach knotting up and thought, Here it comes. "Stone," she supplied, and waited for his reaction.

There was none. "Right, Stone. Alexis, this is Nora Dixon. Her son broke his leg—fell from the loft in Miller's barn."

"He's lucky he didn't break his damn-fool neck!" Nora added. "Now, what will you folks be having?"

"I think a cheeseburger for me. And a chocolate milkshake," Alexis decided in a fit of nostalgia for her childhood eating habits. This place reminded her of the hamburger joints of her youth.

"You know me," Brant said. "Chicken-fried steak and gravy."

"Have it in a minute."

Brant said nothing about her name, and Alexis began to relax. Apparently he hadn't made the connection. Now was the time, she thought, to tell him what she had come here for. She didn't know exactly why, but with Brant she wanted complete honesty. And yet . . . she couldn't bring herself to tell him. The thought of his face turning hard and remote, his brows swooping down in a frown, his mouth a thin, straight line of disapproval, turned her cold inside. She dreaded breaking the fragile chain between them. Later, perhaps, when they went back to Beth's. Maybe it would be easier in the darkness, while they drove along the highway or stopped outside Beth's house. She would not be able to see his expression so well, then, and everything would seem softer, less harsh. But she could say nothing here, in this casual, brightly lit atmosphere, surrounded by people.

Alexis turned the subject to him. "Do you think you'll continue to ranch here?"

Brant shrugged slightly. "I can't think of anything else. When I came back from Vietnam, that was all I wanted to do. I couldn't wait to get back to work on the barns and corrals and to feed the stock. I still don't have any desire to leave the ranch. I feel very . . . satisfied there, doing what I'm doing."

"Well, that is more than most of us can say."

"Tell me about you. That's more interesting."

Alexis hesitated, thinking this could be dangerous ground. "Well, I have two sisters, both younger, and no brothers. Uh, let's see . . ."

"Married? Divorced?"

"No, neither. What about you?"

"No, I never married."

"Well, then, I guess that makes us a couple of old bachelors," Alexis said lightly.

He smiled. "I would hardly classify you as old, particularly in that dress. You look like the newest young addition to a Chinese war lord's concubines."

"You, sir, have a very vivid imagination." Alexis laughed, though her chest tightened crushingly at his words.

She sat with one arm on the table, and Brant began gently to trace her hand and arm with his forefinger. Her breath caught in her throat at his touch, and a warm pulsation fluttered just above her stomach. She could see the gold of his eyes darken with desire, his mouth curve sensuously beneath the mustache, and she wished they were not trapped in this booth.

"Here you are!" Nora's cheerful voice broke the spell. They pulled their hands back from the table as she set down the hot plates, handing Alexis her cheeseburger and Brant the golden-brown, batter-fried meat pattie with cream gravy on top that Texans called chicken-fried steak.

Alexis picked up her burger; the top was shining with melted cheese and butter. She bit into it and tasted the same thick, juicy meat she had known as a youngster.

"How do you like it?" Brant asked.

"It's heavenly—just like the kind I used to get at Meyer's Drugstore."

They ate without much conversation, just enjoying the food and the atmosphere. Alexis found that she rather liked this cafe. It had an air of friendliness, closeness; everyone knew each other. There were no pretensions whatsoever; it was easy to be yourself.

After they had finished, they drove back to Beth's. Brant sat in an almost brooding silence, his eyes on the road, but he kept one hand firmly clasped over Alexis's, his thumb softly rubbing her palm.

"What are you thinking?" Alexis asked.

He grinned. "Nothing fit for your ears, probably."

"What does that mean?"

He glanced toward her, then back to the road. Raising her hand to his lips, he softly kissed the palm, then each finger separately. "I was wondering how soon I could get you into my bed."

Taken aback at his bluntness, Alexis said tartly,

"Don't you think the first consideration is 'if,' not 'when'?"

McClure chuckled slightly and returned her hand to the seat. "Oh, but I won't let myself even consider that possibility. It would be too painful."

Alexis stared at him, but he looked straight ahead, his face immobile. She glanced away to gaze out the window. When the Ford turned into the section road, she was relieved to see the Thompson house looming up on the right.

Smoothly, Brant pulled his sleek car into an available space in the driveway and came around to help her out. They walked toward the rear patio, but before they had reached it, Brant took hold of her arm and drew her to him. Slowly, caressingly, his hands moved over her waist and back. She trembled slightly at his touch.

"Alexis," he said, his mouth lingering over the word, and bent to kiss her.

His lips ground into hers fiercely, hungrily, parting them, and his tongue raked her mouth, luxuriating in its sweetness. Alexis clung to him as he began to explore her neck. His breath against her skin seared like flame while his lips and teeth and tongue evoked little whimpers of pleasure from her throat. Her name sounded like a groan upon his lips, and he kissed her again, dizzyingly. Alexis dug her fingers into his hair as if to hold him there forever, her breath rasping and quick. The world was suddenly a hot, wild kaleidoscope of emotion, and for the first time she felt that her senses were really alive.

Brant's hands moved around her waist and up to cup her breasts, then slid down her abdomen and back to follow the curve of her hips. His fingers pressed into the soft flesh of her buttocks, lifting her into him, so that Alexis felt every hard line and curve of his body, each bone and muscle. She let her hands drift down his arms and shoulders, caressing their taut cording and solid strength. She wanted to feel the satin ripple of his skin, unimpeded by clothing, a thought so blatant that she blushed even here in the dark.

Suddenly Brant released her and stepped back. She could hear his breath struggling in his throat. "I want you," he said baldly.

Alexis pushed back a stray lock of hair, fingers trembling. She was a blur of emotions, soft and weak, but lit from within by a blaze of desire. Remotely, as though she looked at herself from a distance, she knew that she wanted Brant McClure as she had never wanted any other man. It was dazzling, scary. She hardly knew what to do or say or where to look. She felt as though she were tottering on the edge of a cliff.

"Will you come home with me?" he murmured.

She wet her lips nervously. If she didn't tell him now who she was, if she let him make love to her and he found out afterward, he would feel betrayed; he would not sign the lease. He might even hate her. Yet if she told him now, he might despise her still, might turn and walk away from her. Or he might continue the relationship in a businesslike way, cutting off all romance in order not to have it color his decision. She knew he would not go on making love to her in this delightful, dizzying way.

The fire of his lovemaking hummed through her veins, pounding in her temples. I want him, she thought. For the first time in my life, I feel the way a woman is supposed to feel. To hell with Alec, to hell with the lease. Tonight, for once, *I* am going to come first!

Her answer was a low "Yes."

He smiled and with one hand reached out to caress her neck. "You're cold. You'd better run in and get a wrap. I'll tell Beth where we're going. If I don't, she'll have half the highway patrol out looking for you."

They walked across the patio, and Alexis said jokingly, "The proverbial cowboy—stranded without a woman for months on the range."

He laughed. "Not quite months."

"Hours?" she offered suggestively, amazed to hear herself sound so coquettish.

His only answer was a swift, burning look at her as he opened the French doors, and Alexis felt an unfamiliar melting in her loins at the fire in his eyes.

She slipped across the living room and down the hall to her bedroom to get a light sweater. Brant looked around, trying to locate his sister in the crowd.

"Why, hello, there, Brant," a voice said at his elbow, and Brant turned to see Dr. Whiting, a balding, plump man who, from the look of him, had enjoyed an evening filled with drink.

"Jack, how are you?" Brant acknowledged shortly. He didn't want to have to exchange dull pleasantries with a drunken man, in the mood he was in. He felt as impatient and hungry as a teen-ager. Lord, what an effect that woman had on him! He couldn't remember anyone who had sparked such passion in him so quickly. Just one look at her, and he had been lost.

The doctor was not easily ignored, however. "Seems like a year since we saw you, Brant. Why, I was telling Mary Nelle the other day that we hardly ever see you any more."

"Well, I've been busy, you know, harvesting the hay and all . . ."

"Saw you with the Stone girl. Pretty, isn't she?"

"Mmm," Brant assented vaguely.

Jack chuckled jovially. "I tell you what, I wouldn't mind having her explain a few points of law to me. I was just saying to Rusty that it looked like he'd finally found somebody who could persuade you to let go of those oil rights."

"Who? What are you talking about?" Brant turned toward him, puzzled and only half listening.

"I'm talking about Alec Stone's daughter," Jack said with the ponderous patience of a drunk.

"Alexis?" Realization was beginning to dawn on Brant. "Alexis is Alec Stone's daughter?"

"Well, of course she is. Didn't you know?"

"I guess I never put it together," Brant replied tightly, going strangely white around his lips.

"Who better to send up here to persuade you than a pretty woman who is a lawyer at Stone Oil *and* Alec's daughter? That Alec, he's always thinking."

"Yeah," Brant grunted, his voice grim. "He's always thinking."

Alexis appeared in the doorway and started across the room toward Brant, that same radiant smile on her face. He watched her, not moving, his face as blank and still as death. Radiant and false, he thought. Yeah, now he could see some resemblance to her old man, not the hair color, of course, but those purplish-blue eyes and the tall, slender build, the determined chin, the long-fingered, capable hands, that air of authority. So the old man's daughter had played him for a fool, too.

"Hi!" she said gaily as she reached him, and he returned her greeting evenly, guiding her outside once more.

In silence they walked to his car, the gravel of the walk and the driveway crunching beneath their feet. Alexis felt awkward but rejected this feeling as a distortion caused by last-minute jitters.

Gravely, he held open the door for her and then slid in on the other side. For a moment he turned and looked at her, his eyes unfathomable. Alexis shifted a little under his regard. He moved across the seat and took her in his arms, seizing her lips in a long, drowning kiss. Immediately she responded, the flame in her fanned into life again. She wrapped herself around him and strained against his chest, meeting him kiss for kiss.

Brant's hands wandered down her silky legs and under her dress, brazenly exploring her flesh. Alexis gasped a little at his intimate touch, and the thought crossed her mind that they were not very far from the house, that at any minute someone might come out and see them. But his hands were sending wild tremors of delight through her body, and she dismissed the thought. Tonight she would not think or worry. Tonight she wanted nothing but to feel the new pleasures that Brant awoke in her. He pulled her down on the seat beneath him, his knee parting her legs while one hand fumbled with the zipper at the back of her dress. He tugged at her dress and bra until at last he exposed the firm pale globes of her breasts. Gently his fingers moved over their smooth whiteness, circling and teasing the rosy nipples to tautness. Then he bent his head to take one nipple in his mouth and softly rouse her to new heights of passion.

A soft moan escaped Alexis's lips as she slipped gently into the wild vortex of pleasure he created. Brant drew back from her suddenly, and she opened her eyes in faint bewilderment. Above her his face was harsh, his lips a thin, bitter line. A spasm of fear darted through her.

"What—"

"You little bitch!" he growled savagely. "Just how far would you go to get that lease? To my house? To my bed?"

Alexis's face lost all color, stricken with uncomprehending fear. "What are you talking about? Brant, what's wrong?"

"Don't bother to play the innocent with me, Alexis!" he snapped, sitting up and pulling away from her. "I know all about your game. Someone at the party was kind enough, unlike my dear sister, to inform me of who you are—Stone Oil. I should have known that old lecher would pull something like this. Only a Stone would sleep with a man to get a gas lease! My God! Don't any of you have a shred of common decency?"

"That's not true!" Alexis cried, tears starting in her eyes as she struggled into a sitting position. "How dare you say that about me, about my family? You don't even know us."

His lips curled contemptuously and his eyes raked her coldly, making her doubly aware of her dishevelment—her tousled hair and undressed state. "I know everything I need to know about you," Brant said as she hastily fixed her clothing. "I know that everybody else Alec Stone sent up here had failed to get me to sign that damned lease, and that he sent you to wiggle your luscious little butt at me, hoping I'd fall all over myself and give in. How fortunate for him that he has a daughter who is both a lawyer and a whore. What were you planning to do when we got to my house? Pull the lease out of your skirt and say, 'Sign here, and I'll climb into your bed'?"

Furious, humiliated, Alexis struck at him, her plam cracking against his cheek. His face paled, but he did not move.

"How dare you say that about me?" Her voice was low, breathless. "How dare you accuse me of being a whore, when you haven't even bothered to check out the facts? You just jumped to conclusions, believing yourself quite pure, of course, but me—oh, no, I'm beyond redemption. I did not lie to you. You knew my name. I just didn't think it was necessary to drag my business concerns into what I considered a purely romantic situation."

"That's a true Stone reaction. When someone points out your underhanded dealings, hit them. Attack."

"I'm sorry I ever responded to you. I can't imagine how I thought there was anything attractive about your macho, narrow-minded personality. It's obvious you had no real interest in me, or you wouldn't turn so completely against me when you found out that I work for Stone Oil. You are the kind who uses women, who has no real interest in any deeper feeling!"

"I? I used you?" His laugh was short and harsh. "You *are* a cool one. Just like your father. Nothing shames you, does it? You simply turn it around and use it as a weapon. Well, let me make something clear to you, lady. I am *not* going to lease my mineral rights to Stone Oil—any time, any place, for any reason. Nothing you or anyone else in your organization does or says will make me change my mind. Don't even bother to come around again with some other new tricks, because I *will not deal with Stone Oil*. Is that understood?"

"Perfectly," Alexis retorted sarcastically.

"Fine. I hope I don't see you again, Miss Stone. Good night."

Furiously, Alexis yanked open her door and stepped out, flinging it behind her with a crash. As she stalked off toward the house, she heard his car start and then spin away with a roar, sending gravel flying.

Alexis went around to the kitchen entrance to avoid the living room on the way to her bedroom. She didn't want to meet anyone, especially Beth, in the state she was in, her dress crumpled and her face red, her hair a tumbled mess. Quietly, she locked the door behind her and began to undress, flinging her clothes stormily across a chair.

What an unspeakable, awful man! He had discovered her identity while she was getting her sweater, and then, knowing that he hated her for it, he had conducted that fake passionate scene in his car for one reason only: to degrade her, to make her reveal how much power he had over her and her treacherous senses. It embarrassed her even to think about the way she had quivered in his arms like a panting schoolgirl. How could she have been so swept off her feet by such a rude, shallow cowboy?

Well, whatever had caused the bizarre lapse in her behavior, she was certainly over it now. He had destroyed any desire she had had for him with his crudeness and abusive tirade. She had thought he might suspect her of ulterior motives when he found out who she was, but never had she imagined that he would fly into a temper fit. The thought of his vicious words made her burn all over. She knew she hated him now with an intensity equal to the passion he had awakened in her earlier.

So he thought he could shame her, then castigate her vilely and escape unharmed, did he? Alexis began to pace wildly back and forth across her room. No doubt he took her for some delicate, wilting female who would beat a hasty retreat at the first sign of battle. He'd find out otherwise. Oh, yes, he would find out otherwise!

She had not even *begun* to pressure him. Tomorrow she would start her campaign in earnest, and Brant McClure would learn that no slow-witted, chauvinistic cowboy could ever be a match for Alexis Stone!

Chapter 4

Alexis surveyed herself critically in the mirror. She wanted to present exactly the right image this morning: businesslike, no-nonsense, calmly efficient—the opposite of how she had portrayed herself last night. Her luxuriant hair was pulled severely back from her face and coiled in a knot on the nape of her neck. The crisp beige linen suit she wore, with its straight skirt and simply cut, almost mannish jacket, underscored the look she wanted to achieve. Her only concession to femininity was an eggshell-colored blouse of a soft, near-transparent material, and her only adornment was a pair of small gold stud earrings.

Alexis picked up her briefcase and left the bedroom, her face smooth and noncommittal. In the kitchen, Beth greeted her cheerily while scrambling a batch of eggs at the stove.

"Sit down. There's orange juice and coffee ready, and I'll have the eggs up in a minute."

"Um, I'd love some coffee," Alexis said, and poured a cup. "But really, I don't need breakfast. I never eat it."

"It's no trouble, honestly. I make it every morning for us. One more person is no bother. And you *should* eat breakfast. I keep telling my girls that it's the most important meal of the day."

59

Alexis sat down at the table, where five places were already neatly laid, and sighed inwardly. She had hoped to get away this morning without any long discussion with Beth. She didn't know if she was up to Beth's probing questions about last night, nor did she have any desire to reveal how foolishly she had responded to Brant. She couldn't talk to a man's sister about how much she now disliked him.

"Well," Beth said, slightly conspiratorially, and Alexis knew that the dreaded subject was coming up. "How did it go last night? I didn't see a sign of you two after the party began, not even at dinner. I took that to be a good omen."

"Yes, it was at first," Alexis replied slowly. "We got along rather well. We talked and then went to eat at Nora's Cafe."

"Good heavens!" Beth gave a short burst of laughter. "He showed you a real slice of life in Barrett, then!"

"It was nice. Everything was so relaxed and friendly."

"Terrific!" Beth exclaimed, dumping the eggs into a platter and setting it on the table. Her face was glowing with barely suppressed glee. "Oh, Alexis, this is great! You and Brant really got along!" She sat down beside Alexis, eager to hear more.

"Don't get your hopes up, Beth," Alexis said quickly. "I said it went fine *at first*. But later Brant found out who I was. We came back here and somebody told him."

"Uh-oh," Beth moaned, her face beginning to droop.

"Worse than that. He had a fit. He told me not to see him again, that he would never sign with Stone Oil, and he slammed out of the driveway."

"Oh, *no*. Oh, Alexis, I am so sorry. I thought it would be better if he didn't know who you were. It's all my fault. I thought I was being so clever, and here I messed everything up even worse."

"It's not your fault, Beth, not at all. I could have told him any time during the evening who I was and what I was here for. Frankly, the way he reacted, I don't think he would've listened to me even if he'd known who I was from the beginning. Just what is it that he has against Stone Oil? Why is he so adamant about refusing to lease?"

Beth looked uncomfortable and shifted slightly in her chair. "Well, I think the reason has its roots in something personal. Plus, Daddy was always against it, thought it would ruin the land, and Brant feels he has to go along with Daddy's wishes. Besides, Brant is just like him. He's got a thing about not spoiling the land."

Alexis suspected that Beth wasn't telling her the entire story, but she didn't press the issue. The children came romping into the room, followed by Rusty, and the conversation took a lighter turn. Alexis ate hurriedly in order to leave before the others had finished the meal; she didn't want Beth to pursue their conversation further.

"Beth, that was delicious. Thank you," she said, and rose. "Now I have to run. Could I borrow one of your cars?"

"Sure. Take the Riviera." Beth rose also and moved toward a large purse lying on the countertop. After riffling through it, she detached a key from the overloaded key ring and handed it to Alexis. "But must you run off so fast?" she asked.

"I want to catch your brother before he's somewhere on the ranch." Strangely, Brant's name seemed to stick in Alexis's throat, and she could refer to him only indirectly.

"Good idea," Beth agreed. "He ought to be somewhere around the house and barn for a while, but he's usually gone by nine or so, even on Sundays." She gave Alexis directions to the McClure ranch, then smiled and added, "Good luck."

Alexis laughed. "Thanks. I have the feeling I'll need it."

Beth stood for some time after Alexis had left, unconsciously playing with her key ring, her mind far away. The scrape of chairs brought her back to the present as Rusty and the girls got up from the table. She gave the children a quick kiss and waved a cheerful good-bye as they piled into the pickup to accompany Rusty to town. Then she turned, marched decisively to the phone, and dialed her brother's number.

Brant McClure showered, shaved, and dressed with his usual dispatch. Sitting on his bed, he shoved his feet into his worn, faded boots, then clattered down the stairs into the spacious country kitchen. After pulling out a cast-iron skillet onto which he slapped some butter, he filled a kettle with water and put it on the stove to boil. He had gone through these motions many times in his life, and he did them quickly, without thinking.

Funny, he mused, how quiet and still the old house seems this morning. It was this way every day, but usually he didn't notice. He had lived alone for so long and was so used to it, he was surprised now at his awareness of the solitude.

Almost involuntarily, his mind turned to Alexis Stone, and he saw again her soft, burnished mass of hair, felt it beneath his fingers, remembered her fine-boned, elegant face and huge, velvety-blue eyes. Anger spurted up within him. Damn that woman! A Stone, he might have known—a Stone. She was as amoral as her father, that was obvious.

As soon as he had laid eyes on her, he had felt a treacherous flame dart through his loins. All evening long, he had felt like a stallion around a mare in heat, wanting her so badly it hurt, but he had tried to hold back, tried not to rush her or scare her off, giving her time to know him better, maybe to come to want him, too. And all the while she had been leading him on, enticing him for the sake of a gas lease!

Frowning, he dished up his two fried eggs, removed

the toast, and poured hot water into his cup of instant coffee. He didn't want to think about her. It was idiotic to remember the effect she had had on him, or the stab of hurt and anger when he had discovered the game she was playing. The only thing to do was to forget about her completely. Hopefully, he would never have to see her again.

He bolted his food, put the dishes in the sink, and ran hot water over them. Then he sat down to finish his coffee. He grimaced a little; instant coffee was not to his liking. He far preferred perked, but it was pointless to go through the trouble for only one person.

The phone in the kitchen rang, startling him. He snatched it from the wall and growled, "Hello."

"Well, I see you are in a foul mood this morning."

"Hello, Beth. I ought to be, after what you did to me last night. Why didn't you tell me who she was?"

"Well, I thought it was best. That's what I'm calling about. Alexis told me you blew your stack."

"Yeah. Fortunately, Jack Whiting told me about her before I made a complete fool of myself."

"Well, I just wish you had, for once," Beth said with some irritation. "I could strangle that drunken idiot! Honestly, Brant, you need to lose a little of that iron control of yours. Sometimes you're practically inhuman."

"Well, thank you, dear sister." He strove for a sarcastic tone, but rueful amusement won out. He had never been able to stay angry at his younger sister. "Really, Beth, what did you think you were doing?"

"I was *trying* to spark up your life a little. As soon as I met Alexis, I liked her, and I knew those devastating eyes would get to you."

"You mean to tell me you were trying to be a matchmaker between me and Alec Stone's daughter?"

"Yes, I was," Beth retorted stubbornly, and he could almost see the upward thrust of her chin. "You know how I feel about your living out there all alone, with no attachments to anybody. It's bad for you."

"There is Libby," he reminded her in a teasing voice, laughing at her expected snort of disgust.

"I am talking about attachment to a human being, not to a pretty mannequin like Libby Preston. She's just another escape from commitment for you. Anyway, I'm not going to let you sidetrack me with Libby Preston. I wanted you to know it wasn't Alexis's idea not to tell you who she was. It was mine. It was my fault, not hers. So you shouldn't be so mad at Alexis about it."

He sighed, his mouth grim. "Beth, your naiveté astounds me sometimes. Do you honestly think it made any difference that you were eager to fall in with her plans? She came up here prepared to do anything to get that lease from me. No doubt she was very pleased to find you so willing to help arrange things between her and me, but even if you hadn't, she would have found a way. That is one cool, determined woman, believe me. You had nothing to do with the lies she told me last night."

"What lies?"

"Come on, Beth . . ."

"What lies?"

"All right, I'll tell you." His voice was hard, every word a sharp stab. "She told me she wanted to sleep with me, to come home with me. And it wasn't only words. She lied to me with her lips, her body, her every expression."

"Did it ever occur to you that maybe they weren't lies? That maybe she really did want you?"

"Oh, I'm sure it must have added some extra snap to think she was seducing the son of the woman her old man had seduced. No doubt she and Stone had a good laugh about it when they thought it up."

"Brant, you talk about them as if they were some sort of monster!" Beth protested.

"Why shouldn't I? What do you think they are, Beth? Ordinary people? They aren't. They are so separated from the rest of the world by millions of dollars, they don't know what real people are like. Money and power are all that matter to them."

"How do you know?"

"Beth, you were so young, you probably don't remember Alec Stone. I do. He was a very handsome man, tall and elegant like his daughter, with the same deep blue eyes, but he was as cold as a snake and about as trustworthy. He used to come over here, trying to talk Dad into leasing, and all the while he had his eye on Mother. Nothing like stealing a man's wife from him while he's assuring that man how much he can trust Stone Oil! Why do you think Stone took Mother?"

"I guess because he fell for her."

Brant snorted with disgust. "He was *not* overcome with love for our mother. Do you honestly think that some rancher's wife with two kids had more appeal for him than all those lovely, well-kept, sophisticated women he knew back in Dallas? And after Mother left us, he didn't divorce his wife and marry *her,* did he? He dropped her flat in no time. I'll tell you why he did it. It was one of two things. Either he was bored up here and so careless of anyone else's feelings that he wrecked several lives just to relieve his boredom. Or else he was so angry with Dad for refusing to lease to him, for daring to deny him what he wanted, that he did it for revenge. He did it to pay Judson McClure back."

"Brant, you are too hard on them. It was simply a natural attraction between two healthy, good-looking, and restless people."

Brant's tone was icy. "Maybe you don't remember what happened to Dad. Maybe you don't remember the way he aged ten years when Mother left. It broke his heart, and he never really recovered. Till the day he died, a part of his spirit was gone."

Tears choked Beth's voice. "I know, Brant. You think I don't remember our father? I loved him, too, and it hurt me when Mother left, just like it did you and him. I'm not trying to excuse Mother or Mr. Stone. What they did was wrong. I'm only saying it doesn't make them less human. They aren't some kind of monster. People do things like that. People don't control their emotions like you do. And, besides, just because you hate Alec Stone, that doesn't mean his daughter is a carbon copy of him."

"So far, she has given a pretty good imitation."

"Oh, Brant . . ."

"Listen, Beth, I know you did what you thought was right. I know you always want the best for me. But you didn't help me at all where Alexis Stone is concerned. And all your apologies for her and your taking the blame can't change the way I feel. I'm not leasing the mineral rights, and I'm not going to see Alexis again. That's it."

Beth sighed. "Okay. I'm sorry I messed it all up so."

"Don't worry about it. I'll recover. You know that."

"That's what worries me," she said ruefully.

He laughed. "Good-bye, Beth. I have work to do."

Brant hung up the phone and stood for a moment staring at the floor. Absently, he brushed one hand through his thick brown hair, then collected himself, stretched, and started for the side door. Just as he did, a knock sounded at the front door, and with a sigh he headed down the hall to the main entrance.

Directions were simple in the Panhandle, and Alexis found the McClure property easily. Everything was laid out in squares, like a grid, with the requisite section-line roads in evidence except where they had become overgrown from disuse. Only the highways curved; even the streets in town were neat lines and squares. She had to drive almost back to Barrett before she came to the cutoff to 412 that led to Brant's ranch. A few miles later, she approached the stock tank and windmill that Beth had mentioned and turned up the section-line road. Before long, she could see the two-story frame house off to the left. She went off the narrow caliche road and onto an even narrower track.

The McClure house was old and weather-beaten. It had probably been built by Brant's grandfather, but it could have been even older than that. Straight and clean-lined, the building stood out boldly against the nearly barren landscape. It was painted gray and its trim and shutters were white, but obviously many years had passed since it had been repainted, and it wore a tired look.

By contrast, the barn that lay to the north was sturdy and bright, and the corral fence gleamed with new wood. Alexis thought she could understand why Brant's mother had left this grim place, where a barn was considered more important than one's house.

Alexis opened the car door and stepped out, smoothing down her skirt and taking a deep breath. This was going to be the hardest deal she had ever made in her life, and she must be careful not to blow it. She rapped sharply at the front door, and after a few moments she heard the sound of boots on a wooden floor. The door swung open to reveal Brant McClure. Her stomach did a curious flip-flop at the sight of him, and for a moment she could not speak.

Brant scowled at her darkly and snapped, "What do you want?"

Alexis recovered her voice. "I am here to discuss a gas lease with you."

"I thought I told you not to waste your time coming by," he said, his face taut.

"But you've had a night to cool down," Alexis reminded him. "I thought you might be more amenable to reason this morning."

"Look, lady, I'll tell you just what I've told every flunky your father's sent down here. I am not interested in leasing to Stone Oil. And I never will be. That's the beginning and the end of our discussion."

Rudely, he closed the door in her face, and Alexis gasped. The man was totally infuriating! She scampered down the front steps and around the building, certain there was another entrance. Just as she reached a side door, Brant emerged, closing the door behind him. His expression was thunderous, and when he saw her, he looked as if he might explode.

"Damn!" he exclaimed. "What does it take to get rid of you? I don't see how I could be any more plain than I have been!"

"Oh, you were plain enough, all right," Alexis agreed dryly. "Mr. McClure, what I am proposing is that we put aside everything that happened last night, forget our personal feelings, and approach this purely as a business arrangement."

"Purely as a business arrangement," he repeated mockingly, "my answer is no. Now, if you will excuse me, I have a great deal to do."

He strode quickly away from her toward the barn. Alexis hurried after him. Even though she was a tall woman, she could not match his long-legged walk, and she almost had to trot to keep up.

"Mr. McClure, this is the best business deal you could make. Think what you could do with the lease money . . . repair the house, for instance. It is badly in need of painting."

He did not answer her or even turn his head. He pulled open the barn doors and proceeded down the stalls, speaking softly to the three horses that were there, stopping to pat their noses. Then he unlatched their stalls and led them out into the corral, all the while completely ignoring Alexis.

Firmly, Alexis held her temper in check, even though Brant was trying it to the limit. Swallowing the biting words that rose to her lips, she kept pace with him, following him up the wooden ladder into the loft, where he pitched hay for the horses.

"Think of all the things this ranch needs that you could buy with the lease money. And I'm certain we'll strike gas on this property. Alec is convinced of it, and whenever he is that sure, he always turns out to be right. Think what the royalty money would mean. Breeding experiments, expansion, whatever you want. Don't let your stubbornness keep you from having that, nor your hurt feelings over my deception last night."

He turned to her abruptly, his golden eyes flashing fire. "Lady, I have had it with you. Leave me alone! I refuse to sign. Period. I have enough money to do what needs to be done. I am not poverty-stricken. And even if I were broke, I would never sign a lease with Stone Oil. I'd sell this land first—lock, stock, and barrel."

"Yes, and let someone else get the royalty money," Alexis pointed out. "What do you have against oil? The country needs it, Mr. McClure. You know what the Iranian situation is. You know how the Arabs are squeezing us for money. Gas prices are ridiculous because of that. It effects everyone in the country: truckers, farmers, businesses. When you could do something to ease that situation, how can you stand by and do nothing?"

"The gas under my land is not going to save the United States from the Arab oil sheiks," he retorted sarcastically.

"It would help. Every new domestic discovery helps," Alexis argued.

"Reducing our consumption would help a lot more."

"That is not the point. Of course we have to reduce consumption. But we also have to find new sources of oil right here in America!"

Brant turned and climbed down from the loft, with Alexis right on his heels. From the barn he went to a tool shed several feet away. After putting on a pair of heavy work gloves that lay on a shelf, he pulled out a roll of barbed wire and laid it on the ground outside. Next, he picked up a hammer, a box of staples, and a wire cutter and exited the shed.

He then looked wearily at Alexis. "You don't give up, do you? Didn't anyone ever tell you it isn't ladylike to chase a man?"

"That sounds like the sexist sort of remark you might make," Alexis replied heatedly. "You can't defeat a logical argument, so you revert to petty verbal abuse."

He studied her for a moment through narrowed lids. Finally he said, slowly and distinctly, "Miss Stone, you are trespassing on my property. I have tried to stay calm and refrain from threatening you. But you are getting on my nerves. I am not going to lease my land to your father. I doubt that you have any understanding of this, but I love my land. I think it is beautiful, a miracle, a wonder. And I refuse to let some oil company come in here and defile it. I refuse to let my land be raped so that your father can make a buck out of it!"

"But drilling no longer means entirely upsetting the ecological balance," Alexis protested. "We can come in now and drill a well without disturbing your land very much at all."

"Don't try to fool me," he rasped. "I've seen people's land just after the seismograph crew has been on it, and it's worse when they are actually drilling. Huge trucks run all over, killing growth, rutting the ground."

"We can make arrangements in the contract whereby, at our expense, we'll restore the growth to the land when we have finished."

"After the soil has already eroded from lack of ground cover!"

"You are not being reasonable!" Alexis flared. "Think what this could mean to the town of Barrett—the increased business our crews would bring in. That should mean something to a town this size. The restaurants, the motels, the stores all would flourish. And the things *you* would be able to do with the money you receive would also help Barrett. You're depriving your own town of the business sustenance it desperately needs."

"Don't preach to me about Barrett," he growled, picking up his tools and wire and starting toward the garage. "This town doesn't need all that. Some places are not meant to grow, and this is one of them. It's an area with a small population, mostly ranchers and some farmers. What we do around here won't support a town any larger than the one we have. The prosperity that the oil business would bring in would be temporary at best, and would give the people a false idea of what they could make. Then when the oil moved out, the people would be left with what they once had. People would get fired. The new things they bought on the basis of the boom would be unsalable. They'd be worse off than before."

"That is faulty economic thinking," Alexis contended, matching him stride for stride. "The oil business is here to stay. They *can* count on it, if only people like you would be public-spirited enough to give oil a chance! And the extra money they'd earn while the crews are here wouldn't be lost. That means they *would* be better off than before."

Brant swung the wire into the back seat of his jeep and tossed in the tools. Then he turned to face Alexis, his face hard, his eyes as cold as marble. "Let me put it this way. I don't care that most of the people of Barrett are oil-crazy. It won't bother me in the least if they all hate my guts because I don't lease. I intend to do what I want to, what my father would have done, and what my own conscience tells me is the right thing to do. *I am not leasing.* Now, get that through your head. I am going out to help some of my hands with the fences, and when I get back, I don't want to see you here. Is that clear? If the only way I can get rid of you is to call the sheriff and have you arrested for trespassing, I will."

With that, he jumped into his jeep and turned on the ignition. With a roar, he backed out of the garage and left Alexis standing staring after him, hardly able to believe that he had just driven off so rudely.

With a wordless cry of frustration, she stamped her foot angrily on the garage floor. What an insufferable, horrible man he was, so utterly impervious to any kind of reason!

Stormily, she walked to her car, got in, and slammed the door. She wondered how long he would be gone. She had no intention of following his orders to vacate his property. Surely not even he would make such a fool of himself as to call the sheriff. No, she would just wait for him to return. She was not about to give up this easily. Folding her arms, she swung her legs up onto the seat and arranged herself as comfortably as she could, settling down to outwait him.

Three hours later, Brant had still not returned, and Alexis found herself growing more tired, hot, and thirsty by the moment. The October sun was beating through the windows and she rolled them down, to find herself in contention with the annoying, dusty Panhandle wind. And, to top it all off, her stomach was growling with hunger pangs. Alexis began to think that her mission was futile. Brant would probably stay out all day. Since he hadn't taken any food with him, she had hoped that he would come back for lunch, but doubtless he was one of those obnoxious types who could go all day without eating and never notice a thing.

Finally yielding to the clamor of her own stomach, Alexis turned the car around and drove into Barrett. There was little choice in the way of restaurants, just Nora's Cafe and a drive-in across from the high school. Alexis chose Nora's.

Nora greeted her like an old friend, which soothed Alexis's lacerated feelings somewhat. The food was simple, good, and more than ample, and Alexis became so interested in the conversation of two farmers at the table next to hers that she lost all track of time. It was almost two o'clock before she realized that she wasn't getting anything accomplished here.

The jeep was not in sight when Alexis drove up to the McClure ranch, and she got out of her car with a sigh.

There was no longer a speck of shade around the house in which to park her car, and she knew it would be unbearably hot inside the vehicle. She strolled up the front steps to the porch and sat down on an old swing. For a few moments she rocked absently, her eyelids growing heavy. The long-sleeved jacket was too warm for her, so she took it off and folded it over the back of the swing. The blouse was really too sheer, she thought, to be worn without the jacket, but there was no one here to see her, and when she heard Brant's jeep, she could slip it back on.

The warm, somnolent afternoon continued, and before long Alexis leaned her head back against the swing. The gentle rocking, the breeze, the monotonous hum of the insects in the yard lulled her, and soon she dozed off.

"Well, Sleeping Beauty," a harsh voice said, jerking Alexis from her sleep.

Blinking, disoriented, she looked up to find Brant McClure towering over her. He stood with his hands on his hips, his face angry and hard, glistening with sweat. His blue work shirt was damp and opened down the front to reveal his bare chest, covered with curling brown hair that was dotted with tiny drops of sweat. A gleam in Brant's gold eyes unnerved Alexis.

"I must have fallen asleep," she murmured. She straightened up and stretched, trying to appear calm.

"You were supposed to be gone," he snapped, and his burning eyes lowered pointedly to her chest. "I like your wares, ma'am, but the price is too high for me."

Alexis remembered then that she had taken off her jacket and was sitting there in her revealing blouse. A flush stained her cheeks as she picked up her jacket and hastily put it on.

"I didn't realize—I mean, no one was here, and I—" Alexis shut her mouth on her stumbling excuses. She had no need to apologize to this man; she must not show any weakness. Far better to be on the offensive.

"How long have you been standing there before you woke me up?"

A slow, insulting grin spread across his lips. "Oh, I enjoyed the scenery a little first." He leaned against the wooden column of the porch, crossing his arms negligently. "That's a good business suit for you, Alexis. The jacket is all lawyerish, and you can pester and prod and pound on your desk, but if you don't get anywhere with that, you can always take off your jacket and persuade in more subtle ways."

Alexis came off the swing in a single movement, her blue eyes dark. "You are the rudest, most insulting person I have ever met! My father told me you were pigheaded, but he didn't tell me that you had the manners of a pig as well. You accuse me of all kinds of things when you know absolutely nothing about me. And you blindly refuse our offer when you don't know what it is!"

His jaw tightened, and in a dangerously still voice he said, "I know all about your offer. You don't need to spell it out for me. I know that it consists of avarice, money, and deceit. Nothing you could offer would induce me to let Stone Oil destroy my land. Your father and his kind are predators, killers." His eyes flashed fire, and Alexis was suddenly aware of an awesome hatred within him. "I wouldn't let one of his kind get his hands on my land for anything. He destroys everything he touches."

"You don't even know my father!" Alexis cried in astonishment. "How can you be so sure about that? How can you be so sure you know all about him?"

"I do know Alec Stone. I met him when he was here before, when I was twelve. He's a snake, a first-class son of a bitch."

Alexis gasped. How dare he talk about her father like that! She wanted to fly at Brant, clawing and hitting, and it was only with the utmost effort that she restrained herself. She glared at him helplessly, taut as a wire, trembling, and then she noticed that he stood in much the same way she did: tight, barely controlled, an invisible yet palpable energy racing inside him. She suspected that he would have liked nothing better than for her to lash out at him in physical violence. That thought helped cool her seething emotions and set her brain in command once more.

Alexis smiled, a little pityingly. "What a narrow-minded man you are. How did Beth come out so nonjudgmental?"

"Beth is naive," he snapped. "She is foolish enough and inexperienced enough to fall for the act you put on."

Alexis raised her eyebrows condescendingly. "She is a grown woman with two children. Somehow I suspect she can't be all that naive."

"She's been protected all her life," he retorted. "Somebody who loved her—her father, her brother, her husband—was always there to shield her from the hurt, the lies, the predators of the world."

Alexis felt a spasm of ache and envy that she had never known such masculine love and protection, but the feeling was quickly covered by one of irritation. "Perhaps Beth would have appreciated less of your superior male 'protection' and a little more trust."

"What does that mean?"

"It means that Beth told me your father trusted her so little he left all his land to you. Maybe she would rather not have been treated like a child. It's a pretty difficult thing to combat all your life."

"You know nothing about Beth's relationship with our father," he said stiffly. "They loved each other very much."

"And I love *my* father. Therefore, I cannot help but take exception to the vicious things you've been saying about him today," Alexis stated calmly, her head high and her eyes clear and watchful.

"Either you are a tremendous liar or you don't know

the first thing about your father," he remarked in an even tone, but a muscle twitched in his jaw, betraying his banked rage.

"*You* don't know him!" Alexis countered. "You have prejudged him, and you prejudged me because of some warped idea in your head. I don't know where you got it. I don't know why you insist that I came here to offer you my body in exchange for your signing the lease. It all comes from some sick idea you made up and forced onto me."

He looked at her coldly, his eyes like glinting chips of metal, and when he spoke, his voice was clipped and biting. "I know very well what Alec Stone is capable of. I've lived with the results of his whims for quite a few years now. And I know what you are capable of, too. You proved that last night . . . and again today."

Roughly, he reached out and pulled her jacket down over her arms, exposing the swell of her breasts against the thin material of her blouse. At the touch of his hands on her arms, at the nearness of his body, Alexis felt her nipples harden treacherously. A warm flush washed over her face. Beneath the gauzy blouse, the reaction of her body had to be blatantly obvious to Brant. She jerked away from him, straightening her jacket.

"Wearing that blouse, how can you pretend, even to yourself, that you didn't come here to entice me in whatever way you had to so that you'd get your precious lease? If I agreed to the deal right now, you'd be unbuttoning your blouse and heading for the bedroom. You're a whore, Alexis Stone, for all your wealth and power, and Alec Stone is your pimp!"

Alexis choked with impotent fury. She despised the man, longed to batter him with her fists until her wrath had been dissipated. Yet she knew the awful weakness that her body had just displayed; knew, too, the complete mastery over her that he had wrought last night. She sensed suddenly that if they continued this argument now, it would ignite something in them that would only end in her being consumed by flames of passion. Above all else, that must not happen, or she would lose to him utterly.

She pushed past him without a word and walked straight to her car. He remained on the porch watching her as she wheeled the Riviera around and took off down the narrow road at breakneck speed. And inside both the watcher and the watched something seethed and boiled, hurting and remaining unfulfilled.

Chapter 5

Alexis knew that in order to have any hope at all with Brant, she would have to keep a cooler head today than she had yesterday. She had let the things he said about her and her father get to her, and that had given him the upper hand. Yesterday afternoon, after she left Brant's house, she had driven aimlessly for several hours before she returned to Beth's home. Alexis did not feel she could face Beth without revealing her total hatred for the other woman's brother. Finally, she had blown off enough steam, and was able to consider the strategy she should employ with McClure.

Gradually, Alexis realized that he had been intensely attracted to her before. She suspected that below his angry surface there was some feeling for her that she could use. Now she knew she would have no compunction about turning that feeling to her advantage. If she could just stay calm, keep control of her emotions, then eventually he might cool off enough so that an agreement could be reached.

This morning she dressed casually in boots, jeans, and a sky-blue blouse that intensified the color of her eyes, and set out for McClure's ranch once again. Today she intended to be dressed to follow him under any circumstances.

When he did not answer the knock, Alexis skirted the house and went to the corral. There she found him currying a horse, and at the sound of her approach, he looked up. Recognizing her, he straightened and stared at her in pure disbelief.

"You are without a doubt the stubbornest female I ever met," he said brusquely, though a faint glint of amusement flickered in his eyes.

"Yes, I probably am," Alexis agreed, swinging up onto the corral fence to watch him.

"Well, you can keep coming around here every day for the rest of your life if you want to, but that doesn't mean I'll change my mind." He turned back to his work.

"Is that an invitation?" Alexis teased lightly.

The only answer she received was a grunt as he continued currying the horse. For the next few minutes they were silent, and Alexis relaxed a little. At least he wasn't going to throw her off his property immediately, as he had threatened yesterday. She found that sitting on the fence with the fall sun warming her back was rather pleasant. She had never needed a lot of chatter to be content, and she enjoyed watching Brant's skillful, compact movements.

"Do you remember that when you met me, you invited me to go riding with you?"

"So?"

"So I've come to take you up on your offer."

He turned, his face cold. "I have rescinded the offer."

Alexis sighed. "Come on, Brant, can't you bend a little? I promise I won't say a word about leases while we are riding. I would simply like to see your ranch before I leave."

Brant studied her for a moment, his amber eyes wary and thoughtful. "So you are going back to Dallas?"

Alexis shrugged. It was not really a lie; she was going back . . . eventually. "I suppose my father and I will have to accept defeat, for once."

"All right," he said grudgingly, gave the horse a final stroke, then climbed over the fence and went into the barn.

His expression was grim as he saddled and bridled two horses, but Alexis, knowing she had won a small victory in the fight, deliberately ignored his attitude.

"I suppose you don't have the slightest idea how to ride," he growled as he led one of the horses to her.

"Truthfully, I haven't ridden much," she admitted.

Brant's mouth quirked down, indicating his disapproval. "Well, this mare is the most docile horse I have. Bisco won't run away with you, but you'll have to exercise some control over her. Don't get too lax with the reins."

"I won't," Alexis said, putting her foot in the stirrup and pulling herself up into the saddle.

"Too long," Brant declared, looking at the stirrup. "Take your foot out."

Alexis let her leg hang loose as Brant adjusted the stirrup. Then they repeated the process with the other side.

Brant disappeared into the house and returned a moment later with a rifle, which he shoved into a leather scabbard behind his saddle. Alexis raised her eyebrows.

"I promise you won't need to defend yourself against me," she remarked sarcastically, gesturing at the gun. "Or are you planning to stop my bugging you permanently?"

A frosty smile touched his mouth. "Actually, I always carry it in case of an emergency. But now that you mention it, it would be an effective end to my problems with you."

Brant swung into his saddle, and they set off at a sedate trot. The ride was bone-jarring, especially since Alexis had no idea how to post. She was grateful when Brant slowed to a walk, and her horse followed suit. Brant glanced around at her, and she detected a gleam of wicked laughter in his eyes. "Trouble?"

"Nothing except that my teeth are about to fall out," Alexis retorted. Then, determined to be cheerful, she asked, "What kind of cattle do you raise here?"

"Hereford mostly, Angus." His answer was terse, and he did not look at her.

Alexis gritted her teeth and tried again. "How many men work for you?"

"Four or five, besides the foreman. I usually have to hire extra help when the work is heavy, like during roundups or the calving season."

"How big is the ranch?"

An unpleasant smile seamed his face. "As if you didn't know. I imagine Alec Stone knows everything there is to know about me."

Alexis sighed. "I was just trying to be pleasant."

"Why? Why should you try? Why should you care? There is no reason in the world for us to get along. It would be better if we remained in a state of mutual antipathy."

"I bet you have a lot of friends."

"Enough," he answered laconically.

For the moment Alexis gave up her attempts at conversation. The day was as warm as it had been yesterday. She was becoming thirsty and, worst of all, stiff. Her back and legs ached, unaccustomed as she was to riding, and she wished they would stop for a rest.

In order to take her mind off her pains, she returned to conversation. "Are you and Beth close?"

He shrugged. "Depends on what you mean by close. She usually tells me a lot about what she's doing, or her problems."

"But you don't reciprocate," Alexis ventured.

"I'm not real big on gabbing about my problems to the world, no."

"Neither am I. I've always been rather solitary. I spent a lot of time with my studies, my books."

He glanced at her briefly. "Ambitious, huh? The besetting sin of the Stones. You know, I can see that ambition written all over you—the way you hold yourself, like you're about to pounce; the way you listen so intensely, as if nothing must slip by you. You always seem pumped full of voltage."

Alexis bit back a retort. At least he was talking, not frozen in silence or yelling abusively. "I take it you think ambition is bad."

"Not necessarily. Some people don't have enough of it and some have too much. There isn't anything wrong with it, in and of itself. I have ambitions—for improving the stock, for making the ranch profitable and successful."

"None for your personal life?"

At this question he gave her a long, thoughtful look. "I'm not all that interested in my personal life. I don't imagine you are, either."

Alexis shook her head. "Not much." She paused, then asked, "So what makes us different? It sounds to me as if we're rather similar."

"God, I hope not!"

"Did anyone ever tell you how rude and obnoxious you are?"

"I think you did yesterday."

"Apparently it didn't make much of an impression."

"Apparently not," was his easy answer.

Alexis stretched a little, trying to ease the stiffness in her shoulders. She was beginning to wonder when he was going to turn back. She really hadn't had a tour of the ranch in mind when she had suggested that they ride.

"It's only a little farther," Brant said as if reading her thoughts. "I thought I'd show you the creek that runs through the property."

The cottonwood trees lining the creek were a welcome sight, even if the fall weather had stripped them of their leaves. When they reached the water, Alexis dismounted swiftly, anxious to get out of the numbing saddle. To her surprise, her knees buckled under her, and she had to grab at the saddle horn to keep from falling over.

Brant chuckled. "Sore?"

Alexis glared at him, straightened, and tried to walk away from Bisco with as much dignity as she could muster. Behind her, she heard Brant's deep laughter and she whirled around. "I fail to see what is so amusing!"

"I know. You never see yourself as anything but supremely important and serious. Believe me, that walk of yours *is* amusing!"

However, despite his laughter, he moved forward and put one hand under her arm to help her.

"I am perfectly capable of walking by myself!" Alexis snapped, twisting her arm away.

"No doubt," he replied smoothly, and replaced his hand. "But allow me to be a gentleman."

Alexis gave a small snort that was meant to indicate her disbelief, but she did not remove her arm. They strolled down the bank of the creek. It was cooler here, and Alexis could feel the looseness returning to her numbed limbs as she walked. Beside her, Brant seemed a little more human, unbending somewhat for the first time since the disastrous night of the party.

"This is the only creek on the property," he said. "My great-grandfather named it Siler Creek, after one he had known in East Texas. It flows eventually into the north fork of the Red River."

"Your great-grandfather settled the land?"

"Yes, in 1910, when my grandfather was just a boy. He was one of the earliest settlers around here."

"Who built the house? Your great-grandfather?"

He and my grandfather both, in 1922. Originally they only had a dugout. You can see the remains of it in the center of the ranch. Then they added on, built a little wooden house, and turned the dugout into a cellar. That's used by the ranch foreman now. I think they built the big house because my grandfather was about to be married and they needed a lot more room in the house for kids. It was actually my grandfather who built this place up. His father was something of a dreamer, the kind who thought big but never did much. But Granddad was a real doer. He quadrupled the size of the ranch over the years, built the big house, and married the banker's daughter."

"Was that how he got the money to increase the ranch?"

"I don't think so. Oh, maybe part of it. Probably her father loaned him money more readily. But Granddad was an independent old cuss, and he was strong. I remember one time my father wanted to do something after he had a family, and Granddad thought it would hurt the ranch. Boy, they had a bang-up argument, but it was Granddad who won it. My father backed down. I think that was the only time in my life I ever saw him do that."

"So you come from a family of independent, strong-willed old cusses."

"Yeah, I guess so. We are all like that," he agreed.

Alexis felt relaxed; they seemed to be getting along more smoothly. Unthinkingly, she said, "I guess stubbornness must run in families. Alec is stubborn, and so am I."

Her companion stiffened at the mention of her father, and Alexis could have bitten her tongue. Why had she said that just when everything was going so well? "What do you have against my father?" she asked on impulse. "I know he can be rather devious at times, but what did he do that got your back up so?"

Brant regarded her intently, and for a moment she thought he was about to reveal something. Then he replied, "Nothing."

"It can't have been nothing," Alexis countered earnestly. "You speak of him with such absolute hatred. You said he ruined your life."

Brant shrugged. "I was exaggerating."

"Look, I am not a fragile flower. I can take it."

He stopped walking and turned to face her. "Either you're a liar and know all about your father and are just like him, or else this innocent pose is real. If that's the case, there's no point in shattering your illusions."

"Brant, I don't have any illusions."

He shook his head and started back toward the horses. With a sigh, Alexis followed him. His paternal attitude was maddening, and yet . . . why was she so sorry to see this moment of friendship end? After all that he had said to her, surely she could not possibly wish to have any sort of relationship with him . . . could she?

Disturbed by her thoughts, Alexis clambered clumsily into her saddle, Brant giving her a small shove on her bottom. His touch and the wash of weakness it sent through her disturbed her even more. She put her heels into her horse's side, urging the mare into a gallop. Behind her, she heard Brant give a shout, but she rode heedlessly on, aware of his horse's hooves and that he was racing after her.

Never before had Alexis felt quite this sensation as the mare sped along. It was beautiful, freeing, frightening, and yet exciting; it seemed to match her mood. The wind whipped at her tied-back hair, tugging it free and sending it whirling behind her like a bright flame. Suddenly her horse broke and shied, and the reins were wrenched from her hands. She grabbed at the saddle horn, her feet slipping from the stirrups. Bisco twisted and reared, and Alexis slid helplessly backward.

In the next instant she landed with a solid thump that sent all the air rushing from her lungs and shot dazzling sparks across her eyes. For endless seconds she could not breathe, and she knew she would die because she couldn't get any air into her lungs. Frantically, she turned her head to one side, trying to suck in air, still not completely aware of what had happened. There, not ten feet away, lay the coil that had caused her horse to buck in terror. Its tail shaking ominously, its head raised and searching, the rattlesnake inched forward.

Alexis wanted to scream, but the breath would not penetrate her lungs. Feebly, powered by overwhelming fear, her arms and legs began to twitch, and she scrambled to get out of the way. Yet nothing seemed to obey her brain, and now the snake was sliding toward her.

There was the sound of hooves behind her, an explosion, and before her eyes the head of the snake separated from its body, flying off. Gorge rose in her throat, and suddenly she slipped into darkness. Her head lolled back in a faint.

"Alexis!" Brant leaped down from his saddle, the rifle still in his hands. He ran to her still form, dropped the rifle on the ground, and reached for the pulse in her throat. It was still beating strongly and he swallowed in relief. Quickly, he ran his hands over her body, prodding gently for broken bones.

"Alexis," he said again, and this time her eyelids fluttered open and she stared up at him. His face was pale and strained, a frown across his forehead. "Are you all right?"

She nodded weakly, and sucked in the delicious air she had been searching for moments ago. "What . . . what happened?"

"I think Bisco bolted when she saw the snake, and she threw you. You're a damn little fool for galloping like that! You don't know how to ride a horse," he said harshly.

"Don't lecture," she murmured between ragged breaths. "God, I feel like I died."

"Well, you haven't. You just got the wind knocked out of you. Lie there for a second, and then we'll see about moving you."

"I wasn't trying to go anywhere, believe me."

That remark brought a thin, involuntary smile to his lips, and he stood up. "I know it's hard for you, but try not to talk. You'll feel better."

Picking up the rifle, he replaced it in the scabbard behind his saddle. Then he came back to Alexis and squatted down on one knee. Gently, he slid one arm behind her neck and shoulders and propped her up.

"Feeling better?" he asked. Alexis nodded, and he continued. "I don't think any bones are broken. I want you to try to stand up. I'll help you. Okay?"

Her entire back ached, as did her head, but at least everything seemed to move all right. However, as she set her right foot on the ground and tried to shift her weight to it, a pain stabbed through her ankle and she winced.

"What's the matter?" His arms tightened around her, holding her upright.

"My ankle hurts."

He bent down, put his arm under her knees, and easily scooped her up as if she were a baby. At her faint sound of protest, he said gruffly, "Hush. There's no sense in putting any weight on it. Just be quiet, and we'll see what we can do about it at my place."

He carried her to his horse and settled her onto it, then swung up behind her. Cradling her in his arms as he had carried her, he clucked to the animal, and they set off toward the ranch.

It was a much slower journey now than it had been before, especially since every movement jarred Alexis's back unmercifully. Despite the pain, she was uncomfortably aware of the nearness of Brant, of his clean male scent, of his muscled chest against her cheek. His arms encircled her in a warm ring of protection, and she felt lazily content, yet jumping inside with fearful excitement. Just the touch of his powerful body, she realized, was enough to turn her all weak again.

She resented his magnetism and her response. And yet . . . how nice it was to have seen the concerned look on his face, to have heard that light tremble underlying his voice when he knelt beside her and spoke her name. He had been scared because she was

hurt. And now, suddenly, his anger was gone, and he was gentle and kind. With an inner sigh, she wished it would last longer.

"What about my horse?" she asked, her words muffled against his shirt.

Brant drew in a funny little half breath and said, "Oh, don't worry about Bisco. She'll find her way home. We'll probably find her there before us."

In fact, they did. The paint mare stood waiting patiently beside the corral and looked at them as if wondering what had taken them so long.

Alexis had to smile. "I don't think Bisco is exactly aware of the great inconvenience she's caused."

Brant chuckled. "Don't expect a horse to be too concerned about your spills."

He reined up in front of the house and slipped to the ground, easily lifting Alexis down. He carried her to the front porch, and she reached out to open the door for him.

"I feel like we're honeymooners," she joked, and felt his arms become rigid beneath her.

He deposited her on the living-room sofa and left, returning a few moments later with an assortment of first-aid equipment. His concerned manner was gone, and in its place was the mask of a polite stranger. I'd better learn to put a curb on my tongue around Brant McClure, Alexis told herself.

Efficiently, he gave her aspirin and a cool, damp cloth for her head, then removed her boots to feel her ankle gingerly. "No broken bones that I can tell. I imagine it's only a sprain. I'll put this ice bag on it. That's about all there is to do. But if you want, I'll drive you to Dr. Whiting's office and have him look at it."

Alexis shook her head. Beth had told her that it was Jack Whiting who had informed Brant of her identity, and she had an unreasoning but strong aversion to the man. "No, I'm sure I'll be fine."

"Good. Now, if you will excuse me, I have to

unsaddle the horses. I'll come back later and fix us some lunch."

Alexis lay still after he had left, feeling the blessed easing of the ache in her head as the aspirin took effect. Even her back did not seem quite so bad. Carefully, she sat up and put her feet firmly on the floor. She hadn't noticed any pain in that ankle since she had first stepped on it, and she suspected that it wasn't as bad as Brant thought. Slowly, she stood up and gently transferred half her weight onto it. She winced at first but was able to walk across the floor with the merest of limps. Alexis was positive the ankle was strong enough so that she could walk out the door and drive back to Beth's.

But she wasn't ready to let Brant McClure know that just yet. She returned to the couch, and stretching her legs out on the sofa, returned the ice bag to her ankle. She could think of ways she would rather gain some quiet friendliness from Brant, or at least a cessation of hostilities, than from being thrown off a horse. But since the opportunity had arisen, she was not about to let it slip through her fingers. He planned to make them lunch, and perhaps in that time she could forge some inroads on his obstinate attitude about the lease. She certainly wasn't going to volunteer the fact that she was feeling well enough to go back to Beth's.

A small worry at this deception touched her conscience, but she pushed it away. It was only a small lie; her ankle did hurt, and it had been very painful a little while ago. Besides, Brant was simply assuming that it was too bad for her to walk on. She was really doing nothing more than refraining from rocking the boat.

Alexis heard a door closing somewhere in the house, then the clatter of dishes from the kitchen. A few minutes later Brant appeared in the doorway, two plates in his hands.

"I hope you like tuna fish; it was all I could find."

"Love it," Alexis assured him.

"What would you like to drink?"

"Anything. Tea, a Coke, whatever."

He left, and returned shortly with an icy glass of tea. Alexis sipped at it gratefully, suddenly remembering how thirsty she was. "Thank you. It's delicious." She took a bite of her sandwich. "So is this. You're a terrific cook."

He smiled. "It's not exactly the hautest of haute cuisine."

"So who is used to haute cuisine? It's usually hamburgers, pizza, and TV dinners for me."

"What? No chef? Or at least a housekeeper?" he teased, his face relaxed, almost friendly.

"I definitely think you have the wrong idea of my life."

"Really? And what is your life like?"

"Very dull," Alexis said, startled at her own words. Never before had she thought of her life as dull. "I get up at six-thirty and leave at seven-fifteen because of traffic on the Central. I work all day. Usually I get my secretary to bring me a sandwich for lunch. And I go home about eight, unless I have something urgent to finish. I drive home, eat, run a little, relax, and go to bed early."

"All work and no play . . ."

"You should talk."

He laughed shortly. "I suppose you're right. Beth always tells me I do nothing but work. Only most of it doesn't seem like work to me. I do things I really enjoy. Sometimes I feel like I'm on a full-time vacation."

"I used to enjoy what I did very much. But lately I've felt restless and bored. I don't know exactly what it is. I think maybe I'm getting tired of leases and royalty interests, all the estate problems and divisions, the contracts and sales." It amazed Alexis to hear herself telling him these things. She had not spoken of her recent dissatisfaction to anyone, and yet here she was telling Brant McClure, who hated her and her job.

McClure regarded her steadily. "You mean you want to get out of oil?"

"Oh, I don't know. I don't think so. I mean, someday my sisters and I will own it, and one of us ought to know something about it. But I think I'd like to move to another area—the administrative law part, perhaps—that deals with government and regulations."

"Do you do court work?"

"No, I'm not the type for litigation."

"Why not?"

"It makes me too nervous. I'm scared."

"You?" His tone was disbelieving.

"I told you, your picture of me is far from real."

Brant finished his sandwich and stood up. "I think I'll take a look at your ankle." He knelt beside the couch and pushed her pants leg above her ankle, then removed the ice pack. "Very good. It looks like the swelling has gone down a lot. I'm going to probe a little bit more. Tell me if it hurts."

His strong, slender fingers gently explored her ankle, probing carefully around the bone, then moving the foot around. Alexis went liquid inside at his soft touch, the tingling going straight from his fingers clear up to her chest. She felt suddenly flushed, then cold, and she knew that she wanted those fingers to travel up her leg and explore her body ceaselessly in the same caressing way.

Alexis clenched her own fingers. Brant McClure was her enemy, if anyone ever was. He hated her and everything about her, had told her so in very explicit terms. Yet she, like a fool, had sat here revealing things about herself. She couldn't even control her treacherous body, which yearned for his touch without a regard for her mind's commands.

"Ouch!" she snapped, not because what he was doing hurt her, but simply to get him to remove his hands. She had to stop the idiotic way she was feeling, had to regain control of herself.

"That's the place, huh?" he said, and laid her foot back on the couch.

He stood and barely looked at her, jamming his hands into his pockets. The former tautness had returned to his face, and his eyes were as bright and hard as agate. "I'll call Beth, and then I'll take you over there."

Quickly, Brant left the room and strode down the hallway to the kitchen, mentally cursing himself. Why did he let Alexis get to him so? Despite all he knew about her, he had felt the familiar hot stab in his loins when he examined her ankle, and he had wanted to stretch full length against her on the couch, to mold her body to his, to kiss her and caress her, to ease this raging hunger that started up each time he saw her. Already she was working her spell on him, and he was unbending, talking to her, believing her act.

Her fall had broken the barrier between them he had carefully built. The seconds it had taken to catch up to her had seemed endless. He had seen the snake as he came skidding to a stop, and for one heart-stopping moment he had thought he would see her die before his eyes. Thank God, he had brought the rifle. Thank God, his arm and eye had been steady. The warm relief that had flooded him when he knelt beside her and realized she was all right had finished off his reserve.

Brant had tried to recapture that reserve once or twice since he had brought Alexis home, but each time it had slipped away again. That was why he had to take her back to Beth's, had to get her out of the house before his desire betrayed him.

Beth's lilting voice answered the phone, and he plunged in. "Beth, this is Brant. Listen, Alexis got thrown this morning."

Beth gasped. "Oh, no! Is she badly hurt?"

"No, nothing serious. I didn't take her to the doctor. All she has is a sprained ankle, and I've got her on the couch now with an ice pack on it. It still hurts some, but I don't think there'll be any problem."

"Thank heavens!" Beth exclaimed, relieved.

"Anyway, I'm going to drive her back in your car. Can you bring me back to my ranch?"

There was a long pause at the other end, and Brant could almost see Beth's mental wheels spinning. Finally she said, "Well, Brant, I just don't know. I was going to pick the girls up at school and take them to Amarillo to see the orthodontist. He's putting braces on Jenny's teeth. So I won't be here to take you back. Couldn't Alexis just stay there for a while?"

"No, she could not," Brant declared firmly. "I'll bring her back in my car, and you can get this car of yours some other time."

"But, Brant, surely Alexis shouldn't be over here all alone, not with a hurt ankle. How will she get anything to eat? I don't think she should walk on it. And what if she needs help? No, really, Brant, I don't like the idea. I think she should stay with you until we return."

Brant sighed. "And when will that be?"

"Very late tonight. I promised the girls a treat. Rusty is meeting us, and we're going out to eat and to see a movie. So there's no point in your bringing her back until tomorrow."

"Spend the night here? Come on, Beth, cut out the tricks! I know what you're trying to do, and it won't work. I don't want any of your scheming!"

"I'm not scheming," Beth replied with an air of injured innocence. "I told you, I already had all this planned. And I can't cancel Jenny's appointment. It would be six more months before I could get another one. Orthodontist appointments are precious."

"You're still trying to cook up something, Beth, I know you. And I refuse to go along with it."

"Go along with what? Really, Brant, I thought you were mad at the woman. Why should her presence there bother you?"

"Precisely because I *am* mad at her."

"It isn't because you still have a yen for her, is it? And that you're not sure you can stand the test? Isn't it really that you're afraid her attraction might overcome your bitterness?"

"No!"

"Sounds to me like you're scared of her."

"I am not scared of her," Brant said through clenched teeth, thinking that he would cheerfully throttle his little sister if only she were within arm's reach. "Damn it, Beth, you know how I feel about the Stones. How can you saddle me with one of them?"

"I didn't saddle you with her," Beth retorted indignantly. "It was at your ranch that she got thrown, it was your horse, and no doubt it was your carelessness, since you dislike her so much. You'll be lucky if she doesn't sue you."

"For Pete's sake, Beth, will you be serious?"

"I am serious. I told you as seriously as I could that I'm not going to be here the rest of the day and that you'll have to keep Alexis there until tomorrow."

"Beth, if you are lying to me—"

"Honestly, Brant, you are the most suspicious person!"

"With you, I have every reason to be. All right, I'll let her stay here tonight."

"Ah, the gracious host. Alexis will probably be overjoyed at your sacrifice."

"But bright and early tomorrow morning, she is going back."

"Okay. There's no need for you to put on your army voice for me."

"Good-bye." Angrily he clapped the receiver back on the hook. Beth had really gotten to him this time. He didn't believe her little story about the orthodontist for one moment. Oh, she might pick up the girls and Rusty and take off to Amarillo just to make her story convincing, but Brant knew she had concocted the idea on the spur of the moment to force him into a day and evening of proximity to Alexis. Beth had never been above the use of a few little lies if they would smooth the path of one of her schemes.

Pulling his face into a remote, icy mask, Brant walked back into the living room, where Alexis still reclined on the sofa. "I just called Beth, and she said she was going to Amarillo and wouldn't be back until late tonight. So you are going to have to spend the rest of the day here. I'll take you over tomorrow."

Alexis stared at him. Beth had said nothing to her that morning about going out of town. Seeing the obvious reluctance on his face, Alexis retorted automatically, "That's all right. I can stay there without them, surely."

"Don't be an idiot," he said gruffly. "Beth is right. You wouldn't be able to make your meals or call for help if something happened or you got sick. You'll stay here. I have plenty of extra bedrooms."

His domineering tone grated on her nerves, but she had recovered sufficiently from her surprise to realize what Beth was doing. Brant's sister was forcing him to accept Alexis as a guest, hoping that his compulsory hospitality would make him more approachable, more agreeable to Alexis and her proposal. Of course, what Beth wanted was a romantic entanglement, which Alexis knew was impossible now. She and Brant had gone too far to return to that stage. But she was still determined to wrest that lease from him, and being here at his ranch would bring her one step closer to that goal.

Sternly, she repressed the little pangs of guilt that nagged at her for her lies to him, and stifled the desire to throw his grudging offer back in his face. "All right, thank you. Since I don't have much choice, I guess I shall have to be grateful."

"I'm going out to work now. I'll be back in a few hours. Would you like anything before I leave?"

She shook her head. "I think I'll go to sleep."

"All right, then. Good-bye."

He turned on his heel and left. Alexis stared after him, biting her lip, and wondered if she had made a smart move or a large mistake.

Chapter 6

Alexis did, indeed, sleep most of the afternoon. When she awoke, she prowled around the living room, looking at the books that lined the bookshelves and at the pictures on the walls. Her ankle felt a great deal better, and even her back did not ache very much.

She almost wished that she hadn't gone ahead with her plan. Now it made her very uneasy. It had seemed all right when she first thought of it, and even better after Beth had made up a story to aid and abet her. But now—what if he found out? He would have her dead to rights this time about being deceitful. She would be even worse off than before. But there was nothing she could do about it. She could not confess that her ankle was fine.

At the sound of the back door slamming shut, Alexis hopped back onto the couch and waited for Brant to appear. She heard the tread of his boots on the wooden hallway floor, and her stomach constricted in anticipation.

"Hello." He stopped in the doorway and swept his eyes over her.

A shiver ran through her, and she could manage no more than a smile. His hair was damp, and he had peeled off his stained work shirt and slung it over his shoulder. His broad chest glistened with sweat, and

Alexis's eyes were drawn to it. He was so tanned, so hard, the muscles across his stomach and chest like iron . . . There was something about him that was elemental and overpowering.

Brant took off his felt cowboy hat, rubbed the sweat from his brow with his forearm, and smiled at her a little ruefully. "I'm afraid I'm a little dirty. I'll have to clean up before I can fix dinner, if you don't mind."

He had spent the afternoon doing the most physically taxing chores he could find, digging post holes with a couple of his men on the south fence. He had hoped that would rid his mind of Alexis, but one look at her, and he knew it hadn't worked. Alexis looked incredibly vibrant, her eyes the color of the pansies his mother had grown when he was a child. Brant sensed it was going to be a long evening.

After taking a shower, he whipped up a quick dinner of steak and salad, and he and Alexis ate off the low coffee table in the living room. Alexis smiled to herself at the sight of him squatting cross-legged on the floor, dressed in a T-shirt and jeans, barefoot, his hair dark with dampness from his shower. He looked almost boyish. She realized with a start that she wanted to reach out and run her hand through his wet hair.

To turn the direction of her thoughts, she asked brightly, "What did you do this afternoon?"

"Dug a few post holes. I had to replace some of the fencing."

"I thought there was a machine that did that."

"There is, but for the small amount I had to do, there was no point in renting one. Anyhow, I enjoy the exercise."

Under her questioning, he began to unbend further. He spoke of the cattle auctions, of buying and selling stock, of breeding them and doctoring the sick ones, of the myriad ordinary tasks that had to be done to the outbuildings and fences, and to the land itself. Alexis sat wrapped up in the spell of his words, envisioning his lonely, demanding life, the pride and love he felt for his property. Without her quite knowing why, her eyes stung with tears.

"You love this ranch more than anything, don't you?" she asked softly.

Brant looked at her, his expression serious but not closed. "Yes, I do. That's why I won't lease to your father."

Alexis knew with a sinking feeling that no matter what she did, she could never shake his conviction. He would not lease the land to her even if he consented to listen to her reasonable arguments. And she could not bring herself to try any of her father's tactics. She might as well pack up and leave tomorrow and admit to Alec that she had failed.

"I'm going home tomorrow," she announced. "I know you aren't going to give me the lease. But I would truly appreciate it if you'd tell me what you have against my father."

A blaze flickered in his eyes and was gone. "You wouldn't want to know."

"Would you please let me decide that for myself? I am not impressed by your macho attitude, and I assure you I can handle whatever it is."

He sighed, rose, and went to the window to stare out at the bleak Panhandle night, his back to Alexis. "Since you insist . . . When your father was here in 1958 to lease H. R. Thompson's land, he came to our house and tried to lease Dad's land, too, but Dad wouldn't allow it. I remember just the way he looked—tall, with blue-black eyes like yours, and just brimming with energy and drive. He was very charismatic. I admired him, and I couldn't understand why Dad wouldn't do business with him. For a little while I dreamed of working on the oil rigs when I grew up, becoming an independent operator and making my fortune in oil."

He paused, and Alexis said dryly, "Daddy has that effect on people."

"Later, when they started drilling on Thompson's land, he came here quite often, still trying to get Dad to lease him the mineral rights. Sometimes he would be at the house when I got home from school, and at first I was awed and pleased. Then it began to occur to me that something was wrong, that there was no reason for him to be here at that time, but I kept my mouth shut about it. I didn't want to know what was going on. One night I heard Mother and Dad have a shouting match downstairs in the den. I couldn't understand what they were saying, but I had never heard them yell at each other like that. I could hear Alec Stone's name mentioned often, loud and clear. The next day when I got home from school, Mother was gone. I haven't heard from her since."

Brant turned toward Alexis, his eyes hard and dark, glittering with a pain that remained after all these years. "All the time Alec Stone was coming over here and working on Dad, he was having an affair with my mother. She left Dad for him, and, of course, later Stone dropped her flat. He was never particularly interested in her. He was just bored, and no doubt it added a fillip to his pleasure to think he was cuckolding the man who opposed him. It broke my father's heart. He was never the same after that. Some spirit in him died, and for all the love he gave Beth and me, I don't think he ever really enjoyed life again. For a whim, for his own temporary pleasure, Alec Stone broke my father—and that is why I can never forgive him!"

"No." Alexis stared at Brant, her eyes wide. Her brain felt blank. She could think of nothing to say, did not even know what to think. Brant whirled around to gaze out the window again, his back rigid and his arms crossed, closed in on himself.

"I might have known you wouldn't believe it," he said bitterly.

"That's not true!" Alexis denied hotly. "Daddy didn't— He wouldn't!" No, not her father, not Alec, not the man she had always idolized.

Brant turned back to her, his face stamped with

contempt. "How much can you pretend things don't exist, just so you won't tarnish your precious father's image?"

"You were young. You can't be sure that what you thought happened really did happen. Sometimes children get things distorted, confused."

"I wasn't a baby, Alexis. I was twelve, almost a teen-ager. I knew what was going on. Everyone did. Ask Beth, ask anyone who lived in Barrett then. The affair gave the county a whole year's gossip."

"Gossip isn't necessarily true," Alexis observed halfheartedly as Brant faced the window once more. But she was aware of her father's insatiable hunger for everything in life. Why wouldn't that hunger extend to women as well, especially since he was so attractive? Women flocked to him in droves at parties. Though Alexis had thought nothing of her parent's divorce at the time—all her friends' parents were divorcing, and she knew that Alec was hell to live with—now she remembered seeing her mother's face tear-stained long before and long after the divorce, and hearing her mumbled, inarticulate reasons for the separation. Ginny had not wanted to blacken their father in her daughters' eyes. Alexis remembered, too, her mother's words on the phone several nights ago, words that had struck her then as curious: ". . . serious men can be just as unfaithful as fun-loving ones, you know. Sometimes I think the ambitious ones are the worst." The ambitious ones—who else but Alec Stone?

Alexis thought of her sparkling, beautiful stepmother, Laraine, whom Alec had married three short months after the divorce. Had he been having an affair with her? Was that what had triggered the divorce? How strange that she had never thought of this before.

Alexis swallowed and said faintly, "Even if it *is* true, that doesn't mean Alec behaved maliciously. They were just attracted to each other. If you'll remember, there was a good deal of chemistry between us the other night, even though neither of us wanted it. Things like that happen. It doesn't mean that my father set out to ruin your life."

Brant was silent, and she went on. "I'm sorry, Brant. I don't know what else to say. I can't make up for what my father did over twenty years ago. But can't you see that it doesn't make *me* bad?"

He whirled around to face her. "You're just like him. You came up here to use your body to get to me."

"I did not!" Alexis retorted. "No matter what you think, I did *not* do that. Why should whatever he did be settled on me? After all, it wasn't only my father who was involved. Your mother had an equal share in it. Does that automatically make *you* bad?"

Brant offered no reply, merely looked at her from unfathomable amber eyes. Finally he broke and walked from the room. Alexis heard the back door slam, and she leaned against the arm of the sofa with a sigh. It looked as if she was stuck here. She had no idea where Brant had gone or how long he might stay away. But she knew she couldn't seek a vacant bed and thus show him, when he returned, that she was capable of walking around or even climbing stairs. After what she had said, she couldn't let him know that she had lied to him, or he would feel doubly justified in his attitude toward her.

As she lay there, she slowly drifted off to sleep. The next thing she realized, she was being lifted, and her eyelids fluttered open drowsily. Brant's face loomed above her.

"What—"

"Shh. It's all right. I'm taking you up to a bed so you can sleep better," he whispered.

Alexis relaxed, leaning gratefully against his broad chest. The slow, rhythmic pump of his heart beneath her head was soothing, and she felt pleasantly cosseted. Before he reached the room, she was fast asleep again. Gently, he set her on the bed and started to pull the covers around her, but then he stopped, gazing down at

her. It would be uncomfortable for her to sleep in the
dirty clothes she had on, yet he didn't want to awaken
her to undress. For a moment he hesitated. Then, with
a shrug and a set face, he reached out and unsnapped
her jeans. He pulled them down over her slim hips and
legs and tossed them on the floor, then began to
unbutton her blouse. With a grimace, he noticed that
his fingers trembled on the buttons, and he cursed
himself for the tide of desire that rose in him at the sight
of her firm body clothed only in underwear. Damn
the woman!—Why did she have the power to arouse
him so?

He very much wanted to ease the lacy bits of
underwear from her and kiss her awake, to feast his
eyes and hands and mouth on her beauty. What did it
matter who her father was or what she had come here
for? She moved him as no other woman ever had . . .
wasn't that enough?

With a sound of disgust, he tucked her in bed and
pulled the covers over her. He ran one hand through
his thick hair and sighed, then abruptly turned and
walked out of the room.

Alexis awoke in a strange room, and it was a moment
before she got her bearings and remembered where she
was. Vaguely, the memory of Brant's carrying her
upstairs came back to her. She realized then that she
was lying in bed with nothing on but her bra and
panties. When had she undressed? She could not
remember. Had Brant undressed her? A flush rose in
her cheeks at the thought. She was at once embarrassed
and strangely breathless.

There was a soft knock on the door, and the handle
turned. Brant entered the room, balancing a tray with
one hand. He smiled, and it seemed to Alexis that his
face no longer wore that carefully controlled mask.

"Service with a smile," he joked, and brought the
tray to her bed. "Here is your breakfast."

"You shouldn't have," she protested, sitting up and

clutching the sheet to her, intensely aware of her nakedness and the fact that he was responsible for it. "I could have come downstairs."

Brant made no reply. He placed the tray on her lap and poured a cup of coffee from the small pot. There was a second mug on the tray, and he poured himself a cup. He remained standing, watching her, and Alexis felt self-conscious under his scrutiny.

"I—I'm sure my ankle is fine this morning and that I can drive back to Beth's house."

"I've been thinking about that. It would be better if you rested again today, just stayed off it. That way you'll be sure it's healed."

"But I'm going to fly back to Dallas today."

"There's no need to, is there? You could stay another day. I'll carry you down to the living room and you can read and rest there. I have to go up to the north quarter to help the men load some cattle, so I'll be gone."

"No, really," Alexis began again, feeling helplessly trapped in her fabrication. "I'm sure my ankle is just fine. There's no need—"

"I want you to." His voice cut firmly across her words. "Look, I have to get to work, so I can't talk about it now. But I would like you to stay here another day. I can fix us supper again tonight, and we can talk then."

Alexis hesitated, glancing up at him. Brant's face was softer, with an almost pleading look in his eyes. She realized that he was apologizing to her in his own stiff way, that he was saying he was willing to try for a new start. She swallowed, feeling suddenly scared.

"All—all right," she agreed tremulously.

A hint of a smile hovered on his lips. "Good. Eat up, then, while I run a bath for you."

Alexis tackled her breakfast of French toast and cursed herself for having to pretend that her ankle was still sore. How was she supposed to get to the bathroom to take a bath if she couldn't walk? Was Brant going to carry her there, too. Skimpily clothed as she was, she dreaded the thought of being cradled in his arms.

Brant returned and lifted the tray from her lap. Alexis made a gesture of protest when he reached out to pull back the blanket.

"Really, Brant, I'm sure I can hop in there or something. I don't need to be carried."

"Don't be silly," he replied gruffly. "Why should you?"

"I don't have any clothes on!"

"You're wearing some," he said, his eyes suddenly twinkling. "But it won't be a new sight, considering that I saw you that way last evening."

Alexis blushed and muttered, "You had no right to undress me."

Brant shrugged. "I didn't want your jeans getting horse hairs and dirt all over the sheets. If you get right down to it, I saw more of you the other night in the car."

There was a sparkle to his gold eyes, and Alexis turned her head away, unable to face him. He chuckled softly. "I promise I won't be driven to rape you by the sight of your luscious young body."

Alexis did not protest as he pulled back the blanket and lifted her into his arms. She looked studiously away from him, but she could not ignore the feel of his strong arms against her flesh. He had not buttoned his shirt yet, and the bare strip of skin down the middle of his chest seared her where it touched her.

Brant crossed the hall to the bathroom and deposited her on the side of the tub. When he stepped back, Alexis was conscious of a faint pang of disappointment. "While you are bathing," he said, "I'll go up to the attic and see if I can dig up something for you to wear. I'll put your clothes in to wash."

He left, closing the door after him, and Alexis quickly took off her underwear and eased into the hot water. It was deliciously relaxing, making Alexis realize how sore her muscles were from the fall yesterday. For a long while she soaked, daydreaming, until she was jerked from her reverie by the heavy thud of boots outside. The door opened and Brant stood there, some garments in his hands. His eyes slid over her, but Alexis made no attempt to cover her nudity. She knew suddenly that she wanted him to look at her in this way, that she was stirred by the blaze lighting his eyes.

Finally he moved, tossing the clothes onto the countertop. "Here are some shorts of Beth's. I was afraid her dresses and jeans would be too short for you. I found a cane up there, too. I thought you might use it to get around some while I'm gone . . . as long as you don't try to do too much. But I'll carry you downstairs as soon as you're through with your bath. It's easier and safer."

"All right." Alexis was surprised to find that her voice came out normally.

Brant hesitated for another moment and then was gone. Alexis quickly finished bathing and stepped out. She toweled herself dry and put on the clothes that Brant had brought. They fit reasonably well, although the shorts were almost indecently snug and short. Remembering to stand on one foot, she left the bathroom and limped across the hall. Brant stood by the window in her room, absently sliding the cane back and forth in his hands. At the sound of her footsteps, he turned sharply and looked her up and down, a smile playing on his lips.

"I couldn't have made a better choice," he said lightly, and came forward to pick her up.

After carrying her downstairs, he set her on the living-room sofa and placed the cane beside her. "Now, promise me that you won't overdo," he urged with mock sternness.

"I promise," she replied with a small smile, guilt stabbing through her. She felt all kinds of a heel for lying to him when he was being so nice to her. Perversely, it irritated her that he should act this way. It was like having a bad guy turn into a good guy right before your eyes and spoil the plot. Alexis thought that now she knew what the phrase "killing her with kindness" meant.

Brant picked out several paperbacks from the shelves along the wall and dumped them next to her. "I've got to go. See you at lunch."

Alexis turned her attention to the books. They were all novels, which she hadn't had much time for since law school. It was an unaccustomed pleasure to pick through them, examining the jackets to find the most entertaining one. Finally she selected a long saga of a wealthy New York family and was soon lost in the complicated plot of greed and passion.

Brant returned at noon, this time with hamburgers from Nora's Cafe, and Alexis felt another twinge of conscience at his thoughtfulness. He talked breezily, impersonally, about the work he had been doing all morning, recounting in humorous detail the adventures of loading a particularly recalcitrant calf. Alexis smiled, seeing the warm light in his amber eyes, and wondered, with a quirk of anticipation, what was going on with him.

After Brant had left, Alexis returned to her book, but somehow it no longer held any appeal. The main character reminded her too much of her father, and she found her thoughts reverting again and again to Alec. Eventually, she laid the paperback down with a sigh and rose to walk through the house. Since she couldn't get him out of her mind, she decided to give in and think for a while.

The more she thought, the more convinced she was that Brant had told her the truth. The story fitted in very well with her father's personality. The question was, how did she feel about it? Angry? Betrayed? Disillusioned? Or was she simply not fazed by it at all? She really didn't know. She couldn't put her finger on the pulse of her emotions. Surely she had known Alec too long to be shocked by this information; she had witnessed his tough ruthlessness in other matters. It would be silly of her to expect him to be sexually moral. But then, she had never been exactly sensible where her father was concerned.

All her life she'd excused any of his imperfections. If he did something that she would not have done or that she would disapprove of in any other person, she would simply shrug and tell herself that this was Alec. He was different; he was special; he was allowed to do what others could not. He had always been so dynamic that everyone else paled beside him. How could anyone's mores apply to him?

But now, meeting a man like Brant, whose force pulled as strongly as Alec's, a man in whom that same power lay leashed and waiting, but who was, at the same time, honest and principled . . . could she honestly say that her father's magnetism permitted him free rein? A once-firm foundation cracked inside her, and tears formed in her eyes.

"Oh, Daddy!" she whispered aloud. "Oh, Daddy, what gives you the right to hurt people so? How can you trample over them and never care?"

Her churning brain went on. Was Brant truly any different, any better? He had a love and a respect for land that her father would never understand, and he despised Alec for his excesses. But what about his own? He had an illegitimate son, after all. Moreover, he had callously left the child in Vietnam. That hardly bespoke a highly principled man. Perhaps his principles rested in matters other than sex.

Alexis returned to the sofa, frowning. She wondered what the child's mother had looked like. She pictured a fragile Asian beauty, a woman with soft, golden skin, almond eyes, and thick black hair. Alexis envisioned her as petite and beautiful, with elegant little wrists that looked as though they would snap at the slightest pressure, dressed in a peach-colored cheongsam as she opened her door to admit the tall American. Alexis saw Brant's eyes turning hot gold with desire as he looked at the woman; saw him pick her up and carry her to the bed . . . as if she were weightless.

Sternly, Alexis shook her head, clearing the picture from her mind. This was getting ridiculous. What did it matter what the woman looked like, or whether he had slept with her casually for a night or had an ongoing affair with her for months? Brant McClure was nothing to Alexis, now or ever. She couldn't care less what he had done or whom he had done it with. She picked up the book and firmly fixed her thoughts on the page in front of her.

Soon, however, the book slipped from her hand and she stared off into space, recalling what Brant had said last night about his mother. Was his mother's infidelity the reason why he had never had a serious attachment to a woman, not even to the mother of his child?

The slam of the rear door brought Alexis back to the present, and she stretched out hurriedly on the couch. A few seconds later Brant's boots sounded in the hall, and then he stood in the doorway. A half smile touched his face.

"Hello, there," he said, taking off his cowboy hat and wiping the sweat from his forehead. "How have you been doing?"

"Very well, thank you. I've read about half this book. Believe me, it would take your mind off anything."

A genuine smile cracked his face. "What is it?"

"Oh, a story about the rich and unscrupulous. A family of Pennsylvania Stones, so to speak."

His eyebrows shot up, but he said nothing. Tossing his hat onto a chair, he strode over to her and knelt beside her to examine her injury. A jolt went up her leg where his hand touched her, sizzling like electricity. When at last he released her ankle, she breathed a small sigh of relief.

Brant stood up. "It looks a lot better today. Tell you what, you keep on reading, and I'll go upstairs and shower. Then I'll see what I can make for dinner."

"All right," Alexis agreed, still trying to establish control over her rebellious body. It was insane for her to react this way to his mere physical touch.

Dinner appeared to be a repeat of the night before. Wordlessly, Alexis gazed at her plate containing steak and salad. Brant laughed as he lowered his big frame to the floor.

"Looks the same, huh?"

"Yes, rather," Alexis admitted.

"Well, I won't have it said that I don't provide variety," Brant protested mockingly. "Last night was rib-eye, and this is filet."

Alexis nodded. "Oh, I see. Tell me, do you dine on nothing but steak?"

"Well, I can hardly be so disloyal as to eat anything but beef. And steak is the easiest to fix. I never have time for a roast, although sometimes I make hamburgers. Listen, don't knock it. In a restaurant in Dallas you'd pay at least nine dollars for a steak like this. In New York, probably sixteen."

"Oh, I wasn't knocking it," Alexis reassured him. "Merely curious, that's all."

"It's clear that you don't eat enough of it," he said in a lecturing tone. "Too much chicken, fish, and junk food. You're too thin."

"Are you objecting to my figure, sir?" Alexis inquired in a haughty tone.

He ran his gaze carefully over her before speaking, his amber eyes finally resting on her face, a flicker of clear admiration dancing in them. "Oh, no, the shape is fine. I thoroughly approve. I just say there ought to be a little more of it, provided, of course, that you want to be healthy."

Alexis swallowed hard, uncertain how to react to the expression in his eyes. She had seen it before, the night he had almost gone to bed with her. Her fork shook slightly in her hand. That was all behind them; it had to be. All she ought to be concerned with now was the lease. Frighteningly, it seemed that the harder she tried to hold on to her purpose, the more it eluded her. She wasn't even sure that she still wanted the lease, even if he should offer it.

Brant had brought a bottle of red wine with him from the kitchen. He poured her a glassful now, which she nervously drank down. Brant, watching her, took a sip from his own glass. Alexis cut a bite of steak and dutifully chewed it, all the while self-consciously aware of his eyes on her. She swallowed and smiled.

"Delicious," she pronounced, although she had barely tasted the beef. A bright golden flame burned in his leonine eyes, and it disturbed her.

"Tell me about yourself," he commanded, beginning to eat but keeping his unswerving gaze on her.

Alexis laughed weakly, dismayed at the slight tremor in her voice. "You know most of it. I'm twenty-six and a lawyer. My specialty is gas and oil. You know my family." She bit her lip, afraid she had brought up the wrong subject again, and quickly stumbled away from it. "Uh, let's see . . ."

"But what about you?" he prodded. "I want to hear about you. What do you do? What do you like?"

"Well, uh . . . I play tennis some, when I get a chance. I like to read, but I never seem to have enough time for that. I like movies sometimes. Honestly, I can't think of anything. I must be awfully dull, I guess."

"What about men?" His question was soft, but it riveted her attention. His face was blank, almost polite, but his eyes still burned.

"What about them?"

"Are there any in your life? A fiancé, lover, friend?"

"No, not really. I've never been serious about anyone, actually. It worries my mother to death. She thinks I'm going to die an old maid. I'm not engaged. I have been seeing one man fairly often, but there isn't much to it."

"Poor man," he said, his voice indicating anything but sympathy.

In a single fluid motion he rose from his seat on the

floor and came around the coffee table to kneel in front of her, his face level with hers. She watched him, mesmerized, as his hands slid around her neck, securing her head at the nape while his thumb caressed her jawline. Alexis could not speak, could hardly breathe, not daring to break the spell. Slowly, inevitably, his face came closer to hers, until it blocked out everything, and then his lips were touching her mouth. Gently at first, teasing, playing with her, but then increasing in pressure, digging into her, parting her lips.

His tongue swept inside, tasting the pleasure of her. Alexis's head spun, crowded suddenly with contradictory emotions. His mouth was searing and insistent, forcing her backward until her head rested upon the sofa.

"Alexis," he whispered, his breath hot against her cheek. His lips left hers to explore her face and ears, sending ripples of tingles all through her. His hands moved down her body, caressing her through her clothes.

"Wait! What are you doing? Brant, I—" Alexis mumbled confusedly, reeling beneath the intense sensation spreading across her body.

"God, I want you. Ever since the night at the party. I wanted to rape you that night when I found out who you were. I wanted you so bad, and yet I hated you." His words came out in quick, panting breaths as his lips covered her face in brief kisses and slid down her throat to the soft swell of her breasts. "Instead, I came home and fought it, and I've been fighting it ever since. Do you have any idea how you looked in those jeans, the way your bottom curves under, making a man die to touch it? It was all I could do to keep from dragging you into the barn and taking you right there."

His fingers fumbled at her waistband. Alexis struggled to sit up, fighting the whirling confusion in her head. "But, Brant, what about my father? What about—"

"Damn it, I don't care!" he snapped.

Almost reverently, he pushed the blouse off her shoulders and down her arms, then unhooked and pulled away her brassiere. His eyes roamed over her body, drinking her in, and Alexis felt her breath catch in her throat at his gaze. Slowly, gently, his hands touched her stomach and traveled upward, moving with maddening, delightful slowness over her creamy skin.

"What you said to me last night," he said softly, "was true. Because you were Stone's daughter, I never gave you a chance. I assumed from the beginning that you were conniving and wicked, no matter how damned desirable you were. That wasn't fair of me. Forgive me, Alexis, please." For the first time his eyes returned to her face. The hard cynicism was gone; his face was open, flushed with desire, his eyelids heavy over his lion's eyes. "Let me start again."

Alexis could not speak, could only stare at him in tremulous uncertainty. Gently, he bent his head to her, and his mouth trailed kisses of fire across her chest and stomach. A moan escaped her as he took one rosy nipple between his lips and gently worked it to a diamond-hard peak, then repeated this on the other breast. His hand tore at the fastening of her shorts, tugging them from her body.

His lips and tongue and hands seemed everywhere, playing Alexis like a fine instrument, evoking wild sparks of desire in her that she had never known before. She twisted beneath him as he slipped one eager hand inside, exploring and arousing her most secret recesses, experiencing her as no other man had ever done. It was frightening, delightful, too much all at once. Her mind cried that he was her enemy, her opponent, that he was conquering her without a struggle, but her body responded and moved beneath him, yearning for the feel of his hard maleness. Alexis battled in tormented confusion with the two opposite sides of her nature.

Finally, desperately, she shoved herself away from

him, crying out, "Wait! Give me time!" The impetus of
her movement carried her halfway across the floor. He
turned in surprise, following her with his eyes, his face
flushed and his chest rising and falling in great heaves.

She stopped and looked at him, and it was then that
she realized she had run quite easily and was now
standing firmly on both feet. He had to know now that
she had lied. She gasped with horror and glanced down
at her feet, then back up at him, one hand flying to her
mouth to cover the gasp.

Realization pierced his face, heavy with passion. She
knew, miserably, that her flight across the room had
not betrayed her; it was her guilty reaction that had
immediately given her away.

Chapter 7

His face hardened and a gold fire ignited in his eyes. Slowly, menacingly, he rose to his feet and hissed, "You bitch! You lied to me again!"

Alexis swallowed, her words of defense sticking in her throat. He would not listen; passion and rage at her betrayal had driven him beyond reason. His eyes were the hungry, feral eyes of a jungle cat. Cold fear shook her, and she backed away from him intensely aware that she wore nothing. She had to grab her clothes and run, but she froze at the thought of approaching him.

"You little bitch!" The words tore out of him, and he advanced slowly toward her. "This time I demand my due. Lease or no lease, I think I've paid for that sweet whore's body of yours."

"No!" Alexis cried, her voice but a dry whisper. Panic made her whirl to execute a wild dash for the open door.

But he moved, almost more quickly than she could see, and blocked the way. He loomed before her, tall and muscular, his lips drawn back in a savage imitation of a smile. Fear rippled down her body.

"Tell me," he said almost conversationally, except for the steely edge to his voice, "is it that much fun making a fool of us McClures? Does it amuse you to

117

tease me, to hear me pour out my guts to you and know that I've been a blind fool to believe you? Is that how you Stones get your sophisticated kicks, by cutting the heart out of us poor dumb country boys and watching us bleed?"

"No!" Alexis choked out, sobs of terror rising in her throat.

Steadily, he came closer, until at last Alexis broke and ran. His hand lashed out and clamped down cruelly on her wrist, and he flung her against the sofa. She tumbled onto it, full length, upon her back. He stood looking down at her, his face that of a stranger. Her breath came in little panting gasps. Alexis was frozen with fear and could only watch him.

Deliberately, Brant unbuttoned his shirt and let it fall to the floor, revealing his broad, rock-hard chest with its thick mat of curling brown hair that trailed in a V down his stomach and disappeared into his jeans. Alexis closed her eyes weakly, tears clogging her throat. This could not be happening; Brant could not have turned into the brutal maniac she saw before her.

"What's the matter, Alexis?" His teasing voice caressed her name. "Can't you take it? Haven't you ever had to pay up? Haven't you ever lost one of your little games?"

She heard the snap and rasp of his zipper, then the sound of sliding cloth. She opened her eyes to see him standing naked above her, then glanced fearfully at the hard, swollen shaft of his manhood, the weapon with which he would pierce her, the means of his victory over her.

"Please, Brant, no," she whispered. "Don't, please. I swear—" Her voice choked on her sobs.

His laugh was bitter. "You swear what?" he said sarcastically. "Swear whatever you please. I know how worthless your oaths are, Alexis."

He bent, slipping his hand between her thighs. As if that were the signal, Alexis came out of her frozen state and began to struggle. Terror turned her into a clawing, biting, blind animal, and she flung herself at him.

Brant shoved her back onto the couch and threw himself upon her, wrapping his strong legs around hers, grabbing her arms and pulling them together high above her head. She managed to tear one arm away, but with a grunt he clamped a hand on it, then secured her hands behind her back. Fiercely, his mouth came down on hers, and though she struggled to turn her head away, she could not move beneath the force of his kiss. His lips seared into hers, consuming her, conquering her. His tongue lashed in and out, laying claim to the sweet cavity. Roughly, his lips left hers to roam her body. Alexis arched against him, trying to stop him, but the quick rasp of his breath told her that she had succeeded only in inflaming his passion even more.

Her arms ached from their imprisonment behind her back, but his mouth upon her breasts teased hot ripples of desire through her, until her discomfort faded and was lost in the wild betrayal of her senses. Reason receded, and she drifted into a sweet haze of pleasure. His knee parted her legs, and he probed at her, pushing harder and harder until she cried out, her floating cloud of sensual delight ripped by pain. He entered her, filling her, taking over, shoving into her again and again; he was beyond seeing or hearing or feeling compassion in his rush for fulfillment. At last he shuddered at his peak and collapsed heavily against her.

Tears flooded her eyes, pouring out, choking her, but Alexis swallowed the sobs in her throat. Hurt surged within her and mingled with hatred and fear. She refused to give him the satisfaction of crying. She would not let him hear her grief, no matter how many tears flowed from her eyes.

"Alexis," Brant mumbled against her neck, his breath slowing and his taut body relaxing. "You're a virgin. Jesus. A virgin. Alexis." Her name came out a sigh, and she felt him ease into a deeper relaxation. Soon he was asleep.

Carefully, quietly, Alexis slipped from beneath Brant, picked up her garments from the floor, and tiptoed out of the room. In the hall she dressed as rapidly as she could. When she was through, she had to lean against the wall, so greatly had her body begun to tremble with the aftermath of what had happened. Shakily, she wiped the tear tracks from her cheeks and drew in a deep, shuddering breath. She could not afford the luxury of giving way until she had escaped from Brant. Only when she was safe could she let herself go.

The bolt on the front door slid back with a loud click, and Alexis stood perfectly still, listening for a sound from the living room. It did not come, so she turned the knob and stepped out into the night. Like a covering blanket, the darkness enveloped her. She scurried down the porch steps and over to her car. The key was still inside, where she had left it yesterday morning. What an age ago that seemed now.

The Riviera did not start at the first try, and Alexis burst into tears, pumping the accelerator in a frenzy and flooding the engine. He would hear the car noise if she wasn't careful, and she forced herself to regain control. After a couple of seemingly endless minutes, she twisted the key again. This time, the engine sprang to life. Swiftly, she turned the car around and sped down the driveway and onto the section-line road. She covered the caliche road much too fast for safety in the dark, but she was frantic to get away. Not until she was on the highway and racing for Beth's house did she feel even a modicum of safety.

Beth and her family were at home; the cars were there. When Alexis pulled up to the house, her heart leaped in agony. All the lights were out. Everyone must be in bed. She prayed at least one of the doors would be unlocked. She didn't think she could bear to rouse them from their sleep to let her in. Beth's quick eyes would see her disheveled state and tear-stained face, and she would beleaguer her with concerned questions. Alexis knew she wouldn't be able to answer anything without breaking down completely. How could she tell her new, dear friend what Brant had just done!

Fortunately, the back door opened easily, and Alexis sighed with relief that the Thompsons, for all their money, kept to the country custom of unlocked doors. Like a wraith, she slipped through the kitchen and down the hall, feeling her way along the wall, picking out a path by the faint light of the moon. Once in her room, she locked the door, then pulled a chair across and fitted it under the doorknob for extra measure. It was a foolish gesture, she knew, since there was no one here who would attack her, but right now she didn't care about logic and good sense. All she wanted was to feel secure.

Alexis peeled off her clothes and ran water in the bathtub. As she sank into the warm water, she reflected wryly that she was doing the worst thing a woman could do after being raped—washing the evidence away. But then, this was hardly the usual case. After what had gone on earlier in the evening, rape would be almost impossible to prove. And she knew that she could never, never notify the police of what Brant had done. Grimly, she sank into the warm water and proceeded to scrub herself fiercely with a soapy washcloth. She wanted to get rid of the feel of Brant's hands and flesh wherever they had touched her. Emerging from the tub, she dried herself and put on a nightgown, then stumbled to the large bed and crawled between the covers. There, finally, the sobs welled up again in her throat, and she turned her face into her pillow and cried her heart out.

The sun slanting through the window awakened Alexis late the next morning. She yawned and sat up, stretching, and then suddenly fell flat against the

mattress as she recalled the events of the previous
night. Like lightning, emotions stabbed through her in
quick succession: fear, sadness, and fury. Rape. There
was nothing else to call it.

Her mind skittered away from the painful subject,
but she forced herself to remember. She saw again
Brant's narrowed, yellow cat eyes and the way he had
thrown himself between her and the door. He had been
wild, like an animal. A vicious, hate-filled animal.
Alexis shuddered.

A quiet, bitter rage filled her heart. Oh, he had
conquered her, all right. He had done what he wanted
and had paid her back in triplicate for the lie she had
told him; perhaps he had even been paying her back for
the mother her father had taken from him. Most of all,
Alexis suspected, Brant had punished her for the lust
she aroused in him, when he wanted to feel nothing for
her.

He had vanquished her in the age-old manner of
men, had used her body like a whore to prove his
mastery and masculinity. He had taken her virginity,
had turned her first night of love, which should have
been something glorious, into a sordid, painful defeat.
Alexis had never thought much about her virginity, had
not believed she was saving something precious for the
man she loved, but now she realized that she had
longed for a special man to take her and introduce her
gently to love. It should have been a rare and wonderful experience, but Brant McClure had ruined it, had
stained her loss. Damn him! No doubt today he would
go calmly back to work, having cleansed himself of his
anger and frustration.

Alexis hated him for what he had done, for the fear
in herself, for the pain and humiliation he had caused
her. She hated him for having held her helpless and
immobile in his arms. She hated him for the egotistical
male conquest he had achieved and for his domination
over her. She hated him, not least of all, for the
treacherous way he had caused her body to respond to

his lovemaking against her will. After he had subdued her, and before his final violation of her, he had stroked and kissed her into a trembling, passionate submission, and had made her want him even in the midst of her degradation.

She groaned and turned over, burying her face in the pillow. What was she to do? Brant McClure had brought her to her knees; she had lost totally. She, Alexis Stone, the intelligent, confident career woman who had made hard-bitten male attorneys respect her, had lost to a macho, stubborn, stupid cowboy! She swept the pillow from the bed. Suddenly, excitement lit her eyes.

No, she did not have to lose. He had won the last hand, but she had another card to play. She had one more chance to force the lease from him. Alexis had never thought she would use it, but now . . . now she would use anything against Brant McClure. For a moment her stomach curled in fear at the thought of confronting him again, but then she shook her head. No, she wouldn't let that stop her. For her own self-respect, she had to face down her fear and show him that he hadn't really defeated her, hadn't turned her into a shivering, cringing female. She would still stand up and fight him to the last inch.

Quickly, before she could change her mind, Alexis dressed in a charcoal-gray suit and pulled her hair into a severe knot at the nape of her neck. A ring of bruises mottled her wrists where he had gripped them. She pulled her long sleeves over them. She would not allow him to see any signs of his victory.

Next, Alexis repacked her clothes. She would leave today. Once she had checked the room to make sure nothing of hers remained, she lifted her suitcase and started down the hall.

"Alexis!" Beth exclaimed in astonishment as Alexis entered the kitchen. "Are you leaving? What happened? I didn't even know you were here. I thought you were still at Brant's."

Schooling her voice to betray none of her inner turmoil, Alexis said, "I'm going to make one last stab at your brother this morning, and then I'm flying back to Dallas, whether he signs or not."

Beth's face revealed her disappointment. "And here I thought everything was working out. When you didn't come back yesterday, I had hoped . . ." Her voice trailed off wistfully.

Alexis shrugged and shook her head. "I thought it might work out, too, but it didn't. He's tough." A quiver darted through her as she thought of just how tough he was. Would she be able to get the better of him?

"Well, sit down and have some breakfast."

"No, I'm really not hungry."

"At least have a cup of coffee. Let's talk a little before you go. Are you ever coming back?"

"I doubt it. My job doesn't usually take me out of Dallas."

"Oh, I'm so sorry. I really enjoyed having you around. I guess it was stupid of me to hope that you and Brant might hit it off."

Alexis felt a treacherous urge to break down and blurt out her roiling emotions to Beth. She knew she had to get away before she lost control of herself.

"I hate leaving you, too, Beth. You are one of the few friends I've ever had. It was a nice feeling. Do you ever go to Dallas?"

"Not often, but the next time I do, I promise I'll call you."

"Good," Alexis said sincerely. "Now, I really do have to run. I need to see Brant again and then go straight to Dallas. I'm sorry, but I've got so much work to do back there. I'll leave the Riviera at the airstrip for you."

Beth walked her to the door, then waved good-bye as Alexis pulled out of the driveway and set off down the road. With a sigh, Beth turned back to the house.

Alexis and Brant had seemed so perfect together. Why couldn't they have been attracted to each other?

When McClure answered Alexis's firm knock, amazement spread across his face. "Alexis!" He stopped, and they stared at each other for a moment.

At the sight of him, tanned and handsome, Alexis felt a cowardly trembling; for a moment she was seized with a dread that she wouldn't be able to pull it off.

He frowned, a shadow touching his eyes. "Uh . . . about last night, I didn't mean to . . . that is, I didn't know you were, well, a virgin. I never dreamed . . ."

Alexis stiffened, forcing herself to stand tall and unafraid, as cool as ice. Don't let him know, she told herself. Don't let him know what it did to you. Don't give him that satisfaction.

Swiftly she cut into his hesitant speech. "I can't see what difference it makes whether I'm a virgin or quite experienced. Rape is still rape," she said crisply, consciously putting one hand on her hip in a posture she had learned from her father to convey control and indifference.

"Damn it, you lied to me!" he bit back, stung by her attitude and words.

Alexis raised an eyebrow. "And that is a justification for rape? I'm sorry, McClure, but I wouldn't try that line in a court of law if I were you."

His eyes turned hard. "Nothing affects you, does it? You're as cool and calm as an ice cube. Doesn't anything penetrate that tough hide of yours?"

Her smile was slow, taunting. "I'm sorry. Do you like to see fear in your victims? I hate to disappoint you, but I don't scare that easily. It would take more than a display of brute strength to turn me into a cringing female."

His eyes flashed at her words. Damn it, when he awoke this morning, he had felt guilty as hell for abusing her, for letting his anger and passion carry him past reason. Despite her behavior, he'd felt like a cad for taking her by force. Now here she was, obviously unaffected, and she made him feel foolish for his earlier remorse. His actions had mattered nothing to her; her body had no sanctity.

"I don't know what it would take to make you cringe," he said bitingly, "but I doubt that anything could make you a female."

"Oh, was I so unfeminine as not to enjoy the proof of your masculinity?" Alexis mocked. "I presume that's what it was—a demonstration of your superiority due to your greater strength. I *am* sorry. I've never had the time or the interest to play along with men's little ego games."

"It wasn't ego, lady," Brant snapped. "It was pure damn hate."

Inwardly, Alexis flinched. For a moment she wanted to run back to the car. Instead, she forced herself to remain where she was. Keep to the offensive, she told herself. Keep to the offensive.

"I had hoped to conduct these negotiations with some semblance of normalcy and friendliness—"

He laughed shortly. "Is that why you deceived me at every turn? To inspire friendship?"

Alexis plowed on as if he hadn't spoken. "However, you've been determined from the start to taint every discussion with emotion. So I have come to the conclusion that emotion is the only thing that will reach you."

"What are you talking about?" His tone was scornful, but Alexis saw the wariness in his eyes, and her heart gave a hopeful leap. She had him on the defensive now.

"I mean that you have an illegitimate son in Vietnam."

McClure stiffened almost imperceptibly. "So?"

"So I also know that for the past seven or eight years you've been trying to get the child out of there and admitted into America."

"It's no secret," Brant said tightly. "I want the boy to live with me. What does that have to do with you?"

"Stone Oil has a great deal of influence all over the world. Alec thinks he could get the boy out."

McClure's mouth twisted, and he finished the sentence for her. "Provided, of course, that I sign the lease."

Alexis's stomach was in knots, but she kept her voice and face expressionless. "Exactly."

Brant's face darkened, and Alexis could see that he held himself tautly, as though every muscle in his body strained against his control. "You *are* just like your father," he said in a disgusted voice. "For some reason I thought you were a little better, not quite so despicable. But here you are, selling a man's son to him just to get one of your precious leases. You're Alec Stone all over again: no emotion, no morals, no principles."

"You dare to accuse *me* of having no morals?" Alexis snapped heatedly. "After what *you* did last night? You are a vicious, brutal pig, and yet you have the gall to accuse me of not having morals or principles!"

His voice lashed at her like a whip. "At least what I did was done in the heat of passion. There was some feeling to it. It wasn't the calculating torture that you and your father use."

"Oh, I see. What you did was all right because you did it blindly, lashing out cruelly."

"Don't, Alexis," he said through clenched teeth. "Don't drive me too far."

"Oh, now your bursts of temper are *my* fault? Well, let me tell you something, Brant McClure. You say that I'm just like my father, but that's not true. You're the one who's like him. You're the one who goes around taking whatever woman appeals to you, acting like some medieval baron, heedless to anything but your own desires. Maybe Alec *is* a predator, but so are you. Neither one of you cares who or what you destroy along the way in the pursuit of your own pleasure—"

"Shut up!" he growled, his eyes burning dangerously.

But Alexis was too angry to take heed, and she plunged on. "It didn't matter to you that I didn't want you last night, any more than it mattered to my father that he wrecked your family. You don't give a damn about anyone but yourself. You just go merrily on your way, scattering your seed all over the world, with no thought to the consequences. You wanted some woman in Saigon and you took her, and to hell with what might happen to her, to hell with the kid whom you left in the hands of the Communists!"

A spasm contorted his face at her words. Suddenly his hand flashed out, catching Alexis on the cheek and sending her staggering back against the porch wall. For a moment they stared at each other in horror. Alexis put her hand up to her numbed cheek, her eyes wide and tear-filled.

With an inarticulate sound, Brant clenched his fists, folded his arms tight about his body, and turned away from her. "Oh, God, Alexis . . . " His voice was a strained whisper.

Alexis straightened, leaning against the wall to support her shaking knees. Strangely, all fear had left her at his slap. Automatically, she reverted to behavior she'd learned from watching her father. She was filled with a consuming hatred. In her mind there was no thought of running, only the white-hot surge to do battle.

Her voice as she spoke was as cool as if nothing had happened, as remote and unconcerned as a stranger's. "Will you sign the lease?"

He whirled to stare at her, his face torn and puzzled. "Good God, Alexis, does nothing faze you?"

"I'm sorry . . . Did you hope to frighten me away?"

"No! That's not what I meant . . . I just can't believe you are so— Alexis, isn't there even a drop of blood in your veins?"

"Is that what you've been trying to prove?" she

countered, a thin, tight smile touching her lips. "Then you are in for a disappointment. There is blood, all right, but I don't shed it for your amusement. Now, can we return to the matter at hand? If my father can work a deal and get Paul—Huang Li—into the United States, will you sign?"

Brant drew a long breath and gazed beyond the porch, across the wide stretch of fields. Finally, without looking at her, he said tonelessly, "Yes. To get Paul, I'll turn it over to you."

"Good." Alexis felt a curious flatness. She had won . . . Where was the expected elation? "I'll get the papers out of the car."

"Wait." His bitter tone stopped her. "I'm not signing yet. I'll sign when you deliver Paul to me right here at this house, and not before. If I sign now, I have no guarantee that your father will hold up your end of the bargain."

Alexis grimaced. "And if our company goes to all the trouble and expense of getting your son into the country and delivering him to you, how do we know you'll go through with your part of the bargain?"

"I promise I will. You have my word."

"Oh, yes, the vaunted word of Brant McClure. Having witnessed a demonstration of your morals, somehow I find it a little difficult to believe in your high sense of honor."

"Well, you'll just have to," he snapped. "That is all you'll get. I'll sign the lease when you bring me Paul. That's it. Take it or leave it."

"I see." Alexis raised her brows slightly. Despite her words, she believed McClure would stand by what he said. After all, that was part of his Old West code, wasn't it? Anything went—rape, murder, intimidation—but a man's word was inviolate. "All right. I'll accept your deal. I'll send the papers with Paul. Good-bye, Brant."

"Good-bye." He looked at her with flat, marble-hard eyes.

Stiffly, Alexis walked to the car and got in. Switching on the ignition, she backed out and spun off toward the road. Behind her, Brant stood as still as a statue on the porch, watching her departure. Alexis saw him for the last time in her rear-view mirror, then she turned onto the section road.

It didn't take her long to reach the Thompson airstrip. She drove mechanically, all the while churning over in her mind the final confrontation with Brant McClure. She had won, had wrested victory from a man none of her father's flunkies had been able to beat. She had defeated the man who had so defeated her. And yet the taste of victory was like ashes in her mouth.

In her rage, in her determination to defeat him, she had used the one thing she had thought she never would. What did that say about her? Was she really what he had accused her of? Was she really so ambitious that she had allowed nothing to stand in her way? Brant had accused her of not having any emotions. But oh, this dreadful emptiness inside her was surely a refutation of his words. She ached; she was suddenly tormented with doubt.

At the airstrip, Alexis pulled up beside the other Thompson car and cut off the engine. For a moment she looked at her Cessna, telling herself that she had to get in it and fly back to Dallas. Suddenly she thought of the night she had met Brant McClure, of the soft melting way she had felt in his arms, of the glorious spread of warmth throughout her body. How had everything become so twisted? Tears sprang into her eyes, and the Cessna wavered before her.

She leaned her head against the steering wheel, waves of emotion breaking her self-imposed dam and washing over her. She gripped the wheel tightly as sobs shook her unmercifully. She felt as though her world were tumbling around her. Who was there to hold on to? Her father? What a laugh. Her mother? Darrell? The choices became even more ridiculous.

Finally her sobs subsided, and she leaned back against the seat, wiping the tears from her cheeks. Accept it, she told herself; you are alone. It's about time you faced reality. Perhaps McClure was right; maybe I'm incapable of feelings. It certainly seems as if I'm incapable of attracting love and holding it.

Alexis swallowed on a choke and pulled a tissue from her purse to blow her nose. She could not spend the rest of her life sitting in some desolate field in the Panhandle. Whatever awful truths she might have to face, she had to continue with her life. She took a deep breath to settle her jittery nerves, and stepped from the car, pulling her suitcase after her. It was time to return to the world she knew.

Chapter 8

It was strange to land at Addison Airport, to see the familiar Dallas skyline again as she walked across the asphalt parking lot to her Mercedes. Alexis felt as though she were returning from a foreign country, as if her trip had involved great time and distance. She felt oddly out of touch with everything around her. Something was different, and she suspected it was herself.

Alexis drove down Mockingbird to the Central and headed for the office. She hoped that seeing her familiar surroundings would dissipate this peculiar sensation of being adrift. After parking in the spacious underground area of the Stone Building, she took the elevator to the tenth floor, walked down the hall, and stopped at her door.

There it was, the same medium-sized square she had occupied for the past three years. One wall was glass and looked toward downtown Dallas. A credenza stood along another wall, a large oil painting of a brewing thunderstorm above it. A tall metal filing cabinet, two leather-padded chairs, a small bookcase, and Alexis's wide walnut desk and swivel chair completed the furnishings. Books, files, and papers were piled in small stacks in almost every available space—all over her desk, atop the credenza, on the floor around her chair, and even across the top of the wastebasket—a very organized jumble that only Alexis and her secretary, Betty, could understand. All so familiar, so normal, and yet curiously remote.

Alexis set her briefcase on the desk and began riffling through the accumulated papers and mail. Telephone messages were spiked on a steel message nail. She pulled them off and sorted them out: Morgan Stone; Alec; Alec; Jim Whitsell of Whitsell, Courtney, and Harrison; Ruth Dempler from Mobil; Nick Fletcher; Richard Moor in Houston; Macusi about Canada—oh, Lord, not another problem with that well—Ginny; Anne Stowers—who?—the list went on and on.

Firmly, Alexis stuck the messages back on the spike. She'd tackle them later. Right now she didn't have the energy to call all those people. Listlessly, she began to scan the papers on her desk.

"Alexis!" Betty stood in the doorway, file in hand. "I was just about to put this on your desk. I didn't know you were back."

"I just got in. Anything important going on?"

The woman gestured at the desk between them. "Same old stuff. They're having problems with suppliers in Canada . . . again. Macusi's blowing steam about it and says to call him immediately. It seems they've been calling him from Canada every day, and he thinks we ought to get out of our contract with the pipe company. Mobil's got some question on the lease we're doing with them in Crockett. Other than that, and a few minor emergencies, it's been pretty peaceful. Have you been up to see Mr. Stone yet?"

"No, I came by here first."

"Well, you better get up there. He's been calling you almost as often as Frank Macusi."

Alexis half laughed, half sighed. "Maybe I should have stayed in Barrett."

Betty laughed with her. "Oh, sure. You'd die of boredom in three weeks."

"I guess you're right." But somehow, Alexis wasn't

positive about that. "I'm going up to the top floor now," she said. "If Frank calls, tell him I'll get onto that contract with the pipe company as soon as I return. Hopefully, I'll have something by tomorrow. When I do, I'll call him. Okay?" She strode down the hall toward the elevator, Betty at her heels, jotting down instructions on a slip of paper. "Oh, and see if you can find that contract for me and put it on my desk. What else? Call Mobil and tell them I'm really tied up, but I'll get in touch with them either late this afternoon or tomorrow morning."

Pug Walker, who had been the head of the division orders department for years, stood at the receptionist's desk in front of the elevators. He greeted Alexis with the familiarity of an employee who had known her in pigtails. "How goes it, Al?"

"Hi, Pug. I take it everyone's dying and dividing as usual," Alexis said lightly, smiling.

"You don't know the half of it. You wouldn't believe one I got in yesterday. It's such a tangled mess it took the attorney two pages—single-spaced—to explain how it's supposed to go. No supporting documents, of course."

Alexis laughed and punched the button for the elevator. Pug continued. "Boy, you sure looked like your old man just then, walking down the hall with your secretary trotting along, taking down orders. Alec Stone has never wasted even a walk to the elevator."

Alexis smiled, but her heart sank at his words. Just like her old man . . . ambition, drive, and no wasted time. It was crazy. Why should it depress her to discover that she resembled her father? That was what she had always wanted, to be like Alec, to be liked by Alec. It was all so tangled up now. What was it she had really wanted all this time? She no longer thought she knew.

Upstairs, Mrs. Jenkins brightened at the sight of her and buzzed the intercom with great feeling. "Your daughter's here, Mr. Stone. Alexis." Obviously Alec had been bugging her as much as Betty about Alexis's arrival.

Alec Stone's voice boomed out from the speaker. "Yes! Send her in."

Alexis pushed open the massive door and advanced toward her father, swallowing as she did so. She really hadn't prepared herself for this meeting. Hadn't even thought about it. Now, seeing him, she felt a rush of confused emotions. He looked the same. Yet now, knowing what she did, she no longer knew what to think or how to feel. He was her father, but he was a stranger, too, someone she was seeing for the first time through awakened eyes.

"Alexis!" This time he came from around the desk to take her hand and pat it. "How did it go? Tell me." His bright blue eyes, so like her own, stared down at her.

She gave him a weak smile. "Fine, Daddy, just fine. I got the lease."

His laugh rippled through the air and he squeezed her hand hard. "Good girl! I knew you could do it. So you got that stubborn s.o.b.!"

"Well . . . he and I agreed on a deal. He hasn't signed yet. He will if we can get his son back for him, but he refuses to sign till then, for fear we won't follow through."

Alec gave a short grunt of amusement. "Not trusting, eh? Well, will he sign, do you think, when we give him the boy? Or will he back out on us?"

"I think he'll keep his word. He seems the type."

"Well, Alexis, I'm impressed. I really am. I thought you could do it, but those McClures . . . you never know." He sat down behind his desk, a triumphant smile splitting his face.

"Daddy, why didn't you tell me?" Alexis blurted out. "Why didn't you tell me he hated Stone Oil because you once had an affair with his mother?"

The smile vanished as Stone's brows drew together threateningly. "Because I didn't think it was any of your business, that's why."

"You didn't think it mattered that I would be dealing with Brant McClure's intense distrust and hatred without even knowing the reason for it?"

"What good would it have done? You can't change what happened."

"But it is true, isn't it?"

He paused, tapping his fingers on the desk, his eyes studying her. "Yes, it's true that I had an affair with Selena McClure in 1958. It had nothing to do with her son or that land, I can assure you. She was a very pretty woman."

"Did you love her?"

"Love her?" he repeated in astonishment. "God no! She couldn't hold a candle to your mother or to Laraine. She was pretty, but not a beauty like Ginny."

"But she loved you, didn't she? She left her husband and children for you."

He shook his head. "I don't know what she felt for me. I know she was bored stiff with that rigid husband of hers and her backwater life. Selena wanted more excitement than Barrett, Texas, had to offer. She didn't leave her family for me. She left because she couldn't stand to stay there." He paused. "Why this third degree all of a sudden? Surely you must know . . ."

"Know what? That you had affairs all the time? No, as a matter of fact, I didn't. Old Alexis, always too stuck in books to notice what was going on around her."

Her father sighed. "I thought your mother told you. Morgan's attacked me for it more than once. I thought you knew and just weren't as puritanical as Morgan. Al, it had nothing to do with your mother. I loved Ginny. She was the one who wanted the divorce."

"Because you were having an affair with Laraine at the time."

"I won't have you attacking Laraine about this!" he barked.

"I didn't say anything against her. I simply don't understand how you can claim that you always loved

Mother when you were out chasing every other female you could find!"

Alec frowned and rubbed a hand over his forehead. "Alexis, you are a grown woman. Surely you must realize that people have affairs. I thought your generation advocated free-and-easy morals."

"I don't know what my generation advocates," Alexis snapped. "I'm beginning to realize that I was never in touch with anyone my own age. I can understand an affair; I can understand your falling out of love with Ginny or your loving Laraine. She's beautiful and very right for you. I know you two get along better than you and Mother ever did."

"Then what's the problem? Why did this McClure thing get you so stirred up?"

Alexis looked at him blankly. She could hardly say that McClure had made her wonder if her own father was a ruthless man who had broken up a marriage to wreak revenge on Judson McClure, who crumbled hearts and lives like toys for his own pleasure.

"I guess I'm just tired. McClure was a difficult man to deal with. And then when I found out that he had something personal against you, and you hadn't told me about it, I was pretty mad."

Alec smiled. "Well, let's forget it now, huh? You did it, didn't you? No one else could, and I'm very proud of you. Brant McClure is just the same jackass his father was. That man was so caught up in his land, he hardly knew anyone existed. It's all over now. Okay?"

Alexis nodded. "Okay."

"I'll set a few wheels in motion in Washington and Asia to get that kid back here. Oh, I hear they're having trouble on the Canadian wells again."

"Yes. I was going to look into that when I got through here."

"Good. Frank's getting an ulcer over it."

Alexis had started toward the door when her father's voice stopped her. "Oh, wait, I almost forgot. Laraine has got some big shindig planned for a week from

Friday, and she wanted me to invite you. Can you come?"

Her hesitation was almost nonexistent. "Sure. I'll be there."

Feeling as though she were resuming her life after a major absence, Alexis tried to reenter her groove. It was harder than she would ever have imagined.

She dug into her work, and where once she would have lost herself in it, now it seemed merely taxing and time-consuming. No longer did she want to stay late at her desk, and while she analyzed documents for clauses in the company's favor, her mind often drifted. She would think about Ginny or her father or, all too often, Brant McClure.

That was the worst thing. Her mind kept returning to him, to having been violated, to the brief feeling of closeness, to the indescribable passion that had overwhelmed her. Why couldn't she simply forget the man, as he had no doubt forgotten her? Why couldn't she get his handsome face out of her mind?

As she had promised earlier, Alexis went to dinner with her mother one evening. She felt strangely awkward to be with Ginny, knowing now what she did about Alec. Now she better understood her mother's turmoil. It was easier to excuse Ginny's vagueness or her childish mood swings; unquestionably Alec's string of affairs had shredded her confidence and broken her heart. But Alexis could not express such feelings to her mother, and Alexis's new pity made her uneasy all through their time together.

She met Ginny at The Oaks, a quiet, out-of-the-way restaurant with a superb cuisine and an old-fashioned air of elegance that Ginny enjoyed. Ginny, of course, was late, and Alexis was on her second drink before her mother swept in. Even though she was almost fifty, Ginny still had the power to turn heads. Tall, with red-blonde hair and a beautifully sculpted face, she made a striking figure in her expensive, exquisitely simple green dress. The only other person Alexis knew who could cause such immediate attention was Morgan, who resembled their mother closely.

Ginny glided to the table, babbling breathless excuses even as she sat down. A solicitous waiter hovered, impressed by her air of obvious wealth, though she looked up at him uncertainly.

"Would you like a cocktail before dinner, madam?" he intoned.

"Oh. Oh, yes, a gin and tonic, I think," Ginny fluttered, and turned to Alexis. "Or is that a summer drink, dear?"

Alexis shrugged. "Depends on when you want to drink it. If you want it now, then it's an autumn drink."

Ginny laughed. "Alec always used to tell me things like that. I have never learned what one says to waiters or what to tip them. Alec used to say that I shouldn't let it bother me, but I'm not good at bluffing. Uh-oh, here he comes again. Alexis, you take care of things."

Alexis smiled at the man as he placed Ginny's drink carefully on the table, and told him they'd wait a while before ordering. Her mother leaned back against the high, plush booth and breathed a sigh. Ginny was always rushing, was never on time, and when she finally reached wherever she was supposed to be, she would breathe that same little sigh, indicating her relief that somehow she had once again managed to pull it off.

"Well, how was Barrett?" she asked Alexis.

Her daughter stirred uncomfortably. Did Ginny know about the affair Alec had had with Mrs. McClure? Did Barrett awaken bitter memories, or was she completely indifferent to it?

"Oh, all right, I guess," Alexis replied neutrally. "It was just a business deal."

Ginny waved that away with a gesture of one elegant slender hand. Leaning her cheek against her palm, she surveyed Alexis for a moment. "You look different, honey. What is it?"

Alexis felt a betraying blush spread along her cheek-bones, and her mother's eyes glowed green with interest. "Well? Tell. Come on, out with it. Is it a man?"

"Well, it was the man I went to see." Alexis was surprised to hear herself confessing this. "I was a little attracted to him, but he didn't feel the same about me."

"Oh, nonsense! How could he help but be interested in you?" Ginny protested. "You are very pretty, Alexis, especially when you put an effort into looking good. Who is he?"

"Brant McClure," Alexis answered, watching her mother's face for a flicker of recognition. There was none.

"Oh? What does he do? What does he look like?" Ginny was in her element now.

"He's a rancher. He's tall, has brown hair and a mustache and strange, almost gold eyes."

"Oh, yummy! So what's the snag?"

He hates Stone Oil. I practically forced him into the lease and . . . well, he's very angry at me." Alexis edited her story considerably for her mother's benefit. "And now I dislike him, too, after all he said and did."

"Like what?"

"Oh, it's not important," Alexis said airily, knowing her mother would become so upset over the truth that she herself would probably fall to pieces again. "We obviously have nothing in common, no real liking for each other. In fact, I hope I never have to see the man again! It was just— Well, he was the first man I ever remember feeling any interest in."

Ginny's eyes sparkled with her usual optimism. "That's a good sign. Maybe it will help you open up to other men, even though this one didn't work out."

Alexis smiled. "Such as Nick Fletcher?"

"You said it, not I. Have you seen Nick since you returned?" Ginny asked, taking a sip of her drink.

"No, not yet. But I have a date with him Sunday afternoon to play tennis. He called me yesterday."

"Good! You know he is my candidate. I always thought he was the cutest little boy."

"I know, Ginny," Alexis said, refusing to be drawn into a discussion of Nick's merits. She couldn't believe she had revealed as much to her mother as she had; she couldn't remember ever confiding anything to Ginny. Perhaps it was the remorse Alexis felt for not having treated her mother more kindly over the years.

For a moment they sat in silence, Alexis racking her brain for something to say. It was during these awkward pauses that she felt the real distance between them. Finally, she said brightly, "Well, tell me about you. Surely you have some new conquest."

Ginny reached up a hand to smooth back her thick hair, only slightly touched by gray. "Well, there is Wilson Decker."

"Who?"

"Honestly, Alexis, where do you spend your time? He is a representative in Congress."

"Aha! A politician. Watch out for those smooth-tongued types!"

Ginny smiled a deep, secretive smile. "I really think you'd like him, honey. He's devastatingly handsome—iron-gray hair, deep brown eyes, very charming. His wife died about two years ago, and he's definitely *the* catch of Washington and Dallas."

Alexis leaned forward, somewhat intrigued. Her mother had dated a lot in the ten years since the divorce, but this was the most interest she had shown in any one man. "Serious?"

Again there was that inward-looking smile. "Perhaps. What would you think if I was?"

"I think it would be great!" Alexis exclaimed truthfully. "I would love to see you married again. I know you'd be happier."

"Yes, I'm afraid I wasn't cut out to be a gay divorcée," Ginny admitted ruefully. "But it's more than that. Wilson is really someone special. I want you to have dinner with us sometime and get to know him. I'm sure you would approve."

"Well, it doesn't matter whether I do or I don't," Alexis assured her warmly, feeling suddenly closer than ever before to her mother. Had the distance between them always been their differences, or had it really been Alexis's own stubborn clinging to her father that prevented her from appreciating anyone else? "What matters is how you feel about him. If you're happy with him, then I'm all for him. I'd be glad to meet him. You have really piqued my curiosity."

"I know!" Ginny exclaimed suddenly. "You said you'd be playing tennis with Nick on Sunday. Why don't we meet you after your game so we can all have dinner at the club?"

Alexis hesitated briefly. This was an unusual event in her relationship with her mother, and she was a little uncertain how to respond. In the past she would have tried to wiggle out of what sounded like a setup with Nick. What did it matter? Meeting this politician who seemed to have captured her mother's heart might even be fun.

"Ginny, that's a terrific idea. Now, shall we order?"

Alexis went out with Darrell Ingram the following Friday. Seeing him again, she was immediately struck by the differences between him and Brant McClure. Darrell's passive blondness was considered quite handsome by many, but it paled beside the memory of McClure's tough, lean good looks. There was a spice of danger about Brant that was completely missing in Darrell.

Alexis made up her mind to enjoy the evening, but she found her resolution difficult to keep. The play they went to see did not hold her interest, despite Morgan's glowing review of it. Afterward, they went to a nightclub for drinks and dancing, and again Alexis felt rather bored. Even though the club was quiet enough for conversation, since it was an old-fashioned place with a small band, Alexis's mind kept wandering from what Darrell was saying. Irritatingly, her thoughts went all too often to Barrett, Texas, and Brant McClure. Was she never going to stop thinking of that man?

When Darrell took her home, Alexis invited him in for a nightcap out of politeness. Darrell smiled agreeably and took a seat on the couch while Alexis smothered a yawn and went to fix the drinks.

"I missed you," Darrell said, watching her at the bar. "It seems like ages since I saw you last."

"It has been a while, especially since we didn't get to go out last Friday," Alexis acknowledged casually, and glanced over at him. She wondered if he was working up to something; gratuitous compliments were not Darrell's style. He had never made more than a few halfhearted passes at her, and had complied with a gentlemanly air when she turned him down. Actually, she had felt rather piqued more than once at the ease with which he gave up. She suspected he wasn't very attracted to her at all.

She wondered what she would do if he made a pass again. Perhaps the best thing would be to go ahead and sleep with him; maybe it would erase from her mind that dreadful night with McClure. Perhaps Darrell would be able to unleash the powerful emotions that had surged in her at Brant's lovemaking, but Darrell would be gentler, kinder. She studied him for a moment, her eyes narrowed. Then, quite suddenly, she wanted to giggle. Somehow, she could not imagine Darrell ever being strong enough to counteract the effect McClure had had on her. Why, she was frankly bored just talking to Ingram! In fact, the more she thought about it, the stranger it was that she even bothered to go out with him.

Alexis strolled over to the couch and handed Darrell his Scotch and water. He took the drink, and with his other hand grasped her wrist and tugged her gently down onto the couch beside him. He raised his glass in a joking salute to her. "To you, Alexis," he said lightly. "I hope it won't be so long again before we see each other."

Alexis studied the pattern in her skirt as she took a sip from her drink. It seemed crazy to continue this anemic relationship. Finally, she cleared her throat and looked at him. "Darrell, I've been wanting to talk to you about something all evening. We've been seeing each other for several months now, and this relationship isn't going anywhere. I like you. It's just that— well, I don't feel anything deeper for you. I don't really have any interest in a romantic relationship, and I don't want to hurt your feelings. Sometimes I think I'm not really capable of having a deep relationship with anyone. But it isn't fair for you to continue to waste your time seeing me. So I've come to the decision that we should stop seeing each other."

There was a stunned look on Ingram's face as he stared at her. It took a moment for her words to penetrate. Then he swallowed and said, "Alexis, this is awfully sudden. What happened to you in Barrett?"

"Nothing happened," Alexis lied.

"But you weren't like this before you left," Darrell insisted. "I thought everything was fine between us."

"I don't have any problem with you, Darrell," Alexis explained. "I just don't think that we have anything going for us, or that we ever will. It seems to me that it's a dead-end sort of thing and that we should call it quits right now. I really think it would be for the best, Darrell."

For a moment he said nothing, just glanced away from her and back again once or twice. Finally he shrugged. "If that's the way you want it, Alexis, you know I won't fight it. I don't quite understand what brought this on. I don't want to stop seeing you, but I'll respect your wishes in the matter. If you . . . if you should change your mind, I'd like to try again."

Alexis shook her head firmly. "No, Darrell, I really don't think there's any chance of my changing my mind. You know me—I almost never do."

Awkwardly, Darrell stood up, leaving his half-finished drink on the coffee table. He glanced at her again. "I guess I'll be going, then. If you ever need me—well, you know my number. Good-bye, Alexis."

"Good-bye, Darrell." Alexis was surprised at how little she felt for him. She had seen him for several months, had dated him exclusively, and yet she felt no more about his leaving than she would about one of the employees quitting. In fact, she was sure she would be more distressed if her secretary were to say good-bye. Was she really as cold as Brant had accused her of being?

Slowly, she trailed behind Darrell to the front door, locking it after him. She sighed and leaned her forehead against the door. It was a relief to get rid of him, yet she felt a stab of guilt that she could be so businesslike toward the man she had dated for four months.

"Hey! What's the matter with you?" Nick Fletcher's voice rang across the court. "You're playing like hell."

Alexis lowered her racket and drew one hand across her sweating brow. "What do you mean?" she laughed. "You always beat me."

Fletcher laughed back and strolled across the court toward her, tanned and remarkably handsome in his sparkling tennis whites. "That's true. But I usually don't beat you quite so badly."

"I guess the good life you lead is paying off," Alexis replied flippantly.

Nick smiled and ran a hand through his crisp black locks. He was, Alexis reflected, every girl's dream. Twenty-eight years old, he was darkly handsome, athletic, and a charming companion. He was also, she reminded herself, an idle playboy, the sort of man who had the talent to enjoy a professional tennis career but who didn't want to put forth the effort, the kind who had the brains to do anything he chose, but chose to do nothing. Nick was a charmer, all right, but not the sort of man for her.

"I know," Nick replied. "That is why you ought to take me up on one of my offers sometime. It's amazing how dancing until the small hours of the morning will help your tennis game."

Alexis laughed, "But not my job, I'm afraid."

"Why don't we quit playing? It's almost five, and aren't we supposed to meet your mother and her new amour about now?"

"Yes, let's go."

They started off the court, toward the elegant, glass-enclosed clubhouse. As they walked, Alexis asked, "Do you know this Decker guy?"

"Me? Not a chance. You know I avoid political types as much as I can. But I understand he's a good-looking guy, quite a ladies' man. 'Course, your mother is about the prettiest middle-aged woman I've ever seen. They should make a striking couple."

"Ginny sounded more excited about him than I've heard her sound since she and Alec got divorced."

"Well, I hope it works out for them. She's always been on my side where you're concerned."

"Tell me about it!" Alexis laughed. "She's forever going on about what a charming young boy you are. I think she sees you as sort of a cross between Little Lord Fauntleroy and Cary Grant."

Nick threw back his head and roared. "Trust Ginny to make something dramatic out of me!"

They were silent for a few moments, and then, with an odd edge to his voice, Nick asked, "Is something the matter with you, Alexis? You don't look the same."

Alexis glanced at him, startled. Damn his perceptiveness! "No. What do you mean? How do I look?"

He shook his head. "I don't know. There's something about your eyes. Something in your face that just looks—I don't know exactly what."

"Probably tired and frustrated," Alexis quipped. "That job in Barrett was a real killer."

"Well, if you have any problems, you know you can come to good old Nick here." He took hold of her arm and pulled her to a stop. His face was serious as he gazed at her. "Look, Alexis, I really mean it. I know you think I'm a prodigal son, not capable of doing very much, but I *am* your friend. I want you to know I'd do anything for you if you needed it. So if you have some kind of trouble, come to me, okay?"

Alexis nodded and smiled. "Okay."

"There you are!" Ginny's vibrant voice cut through the air. The two of them turned to see her coming down the clubhouse steps toward them in a swirl of print chiffon, her face alive with excitement. "Wilson and I just arrived a few minutes ago. He's in the bar getting us drinks. Come on, we're sitting up here on the terrace."

She led them to an umbrella-covered table that overlooked the swimming pool, and they sat down on gaily colored lawn chairs. Ginny and Nick struck up an immediate, inconsequential conversation, until Wilson Decker returned.

"Wilson!" Ginny cried, holding out her hand to the man who approached them. "This is my daughter Alexis, my oldest. And this is Nick Fletcher. His father is Robert Fletcher. I don't know if you know him."

"Why, of course I know Robert," Decker said smoothly, putting the drinks on the table and extending his hand to Nick. "Pleased to meet you, Nick, Alexis. Your mother speaks of you often, Alexis."

Decker was a tall, broad-shouldered man with silver-gray hair and liquid brown eyes. Ginny had described him well, but she had not been able to convey the charisma that floated about him. Alexis imagined that here was a politician, who, if he chose to, could go far.

"Here's your gin and tonic, Ginny. Could I get you two anything?"

Nick rose. "No, that's all right. I'll go get us something. What do you want, Alexis?"

"Oh, a big glass of iced tea. I'm dying of thirst."

Nick left, and Alexis watched as Wilson Decker sat down, gently taking her mother's hand with assurance. He turned to smile at Alexis. "How are things at Stone Oil? Your mother tells me you're an attorney there."

"Yes, I am. We're having the usual crises. It's not an oil company unless you have one every few days."

"Yes, oil is a risky business, so I'm told. Personally, I've always stayed away from it."

"What business are you in—I mean, besides being a representative?"

"Construction. I know Robert Fletcher from working together on the West End Shopping Center deal. Robert is a very sharp man, but I've never met his son. Does Nick work with his dad?"

Alexis chuckled. "Hardly. Nick believes in living off his unearned wealth."

"Now, Alexis, you're being unfair," Ginny protested.

"Nick is my mother's favorite," Alexis explained to Decker. "Don't ever say anything against him."

"That's not true," Ginny said. "It's just that you run him down too much. Simply because he isn't ambitious like all those oil men and lawyers you know. He is a very nice young man, and he has quite a few interests."

"Oh?" Alexis's voice rose in a question. "Like what? Tennis?"

"Don't be snappy. Nick has many worthwhile hobbies," Ginny insisted defensively.

"Yes, I know about his hobbies," Alexis remarked with a glint of laughter in her eyes. "Such as amateur sports-car racing, expeditions into the Amazon, kayaking, partying, women . . ."

"That isn't what I mean, and you know it," Ginny retorted. "I'm talking about his photography, his painting . . . Why, he even does charity work."

"Now, now, Ginny." Nick's amused voice sounded behind them. "Stop or you'll ruin my reputation."

"Oh, you!" Ginny regarded him warmly.

"Don't worry, Nick," Alexis said. "I happen to know that the main charity you were interested in was Susan Hammons, who was running the auction."

Nick grinned the lopsided smile that had captured many a woman's heart and sat down beside her. "As usual, Alexis, you got me there."

As always when either Nick or Ginny was present, the conversation flowed smoothly. Alexis was amazed, not for the first time, at the ease with which they handled themselves socially. She hated to think of how often she had sat tongue-tied while silence hung like doom over a group.

Almost an hour passed before they moved into the cool green and white dining room to eat, and Alexis was astonished that she had sat so comfortably for so long with Ginny and Nick. Dinner went by quickly on a steady stream of light, amusing chatter. Alexis decided that she rather liked Wilson Decker, especially as a candidate for her mother's heart. He was considerate of her but did not seem to take over. He allowed her at least an opportunity to do things for herself before he offered to help. Alexis realized with a start that her mother seemed more self-sufficient with him, less clinging and helpless. Alec, of course, had always been too domineering, had told her exactly what to do. But, looking back, Alexis saw that she and Morgan had also encouraged Ginny's helplessness by doing things for her whenever she had seemed confused or incompetent.

After the dinner was over, Alexis said good-bye to Decker with genuine warmth. Then, hugging her mother, she whispered, "I approve."

Ginny chuckled and gave her a wink. "So do I."

Nick drove her home, his Porsche roaring down the wide streets of North Dallas, and followed her inside for a nightcap, taking the liberty of an old friend who did not need an invitation. Alexis poured him a shot of Jack Daniels; she, too, did not have to ask.

He settled into a swivel chair with a sigh of contentment and said, "Okay, now tell me what happened in Barrett."

"What do you mean?" Alexis countered, startled.

"You know what I mean. You look tired or sick or something."

"It was trying," Alexis admitted, glancing away from his too-perceptive eyes. "Maybe I need a vacation."

"Hear, hear." Nick held up his glass in a salute. "It's about time you took one. Tell me, have you ever had one since you started work?"

Ruefully, Alexis smiled and shook her head.

Nick sighed in mock despair. "Really, Alexis, what am I going to do with you?"

"Probably nothing," Alexis said frankly. "You've been trying to change my wicked ways ever since I can remember, and you have yet to succeed."

"I know. Why is it that you're the only female who is totally immune to my puckish charm?"

She laughed. "You know good and well that the only reason you pursue me is because *I* am impervious to your line."

"Untrue!" Nick denied with a laugh. "You have always been the love of my life."

"Nick, be serious."

"I am." Suddenly his voice lowered, its usual tone of mockery absent. "Alexis, give me a chance. Can't you stop seeing me as your good old buddy from childhood, the prodigal son you've scolded and helped all these years?" He leaned forward and took her hand, his dark brown eyes almost black in their intensity. "Alexis, I am perfectly serious. I have never really cared for any other woman but you. I'm tired of hanging around, being your friend, treating my feelings as a joke. I love you."

Alexis withdrew her hand and rose. "Nick, please don't."

"Why? Why won't you give me a chance? You don't really feel anything for that zero Darrell Ingram, do you?"

"Good heavens, no!" Alexis exclaimed. "In fact, I split up with him the other day."

"Good. At least I know you haven't totally lost your mind."

"That's unkind, Nick," Alexis scolded mildly.

"Whoever said I was kind?" Nick retorted. "Now, no getting off the subject, Alexis. I want to know what you have against me."

"Oh, Nick, I don't have anything against you." Alexis sighed. "I really, really like you. I have ever since we were kids. But that isn't love, not the romantic kind, at least."

"Only because you insist on keeping us in that same kids' relationship."

"Nick, I'm sorry. I never realized until recently that you actually felt anything like that for me. I always thought you were kidding around for the sake of your image."

"I don't give a damn about my image," he growled.

"Nick, I never meant to hurt you. I'm very fond of you, I enjoy being with you, and I feel you are my good friend. But I simply don't love you. I don't feel that spark, or whatever. We're too different. Believe me, I'd drive you nuts in two weeks."

He grinned. "I'll take the chance."

"Oh, Nick," she groaned.

"Okay, okay, I'm sorry." He sighed. "Well, at least I tried. I guess it's back to the old Ronald Reagan role for me."

"Ronald Reagan?"

"Yeah, you know. He was the one who was always following Bette Davis or somebody around, being her good friend, while George Brent or Paul Heinreid always made off with her."

"You dope," Alexis teased softly.

"Well, you know how we playboys are when our

hearts are finally captured . . . we go soft in the head."
He downed his drink and stood up. "I better get going.
You look like you could use some rest. Don't let Alec
work you too hard."

She followed him to the door, where he bent and
placed a light kiss on her forehead. "The offer is always
open, you know," he said quietly. "If somebody else
breaks your heart and you need someone to mend it, or
if you ever get tired of living in that ice castle, just let
me know."

Alexis smiled. "You'll be the first, I promise."

Chapter 9

Alexis pulled up in front of the crisp white Colonial mansion set back imposingly from the street, its emerald-green, carefully manicured lawn sloping down to the thoroughfare. This was her home . . . or had been until the divorce. Ginny had said she could not bear to remain there, and had let Alec have it as part of the divorce settlement, while she and the girls had moved into a modern house out on Walnut Hill. But to Alexis the split-level residence on Walnut Hill had been only the place where she stayed during vacations from college or law school. This mansion in the older and posher neighborhood of Highland Park, where Alec now lived with his second wife, was really her home. It seemed odd to return to it as a guest.

She got out of her car and began the long walk up the tiered brick sidewalk to the front door. Nervously, she smoothed down her floor-length, sea-green dress and patted her hair, which she had swept up into a loose pompadour style reminiscent of the turn of the century. She knew that she looked as well as she could; the high collar accentuated her slender throat, and the color went well with her hair and skin tones. The dress was simple and tailored, but the glossy sheen of the material gave it a luxurious look.

It was not anxiety about her appearance that prompted her nervous gestures. It was simply that she always dreaded going to one of Laraine's parties. Not that Alexis had anything against Laraine, who was hardly the wicked stepmother of folklore. She was rather selfish and vain, but then, Alexis had grown up around a great number of people like that. She was not a hardhearted person, either, and Alexis thought that Laraine had a genuine liking for her. Sometimes Alexis even enjoyed the woman's brittle, sarcastic humor.

The problem was that Alexis hated parties, and the bigger they were, the more she despised them. Laraine's affairs were always huge. Alexis had never been a master of the social graces, and she felt awkward in conversations that revolved around clothes, jewels, scandal, and entertainment. The crush of people overwhelmed her, though she fought to hide this feeling. To make matters worse, most of the people there would be Laraine's age, not hers, and she probably wouldn't know them, or only slightly. She wished that Laraine had invited Morgan so she would have someone to talk to, but Laraine resented Morgan and seldom included her. Laraine didn't like the way Morgan freely took Alec to task. Moreover, Laraine's glistening blonde beauty could not withstand the comparison to Morgan's youthful vibrancy. Morgan's rich auburn hair and emerald-green eyes captured everyone's gaze. In all fairness, though, Alexis had to admit that Morgan had never been very nice to Laraine, whom she resented for having replaced Ginny.

Taking a deep breath, like a swimmer going underwater, Alexis rang the doorbell. A moment later an efficient servant opened the door, and Alexis entered, smiling.

"Alexis, darling!" Laraine walked across the marble hallway, holding out both her hands to Alexis. She was dressed in a long blue gown that shimmered under the lights and showed off her statuesque figure to perfection. Her golden hair was swept up into a flawless French chignon. Sapphires gleamed in her earlobes. She was a picture of cultivated beauty and wealth. A proper prize for Alec's collection, Alexis thought grimly before rebuking herself.

"Hello, Laraine." Alexis avoided looking at the crowd of people that swamped the living and dining rooms, and the hall. The only clear spot seemed to be the staircase that wound gracefully up to the second floor. "How are you? Thank you for inviting me."

"Oh, I always love to have you, dear, you know that," Laraine said, putting her hands on Alexis's shoulders and laying her smooth cheek against Alexis's. "Alec tells me you did beautifully on that tough assignment he gave you. I was so pleased, and so was Alec. He is really very proud of you, you know."

The two women chatted for a few moments about inconsequential things while Laraine led Alexis around, introducing her to various people. Finally Alexis asked, "Where is Daddy?"

Laraine shrugged. "Who knows? He was closeted in his study with Bill McHenry for a while, then I saw him over by the bar. But the telephone rang a minute ago, so he may very well be talking on it. You know him. It's hard to keep track of him. Oh, there's Maressa Bolton. Let me introduce you to her. She's been after me all evening to meet you."

"Why?"

Laraine grimaced. "Lord only knows. Half the time Maressa herself doesn't know why she does things. She's a big clubwoman, so she probably wants to pressure you into speaking to some group or other of hers. She always wants me to join something, and I just detest clubs. There is absolutely nothing more stultifying than a garden club, unless it's a ladies' auxiliary."

Alexis laughed, and Laraine guided her to a large woman attired in an outmoded black dress. She was hardly Laraine's type, so Alexis knew she must have been invited for some business reason. Much as Laraine had predicted, Maressa immediately set about convincing Alexis to speak at a women's luncheon. Alexis hated speaking in front of groups, but she agreed. After all, the women's groups always wanted women to speak, and there weren't that many around in positions of authority. Besides, it would be good publicity for Stone Oil, and an oil company certainly could use all the good publicity it could get, no matter how small.

After Alexis had agreed to speak, Maressa went into a long, boring monologue about her favorite pastime: growing tropical flowers. Alexis smothered a yawn and put on an interested face. She didn't see her father enter the room and sweep the crowd with his eyes.

"Is Alexis here yet?" he asked Laraine, who had come up to him as soon as he appeared in the doorway.

"Yes, she's over there talking to Maressa Bolton. Poor thing, I'd better rescue her soon."

Alec smiled down at Laraine. She was everything a man could ask for in a wife. She was pretty, intelligent, terrific at organization, able to entertain at a moment's notice, and a real wizard at mixing groups of people and keeping a party going to everyone's satisfaction. No one could have been a better hostess. She was the only woman he knew who could measure up to his exacting standards. Which was why it perplexed him at times that he still thought with longing of the flighty, vivacious, beautiful woman who had been his first wife. He had spoken the truth to Alexis when he said he had always loved Ginny. For all her faults and inadequacies, for all his affairs, he had loved her throughout their marriage. Sometimes he wondered if he didn't love her still.

"I congratulate you, Laraine. It's a wonderful party, as always."

"Thank you. I do think it's going rather well, especially since I couldn't find a way to avoid asking

Patty Benningfield *and* her ex-husband. Fortunately, they've managed to stay at opposite ends of the house."

Alec chuckled. "I think there's been less fireworks tonight than when we invited them as a married couple." He glanced over to where Alexis stood, still in conversation with Mrs. Bolton, and studied her silently for a moment. "Alexis looks rather well tonight, don't you think?"

"Yes. That shade of green is divine on her, makes her glow like a jewel." She cast her husband a small sideways glance. "Dear, don't you think Alexis is looking a little tired, though? Don't you ever give that girl a vacation?"

Alec seemed a little surprised, and he shrugged. "Heavens, I don't know. I presume she's taken a vacation. I don't know anything about it."

"Well, I'll lay money that she hasn't had one in at least two years. Frankly, she looks very drawn and thin to me."

Alec smiled at her. "You really like Alexis, don't you?"

Laraine tilted her head thoughtfully. "Yes, I guess I do. She is a sweet girl, and she's always been very nice to me."

"That may be true, but I've never been able to figure her out. I can understand what Morgan does better."

His wife smiled. "That might be because Morgan acts more like you expect a woman to act. I don't think Alexis would puzzle you so much if she were a man."

"Maybe not, but she isn't. It's funny, Laraine, but I just can't seem to get close to her. She never argues with me or tells me off the way Morgan does. Yet I feel a warmth with Morgan, even when she's hating my guts, that I don't with Alexis. She's all wrapped up in herself and her job. I don't feel I can hug her, like I do Morgan, or take her out to dinner and have a good time with her. She's too aloof."

"Has it ever occurred to you that Alexis is more like you? She has the same drive, the same intellect, the same wall against the world." Alec frowned but said nothing, and Laraine continued. "I think Alexis absolutely worships you, Alec, and you've never realized it. I think she works herself to the point of exhaustion because she wants your approval." There was a touch of sadness in Laraine's eyes as she spoke. She knew all too well the hurt of striving for Alec Stone's approval and inexplicably coming up second.

"She has always had my approval," Alec said.

"I don't think she realizes it, though."

He stared at Laraine for a moment, then murmured, "Perhaps you are right." His gaze went back to his daughter. "Maybe she does need a vacation."

Laraine started to say something, then stopped. When she married Alec Stone, she had made a vow not to interfere with him and his children; she had always hated meddling stepmothers.

"Why don't you say hello to her and get her away from Maressa? I have to check on the refreshments."

"All right." He moved across the room to his daughter's side and neatly inserted himself between the twosome.

"Daddy!" There was relief as well as happiness in Alexis's voice when she saw him.

"Hello, dear." He clasped her arm firmly. "Good evening, Maressa. I hope you will excuse us. I haven't had a chance to visit with my daughter since she arrived."

"Thank you," Alexis whispered as he led her toward the hallway. "I felt like I was going under for the third time."

"She is something of a bore," Alec agreed. "Unfortunately, her husband is a very important judge."

They fell into a short silence, broken by Alec's inquiring, somewhat awkwardly, "Did you calm Macusi down?"

"Oh, yes, I think we'll be able to get out of the contract, like he wants." Alexis paused, then asked casually, "How are things going with the McClure boy?"

"I talked to some people in Washington about it, and they said they'll do everything they can to expedite matters. I've also let slip through foreign channels that we want the child and are willing to grease a few palms in order to get him. It may turn out that we'll have to hire a group of kidnappers to free him, but I think the government sources will work."

"Good."

"Oh, there's Dick Holcomb. Do you know him?"

"I don't think so. Which one is he?"

"The balding guy right there. He's the president of one of our tool suppliers. Good man to know. Come on, I'll introduce you to him."

Alec pulled to a stop beside the man he had indicated and introduced Alexis. A few minutes later he eased out of the group and went on to another. That was his way. He felt he had to circulate and keep as many people happy as possible. Even so, regret pierced Alexis, and she wished that Alec had stayed a little longer. In all her life she could not recall having a lengthy conversation with her father.

After a few moments of polite listening, she excused herself and drifted through the rooms, looking for a familiar face. When none turned up, she went to the staircase and mounted the steps. Suddenly she could no longer bear to face the mass of strangers, and she felt the urge to see her room again.

Laraine had redecorated when she moved into the house—more than once, in fact. Alexis entered her old bedroom, which had been plain, with mahogany furniture and a small study attached, to find that Laraine had turned it into a crafts room, gaily splashed with bright colors. Hardly able to believe her eyes, Alexis glanced slowly around, staring at every modernistic, loud piece of furniture. The effect was not altogether displeasing, though Laraine obviously lacked the decorating talents that Ginny had. Still, it hit Alexis hard that there was nothing left of her old room. It was no longer home.

With a sigh, she sat down on a large floor cushion and leaned up against the wall. If she closed her eyes, she could remember herself here, bending over the desk while studying for a test, or trying on a new dress before the full-length mirror. A stubborn tear oozed beneath her eyelid and crawled down her cheek. It was unnerving to see her entire past obliterated like this. She wondered what had happened to some of the things she had left here—memorabilia that she hadn't wanted at the time. Had they simply been tossed out? She wished that she had taken some things with her that were really dear.

Alexis took another look around before leaving. There was no point in mooning about in a place where nothing was the same. Slowly, she went downstairs and tried to mingle again, but with no great success. She glanced at her watch and decided enough time had passed so that she could go without appearing rude.

Alexis found her stepmother, and pleading exhaustion, said that she was going home early to sleep.

Laraine smiled and patted her arm. "I was just telling Alec that I thought you looked tired. You shouldn't work so hard. Go on home—that's fine. I'm glad you came."

"Thank you."

Alexis slipped out the front door and went quickly down the walk. On the street, she paused and turned to look at the house before climbing into her car. For a long time this had been her home, and now it was as removed from her as a stranger's house. Like everything else in her life these days, it no longer seemed to fit.

"Alexis!" Morgan's voice bubbled out over the phone the next morning. "What have you been doing? It's been ages since I've seen you!"

Alexis had to smile. Morgan had a lilting, vibrant voice that could make anyone smile. "Hello, Morgan. I've been up in Barrett, and then I had a ton of work to do when I got back."

"Barrett?" Morgan repeated. "Lord, how dull can you get? Listen, I was thinking of going shopping this afternoon. Want to come with me? Maybe we could have lunch first."

"Okay," Alexis agreed. She had no real desire to tromp around shopping, but maybe a visit with Morgan would lift her sagging spirits. "When?"

"I just got up. I couldn't make it before eleven-thirty."

"Sounds good. Where shall I meet you?"

"How about Brennan's?"

"Fine. I'll see you there."

They said good-bye, and Alexis got up to shower and wash her hair. Then she padded downstairs for a leisurely cup of coffee and the morning newspaper. Afterward, she dried and brushed her hair and slipped into slacks and a deep blue top.

As always, Alexis was early and Morgan was late. Alexis parked at One Main Place and strolled down to Brennan's, which lay beside the sunken courtyard. A tuxedoed maitre d' quickly showed her to a small table beside the window. Alexis ordered a Bloody Mary and passed the time staring out into the courtyard or glancing around the narrow, elegant restaurant. Everything about the place bespoke quiet, tasteful wealth, from the sparkling mirrors and the crystal chandeliers to the solicitous waiters. A four-man Dixieland jazz band strolled through the room, stopping to play at random tables.

When at last Morgan appeared, breathless and smiling, she made an effective entrance. She wore brown slacks and a matching top that showed off her perfect figure. She had braided her long auburn hair and wound it into a bun at the nape of her neck, the severe hairdo emphasizing the fine-boned beauty of her face. Her emerald-green eyes were wide, fringed with dark lashes, and arched by delicate brown brows. Alexis had to smile at the sensation she caused as she moved across the floor to Alexis's table.

"My, you look beautiful this morning," Alexis said when her sister sat down.

"Do I? Thank you. It's so nice to hear someone say that who isn't after my money or a roll in the hay."

Alexis laughed. Morgan always kept a firm grip on reality. Despite her riches and beauty, she wasn't likely to get carried away by compliments.

"I must say you look rather nice yourself," Morgan added, settling back in her chair. "So tell me, how has the world been treating you?"

"All right, I guess. I got a very important lease in Barrett."

"Good. I bet Daddy was pleased."

"Yes." Alexis shot a speculative glance at her sister. She wondered how much Morgan knew about their father's infidelities. Morgan had been much more a confidante of their mother's, but Alexis wasn't sure if Ginny would have told even Morgan about that. On the other hand, Alec had said that Morgan had berated him for his affairs.

Morgan ordered a Bloody Mary and began to peruse the menu. "Have you seen Ginny's new flame?" she asked casually.

"Yes, I met him the other day. Nick and I had dinner with them at the club."

"What did you think of him?"

"He's attractive. I liked him."

"Me, too. I think Ginny's finally landed a live one there." Her green eyes sparkled at Alexis. "What a gorgeous man! I could almost work up a father-figure complex over him." Alexis laughed, and Morgan looked at the menu again. "What are you getting?"

"Eggs Benedict."

"I was thinking about having Bananas Foster."

"That's all?"

Morgan wrinkled her nose in a grimace. "No, I'll get some sort of breakfast that's healthy, I suppose, but the important thing is whether or not to have Bananas Foster."

"That's too sweet for me. I'd prefer Cherries Jubilee."

Morgan shook her head sadly. "They're both too full of calories. Everything here is." She sighed and patted her stomach. "I gained three pounds in Mexico. I absolutely stuffed myself. So I guess I'd better restrain myself this morning."

"Well, if it's any help, I will, too," Alexis offered.

"But that's not fair. You don't care about desserts anyway!" Morgan wailed, and Alexis had to laugh at her sister's comically woebegone face.

"Morgan . . ." Alexis began, tracing a design on the table with her fingernail and watching it carefully. "What do you know about Mama and Daddy's divorce?"

Morgan laid down the menu. "What do you mean?" she asked warily.

"I mean, do you know what it was really about? Why did Ginny leave him?"

Morgan shrugged and looked away. "How should I know?"

"Well, you must know something, or you wouldn't be getting so shifty about it," Alexis replied firmly.

Morgan sighed. "Well, if you insist, I think it was over the blonde bombshell who is his present wife."

"Morgan, Laraine's a perfectly nice woman. Why are you always so nasty to her?"

"Because of the divorce," Morgan answered quickly. "Daddy was having an affair with her, and Ginny couldn't take it. Actually, I don't dislike Laraine as much as I used to. Sometimes I even feel kind of sorry for her. She'll never have Daddy's love, any more than anyone else will."

"What does that mean?"

"Al, are you trying to get into a fight with me? I

know how crazy you are about Daddy. I don't want to badmouth him to you."

"I found out some things about him in Barrett, and I don't think I'm likely to be shocked by anything you say about him."

"Well, I think that Alec Stone loves himself and his business above all else. Ginny was always a poor third, but I think Laraine is a poor fourth. Daddy once told me he wished that he and Ginny hadn't gotten divorced."

"Morgan, have you ever heard . . . that maybe Daddy had a number of affairs during those years?"

Morgan regarded Alexis through narrowed green eyes. Finally she said, "So you figured it out at last."

"You knew about it?"

"Alexis, *everyone* knew about it except you. You always had your head buried in some book and never had any idea what was going on around you. The affairs broke Ginny's heart."

Alexis sighed. "I'm pretty slow on the uptake, huh?"

Morgan grinned. "You're just different. People like me, we thrive on gossip. I can't rest unless I know everything that's going on. You've never been very interested in the human side of things. Besides, you never could see anything wrong with Daddy."

Their conversation came to a halt while the waiter took their orders. After he had left, Alexis sat quietly for a few moments, playing with her glass, before she spoke in an almost plaintive tone. "Am I like him, Morgan? Am I like Daddy? I know I'm not like Ginny at all."

Morgan frowned and bit her lip. "If you mean, are you exactly like him, then no. You aren't arrogant or oblivious to other people's feelings. But you are smart like him and interested in business. You're determined, and you follow things through. You aren't a social butterfly like Ginny or me. You have more sense."

"You have sense!" Alexis cried staunchly, and Morgan chuckled.

"Alexis, you are loyal. I forgot that. You're loyal to the bitter end. You know I'm as senseless and useless as Nick Fletcher."

"You aren't quite as extravagant."

"Well, perhaps. But let's not get off the subject. We were talking about you. Are you worried that maybe you're like Daddy? Did somebody say that?"

Alexis smiled ruefully. "As a matter of fact, somebody did. I believe he said I was a carbon copy of Alec Stone."

"Oh, that's not true. Whoever he is, he's crazy."

"He's the guy I got the lease from. He hates Daddy because Daddy had an affair with his mother, and his mother left him and his father and sister."

"Oh, so that's how you found out about all the goings-on. But what does that have to do with you?"

"Well, he claimed I was just like Alec, that I was ruthless."

"Sounds like he has it in for both of you," Morgan observed. "Even I'm not *that* hard on Daddy. Don't worry about it. This man sounds like a nut."

"Only about the Stones. I started worrying because I did do some awful things to him, I guess, trying to get him to sign the lease. I tricked him a couple of times . . . but he was just as bad! He was always accusing me of all sorts of stuff and—" Alexis stopped and took a swallow of her drink.

"Come on, tell Morgan," her sister said gently. "You know I can take it. Nothing shocks me."

To her surprise, Alexis found the whole story of her relationship with Brant McClure tumbling from her lips, from the first meeting to the final, bitter parting. Morgan sat silently, her eyes fixed on her sister's drawn face, until Alexis finally wound down.

"It sounds like quite a time," Morgan commented dryly. "Frankly, Alexis, the state you two were in, I wouldn't take what you did or said very seriously. It sounds like it was a highly volatile situation, and you didn't have the time or the distance to cool down. In fact, I wouldn't be surprised if the two of you have a real strong thing going."

"What are you talking about? We despise each other! All that was at the very beginning, before I found out what he was like."

Morgan raised her eyebrows but made no comment.

Alexis continued. "Morgan, ever since I came back, I've been worrying about what happened with Brant, about what I did and the way I felt about him. I really liked him at first, and then it all fell apart. I went out with Darrell last week, and suddenly I looked at him and thought, what am I doing? I don't even like him! Morgan, I just have this terrible feeling that I don't know how to relate to men."

"Men are weird," Morgan allowed. "Who can relate to them? Most of the time they don't make any sense. How could anyone relate to that?"

"Well, I don't feel comfortable with men—in a social situation, I mean. I can deal with them fine at the office, but that's different. I don't know how to act or how to attract them, what to say or what to do. When I was in Barrett, I realized that I never had a normal girlhood. I never acted like a silly, giggling teen-ager. And I never dated, because I wasn't interested in boys.

"But now . . . I feel I've missed out on something, as if a basic part of most people's education is lacking in me. The social part, the men and dating part."

"It isn't too late to learn," Morgan assured her.

"I think maybe it is. Sometimes there are certain stages in your development that you miss, and you can't ever make them up. They're missing forever. I'm afraid that maybe that's the way it is with me. Something is lacking in me regarding men, and I'll never be able to relate to them like other women do. I read an article once about a study they did on a group of convicts, and they discovered that a lot of them never crawled as babies. They missed that stage, and it screwed up the rest of their lives."

Morgan grimaced. "Don't be a dope, Alexis. What

does crawling around have to do with anything? You can deal with men as well as anybody. All you have to do is make a little effort.''

"Like how?"

"Well, this McClure guy is in Barrett, so that pretty well puts him out of the picture. Besides, that situation is too tangled up by now to make very much out of it. So I suggest you start with somebody here—like Nick Fletcher.''

"You sound like Ginny," Alexis said disgustedly.

"Look, Alexis, you're asking for social advice here, not for business smarts. Who knows better about socializing—Ginny and me, or you?"

Alexis shrugged. "Okay, I'll listen. What's your advice about Nick Fletcher?"

"Nick's a nice guy, and he's crazy about you. I know you think he's a hopeless lightweight, and maybe he is. But he loves you, or hasn't that fact penetrated your thick Stone skull yet?"

"Oh, it penetrated, all right. But I don't want to get attached to a playboy, Morgan. What good will that do me?"

"Experience teaches," Morgan proclaimed, a mockingly wise expression on her face.

"Well, he's been taught a lot, then," Alexis retorted.

Morgan laughed. "Probably so, but personally, I think someone like him, someone who knows about women and what they like, would be the perfect person for you. You don't have to run over to his house and hop in bed with him and cry, 'I love you, Nick.' All I'm saying is that you should give him a chance. Go out with him, let him work that Fletcher charm on you. Give yourself a chance, too. I'd lay odds that if you let yourself go with him, put yourself in his hands, he'd turn your whole life around.''

Alexis sighed and shook her head. "I don't know, Morgan . . .''

"It's not just that you don't know how to relate to men," Morgan went on firmly, "you're scared of them, too. All your life you've held them at bay, except for a few like Darrell Ingram whom you knew you were in no danger with. But men like Nick who could really reach you, you put up a wall against. You won't let that guy even get close to you."

"Maybe you're right," Alexis conceded reluctantly. "I'll think about it."

Morgan rolled her eyes in exasperation, but she was stopped from saying anything more by the arrival of their lunch. Silently they dived into the delicious food. After Morgan had time to think, she realized the futility of arguing further with her sister. Alexis had something to think about, and that was the best that could be hoped for now. It would only set Alexis more firmly against the idea if she kept harping on it.

So when Morgan began to talk again, she steered clear of the subject of Nick Fletcher or of Alexis's problems with men. Throughout the meal and all during the afternoon of shopping, she concentrated on making light and amusing chatter. After all, the way Alexis looked, she could use a little cheering up more than anything else.

The following Friday, the shrill buzz of the phone on her desk cut through Alexis's attention on the paper before her, and she groped for the receiver, her eyes still focused on the document.

"Alexis Stone," she said automatically.

"Alexis, this is Beth."

"Beth!" Alexis cried with genuine delight. "How nice to hear from you! What are you doing?"

"Well, right now I'm sitting in my room at the Hyatt Regency. In a few minutes Rusty and I are going to eat up in that wild thing that looks like a golf ball."

Alexis smiled at Beth's description of the Regency's tower, which did rather resemble a huge golf ball on top of an enormously long tee. "So you're both here in Dallas?"

"Yes. I finally managed to convince Rusty to bring

me to Dallas for some shopping. Of course, the only way I could work it was for him to decide that he wanted to see the Cowboy game on Sunday. But today and tomorrow I intend to gorge myself completely on shopping."

Alexis chuckled. "I'm sure North Park will never be the same."

"I know that you're working today, but I was hoping maybe I could persuade you to come with me tomorrow," Beth continued.

"Well, I just finished a marathon of shopping last Saturday with my sister, but for you I'll tackle it again."

Beth's laughter vaulted upward. "Great! That's the mark of a true friend, I'll tell you. When we're through, I thought you might join us for dinner. I've made Rusty promise that he'll take me to a Japanese restaurant and then to an honest-to-gosh nightclub. You'll come with us."

"Okay, that sounds great."

"Terrific. Oh, dear, I have to get off now. Rusty is ready to leave and is standing by the door, tapping his foot and looking at his watch."

"I'll come by and pick you up tomorrow morning, if that's okay. What time?"

"Ah, about nine-thirty, say. I'll be in the lobby."

Again Alexis chuckled. "Which one?"

"Oh, dear, there are a million of them, aren't there? I'll just wait in my room. It's all too much for a country girl like me."

"Okay, see you then."

Alexis hung up the phone, a smile still tracing her lips. It was good to hear Beth's voice again. Alexis had wanted to ask her about Brant. It had been a struggle to bite the words back. But in any case, it really didn't matter a bit to Alexis what Brant was doing. Still, as she bent her head over her work again, she could not help but wonder if by some chance he had accompanied them to see the game. But no, that was silly. That character wouldn't leave his ranch for something as frivolous as a football game. In fact, she didn't think he would leave his ranch for much of anything at all.

Three hours later, after a quick pastrami sandwich that her secretary had brought her for lunch, Alexis was still seated at her desk, immersed in what she was reading and in the notes scrawled across her legal pad. Her forehead was knotted in concentration.

Not wanting to talk, she didn't look up when she heard footsteps stop at her door. A drawling masculine voice cut through her thoughts. "Didn't anybody ever tell you that frowning like that causes wrinkles? You'll be old before your time, lady."

Alexis's head jerked up, and she stared at the man lounging in the doorway, his casual clothes and brown skin at odds with the atmosphere of the law office. Her pen slid nervelessly from her fingers as she gaped at him.

Brant McClure!

Chapter 10

Shakily, Alexis stood up. "I—that is—you startled me. I didn't expect to see you here."

"I came up with Rusty and Beth to go to a Cowboy game. There's nothing much going on at the ranch this time of year." He straightened and moved into the office, closing the door behind him.

Hot, stabbing fingers of fear and excitement clutched at her stomach. "Why did you close the door! I prefer it open."

"Because I came to talk about something private," he said, lowering himself into the leather chair across from her desk. "Don't you usually close the door when you have private matters to discuss?"

Alexis gradually unclenched her fists and sat down, comforted by the width of walnut desk that separated them. It was funny, she thought irrelevantly, how much he looked the same, how well she knew his face, yet how much she saw now that she had forgotten or never noticed before. It seemed an age since their last confrontation, or as recent as yesterday.

"What is it you want to discuss?" she asked, forcing her voice to be calm, even though her insides were jumping under his steady amber gaze. Why had he come to Dallas? What did he want with her? She had thought she would never have to see him again.

"Our deal. Or have you forgotten it?" His expression was cold and set, his tone snide.

"Of course not. But these things take time. It's only been a couple of weeks."

He shrugged. "I thought while I was here I might as well bring this by." He tossed a large envelope onto her desk. "Those are a bunch of papers somebody from Dallas sent me to fill out and sign for the government. I already did that years ago, but I completed them again."

Alexis glanced at the return address on the envelope. "But this is from Jim Shanklin, one of my father's—"

"Flunkies," Brant cut in. "I know, but I prefer to go straight to the horse's mouth."

"I hardly think I qualify for that description, though I suppose I should be grateful you didn't suggest some other part of the anatomy," Alexis remarked dryly.

Her words brought a reluctant smile to Brant's face, but he said only, "I figured you could deliver these to this Shanklin guy and then tell me exactly what's going on regarding Paul. Can you get him out? And if so, when?"

"Really, Brant, this is hardly my territory. I turned the matter over to my father, and I haven't heard anything about it since."

"Well, find out something, then."

Her toes itched to start tapping impatiently. As always, he was succeeding in arousing her ire. However, she kept a firm clamp on her feelings and smiled at him. "I'll call his office and see what I can learn."

Alexis picked up the receiver and tapped out the extension number of her father's secretary. "Mrs. Jenkins, this is Alexis. Is my father in?"

"Yes, he just arrived," the woman answered. "Would you like to talk to him?"

"Please."

A moment later her father's deep voice came on the line. "Yes, Alexis, what is it?"

"Mr. Brant McClure is in my office right now, and he

would like to know what the status is on our offer. Do you have anything to tell him?"

There was a slight pause at the other end, and then Alec said, "Sure. I don't have much, but bring him up here. I'll be happy to talk to him."

Alexis's eyes widened, but before she could think of an objection, her father had clicked off. Slowly, she replaced the receiver and turned to Brant.

"He said I should bring you up to his office and he'd be glad to talk to you." Alexis conveyed the message and watched for McClure's reaction.

His expression remained the same, except for the lifting of one eyebrow. "So," he murmured thoughtfully, "I get a chance to see Alec Stone . . . again. I can hardly pass that up, can I?"

"All right." Alexis buzzed Betty and told her that she would be out of the office for the next few minutes and to take all calls. Then she rose and led the way down the hall to the elevators.

As they sped up to the top floor, Alexis's nerves were stretched tight. The elevator space was entirely too small to be confined with Brant McClure; his presence was almost overpowering. The situation wasn't helped any by the fact that the elevator was lined with mirrors, so that everywhere she looked, there he was.

Alexis dreaded the upcoming meeting between McClure and her father. She had no idea what Brant might do. He was a violent, unpredictable man. No doubt Alec, with his supreme confidence, felt certain he could win McClure over despite his hostile attitude. Alec had a lot of charm, but Alexis doubted if that asset would be enough to sway Brant. Above all, she didn't want to be in the middle when those two implacable men got into an argument.

Surreptitiously, Alexis glanced at Brant, and she almost jumped when she saw him looking straight at her, his eyes alight with a golden flame. Then, suddenly, the light was gone, and his eyes were as hard as marble as they surveyed her. Alexis swallowed, and when the elevator doors opened, she stepped out gratefully. She would see him to the office, and then she would get out as quickly as she could. That way she would avoid the clash that was bound to occur.

Mrs. Jenkins smiled at them from behind her desk and waved them toward the inner office. Alexis returned the smile as she opened the door and ushered Brant inside.

Alec Stone stood up and moved out from behind his desk to greet them. Alexis looked sideways at Brant to catch his reaction, but his face revealed nothing.

"Well, well, so this is Brant McClure," her father said heartily. "Last time I saw you, you were just a boy."

Brant ignored the proffered hand. "Yes. That was when you were . . . seeing my mother."

Stone raised an eyebrow and glanced at his daughter with renewed respect. This man had indeed been a tough nut to crack. "Sit down and tell me what I can do for you."

Without hesitation, Brant chose the chair closest to Alec. So much for intimidation, Alexis thought with amusement as she settled herself to watch the show. As soon as she had observed the greeting that passed between the two men, she had rejected her former decision to leave. It was so rare an occasion to see her father meet his match.

"I made an agreement with your daughter that I would sign the lease if you would bring my son to the United States. I want to know what has been done about it." Brant's words were crisp and short.

"Now, you have to understand, Brant, that these things take a long time. There are some pretty delicate negotiations involved."

"I realize that, Mr. Stone," McClure went on unhesitatingly. "I just want to know what has happened so far. I like to be kept informed."

"Yes, I can see that. That's always wise, of course. I put one of my assistants, Jim Shanklin, on it, and I talked to a few people in the State Department myself. I can safely say that our firm's foreign office is now actively working on negotiating your son's release. The time factor is dependent on how stubborn the Vietnamese are. For extra insurance, I have a little influence with some other embassies, and they have agreed to do all they can to pressure the Vietnamese government into giving the boy up . . . and quickly. But I have no definite word yet."

"I see."

"Of course, as soon as I know something more specific, I'll contact you. Does that answer your question?"

Brant paused for a moment, then replied, "Yes, I think it does."

"Good. May I say that we certainly are happy to have you with us. I think there's a sizable gas deposit under your land. I'm hoping for a long-producing well. Now, let me invite you to have supper this evening with me and my wife, and Alexis, of course. Laraine would love to meet you."

"No," Brant said firmly, rising to his feet. "You know my feelings about you and this organization, Mr. Stone, and they aren't going to change because you came up with something important enough to me to bribe me into signing your lease. I am not 'with' you. I am not part of your team, and I never will be. I couldn't care less what your hopes are for gas beneath my land. If it weren't for Paul, believe me, you wouldn't be drilling there. Now, if you will excuse me . . ."

Alec made no response, a look of astonishment covering his face. He glanced toward his daughter as McClure walked to the door. Alexis shrugged and quirked her eyebrows. At the door, Brant turned and looked at Alexis, obviously waiting for her to join him. Not really knowing why she did it, Alexis rose and followed him out. She walked silently beside him to the elevator, her lips twitching treacherously, threatening to break into a smile. It occurred to her that she had never seen that look of total amazement on Alec Stone's face before, and she was delighted to have been a witness to it. If anyone but Brant had been with her now, she would have been unable to restrain her laughter.

When the elevator reached her floor, Brant stepped out with her. Alexis looked at him in surprise. "Aren't you going on down?" she asked bluntly. "Or did you have something else you wanted to say to me?"

Brant frowned slightly. "No, I guess not." He paused for a moment, watching her, then turned abruptly and said, "Good-bye, Alexis." He punched the elevator button and the doors slid open smoothly. Without a backward glance, he stepped inside, and the doors closed behind him.

Alexis stood there staring at the closed doors, her stomach sinking.

Brant left the Stone Building and drove quickly to the bars on Greenville Avenue. It was four-thirty, and the happy hour should be starting about now. He thought he could certainly use a drink.

Alec Stone. He had finally met Alec Stone again, and he felt strangely empty. It was like meeting one's dragon after years and years of arming against it, and then discovering that the dragon was only a man. When Alexis had asked him if he wanted to go upstairs and put his remarks to Stone himself, his stomach had leaped with excitement. When he had gotten there, he had seen a hard, sharp, wealthy man, but a man nevertheless. Nowhere had there been the all-powerful, ruthless giant who had loomed so large all the years of his adolescence. Brant had told Stone what he thought of him, and amazingly, with that, all the old, roiling hatred and envy had vanished. Now he felt empty and a little tired.

Brant downed a beer quickly and called for another. He remembered the faint amusement on Alexis's face in the elevator, and he smiled. It had tickled her to see the old man told off like that. He wondered if she was really scared of Stone. Damn, she looked terrific like that—all tart and sweet mixed together, like a peach in summer. He took another pull of his beer and let his mind linger on the thought of Alexis Stone. The truth was, most of the time in Stone's office Brant had paid less attention to what the old man had said and more to Alexis's shapely crossed legs.

It was a dumb thing to do, he told himself, coming down here with Beth and Rusty. He hadn't come for the Cowboy game; he could see it better on his TV set than at the stadium. And, he hadn't come to find out about Paul, either; he could have done that over the phone. No, it was because, for the last two weeks, he had been tossing and turning in his bed at night and waking up in a sweat from dreaming of Alexis. After all that had happened, he could not get her out of his mind.

When Beth had asked him if he wanted to come along, he had jumped at the idea, telling himself that he would have a chance to find out about Paul. But deep down he had known that something in him ached to see Alexis again. And when, finally, he had seen her in that dusky-rose dress that clung softly to her breasts and put a glow in her complexion, he had realized it was more difficult to see her than to dream about her. Maybe he had hoped that seeing her would cure him; maybe he had believed that somehow she had changed, that she had forgiven him for his animalistic attack on her, that she had regretted her lies. Admit it, he told himself. You wanted her to cry out with glee when she saw you, and throw herself into your arms!

Whatever he had wanted, it had not happened. The desire only pulsed stronger in his veins, glaringly pointing out the futility of it all. Alexis Stone was a million miles away from him in all the ways that mattered. She might as well be on a different planet, for all the hope there was for them. Nothing could come of it, except deeper pain. He raised his hand to the bartender for another drink. Perhaps if he stayed here long enough, he could blot her out entirely.

Beth was full of chatter when Alexis picked her up at the hotel the next morning. Alexis had not spent a very restful night; images of Brant McClure had disturbed her sleep. But obviously Beth had not suffered from any lack of sleep; she was bright-eyed and full of bounce.

"Oh, it's so good to see you!" she exclaimed, squeezing her friend's arm. "It seems absolutely years since I saw you, even though I know it's been only two weeks. You'll never guess what happened. Mary Nelle Whiting, the doctor's wife, left him and filed for divorce last week."

"I can't say that tears me up," Alexis said dryly.

"No, I guess not. Me, either, except now I'm afraid he'll move out of Barrett and we won't have a doctor any more. Say, did my brother see you yesterday?"

"Yes, he came to the office," Alexis replied noncommittally.

"I told Rusty that was where he'd slipped off to. We couldn't figure out what had happened to him. Rusty thought Brant was trying to avoid going shopping . . . There's probably some truth in that, too. But boy, did he come back last night with one tied on! I heard him stumbling around in his room about one o'clock in the morning, so I went to see him. Was he ever crocked! What did you two do?"

"Don't look at me!" Alexis retorted. "I didn't see him after he left my office about four or five."

"Mmm . . . drowning his sorrows, no doubt," Beth mused.

"Now, what does that mean?"

"I think my esteemed brother has really got a thing about you."

"He certainly has a peculiar way of showing it."

"Oh, he's fighting it, all right," Beth agreed. "But I think, for once, he isn't winning."

Alexis cast her a disbelieving look, and Beth abandoned the subject.

"I covered the mall at North Park yesterday," she announced. "Let's try somewhere else."

They went to the Quadrangle, the European Crossroads, and the Olla Podrida, and by the end of the day Alexis felt as if she had been caught up in a whirlwind. She had bought only a lovely little metal sculpture, a pair of silver earrings, and a peacock-blue dress that Beth had insisted she try on. Once she had donned the soft, clinging dress, she couldn't resist it.

"You simply must wear it tonight," Beth declared, and laughing, Alexis agreed.

Suddenly Alexis was flooded with suspicion, and she glanced at her friend through narrowed eyes. "Is Brant coming with us tonight?" Beth's expression immediately became so shifty that Alexis knew she had hit on the truth. "Beth, you know it will be an impossible situation! How could you?"

"Well, I couldn't tell Brant that he couldn't eat with us," Beth protested. "He is my brother, after all."

"True, but I bet you didn't tell him that I was going to be there."

"I did so!"

"And what did he say?"

"Well, he wasn't terribly agreeable, but he finally said it was all right."

"Beth, I don't think I should come."

"Now look, if Brant will be reasonable, please don't you get all sticky," Beth pleaded. "We need to have a couple, not one person, with us. I want to go dancing. Please, Alexis, say yes. It will be terribly awkward without you, and just imagine what Brant will think if you don't come because he's there. Why, it could blow your whole deal!"

"Now you sound like my father," Alexis said peevishly. "Oh, all right, Beth, I'll come, but I warn you, I don't think it will be a pleasant evening."

"Nonsense. It's going to be grand. Especially if you wear that dress."

"Okay, okay," Alexis capitulated laughingly.

Alexis had to admit that once she was dressed up, with makeup and her hair a tumbling, shining mass of curls, she did look pretty, almost striking. A triumphant little voice inside her declared that this time Brant McClure would be sorry for the way he had treated her.

She soon discovered, however, that that hope had been in vain. From the moment she walked into the bar of the Japanese restaurant where she was to meet Beth and family, Brant was surly and nontalkative. Alexis glanced at Beth, who raised her eyebrows in exasperation and shrugged as if to say she had never understood her brother's moods.

After Brant had established that he had no wish to participate in the conversation, Alexis steadfastly ignored him throughout the meal. This was not an easy thing to do, since they sat side by side at the small table, their chairs jammed so close together that their thighs touched.

Nevertheless, Alexis did her best to concentrate on the performance of the waiter, who sliced and stir-fried their food right at the table. Now and then, if she made the slightest move, her leg would brush against Brant's, and she would quickly jerk away.

She was grateful when dinner was over at last. Beth wanted to move on to a nightclub. Alexis selected a plush bar with a small dance band. Tonight she simply did not feel up to the raucous beat of a disco or the studied rusticness of a country-Western place.

Beth was charmed by the club, but Alexis found herself in worse shape there than at dinner. Rusty and

Beth spent most of their time on the dance floor, leaving Brant and Alexis alone in the padded booth that curved around the minuscule bar table. Alexis wished that she hadn't chosen so quiet a place; at least the noise of a disco would have covered up this dreadful silence between them.

"How is the ranch?" she asked, determined to be polite.

He shrugged. "Okay, I guess. Good as it can be."

That statement effectively stopped any communication for a while, and Alexis stared fixedly at the dance floor, her mind darting about for a lengthier topic. Finally, exasperated, she demanded, "Why did you agree to come tonight if you knew you were just going to put a gloom on everything?"

He shot a glance at her. "I don't happen to feel like talking."

"Oh, that's right, I forgot," Alexis said tightly. "Beth told me you had quite a hangover."

"Beth's mouth can be like the Grand Canyon at times," Brant snapped.

"If you don't want people to talk about it, you shouldn't get roaring drunk," Alexis proclaimed, hearing with horror even as she spoke the primly smug tone of her voice.

"Do you like to fight, or what?"

"I don't know what you mean."

"Well, you keep picking at me like you're hoping to goad me into something."

"I was hoping to force you to speak a little," Alexis retorted.

"All right, if it bugs you so much, we'll carry on a nice, polite conversation. What would you like to discuss? The weather? Let's see, it's November now, isn't it? Still pretty warm here for November. In Barrett, it's getting mighty crisp."

"Thank you. I can do without the weather report."

"What do you want, then?"

"I thought perhaps we could talk about something like two normal adults, but I see that's impossible with you."

"Lady, there is nothing I want to talk to you about," he replied rudely, staring down at his drink. "I found out what I wanted to know in your office yesterday."

Fortunately for Alexis's temper, Beth and her husband returned, laughing and breathless. "Oh, this is great!" Beth exclaimed, flopping down beside them. "Why don't you two get out and try it? If an old fogy like Rusty can do it, so can you."

Rusty grinned and agreed. "That's right. The only thing I ever learned how to do was the Texas Two-Step."

"And the Cotton-Eyed Joe," Beth added.

"Oh, well, I should have taken you to Whiskey River, then," Alexis laughed, "or to the Longhorn Ballroom."

The conversation turned to the Cowboy game, and Brant carefully stayed out of it. After a few minutes Rusty and Beth got up to dance again, and Alexis was left once more with her silent companion. This time she was determined to make no greater effort than he, so she stared into space.

Abruptly, Brant said, "Let's dance," and led her from the booth.

Startled, Alexis followed him onto the floor and moved into his arms. This, she realized, was the biggest mistake she had made in a long time. He held her close, though impersonally, and his skin seared hers where they touched. She was enveloped by him, enclosed in his strength. Her head was full of the warmth of his body, of the crisp male scent of aftershave and soap that emanated from him.

When Alexis realized that she was leaning against Brant, resting her cheek against the smooth fabric of his shirt, she pulled away. Like iron, his arms tightened around her, drawing her hard against him. She felt his breath against her hair and heard a soft, muffled curse break from him. White-hot tingles shot over her body as his hand pushed its way into the thick mass of her hair and rested against the back of her neck. Alexis felt faint and warm, but she knew that she wouldn't leave this place, this moment, for anything.

The music ended and they drew apart shakily, both avoiding the other's eyes as if to conceal a shameful secret. Alexis turned and walked back to their table, sensing his presence behind her.

Before she could sit down, McClure grasped her wrist. She looked up at him questioningly and saw in his eyes the same gold fire that had surprised her yesterday. The shock of its intensity made her gasp. Then his face swooped down, his mouth covering hers and cutting off her breath in a devouring kiss. His arms went around her, grinding her body into his, flattening her breasts against his firm chest. Ruthlessly, his lips possessed hers, his tongue exploring, tasting, the recesses of her mouth. It seemed an eternity before he released her, tearing his arms from her as if he were in pain.

"What are you trying to do to me?" he asked hoarsely. In the dim, flickering light of the club, the bones of his face stood out harshly, and his eyes glittered. "What do you want?"

Alexis shook her head, feeling weak and close to tears, uncertain of anything in this spinning, crazy world.

His voice was low and tortured as he rasped, "All I want is to forget that you ever happened to me. Damn you!"

With that, he wheeled away from her, striding through the club and out the door. Shaken, Alexis sat down and put her head in her hands, trying to pull herself together, to compose herself into some semblance of normality. What was there about Brant McClure that he could confuse her so, could so utterly destroy all her resistance? She knew, with a sick feeling in her stomach, that if he had not stormed out, if he had taken her hand in his, she would have gone with him. Would have gone and gladly, bonelessly, given herself up to his expert lovemaking.

"Alexis, what's the matter?" Beth's concerned voice cut into her thoughts. "Are you all right? Where is Brant?"

Taking a deep breath and hoping she looked calmer than she felt, Alexis lifted her head. "He left. Yes, I'm okay. We had another one of our rounds, I'm afraid."

"Oh, no," Beth moaned, and sat down. "Was it very bad? I'm so sorry. When I saw you two dancing, I thought maybe you were going to work it out, you looked so happy and good together."

Alexis gave a dry chuckle. "We worked it out as we always seem to—badly."

"Maybe if you stopped meddling, Beth," her husband put in, settling his long form into the booth, "and let things take their natural course, there wouldn't be so many problems."

"If I let Brant take *his* natural course, he would never do anything. He refuses to be happy." Beth's voice sounded treacherously close to tears. "Oh, I'm sorry, Alexis. Maybe I did screw everything up. My father always told me I pushed too hard about everything."

Alexis smiled wanly at her friend. "Don't feel bad. I know how much you want Brant to fall for me. I'm afraid, though, that it is simply not in the cards. We don't suit each other at all."

"It could be that you two are too much alike, and that's why you keep running into such problems," Rusty mused.

Beth smiled and clasped her husband's hand. "I think you're right, honey."

"Well, whatever it is, Beth, I think you might as well give up. Brant and I are not likely to get together on anything."

"But I just know that you two feel something for each other. I can see it in your eyes . . . and in his. As soon as you walked into the restaurant tonight, Brant's eyes lit up like somebody had turned a switch on in him."

"Once in a while we seem to have a certain mutual physical attraction," Alexis explained wryly. "But that can't overshadow the fact that we can't stand each other."

Beth looked crestfallen, and Alexis had to laugh at her expression. "I'm sorry, Beth. I know he is your brother. But he and I are like oil and water."

"Okay, I give up." Beth raised her hands in surrender. "I promise I won't try to throw the two of you together again. I guess even *I* have to admit defeat sometime."

"Thank you. Now, if you two don't mind, I'm going home. You all enjoy yourselves."

"Sure. Bye, honey." Beth gave her friend a little hug. "Next time I'm in Dallas I'll call you. Okay?"

"Okay. Bye, Beth. Bye, Rusty."

Alexis went swiftly to her car in the parking lot and started for home. She tried to keep her mind on the traffic and her driving. There was a hard lump in her chest that seemed to be pushing its way out of her throat, but she kept swallowing it down. Not until she was safely inside her own home did she relax her hold on herself and let the flood of tears gush forth. Like a child, she threw herself on her bed and sobbed until the tears were spent. And even then she didn't know what she had been crying about.

Chapter 11

November slipped by, with nothing further heard from Brant. Alexis clung to her work, but no longer could it occupy her heart and soul. She fell into fits of depression from which she would angrily wrench herself and then settle firmly on an even course. Nick continued to ask her out, and she found herself accepting him more often. He was someone who genuinely liked her, and it was easy to go along with him and ignore the possible consequences. There were even times when she thought that maybe Morgan was right, that if she let Nick take over her love life, she would fall in love with him and discover an emotional richness she had never known. But she wasn't ready to commit herself to that. She liked Nick too much to back out once she had started on that track, and she had to be sure.

The first week in December, Alexis answered the phone and heard Alec's voice at the other end, his excitement barely muted. "Alexis, we've got him!"

"Who?" she asked, puzzled.

"Who! Whom have I been trying to get into this country for the last month?"

Alexis's stomach did a flip. "Paul McClure?"

"That's right. I just got a call from Manila, where he's landed, and tomorrow they're going to send him on to Hawaii. Of course, he'll have to get some shots before they let him go. Anyway, the government wants to turn him over to a representative of Stone Oil in Hawaii. They don't want to have their hands in this any longer than necessary."

"Hawaii . . ." Alexis mused. "So is Garrett going to pick him up?"

"No, you are," Alec answered.

"What?"

"You heard me. I want you to fly to Hawaii tomorrow, or the day after at the latest, and bring him back."

"But, Daddy, I can't!" Alexis protested. "I have a million things to do. I can't possibly leave now."

"Don't give me that. Clear up the most immediate stuff this afternoon, put back what can wait, and turn the rest of it over to somebody else. You must have learned how to delegate."

"Well, yes, I could do it, of course, but why? Why pay one of your corporate attorneys to pick up a child, something anyone could handle?"

Alec sighed. "But not anyone can handle this. Alexis, I don't want the details of this deal spread around. I don't even want Garrett to know what's really going on. You know how the public would howl if they found out about how I've been leaning on our government and some other countries as well. This is secret, Alexis, and a priority. I want that lease as soon as possible. I want to start drilling. This has been a pet project of mine for years. Besides, can you see Garrett taking care of a nine-year-old kid? He wouldn't have the first idea what to do. This would work better with a woman handling it."

"Careful, Daddy, your male chauvinism is showing. And what do *I* know about children? Probably about as much as Garrett. At least he's a father, isn't he? I've never been around a kid in my life except Cara, and you know I never took care of her."

"I don't care. You can handle it best, and I want you

to go. This is your deal, and you should be the one to carry it through to the end. Get the boy, bring him back, and take him to McClure. Hell, Alexis, most people would be jumping at the chance to get a company-paid trip to Hawaii in December. Take a week off. When did you last have a vacation?"

Alexis sighed. "You know I haven't taken one since I came to work."

"So this is your golden opportunity. I order you to take a week off as long as it's in Hawaii. Laraine said she thought you were looking run down. You are at the point of exhaustion, and I am kicking you out for a week. Okay?"

Alexis sighed. "Okay."

"Good. Have a nice trip. Call me when you get back."

Well, that was that. Alexis put down the phone with less-than-steady fingers. The time had come. Brant McClure's child was here, and soon she would have to face Brant again and get him to sign the lease. That was frightening enough, but she dreaded almost as much having to meet the child and spend a week with him in Hawaii before taking him to McClure. What did one do with a little boy? She hadn't been teasing when she told her father that she knew absolutely nothing about children. She couldn't remember ever having taken care of one for even an hour.

Fortunately, Alexis was too busy the rest of the day to worry about what was approaching. She went into a whirlwind of activity—making calls, checking her files, canceling appointments, farming out what assignments were immediate, and putting those she could on the back burner. Betty booked her on a flight to Hawaii at two o'clock the next afternoon.

Alexis stayed at the office until almost ten that evening, mopping up her affairs. Finally she rose and stretched, rolling her aching shoulders. She picked up a pile of messages for Betty and dropped them on her desk as she went out. What with packing and getting out to the Dallas-Fort Worth airport, she wouldn't have time to come to the office tomorrow morning. Wearily, she got into her car and drove home. There she ate a quick snack before tumbling into bed.

The next morning was a rush of packing and telephone calls, and by the time Alexis had her bags in the car and was on the way to the airport, she felt as if she had been running in a marathon. She was also relatively certain she had forgotten something terribly important. Well, no matter, she could always buy anything she forgot.

Alexis had brought her briefcase full of papers so that she could do some work on the plane, but as she walked through the American Airlines terminal, she decided that she wasn't up to facing legal problems right now. On impulse, she stopped at one of the bookshops and bought a juicy-looking mystery. That ought to take her mind off her personal concerns.

Alexis slept much of the way to Los Angeles, then read and dozed during the long flight to Honolulu. She hated the boredom on long flights, hated the confinement, even in first class. It was difficult for her to relax and read or listen to music or watch the movie. For too long, she had been used to having a note pad and a phone close by so that she could dictate letters, make notes and phone calls, give instructions, ask questions. At times she hated the phone and the intrusions it made on her life, but when she was marooned without it, as now, she felt almost encaged.

Max Garrett, who was in charge of Stone Oil's operations in Hawaii, personally met her at the airport. She knew it was a gesture made to Alec Stone's daughter, not to one of his lawyers. Everyone thought she had much more influence with Alec than she would ever have.

Garrett drove Alexis to the grand old Royal Hawaiian, where he had booked a suite of rooms for her for the week. Alexis gasped with amazement as they approached the hotel and its beautifully landscaped grounds. The hotel was a bright, almost watermelon-pink stucco, with a huge banyan tree in the courtyard. The effect was dazzling, tropical, and yet elegant. Inside, the lobby was as plush as the exterior promised, with beautiful marble columns and lush carpets.

Garrett left her to relax and clean up before joining him and his wife, Ellen, for a drink and dinner. Alexis was exhausted from the endless flight, during which the time had steadily become earlier. It was the middle of the night at home. Frankly, she didn't want to eat anything; she wanted only to tumble into bed. But she couldn't insult the chief of operations for Hawaii, so she forced a smile and agreed to meet the couple later.

All through dinner the conversation was light, and though Max hinted delicately, more than once, at the reason for her visit, Alexis simply smiled and failed to elaborate.

Finally he said, "A fellow from Immigration called me this afternoon and said you could pick up the child tomorrow morning. Here's the man's name and address. Would you like me to arrange for a driver to take you?"

"No, thank you. I don't think this would qualify as company business. It's a personal favor for a friend of mine. A taxi will be fine, I'm sure."

"Well, if there is anything I can do while you're here, just let me know. Otherwise, we'll leave you alone and let you get some sun."

"That sounds absolutely wonderful."

"Oh, by the way," Ellen put in, "we're having a small party at our house this Friday. If you could come, we'd love to have you."

"Yes, I'd like that. It sounds very nice." Alexis was positive she could get a baby sitter at the hotel to take care of the boy while she was gone. It wouldn't hurt to do a little politicking with the group out here. It never did, so Alec told her.

She barely managed to cover a yawn with her hand.

"Excuse me. I think that wild fruit punch did me in. I hate to break this up, but I really must get to bed. I'm still running on Dallas time."

"Of course," Ellen said sympathetically. "We should have thought of that. You must be exhausted."

They said their good-byes, and Alexis was able at last to flop wearily into bed and go to sleep.

The next morning Alexis awoke just as the sun broke over the horizon. Now her time would be messed up for another day, she thought, then shrugged and went to the sliding glass door that opened onto the balcony. The pale lemon sun hung low, barely topping Diamond Head, off to the right. Before her lay the clear blue ocean and a stretch of sparkling white beach. To the left, the land rose toward the mountains, at whose base flowed a verdant canal. Everywhere grew riots of Vanda orchids, ginger, and frangipani, their odors drifting to her on the air. She leaned against the railing, drinking in the lovely view. It looked so clear, so freshly clean, as if it had just been painted with virgin watercolors.

After a few minutes she went inside to put on a bathing suit for a quick swim in the hotel pool. Now that she was here, the idea of a week's vacation held more appeal. Back in Dallas, she had toyed with the idea of bringing Paul straight to Texas and not wasting a week in Hawaii. But now the thought of a good rest was rather welcome. Besides, the poor child had been flying through time zones just as she had, and no doubt he would be exhausted and confused, too. He could use a few days to recuperate before he made the big jump to the mainland.

After her swim, Alexis showered, dressed, and ate, then caught a taxi to the address Garrett had given her. Once inside the building, she was shuttled from office to office for almost an hour while documents were pulled and sorted and catalogued and signed. She was certain that all the paper work had been done long ago and that there was no logical reason for the delay. Her irritation grew with each passing minute. She was about to blast into the bored-looking woman sitting opposite her behind a desk when the door opened and a man entered.

"Miss Stone? Here is Paul McClure." He made a motion to someone behind him.

A little boy walked slowly into the room, his eyes carefully on the floor and his steps extremely hesitant. Something clutched at Alexis's heart at the sight of him, so small and frail in his baggy khaki shorts and loose-fitting shirt.

"Paul?" she said, rising, her former fear of meeting him inexplicably gone.

"I imagine he will respond better if you use his Vietnamese name," the man told her kindly.

"Are you sure this boy is the right one?" Alexis asked, staring at the bony child, whose thick black hair hung almost to his chin. His head was still down, so that she could not see his face. "He looks so little!"

"It's him, all right. They're small people, and I doubt he's ever had the proper nutrition."

"Well, he will now." Alexis stuck out her jaw mutinously, an expression that more than one lawyer had come to know and dread.

Softly, so as not to frighten Paul any more then he already was, she walked across the office and knelt before him. "Huang Li?" Still he did not look up. "My name is Alexis. I've come to take you home."

She reached out a hand and tilted his chin up. He did not resist her, although he immediately cast his eyes down. Alexis studied his face. Yes, she could see traces of Brant in the strong bones that belied his fragile build. For an instant, when his eyes had flashed up at her and then back to the floor, she had seen that they were not Asian black, but dark brown, ringed with a band of gold around the pupil—a darker version of Brant's eyes.

"Could you sign this paper, Miss Stone, to show that

you have taken custody of the child?" the Immigration official asked, holding out a clipboard.

"Yes, of course." Alexis took the board and signed with a quick, irritated stroke. "Now, Paul," she said to the silent child, grasping him firmly by the hand, "let's go home."

His hand lay limply in hers, unresisting, but not trustingly clasping, either. Alexis set off down the hall with him, his eyes still timidly on the ground. Poor thing, she thought, he must be terrified by these wild, abrupt changes in his life. It was no wonder that he was scared.

As they rode back to the hotel, Alexis made several more attempts at conversation, but the boy did not answer. After a while he began to look at her, but when Alexis spoke to him, she could read the lack of comprehension in his eyes. For the first time it struck her that, of course, Paul could not speak English! Besides his fear, he had absolutely no idea what she was saying. She sighed. That made the situation a little sticky.

When she reached the hotel, Paul hung back a little. Again Alexis took a firm grip of his hand, and he followed her without a murmur. Looking down at him, she saw his eyes widen as they entered the huge, ornate lobby, and almost imperceptibly, he moved closer to her.

"It's okay," Alexis said, hoping the comforting tone of her voice would get through to him even if he didn't understand the words.

Once inside their suite, she let go of his hand so that he would have a chance to explore, but he merely stood where she left him, eyes cast down, clasped tightly in front of him. Alexis frowned, not sure what to do. He was scared to death and lost . . . but how did one counteract that?

With a shrug, she stepped to the phone. First things first—she had to get someone to interpret for them. She flipped through the phone book, found the Stone Oil offices, and called Garrett.

"Hello, this is Alexis Stone. You said to call on you if I needed help, so here I am."

"Sure. What's the problem?"

"Well, this child I picked up for a friend of mine . . . he's Vietnamese, and he doesn't speak a word of English! I'm in a real bind, because he's in my care for the rest of the week and I can't talk to him. Do you know anyone I could hire as an interpreter and who could start teaching him English?"

Garrett laughed and said, "Not personally, but I'll call the international division. They'll know someone. Shall I go ahead and hire him?"

"Sure. Just tell him to come to my suite as quickly as possible. I'll be up here struggling with sign language."

Alexis hung up and turned back to Paul. He stood in the same place, although his head was higher and he was casting quick, almost furtive glances around the room.

"Well, Paul, how do you like it? This is where we're going to stay for a week. This is the sitting room." She had made up her mind to talk to him as if he could understand. After all, one talked to pets, even though they didn't know what one was saying. Something about the tone or the rhythm must get through to them. "That is my room, through that door, and that is your room, through the opposite door. Would you like to see them?"

She went to him and squatted down so that their faces were level. Firmly, she put her hands on either side of his face and raised it. He looked at her, and then his eyes skittered nervously away.

"No, you must look at me," she said, and gently tapped her forefinger beside his eyes. When he looked at her again, she nodded. "Good. No, don't look away. If we're going to get along by sign language, you must keep your eyes on me." She continued to direct his attention back to her face, making gestures between his eyes and hers, until finally he held his gaze on her, although his face was turned slightly away.

"That's better," Alexis told him, smiling reassuringly. "Now, then, let's introduce ourselves. My name is Alexis." She pointed a forefinger at her chest and repeated her name several times. He looked puzzled. She pointed a finger at him and said, "Paul," then pointed to herself and said, "Alexis." She sighed. "No, I guess that won't do it, either. Huang Li." She pointed at him and then at herself. "Alexis."

She could see the spark of understanding in his dark brown eyes, and for the first time his lips moved, trying unsuccessfully to repeat her name.

"Mmm, that's kind of a tough one, isn't it? I know. Just call me Allie. *Allie.*"

This was a little easier for him, although he made it sound more like "Ahri."

"Good. Now, how would you like to look around?" Alexis rose and took his hand.

She hadn't paid any attention to the furnishings last night, but now she could see that the elegant white French Provincial love seat and chairs and the plush carpeting would be very overpowering to a shy, scared little boy. She led him into her bedroom, which, while decorated with the same imposing furniture, was at least smaller. She walked around it with him, making circling gestures and pointing to herself and repeating her name. He watched her intently, nodding, but she wasn't sure if he really understood or if he merely wanted to please her. Then she took him into her large bathroom, and his eyes grew wide and round with awe. The sink was made of gold-veined marble, and golden faucets adorned it. A wide, tall mirror stretched above the sink, and the tub, although porcelain, was wide and deep and sparkling. Hesitantly, his hand moved toward the tub, and then he jerked it back.

"It's okay," Alexis reassured him. "Go ahead and

touch it." She took his free hand and placed it on the tub. His face shining with wonder, he stroked it gingerly. Alexis felt tears sting at the back of her eyes, and a lump swelled in her throat. Poor baby, she thought, and unconsciously, she put a hand on his head and stroked his thick black hair.

Next, she led him back through the sitting room and into his room. It was really far too imposing for a child, since it was as large and luxurious as her own, with the same heavy drapes and plush carpet and expensive furniture. But what else could she do? She seriously doubted that suites such as this contained a room that was small and plain.

"This is your room," she told him, making the same sweeping gestures and pointing to him, saying his name. Paul looked puzzled. Alexis imagined that his brain could not quite accept what he thought she was saying. She dropped the matter and took him into his bathroom. Again she told him that this was his. He cast her a careful, measuring glance, and for the first time he moved away from her. Alexis released his hand instantly, and he began to walk slowly around the bathroom, touching, looking, now and then glancing back at Alexis to make sure he was doing all right.

"Would you like to explore your room a little?" Alexis asked. "I'll give you some time by yourself to look around."

However, as she went back into the sitting room, she found that he was close at her heels. She sat down and looked at him awkwardly. What was she to do? He remained standing beside her. Alexis patted the chair next to her. "Go on, sit down. It's all right." He glanced at her and carefully poised himself on the edge of the seat.

Alexis bit her lip. He looked so pitiful and unsure on the chair's edge that she wanted to cry. What a sad, frightened little thing he was. She hated to think what had happened to him in Vietnam. And then to experi-

ence a sudden, inexplicable uprooting from his familiar
world, to be tossed among foreigners and surrounded
by a babble he could not understand, with no idea what
would happen to him . . . It was enough to scare
anyone out of his wits. That he didn't cry and scream in
terror seemed to her the most pitiful. He had learned to
accept the frightening as normal, to close himself up
and not make a sound.

Her stomach growled hungrily. At least lunch would
take a while, and maybe by then the interpreter would
have arrived.

"Are you hungry?" she asked Paul, rubbing her
stomach and making signs of eating. "Hungry?"

A faint gleam touched his eyes, and he nodded shyly.
Alexis smiled. "Good, then we'll go downstairs. No,
wait, maybe I'd better have the food sent up here." The
people in the restaurant would probably make Paul
more shy and nervous. She picked up a room-service
menu and pondered over it, wondering what he would
like. She settled on a shrimp casserole that came with
rice and tea. At least these would be familiar to him.
She also ordered a small fruit salad. It was unlikely that
his nutrition had ever been very good, and she might as
well start giving him a balanced diet. For herself, she
ordered a chef's salad.

When the bellhop brought their meal, Paul stood
still, eyeing the food with longing, but not making a
move until Alexis pointed to the chair she had pulled
up for him. Then he hopped into it quickly and
surveyed the feast before him with wide eyes. Alexis
offered him the halved egg from her salad, which he
gobbled down. She realized that he probably didn't
know how to use the flatware, so she took his fork and
placed it in his hand, demonstrating how to pick up
food and carry it to his mouth. His handling of the fork
was not a highly successful venture, and he dropped as
much as he put into his mouth. Alexis noticed that he
used his fingers surreptitiously to help the food along,

and she wished she had thought to order him chopsticks. But maybe it was better that he got acquainted with the fork from the start.

Paul ate with lightning speed, stuffing his food down as quickly as he could. Alexis doubted that he chewed half of it, and she thought he had eaten far too much. Her suspicions were confirmed a few minutes later when a good portion of his lunch came tumbling back up. With a sigh, she cleaned up the mess, thinking to herself that she was certainly getting a fast education in the care of children.

After lunch they again sat awkwardly beside each other, and Alexis wondered what on earth they should do. Should he take a nap? But surely nine was too old for a nap. Well, if not that, what then? They could go down to the beach. After all, here they were in a prime resort, and it was stupid to be spending their time inside the hotel. The next logical step was to buy him swimming trunks.

In fact, the best thing to do was to go shopping for clothes of all kinds for him. He had nothing but the unattractive outfit on his back, so he needed lots of things besides swimming trunks—underwear, shorts, cool little tops, jeans, shirts.

"How would you like to go shopping, young man?" Alexis asked cheerfully. "The way you look, though, I would hate to take you into a store. The next thing on the agenda should definitely be a bath."

Paul looked at her uncomprehendingly, but followed when she rose and went into his bathroom. She ran a tub full of water, indicated that she wanted him to undress, and then popped him into the water. Alexis had expected him to howl at that, but his fascination with the sparkling tub continued, and he was quite happy to sit in it, although he made no move to wash himself. Feeling like a complete novice, Alexis soaped a washcloth and began to scrub him. He submitted to her ministrations without protest and even let her wash his hair, although he gasped and struggled at having his head dunked to rinse the soap out. After she had finished, Paul looked a great deal cleaner and the bathtub a great deal dirtier.

When he stepped out Alexis wrapped a large towel around him. Now that Paul was clean, she hated the thought of putting the same grubby clothes on him, but he had nothing else to wear.

Wealth had its privileges, she decided, and phoned the expensive store in the lobby to order a set of underwear, shorts, and a top for a small nine-year-old boy to be delivered to her room. Before long, a saleswoman from the shop arrived, clothes in hand, and Alexis helped Paul dress. He was quite taken with the garments, every once in a while looking down at them or softly stroking the material with one hand.

"Like that? Would you like some more? Good, then let's go."

Alexis again took him by the hand, and for the first time she felt his fingers curl around hers. A strange sweetness swelled in her chest, and she smiled down at him. "I think we'll make it all right, Paul."

Alexis spent a pleasant afternoon roaming the stores of Honolulu with her charge, buying sandals, shoes, trousers, shirts, shorts, brightly colored T-shirts with the names and forms of superheroes emblazoned on the front, pajamas, even a toothbrush.

As the day wore on, Paul became more comfortable in her presence, more animated, although it was obvious that the crowds and strange places scared him. Sometimes he would get carried away enough to exclaim over a garment that particularly delighted him, and once he even grinned at Alexis as he tried on a pair of sandals.

When they entered the lobby of the hotel and started toward the elevators, a small Oriental man rose from his seat and addressed Alexis tentatively. "Are you by chance Miss Alexis Stone?"

"Yes, I am."

"Mr. Garrett told me that you wished an interpreter."

"Yes! Oh, I am so sorry! Have you been waiting here long? I got caught up in buying Paul some clothes, and I completely forgot that you might come this afternoon."

"It's no problem. I've been here an hour, no more. My name is Raymond Chang. I am a professor of Oriental languages at the university, and sometimes I do a particularly difficult job of translating for Stone Oil. I understand that you need an interpreter in Vietnamese."

"Yes. This is Paul McClure. His father is a friend of mine who lives in the States, and since I was coming over here on vacation, I promised him I would pick Paul up. Paul has lived all his life in Vietnam, and I'm afraid he and I don't understand a word the other says. But, you see, I need someone full time for a week. I mean, with your being a professor at the university, will you be able . . ."

"Yes, I think so. Ordinarily, I would recommend one of my better students, but the course work is over for the semester, and everyone is studying for final exams. At the moment I have little to do, no courses to teach. I will be happy to oblige you."

"Great. I'll pay you for your time, the same amount Stone Oil does. Is that fair?"

"More than fair, Miss Stone."

"Please call me Alexis. Could you come up to our rooms now so that we could talk for a few minutes about what we're going to do?"

"Certainly."

As they rode up in the elevator, Dr. Chang bent down and said something to Paul in his native language. Paul gave him that familiar sideways flicker of a glance and answered in a soft voice.

"We have introduced ourselves," Professor Chang explained to Alexis.

"I would really like to have you here as much as possible during the day," Alexis said when they entered the suite. "I'm going to be here a week, and I'd like you to spend some time each day teaching Paul English as well as interpreting for us. He's going to be living in Texas, and he needs to learn the language."

"I see. Fortunately, children are quick at languages. I shall spend, say, three hours, well spaced during the day, teaching him English. I shall try to teach him enough to get by, common words and phrases, but, of course, he will need a great deal of tutoring once he gets to the mainland."

"I understand that, and I'm sure we'll be able to find someone there to help him." Alexis thought to herself that Brant would have to go far afield from Barrett to find a tutor for his son. "I know it's late, but if you could stay a few minutes, I would really appreciate your explaining to Paul what is happening. I'm sure he is horribly confused and scared."

"Yes, I would be glad to."

Quickly, Alexis told him that Paul's father had been a soldier in Vietnam and that he had tried for many years to bring the boy to the States.

"Brant finally got him into the country, and now I'm going to take Paul home to his father. Tell him, please, that I want to be his friend and to help him. I know he must be scared, but he'll like it with his father. Oh, and tell him that his name here is Paul McClure."

The boy listened solemnly as the older man spoke to him, nodding now and then at a question from Dr. Chang. Then the professor turned to Alexis. "I have told him all that, and I think he understands . . . at least with his brain. It will take some time for his feelings to adjust. It isn't an easy thing to accept."

"I agree," Alexis said with a sigh. "I don't know why Brant didn't take Paul with him when he left Vietnam."

Dr. Chang shrugged. "Sometimes we don't act at the right time, but unfortunately, we always find that out too late."

Alexis smiled. "Isn't that the truth! Thank you so much, Dr. Chang."

"It is my pleasure. I'll be here tomorrow morning at nine o'clock, shall we say?"

"That's fine. Oh, and one other thing. I thought maybe if you could teach me a little Vietnamese while you are teaching Paul, that might make his lessons a little more fun. And maybe we could communicate better."

"Certainly. That sounds like a good idea."

After he had departed, Alexis ordered another meal for herself and Paul, and this time she requested chopsticks for the boy. During dinner she pointed out the different foods and named them for him. Afterward, Paul yawned so wide it almost cracked his jaw. Alexis found his pajamas in the multitude of parcels they had brought back with them. Later, when he thought she wasn't watching, Alexis caught a glimpse of him looking at himself in the bedroom mirror and smiling.

She turned down the covers of his bed and panto-mimed sleep until a giggle finally burst from him. He got into bed, and Alexis tucked him in. As she leaned over him, he reached up hesitantly and touched a lock of her hair. Alexis did not move as he gently stroked her hair, his face shining with wonder. She realized that he had probably never seen hair the color of hers before. With a smile, she bent and placed a kiss on his forehead.

"There you go," she said. "You're going to be fine now. Tomorrow Dr. Chang will return and help us talk to each other. And we'll go to the beach. How will you like that? I wonder if you know how to swim. Well, no matter, I'll teach you. It will be a blast, I promise. Now, good night."

Alexis watched a couple of programs on TV, grew bored, and went to bed. She read some more of the mystery novel she had bought for the plane trip before yawning and turning off the light. It had been a long day for her, too. After all, she had gotten up at dawn this morning. Maybe in another day she would be recovered from her jet lag.

Alexis slipped easily into sleep. Almost three hours later her eyes flew open, and she found herself staring blankly into the darkness, her heart pounding, wondering what had awakened her. Then she heard the sound that had cut short her sleep—a loud, high, piercing scream that came from Paul's room.

Chapter 12

Like a shot, Alexis flew out of bed and raced through the sitting room. She cracked her shin sharply on the low coffee table and groped around it, cursing under her breath. The high-pitched cries continued without stopping, even after she had burst into Paul's room and switched on the light.

Paul was sitting straight up in bed, his eyes open and staring sightlessly, his face contorted. Screams and racking sobs shook his small form. Alexis uttered a low cry and ran toward him.

"Paul, Paul, it's me, Alexis," she said, sitting on the bed and touching his shoulder. He was rigid, still sobbing, and she put her arms firmly around him, pulling him against her. She stroked his back and rocked him, murmuring soft, meaningless sounds of comfort. For a time he remained stiff, unyielding in his terror, and then suddenly his thin body gave in and he pressed himself even more tightly against hers, his arms wrapping like vines around her neck.

"There, there, Paul," she whispered against his ear as she rocked him back and forth. "It's okay, it's all right. I won't let anybody get you. It was only a nightmare."

For a long time she sat that way, holding him close, until at last his sobs began to subside. How frail his body was in her arms, what a precious, fragile piece of humanity. She rested her cheek against the silken hair of his head.

"It's all right," she told him again. "I'm here. I'll take care of you."

Paul stopped crying but clung to her like a leech. Alexis stretched out on his bed, cradling him in her arms, and gradually she felt his body melt into slumber. She started to get up and return to her own bed, but realized he might awaken in terror again. So she closed her eyes and drifted off to sleep, still cuddling him.

After that night, Paul seemed to accept her completely. He was always on her heels wherever she went. They studied together with Raymond Chang, and often included him in their other activities. They went to the beach, where Paul sat for a long time, staring at both the ocean and the sea of people around him. He did not approach the water until Alexis took him by the hand and led him into it. After his initial surprise, he giggled delightedly and cavorted with her in the warm waves. At other times Alexis gave him swimming lessons in the pool.

Alexis called Ellen Garrett and told her that she would be unable to attend their party. She didn't want to leave Paul with a stranger for fear he might have another nightmare.

One evening, much to their mutual delight, she and Paul attended a luau on the beach. The music, the color, the dances, fascinated them, and they gorged themselves on the rich food.

Alexis thought she probably should take in the usual tourist attractions, such as the Polynesian cultural exhibits, Pearl Harbor, and some of the other islands. But she was having so much fun doing exactly what she was doing that she had no interest in anything else. The weariness that had settled on her in Dallas melted away in the warm sun and salty water of Honolulu, and she felt happier, more refreshed, than she could remember feeling in a very long time. All she wanted to do was to lie on the beach and sun herself and play with Paul, who grew livelier every day.

In the beginning, Paul had bolted his food as if he believed he would never eat again, and invariably he became sick. The problem wasn't solved until Alexis let him secrete a piece of fruit, which she told him was his to save. From then on, he ate normally.

His progress in English was amazing. By the end of the week he and Alexis were able to communicate, brokenly, with a combination of his English and the smattering of Vietnamese words she had learned from Dr. Chang, as well as with much gesturing. Dr. Chang still had to interpret for anything complex, but, by and large, Alexis and Paul were able to understand each other.

At first Alexis probed into his background, asking the professor to inquire about his mother. It had occurred to her that no thought had been given to the poor mother's feelings about Paul's departure. Had the woman's son been ripped callously from her arms?

When Dr. Chang asked Paul the question, the boy's forehead knotted and he looked down, mumbling a reply. Dr. Chang looked at Alexis. "He says he doesn't know his mother. I don't understand exactly, but apparently—for the past few years, at least—he has been raised by someone else, a relative of some sort. I don't know if his mother died or abandoned him. He says only that he doesn't remember."

"Ask him about his nightmares. He wakes up screaming. What is that all about?" Even though Alexis had had a rollaway bed put in her room for Paul so that he wouldn't be alone in the night, he had awakened twice, screaming as he had before. During those instances he had been more easily calmed by her presence, but she worried about the cause of his nightmares.

Paul frowned even harder at the man's question, and his lower lip trembled perceptibly. He answered, but in a voice that was low and reluctant.

Dr. Chang shrugged at Alexis. "He doesn't want to talk about it. I think maybe it's too hard on him. He just says that he gets scared, that somebody chases him."

Alexis sighed. "I wish I knew what was at the root of it."

"Well, this child was born during a war. I would imagine that, for the first few years of his life, he saw some unspeakable things, things that would be difficult for an adult to see and still keep his sanity. Who knows what Paul has experienced? Poverty, bombs exploding, enemy soldiers occupying the place where he lived? Perhaps his mother was killed before his eyes. Maybe he saw maimings, tortures, fire . . . It could be any number of things. I'm no child psychiatrist, of course, but I'd say the best thing at the moment is to give him love and security and hope that the bad memories fade. I don't think he is ready to face them yet."

Alexis nodded. "You are probably right." After this discussion, she attempted no further searching into Paul's background.

At the end of the week, when they left the hotel and headed for the airport, Alexis felt strangely sad. I should be happy, she told herself sternly, happy because I'm going back to work and will relieve myself of the burden of looking after a child. I should be happy for Paul, who's going to a home with his father where he'll never want again.

She was pleased to see the way Paul walked beside her once they had arrived at the airport. His hand firmly in hers, he held his head up and looked around in delight at the new wonders that assaulted his vision.

Yet Alexis could not shake her sense of sadness. All during the flight across the ocean, while Paul napped or happily colored in a book, she sat staring into space, unable to concentrate on her novel or on the pile of papers that still lay untouched in her briefcase. She was conscious only of the lump in her chest that was growing heavier with each passing mile.

Would Paul never want for anything, really? she asked herself. Oh, Brant could provide all the necessities; there was no doubt about that. But could that cold, remote man give his son the love he so desperately needed? Could Brant give him the happiness he deserved? And what about his education? Paul required a great deal of tutoring, not only in English, but also in reading, writing, math, geography, science—in fact, in everything that other nine-year-olds were learning in school. Perhaps Brant could find a full-time tutor in Barrett who could teach Paul the school subjects he had missed, but Alexis knew that Brant would never find a Vietnamese-speaking person to help Paul with English. And if that essential requirement wasn't met, Paul would never learn the rest of it.

It was then that a dazzling idea occurred to her. *She* could find a Vietnamese tutor in Dallas! There were plenty of Vietnamese immigrants there. Paul could stay with her for a few weeks before going to Barrett, and that way he could take lessons in English and become proficient enough so that when he arrived at Brant's he would be able to learn the other courses. It would mean only a few weeks more, and considering how long Brant had waited for him, surely a while longer wouldn't make any difference. Alexis hadn't had time to call Brant before she had left for Hawaii. If she didn't call him until she was ready to deliver Paul, Brant need never know how much time had elapsed.

A warm relief flooded over her, and she smiled inwardly. That was the perfect solution. It would give Paul the opportunity to adjust more fully. She could show him some of Dallas, let him get a hint, bit by bit, of what America was all about. He could absorb everything more gradually, and the shock of the new country and of the eventual absence of the one person he knew here would be lessened.

Alexis settled back in her seat and picked up her novel. It was more readable now that she had worked things out in her mind. Paul would be happier this way, she told herself, and sternly pushed down the niggling inner voice that said she didn't want to give Paul up because he was a tie to his father.

After the heat of Hawaii, Dallas was bitingly cold. Paul, dressed only in slacks and a shirt, shivered as they walked from the Surtrans station to Alexis's car. Alexis made a mental note to buy some warmer clothes for him tomorrow. She drove straight home, and while Paul spent the evening exploring her condominium, reassuring himself by periodic returns to her side, Alexis set about locating a tutor.

Betty's church had sponsored several Vietnamese refugee families in the early seventies. When she called her secretary at home, Betty immediately released a flood of information about what had been going on at the office during Alexis's absence.

"Hold it, I don't want to hear about all that," Alexis cut in. "You can tell me tomorrow afternoon when I come in." Ignoring the stunned silence on the other end of the phone, she went on. "What I want to know is the name of your minister. Didn't your church sponsor some Vietnamese refugees?"

"Yes," Betty replied, and gave Alexis the minister's name in the tone of one humoring the insane.

"Thanks," Alexis said, and hung up before the woman could start in on the office again. Alexis had absolutely no desire to hear about Stone Oil tonight.

The minister, fortunately, was able to give her the name of a Vietnamese woman who he thought would be perfect. A widow for several years, she had recently married an American. Her name was Mai Norton.

Alexis quickly dialed the number he had given her. A woman with a faint, lilting accent answered the phone.

"Could I speak to Mrs. Mai Norton?" Alexis asked.

"This is Mai Norton."

"My name is Alexis Stone, and your name was given to me by Reverend Barker."

"Yes?"

"I need someone to tutor a nine-year-old Vietnamese boy for the next two or three weeks. He knows very little English and has just come here from Vietnam. Reverend Barker said you might consider the job."

"Certainly," Mrs. Norton said pleasantly. "When would you want me to start?"

"Tomorrow, hopefully. I work during the day, so I'd like you to keep him all day, either here or at your home, and teach him as much English as you possibly can. I will pay you very well."

"That sounds agreeable to me."

Quickly, Alexis arranged the terms of her employment. Mrs. Norton would come to Alexis's condominium the next day at noon. With a satisfied smile, Alexis hung up the phone.

In the morning, Alexis took Paul on a rapid whirl of shopping for warmer trousers, shirts, some sweaters, and a coat. She ignored the voice within that reminded her that Brant certainly could buy him a coat, maybe even looked forward to doing that. Her rationalization was that she had plenty of money, more than she would ever spend, and it was fun to buy the child things. Let Brant buy him a coat, too, if he wanted.

Afterward, they stopped at a fast-food place, where Paul had his first American hamburger and a Coke. He took to them with the alacrity of any child, and Alexis beamed with pleasure.

When Mrs. Norton arrived and Alexis prepared to leave for work, Paul clouded up. His fingers knotted into fists at the end of his rigid little arms. Alexis thought she had succeeded in explaining things to him the evening before. She turned helplessly to the Oriental woman.

"Mrs. Norton, can you explain to him that I'll be back later this afternoon? Please convince him I'm not leaving forever!"

Mrs. Norton spoke to the boy and he nodded, but his

eyes were downcast and the tilt of his chin was almost mulish. A huge lump rose in Alexis's throat. She wanted to put down her briefcase and declare that she would stay. Instead, she gave Paul a big hug, tousled his hair, and went out the door.

Much as she had expected, Alexis was greeted by a huge pile of papers on her desk, and she dived into them nonstop. Her father had told her to call him as soon as she came back, but since she had so much to do, she decided not to phone him. After all, there was really nothing urgent he needed to know about Paul, and he would probably want her to take the boy up to Barrett immediately so that he could get the lease.

Even though there was a great deal left undone by the end of the day, Alexis did not stay late to finish it up. She had told Mrs. Norton that she would be home by six. When Paul saw her, he flung himself at her like a pint-sized tornado, gibbering delightedly in his native tongue.

Alexis knelt and hugged him hard, laughing with tears in her eyes at his greeting.

"He is a very smart boy," Mrs. Norton told her. "He learns quickly. He is also very nice. Very nice."

"Oh, thank you, Mrs. Norton. You don't know how I appreciate this. And you'll be here tomorrow at eight?"

"Yes, of course," the woman replied in a slightly stilted accent. She said good-bye to Paul, picked up her purse, and left.

Alexis turned to Paul. "Now, skunk, how about some dinner? What would you like?"

Paul smiled and said proudly, "Hamburger."

"Alexis!" Her father's voice was stamped with irritation. "Where the hell have you been? Mrs. Jenkins told me she saw you in the building yesterday!"

"Yes, that's true," Alexis acknowledged, then held the receiver away from her for the ear-splitting response.

"Why didn't you come up here?" he thundered. "I

thought I told you I wanted to see you as soon as you returned!"

"I didn't think it was that urgent, frankly. I didn't find out anything new or startling. I just brought Paul McClure home, that's all. I had a lot of work on my desk that needed to get done, and I thought that was more pressing."

"Alexis, when I tell you that I want to see you, I expect you to follow my orders!"

"I didn't realize it was an order," Alexis returned coolly, suddenly angrier with Alec than she had ever been before. "I thought perhaps it was a gesture of fatherly affection to a daughter going away on a vacation."

The cold sarcasm in her tone brought Alec up short. "All right, maybe I got a little hot under the collar about it. The Canadian well and that mess with the Purcer Number One out in the Permian Basin have got me really on edge."

"I can understand that," Alexis replied, unbending very little. She knew there was more fight ahead over taking Paul to Barrett.

"Well, how is the kid?"

"He was a pitiful little thing, undernourished and shabby, and he couldn't speak a word of English. I got a tutor for him while we were there, and he's already beginning to speak English."

"When are you going to take him to McClure?"

"In two or three weeks. I have a lot of things I need to finish up first, and besides, I've found a tutor for him here. He really needs some more training in the language, and you know there won't be anybody in Barrett for that."

"That is McClure's problem," her father said testily. She could sense that he was keeping his anger barely in check. "I want that lease as soon as you can get it."

"I simply can't go yet," Alexis stated flatly. "I have other things to do. I'll take him there before Christmas."

"Alexis, you know how much I want that lease. That is the most important thing you have to do!"

"Oh, I beg to differ with you. I think the Purcer deal is far more important. I know that the McClure lease is a pet project of yours, but we've already drilled and hit oil on the Permian Basin well, and now there's a problem with the title that's suddenly cropped up. We have oil ready to pipe there, if only we can resolve the title dispute. McClure is still an unknown."

Alec sighed. "I guess you're right. Take care of the Purcer well first, but as soon as you're done with it, get that boy up to McClure and bring me back that lease!"

"I will. I promise," Alexis said, and hung up. She felt victorious. It was not often that she came out on top in an argument with her father.

Each day when Alexis returned from work, Paul's confidence was further strengthened, until soon he no longer looked frightened when she left in the morning. His personality blossomed before her eyes; almost daily he grew happier, more prone to laughter, more blessed with good spirits.

During her time off, Alexis tried to show Paul as much as she could of the American way of life. She took him to the Fair Park museums, to her office, and to the restaurant on top of the Regency's tower to show him the Dallas skyline. One weekend they attended the most American, Texan, Dallasite activity she could think of: a Dallas Cowboys football game.

She lassoed Nick into taking them, since there were no tickets left for sale, and she knew his family had several good seats in the lower tier.

When she asked him, he laughed and said, "Well, of course I will. I may have to dump a gorgeous blonde, but you know me: always your servant. But tell me, why aren't you using Stone Oil's box? Don't they have one of those luxurious glass-enclosed things with a bar and TV?"

"Yes, but I don't want Paul to see it from there. That's too removed for him to get the real feel of the game. I want to be down in the stands with all the people and the noise and everything."

"Slumming it, huh? Who is this Paul kid, anyway?"

"Oh, just a boy I'm taking care of for a few weeks for a friend."

"You? Taking care of a child? Somehow that stretches my imagination."

"Then your imagination needs more elasticity," Alexis snapped. "He's from Vietnam, and is staying here so that he can be tutored in English. His father lives in an out-of-the-way place."

"Not Barrett, by any chance?" Nick asked softly.

"What is that supposed to mean?"

"That I think something more is going on here than meets the eye. You've been different ever since you came back from Barrett. Do you realize that twice, now, I've called your house before eight o'clock and you were actually there, instead of at the office?"

"I have to get home because the woman who takes care of Paul leaves at six."

"Tell me something. Why are you waxing so maternal? Who is the father of this kid?"

"His name is Brant McClure, though I don't really think it's any business of yours. And I don't know why you are being so sarcastic over my keeping a nine-year-old boy for a few weeks!"

"Okay, okay, don't bite my head off. Just a little self-interested curiosity, that's all. I promise I'll get off the subject entirely."

"Good. Then I'll see you Sunday?"

"Right. The game starts at three-fifteen. I'll be at your house at, oh, one-thirty."

Nick was, as always, a charming companion, winning over even the shy Paul with his light, friendly conversation. To keep the child entertained during the serpentine wait to enter the parking lot, he made up a long, outrageous fairy tale with a hero named Herman.

Herman, it seemed, got into a great deal of trouble,

including breaking his piggy bank, losing his baseball cards, and getting lost in the woods. Paul hung breathlessly on Nick's words, his eyes round with anticipation.

". . . so there Herman was, and the dark was coming on, and up in one tree he saw a big old owl that suddenly opened his eyes and said, 'Whoooooo are you?'"

Paul giggled. "Owls don't talk. They birds!"

Nick regarded him with mock severity. "Listen, who's telling this story, you or me?"

Paul laughed again. "You."

"Well, all right. This owl talked. Herman, being a little boy like you, wasn't used to talking owls, and he ran off through the woods. He went crashing into trees and tripping all over his feet. All of a sudden he came to a big hill. He fell down, and he went rolling, over and over, all the way down the hill. And when he came to the bottom, you know what?"

"What?"

"He woke up and found he was on the floor beside his bed. It had all been a big, bad dream."

Paul laughed and clapped his hands in glee. "More!"

"Oh, no," Nick protested. "My throat's too dry as it is. Alexis, sweetheart, give me a beer out of that cooler."

"Just one more," Paul pleaded.

"This kid's a tyrant! I tell you what, I'll give you another story on the way back from the stadium. How's that?"

"Okay," Paul agreed, and subsided.

Alexis dug into the icy cooler and pulled out a can of beer for Nick. Removing the tab and handing the can to him, she declared in a professorial tone, "You know that beer is bad for you in the heat, don't you? It takes water out of your system, rather than adding to it."

Nick shot her an amused glance and shook his head. "Alexis, if I ever need a useless piece of information, I'll come to you."

Alexis smiled back at him; it was difficult to be

serious with Nick. "I didn't know you had such a way with kids," she teased.

"Ah, but there are many things you don't know about me," he intoned mysteriously.

"Well, I do know that it was sweet of you to do this for me."

Nick shrugged, and his usually dancing eyes turned suddenly serious. "I'd rather be with you," he told her simply. Then the planes of his face shifted, and he was once again a chameleon. "Say, Alexis, have you ever thought of adopting me and Paul? I think we'd make a great team. I'd even keep your bed warm."

"Every night?" Alexis said skeptically.

Nick put his hand to his heart in a hurt gesture. "Alexis, you are so suspicious. What's one or two nights among friends?"

Alexis rolled her eyes, and Nick laughed. He picked up her hand and placed a light kiss on the back of it. "I'm really not such a cad."

Once he had parked the car, they began the long trek into the stadium. The game held Paul's attention throughout, although Alexis was plagued to death by questions from him on every aspect of the event. Even Nick's plying him with refreshments and souvenirs did not distract him.

Paul had been learning rapidly with the aid of Mrs. Norton, and whenever he wasn't studying with her or doing something with Alexis, he was rooted in front of the television set, which not only kept him spellbound but also spewed English at him continually. Now, buoyed by an almost constant bombardment of English, he was becoming fairly verbal in it, although at times he displayed the rather stilted speech pattern of Mrs. Norton. His improvement in language facility was matched by an upsurge of questions.

The day after the game, as he and Alexis sat at the dinner table, he began a new set of questions about his father and the ranch. This was his favorite topic, and there were times when Alexis's patience and imagina-

tion were stretched to their limits. To speak about
Brant McClure without lessening him in his son's eyes
was no easy task.

"How big is Father?" Paul asked now.

"He is very big, quite tall. I'd say he is about six feet,
four inches."

"What is that?"

"About this much taller than I." Alexis demon-
strated with her hands.

"Wow!" Paul exclaimed and whistled, another talent
he had picked up from television.

Alexis smiled. It was good to see him acting like
other little boys.

"When I go see him?"

"Soon."

"I like it? How ranch look?"

"It is quite big, and most of the land is very flat.
There are very few trees or bushes. It's almost barren."

"What is that?"

"Very little grows there."

"I see. Why named ranch?"

"I don't know. Why are you called Paul? That's just
the name for the type of land it is. See, a place where
you grow things like corn or vegetables or wheat is
called a farm, but a big place where you raise animals is
called a ranch."

"Does he have a house?"

"Yes."

"I have a room, like here?"

"Yes." She reached over and ruffled his hair affec-
tionately. Paul had slept in his own room ever since
they had come back from Hawaii. It was a smaller,
simpler affair than the room in the hotel, and he had
adjusted to it quite well. Over a week had passed
without a recurrence of one of his nightmares, and
before that they had come less and less frequently. She
hoped that his move to the ranch would not impede his
progress.

"Is house big as this one?"

"Oh, it is much bigger."

His eyes widened at that, and he pondered the idea for a moment. Alexis studied him fondly, her gaze caressing his brown eyes, too round and light to be purely Asian, and his strong facial features, another indication of his mixed ancestry. Suddenly a sharp ache darted through her. Soon she would have to take him to Barrett, and she realized she would miss him very much.

Alexis wondered if perhaps it had been a mistake to keep Paul with her these past weeks. She had grown so close to him. But now there was no reason for him to stay with her. His English was vastly improved, and she imagined an English-speaking tutor would be fine for him now. McClure could find someone to teach Paul the school fundamentals that he had missed. He ought to be with his father, not with her. Besides, she had done all she could on the Purcer deal. She no longer had an excuse not to take him.

She had toyed with the idea of keeping him through Christmas. She very much wanted to have him for the holiday, and she had bought him several presents. But when she thought about it logically, impersonally, she knew it was a cruel thing to do. Brant McClure was his father; she was nothing to Paul really. In order to get the boy, McClure had done something that rankled at his very soul. No doubt he wanted Paul for Christmas, too, and although Alexis found it hard to believe that his feelings for the child ran very deep, it was wrong of her to keep him from his son.

"Paul," she asked quietly, "how would you like to go see your father very soon?"

"When?"

"Well, in four more days it will be Christmas. I thought we might go before then. I imagine he would like to have you there for the holiday."

"I like it," Paul said firmly. "Will I really ride a horse?"

"Yes."

"Can I wear boots?"

"I wouldn't be surprised."

He was silent for a moment, then frowned. "You go with me?"

"Yes, I'll take you there."

"You stay?"

"No." Alexis heard her voice shake alarmingly on the word. "I have to come back here to live. I can't live there."

"Why not? I want you to."

"Because my job is here. Because your daddy and I— Well, sometimes we don't get along very well."

A funny, pinched look came over Paul's face, but he said nothing, merely left the table and went to the living room to watch television. Alexis stared after him with a lump in her throat. Had she done something wrong to him, too, by keeping him? Had she let him become too attached to her, knowing that he wouldn't see her again? When the security of her presence was removed, would he be worse off than before?

Chapter 13

That evening, after she had put Paul to bed, Alexis called Brant's number. She noticed that her fingers shook a little as she pushed the buttons. No matter what the reason, she dreaded talking with him after the fiasco of their last meeting.

"Hello?" His familiar, deep voice sent an icy quiver through her, and for a moment Alexis was afraid she wouldn't be able to speak.

"Brant?" she said finally, pushing her hair back nervously. "This is Alexis Stone."

There was a long pause on the other end before he finally responded. "Yes?"

She began to roll the telephone cord between her fingers. "I called to tell you that we have Paul."

"Paul?" Brant sounded almost dazed, and Alexis wondered if he had never really expected them to get his son back. Was he thinking now of what he would have to do to hold up his end of the bargain? "What do you mean, you have him? Where?" His voice was recovering now, picking up its old, hard tone.

"He's here with me in Dallas. I wanted to know if you'd like me to bring him up before Christmas or after."

"Before, of course! Immediately, in fact. Bring him tomorrow."

"Well, I don't think I can get off on such short notice . . ."

"Don't be an idiot!" McClure snapped back at her. "You own the damn company! You can do whatever you like."

Alexis clenched her hand around the cord, fighting the anger that rushed in her at his tone. "I have some things I have to clear up first. I do have work to do. I am not exactly a figurehead at the office."

"Alexis, either you bring my son up here tomorrow or I'll fly down tonight and get him."

"All right, all right," Alexis agreed with annoyance. She wanted to have at least one more day with Paul. "I'll bring him tomorrow. I'll probably drive, so don't expect us until late afternoon."

"Okay," he said, then paused. "How is he? How does he look?"

"He looks fine. He is a very handsome boy."

"I mean, is he sick or anything?"

"He didn't look like he'd had the best diet ever," Alexis replied bluntly. She refused to protect Brant from the reality of his leaving the boy in Vietnam. "However, he's better now. I bought him some clothes; he had only the things he was wearing. And he has eaten quite a bit."

A wavering sigh came through the wire, and then Brant said, "Okay. I'll see you tomorrow, then. And . . . thank you."

"You're welcome."

Alexis had decided to drive to Barrett because she wanted to give Paul the chance to see the landscape as it changed to the tough, western ground of the Panhandle. She rose early the next morning and called Betty to tell her that she wouldn't be in for a few days. After leaving Paul at Brant's, she thought she would drive to Colorado and spend her Christmas vacation skiing. The taste of one week's vacation had encouraged her to try another, and she imagined that she would desperately need something fun to do once Paul was gone.

After she spoke to Betty, she dialed Morgan's number and got her sister out of bed unusually early.

"How can you sound so cheerful at this hour? Good Lord, Alexis, it's only seven-thirty!" Morgan grumbled.

Alexis laughed. "Sorry about that, Morgan. But I'm fixing to leave town on another vacation, and I need to borrow your skiing equipment."

"What?" Morgan sounded more awake now. "Have you gone off the deep end? Two weeks of vacation in one year?"

"Don't be sarcastic," Alexis chided with mock primness. "Can I borrow your skis?"

"Do you have a ski rack for your car?"

"No."

"Then I doubt you'll be able to carry them. I tell you what, just rent them there. You can have the rest of my stuff, though."

"Okay. You're a love. I'll be over in about thirty minutes."

"Thirty minutes!" Morgan cried. "Alexis, haven't you ever heard of sleep?"

"No. See you," Alexis said cheerfully, and hung up.

Despite the fact that she would be seeing Paul for the last time today, she felt in uncommonly good spirits. Perhaps it was the prospect of another vacation, or possibly just relief at being rid of Brant McClure at last. Whatever it was, she hummed as she brushed her hair and pulled on a pair of jeans and a new, brilliant turquoise sweater that turned her eyes electric-blue. She took a little extra care with her looks this morning, dabbing on mascara and a touch of blush-on powder, and debating over which shade of lipstick to wear.

After breakfast, she went downstairs and loaded the back seat of the Mercedes with the neatly wrapped presents she had bought Paul for Christmas, as well as his new green bicycle. Her luggage and Paul's she put in the trunk, and they set out for Morgan's apartment.

Alexis greeted the doorman at the high-rise on Turtle Creek and went up in the elevator. A sleepy Morgan greeted her at the door.

"My goodness, what are you all dolled up for?" Morgan asked, waving her and Paul inside.

"What do you mean? I'm only wearing Levi's and a sweater."

"But such a sweater. And actual makeup. Who are you meeting at this ski resort?"

"Nobody," Alexis laughed. "I guess I just want to look good for Paul's last day with me."

"His last day?"

"Yes. I'm taking him up to his father before I go on vacation."

"I see," Morgan said in a knowing tone, and shot her sister a shrewd glance. "So the noble cowboy is the one who's inspired all this beauty."

"No! What a ridiculous idea!" Alexis protested. "I wouldn't do a thing to look attractive for him!"

Morgan made no comment, merely lifted her eyebrows and led Alexis into her bedroom for the ski gear. Paul carried the boots and Alexis took the suitcase full of clothes. In moments they were on their way to Barrett.

It was almost five in the afternoon when Alexis turned into the section-line road that led to Brant's house. Everything looked so achingly familiar that her heart twisted. Surely she had not missed this place! No, it was only losing Paul, she told herself. Brant would probably be even more astonished than Nick if he knew how she felt about Paul. She would be a fool, she thought grimly, to let him know that, for she was certain he would take advantage of it somehow.

At the sound of her car on the graveled driveway, the front door flung open, and Brant McClure appeared on the porch. Alexis pulled to a halt and turned off the engine. Brant walked down the steps to the Mercedes, as lean and powerful as ever in his rough denim trousers and jacket. Alexis felt a wild tingle jar her nerves at the sight of him.

Angry at her own traitorous reaction, she snapped open the car door and stepped out. "Hello, Brant."

He nodded briefly at her. "Alexis." He had stopped two or three feet from the car, and now he ran his palms down the sides of his thighs before he came forward and opened the passenger door.

Paul did not get out immediately, but remained sitting inside, taking in the tall stranger with wide eyes. He had been quiet all day, and Alexis knew that his future was looming frighteningly in front of him all over again.

"Paul," she said gently, to ease his fear, "this is your daddy. Brant, this is Paul."

Brant glanced up at her, his eyes bright gold. "I think I know my own son, thank you," he grunted.

Alexis shrugged and quirked her eyebrows. Getting his son back certainly had not mellowed him any. She watched him squat beside the car and put his hands on Paul's shoulders. Swiftly, Paul scooted away from him and popped out of the door on Alexis's side, coming to stand by her and clasping her hand tightly.

A spasm of pain swept Brant's face and was gone, quickly. He rose and said with false cheer, "A little too fast for you, huh? Well, I can understand that, Paul. I've been waiting for you for years, but you don't even know me. Why don't we go inside and have a Coke and talk for a while?"

"I think that would be a nice idea," Alexis offered when Paul remained silent. "Don't you, Paul?"

Mutely, the boy nodded. The three of them entered the house, Brant keeping a careful distance from Alexis and Paul. Alexis glanced casually into the living room as she passed it. Remembering what had happened in there, she blushed, feeling again the rough touch of his skin, the caress of his skillful mouth. She could not keep from looking toward Brant, and she saw mirrored in his eyes the same memory. Instantly, she turned away, the heat rising higher in her face.

In the kitchen, Brant poured out drinks, and they sat in an awkward silence. Finally Brant leaned across the table and spoke a few quiet words to Paul in Vietnamese. Alexis recognized them from her brief lessons as a greeting. Paul's face visibly lightened, and Brant began to talk about all the things that he and his son were going to do together. Paul listened with a definite spark of interest in his eyes, but he remained mute and as close to Alexis's side as possible.

"Tomorrow we can drive around and I'll show you the ranch. Would you like that? And I'll teach you to ride a horse. We could go to Amarillo for the cattle auction. I bet you'd like that, wouldn't you? It's a big place, has lots of animals. Maybe we could go to the Palo Duro Canyon. You've never seen anything like that. I guarantee you, Paul, we're going to have a lot of fun."

When Paul still said nothing, Alexis tried to fill the gap. "Paul really needs a lot of private tutoring, Brant . . . in reading and writing and all the school subjects."

"I know," he said shortly. "I've already put ads in newspapers around the state for a teacher to live here."

"Good." Alexis found it difficult to keep a conversation going when Brant persisted in his brusque, flattening way of talking. It was ridiculous to sit here and add to the stiffness of the group, to intrude on a family occasion. She ought to leave now, just finish her assignment and disappear.

Alexis rose. "I'll go out and get the papers for you to sign."

Brant's mouth twisted at her words. When she returned with two copies of the lease, he took the blue-backed documents and casually flipped through them, looking for the last page. Taking a pen from his pocket, he scrawled his name first on one copy, then on the other.

"Aren't you going to read it before you sign?" Alexis asked sardonically. "I figured you would check into every little item you thought we would cheat you on."

His lip curled as he replied, "What difference does it make? I already promised you I would sign. Whatever you've done to me in that lease, I've agreed to it."

"Well it *is* a standard contract," Alexis assured him. "You'll get one-eighth, of course."

Contemptuously, he tossed the two documents on the table. "Well, there it is. Now you have your blood money."

The tension between them was thick. Alexis would have liked to hurl a caustic remark at him, but Paul's fearful look told her that he, too, felt the mood in the air, so she swallowed her words and put the lease copies in her briefcase.

"Why don't you get Paul's things out of the car?" she suggested to Brant.

He rose, and they all three trailed outside, Paul dogging Alexis's heels. She opened the trunk and pointed out Paul's suitcases.

"You must have bought him a complete wardrobe," Brant commented, noting the amount of luggage.

Alexis shrugged and went to the rear door. "Here are his Christmas presents from me."

Brant peered into the back seat with a look of surprise, but said nothing. He took out the packages and carried them to the front porch, then came back for the bike. Catching sight of a tag on the small package resting on top, he frowned slightly.

" 'Nick,' " he read. "Who's Nick?"

"Nick Fletcher. He's a friend of mine who met Paul," Alexis said.

"I like Nick," Paul piped up, and Alexis almost groaned at the inopportune time he had chosen to say something. "He give me flag that say Cowboys, and white football with blue rings. We go to football game."

Brant's face darkened thunderously, and he glared at Alexis. "A football game! How long have you had him? Why didn't you let me know?"

Alexis decided that now was the time to leave, before Brant had worked himself up into a real rage. That was all Paul needed to set him back three weeks.

"I have to go," she announced, not answering him, and turned to Paul. "I'm going now. I know you and your daddy will have a lot of fun here."

"Don't go," Paul pleaded, his big eyes wet with tears, his lips beginning to quiver. "Stay?"

"I can't Paul. You know I live in Dallas."

"You live here." He swung toward his father. "She live here, too?"

"I don't think so," Brant said grimly, his face drawn.

"I have a job in Dallas," Alexis reminded Paul. "I can't just leave that." She knelt and took him in her arms, squeezing him to her as hard as she could. Pain slashed through her chest, and unshed tears welled up in a block in her throat. Never had she imagined that this leave-taking would be so painful. "I love you," she whispered softly, then stood up and began to move rapidly away.

Before she could get around the car, however, Paul had catapulted after her, throwing his slight frame against her and wrapping his arms around her waist, holding on for dear life.

"No go," he sobbed against her. "Please, do not go. Take me. Please, please!"

"Paul, I must—" she began, her throat thick.

Brant interrupted her, launching himself forward like a rocket, his eyes blazing. "Goddamn it, what have you done to him?" he growled menacingly.

Paul's sobs became louder, more high-pitched. "No go! No go!" he screamed.

Alexis clutched him to her, her heart turning over at his terror. "It's all right, Paul, it's all right," she murmured soothingly.

"Alexis Stone, I've figured you for some pretty awful things, but I never thought you would pull a stunt like this!" Brant's voice cut at her like a knife. "You've turned my own son against me! What in hell did you do? What did you say to him to make him so scared of me? And just how long have you had him, anyway?"

"Three weeks," Alexis hissed back.

"Three weeks! My God, you kept my son for three weeks without even letting me know he was here!" Brant roared, his face contorted with fury. "Knowing how much I wanted him, you decided to take your revenge by keeping him from me! Three weeks you had him, and you told him things about me so he'd be afraid to stay here! Damn you!" He spun around in helpless wrath and slammed his fists repeatedly on the roof of her car.

Paul flinched at the crash and began to wail more loudly. Alexis pressed him against her body, covering his exposed ear with her hand.

"What in hell do you think you are doing?" she rasped. "I haven't done a thing to Paul to make him fear you. You handle that very nicely yourself. How do you think all this ranting and raving of yours is affecting him? Do you think that sort of behavior is encouraging him to stay with you? Anybody would be scared of you, especially a poor little kid like him! When he got off that plane, he was so terrified of everything he couldn't even look up. What kind of life do you think he's had? Don't you realize the horrid things he's seen and experienced? The poverty, the war, the killings? It's no wonder he's afraid! I think I've done a pretty good job of bringing him out of it, but all your yelling and pounding of car roofs has probably wiped out every bit of good I've done. Damn you, Brant, do you have to bully *everyone*?"

At her words, Brant paled beneath his tan. He slumped against the car and ran a hand through his thick hair. "God, I've waited for so long to see him . . . and to have him hate me, fear me, want to leave . . . I can hardly stand it." His voice was muffled, despairing.

Alexis felt a spurt of pity for the man. "He doesn't hate you, Brant. And if you'll calm down and act normally, I don't think he'll fear you, either. Paul was very excited about coming to see you—he kept asking me questions about the ranch and what you were like. You are his father; he wants you, too. It's just that he's scared for me to leave. I am the most secure, known element in his life right now, and he doesn't want to lose that. Brant, think a minute. Paul's been ripped from the only world he's known and placed in a totally alien one. He's been abandoned by everyone throughout his nine years—his mother, the relatives he lived with, you. So of course he's devastated because I'm about to abandon him, too."

Raw pain flashed through Brant's eyes, and he looked away from her. His jaw set, and as though the words were being torn from him he asked, "Alexis, would you stay here for a while? Just until he gets more accustomed to the place, less scared of me?" He paused, but she did not answer. He swallowed and went on. "Please, for Paul's sake. Do you want me to humble myself, beg you to stay?"

"Of course not," Alexis breathed, and felt a strange warmth creep through her body. How wonderful it would be not to have to give Paul up yet. "You startled me. I didn't know what to say. Of course I can stay. I was planning on taking next week as a vacation, anyway, and then there's New Year's. I can stay that long."

"Thank you," he said gruffly, and brushed past without looking at her, picking up Paul's suitcases and carrying them inside.

Alexis knelt beside Paul, setting herself to the task of comforting the boy and assuring him that she would remain there for a while. It would be difficult to be around Brant for a week, with all his barbs and innuendoes, but she could sense excitement growing within her, too. It was because of the opportunity to spend another week with Paul, she told herself. She was doing this for Paul.

After a time, Paul quieted, his tears subsiding into hiccups. He wiped at his cheeks with the backs of his hands. "You really stay?"

"Yes, for a while, but not forever. I have to go to Dallas in a week or so. But until you get to know this place and your father better, I thought I would stay."

He smiled. "Now it be fun."

"Yes, and it will be fun with your father, too."

His eyes clouded a little. "He yelled."

"He was upset because you said you wanted to go with me. He loves you very much, and he has waited a long time for you to come. It hurt him that you didn't want to stay. That's all. He'll be very nice to you, I'm sure of it." He'd better be, she muttered to herself.

Brant returned to take her luggage out of the car and into the house. He neither looked at her nor spoke. Alexis sighed. This was going to be a very trying week. With her hand on Paul's shoulder, she and the boy followed him inside.

Brant disappeared up the stairs. Alexis and Paul went into the living room and sat down. A few moments later Brant appeared in the doorway. Alexis glanced up to see him regarding her with an unfathomable look in his eyes.

"I thought we would go to Nora's for dinner tonight," he offered tersely.

"Sounds good," Alexis said.

Paul, who had regained some of his former spirits now that he was assured of Alexis's staying, asked, "What's that?"

"Don't worry," Alexis told him. "You'll love it. Nora makes your favorite."

"Hamburger!" Paul cried out gleefully, and grinned.

Brant smiled at his expression. "I can see you are a true American already." He paused for a moment.

"Paul, I want to apologize for yelling before. I didn't mean to frighten you. I . . . I was unhappy."

"Because I wanted to leave," Paul deduced, his stilted accent and grave face making him look older than his years.

"Yes," Brant admitted.

"That's okay. I not going," Paul reassured him solemnly.

Alexis choked back a laugh. Across Paul's head, her eyes met Brant's and saw mirrored there a furtive amusement.

"Good. And Alexis isn't going anywhere, and neither am I. So I guess that makes us all pretty stationary people."

Paul frowned. "What that mean—station—station—?"

"Stationary," Brant repeated. "It means still, staying put not moving." Paul nodded his understanding, and Brant said, "Let's go. You ready?"

"Sure."

When they arrived at the cafe, Nora smiled and waved at them. Brant took his customary corner booth, and in a few moments Nora hurried over.

"Miss Stone, boy, it sure is good to see you back!" she exclaimed as she handed out menus.

"Call me Alexis," Alexis said, smiling. "Thank you. It's good to see you again, too. I can hardly wait to get my hands on one of those hamburgers of yours."

Nora laughed and leaned over toward Paul. "And who is this fine-looking young fellow?"

"This is Paul," Alexis told her, ruffling the boy's hair. "And I imagine he rather fancies one of your hamburgers, too."

"Well, he'll sure get one, then," Nora promised heartily. "He certainly is a cute little thing. Does he belong to you, Alexis?"

"No, Nora," Brant said, "he belongs to me. This is my son, Paul. He's going to be staying with me now."

The other woman's eyes widened, and Alexis suspected that Nora barely kept her mouth from dropping open in amazement. However, she managed to gulp out, "Well, ain't that nice? Now, what about you, Brant? The usual?"

"Yes, thank you." His face was carefully blank.

After Nora had left the table, Alexis remarked, with a hint of laughter in her voice, "For someone from a small town, you sure don't mind laying yourself open for gossip."

Brant shrugged. "Everyone here loves to gossip; it's the sole recreation. I've never paid any attention to it. I do as I like, and what others think is their problem."

"A nice attitude, if you can handle it. I'm not so sure I could," Alexis observed wryly.

He looked at her, his amber eyes dark and unreadable. "I wouldn't count on that. Somehow I think you would manage."

"Is that a compliment?"

He shrugged again. "Depends on how you want to take it."

"Well, Morgan always tells me that if you have a choice, you should take it the best way you can."

"Who's Morgan?"

"My sister."

"Funny name for a girl."

"Daddy wanted a boy. He had planned to name me Alec, but I had the temerity to turn out to be a girl. Then he gave Morgan one of those vague men-women names."

"Didn't your mother have any say in the matter?"

Alexis gave a mild snort. "Not much. She got to name Cara, though, who came along five years after Morgan. By that time I think Daddy had given up on a boy. He just washed his hands of the whole business with Cara."

"Doesn't sound too pleasant for Cara."

Alexis frowned. "I don't know. Mother and Daddy

both love her—we all do. But she has always been a little different. Younger than Morgan and I, she was practically an only child. Morgan is like Ginny—my mother—and I . . . well, as you said yourself, I'm a chip off the old block. But Cara was never like either one of them."

"Maybe she's the only one of you three to come up with an identity of her own."

His words stung, but Alexis didn't have the energy to make a quick retort. She merely said, "Could be."

Paul had obviously had his fill of listening to their adult conversation, for he piped up now, asking, "Can we really ride around ranch tomorrow?"

Alexis smiled. This was a sentence loaded with *r*'s, which he found difficult to get his tongue around. It sounded like a tongue twister, and he must have thought it out carefully before saying it.

"Sure, if you want to," Brant answered. Alexis glimpsed a look of eager love in his eyes that was almost painful to see.

"Can we see cows?" Paul pressed his advantage.

"Sure. We'll see the cows, and I'll show you the horses, too. And a windmill. Would you like to climb a windmill?"

"What?" Paul frowned at the unfamiliar word.

"You know," Alexis said, "that tall structure I showed you today as we were driving, with the big fan on top."

"Oh, yes!" Paul exclaimed, excited at this prospect.

"And I'll show you the stock tanks and the corrals and the chutes for loading."

"Oh, boy!" Paul's eyes were sparkling at the thought of all the new delights that awaited him.

"I don't think it will take him long to get acclimated," Alexis commented, and Brant smiled.

Nora brought their dinner, which they dived into hungrily, conversation forgotten. When they had finished, Brant stood up and reached into his tight jeans for some money. Alexis was suddenly conscious of his molded thigh beneath the rough material, of the lean look that the denims gave him, riding low on his hips. He walked to the cashier's counter, his stride long and sure. Alexis watched him, hearing the familiar thud of his boot heels, and a hot yearning curled in her stomach. She remembered their last meeting: the hard, passionate kiss he had given her, the way his body had molded itself against hers.

"Alexis?" She looked up at him, startled out of her reverie. "You coming?"

"Oh, yes." She flushed and rose, Paul beside her. "It was delicious!" she called to Nora, who nodded and smiled.

Brant opened the door for Alexis and guided her out, his hand warm and big against the small of her back. All the way home she had the feeling that the space inside the Ford was shrinking, becoming consumed inch by inch, by the power of Brant's masculine presence. She wished she could roll down the window and let in some air, but the Panhandle night was too frosty to do that.

She glanced over at him. He looked straight ahead, and in the dim light his face was a mask of planes and shadows. Alexis shivered and the breath caught in her throat. How could she ever manage to spend a whole week in the same house with him? And how could she still feel those tingles of desire after all he had said and done to her?

Only Paul's occasional chatter broke the silence, and even that died down as the ride began to lull him. By the time they had reached the house, he was fighting to keep his lids from closing.

"I think I'd better put this guy straight to bed," Alexis said, and Brant laughed in agreement.

Brant followed them up the stairs and showed her which room was Paul's. Alexis looked around, amazed at what Brant had done. The room had obviously been redecorated for a small boy. The wallpaper and matching bedspread teemed with pictures from *Star Wars;* the furniture was sturdy and sized for a child. A toy chest rested against one wall, and beside it sat a model of a frontier fort, complete with blue-uniformed soldiers and warring Indians. Alexis glanced into the adjoining bathroom and saw that a child's toothbrush already hung there.

Tears bit at the back of her eyes. What love and care and expectation had gone into this room! He must have started putting it together shortly after they had made their deal. It was the tender gift of an adoring father. Alexis could not reconcile the man who had done this with the man who had callously abandoned his son in Vietnam. Where, and who, was the real Brant McClure?

She and Brant unpacked Paul's suitcases and put his clothes away. Paul offered no resistance when his father helped him into his pajamas. Then Brant stepped back as Alexis tucked Paul in and kissed his forehead. She walked out of the room, but Brant lingered a moment longer, studying his son, whose eyes were already closing. While Alexis watched from the doorway, Brant reached out and tenderly pushed a stray lock of hair off the boy's face. Alexis swallowed against the lump of pity and warmth that rose in her throat.

Brant turned and left the room. For a moment he and Alexis stood awkwardly in the hall. She knew that she didn't want to go downstairs and spend the rest of the evening alone with Brant McClure. Her emotions were too stirred to allow that to happen. Yet it was absurdly early to go to bed.

He seemed as uncertain and ill at ease as she, looking down as he did at the floor and shifting his weight slightly. She could see the tautness of his muscles beneath his flannel shirt.

"Where am I supposed to sleep?" she asked.

He gestured toward the room across the hall. "I put your luggage in the same room you had before."

Alexis hesitated, then said, "I guess I'll get ready for bed. We left early this morning, and I'm a little tired."

Brant didn't respond, merely nodded and started down the hall to the staircase. Alexis went quickly into the room and closed the door behind her. She felt as if she had escaped from something.

to hide in the dark.

Chapter 14

Alexis awoke slowly, the pale winter sunshine piercing her sleep. She blinked, orienting herself, and sat up. She hadn't slept well the night before, and she didn't feel quite up to facing a day with Brant. Sleep had been very elusive; she had gone to bed too early and then had tossed and turned, thinking about Brant and the impossible situation the next week presented. Once she had finally fallen asleep, Paul had awakened her with one of his nightmares.

Alexis had come to with a start and hurried into Paul's room, taking him in her arms and comforting him. Brant had stood in the doorway watching them for a few minutes, and even though she had been absorbed with Paul, she had been uncomfortably aware of the sheer, clinging material of her nightgown. Fortunately, Brant had left without a word, and when Paul had quieted down, Alexis had slid back to her room, where she had lain wide awake for almost an hour, staring at the ceiling until sleep overtook her.

Now the door to her bedroom opened slightly, and Paul's dark head peered cautiously around. Alexis smiled and said, "I'm up. Come on in, Paul."

The door opened all the way, and Paul scampered into the room and bounded up beside her on the bed. "I am hungry," he announced.

"Ready for some breakfast?" Alexis asked, and he nodded.

"We are going around the ranch today," he told her, his dark eyes shining with excitement. "I like that. Don't you, Allie?"

"Oh, yes," Alexis lied stoutly. "It'll be a lot of fun."

"And Christmas tree!"

"What?"

"Daddy says we get Christmas tree."

"Well, good. With all that to do, I guess you'd better run back to your room and get dressed."

"Okay." He jumped off the bed and left as quickly as he had come.

Brant was silent all throughout breakfast and the ride into Barrett to find a Christmas tree. Alexis shrugged off his rudeness and occupied herself by staring out the window or answering Paul's eager questions. When they reached the corner lot where the cut pine and cedar trees lay in rows, Paul dashed out of the car and ran ahead of them, hunting intently for a tree.

As Alexis moved to follow him, Brant placed a hand on her arm and asked, "Does Paul have nightmares often?"

"He had them three times the first week. They've decreased since then. Last night was the first time he had one in several days."

"What is he scared of?"

"I don't know. He doesn't like to talk about it. He just says that big men were chasing him."

"I saw you go in to him." There was an edgy note to his voice that made Alexis bristle.

"Yes, I did," she said, clipping off her words. She wasn't sure what he was implying, but she was positive she didn't appreciate his tone.

"You do everything you can to hold him to you, don't you?" Brant remarked quietly.

Alexis jerked her arm from his grasp. "Just what do you expect me to do? Let him scream in terror and never lift a hand to comfort him?"

Brant grimaced. "No, of course not."

"Then what are you talking about? What else could I do?"

Brant drew his brows together and started to speak, but Paul came running up to them full tilt, babbling about a tree, and Brant snapped his mouth shut.

They followed Paul to the tree and examined it. Brant indicated a hole in one side, and Paul stepped back a little, biting his lip.

"But that's okay," Brant hastened to reassure him, "if that's the one you want. Do you like this tree better than all the others?"

Paul nodded, and Brant said, "Then that's the one we'll get."

Brant continued to be surly and uncommunicative all morning long, even while he set up the tree in the living room and hauled all the old ornaments out of the attic. Alexis could not imagine less of the spirit of Christmas as they hung the glass balls and icicles. She felt as prickly as a cactus and wished that she could return to bed, get up, and start everything all over again.

However, Paul was entranced with the fragile decorations, and his eyes widened in amazement when Brant turned on the lights that made the tree sparkle with different colors. Brant lifted him up to set the angel securely on the top. Paul eagerly affixed ornaments and scattered tinsel everywhere.

When the tree was finished, he insisted that Alexis accompany them on a tour of the ranch. So, after lunch, Alexis put on her coat with a sigh and followed Brant and Paul out to the jeep.

They started across the land, and Alexis held on to the door, feeling as if every jolt and bounce were designed to sever her head from her body. Paul laughed with delight and poured out his eternal questions.

"What is that?"

"It's a gully," Brant told him. "Sometimes when it rains, water comes through there. Over the years the water has cut that big cleft in the ground. When we get over this rise ahead, Paul, look sharp. You'll probably see some of my cattle."

Sure enough, they did, and Paul began to bounce excitedly in his seat, peering through the window at the animals, which stared placidly back. "Look, Allie, look!" he cried. "What are those things in their ears?" he asked his father, pointing.

"Tags. That's how we identify them. That's how I know they are mine."

"Oh. Doesn't it hurt?"

"Not any more than branding, I don't think." Brant then had to explain what branding meant.

They drove past the cattle, then circled back. Brant stared intently at them, frowning. "I don't like the look of that one's eye," he said, stopping the jeep and getting out.

Alexis sighed, leaned her head against the window, and closed her eyes. She wished she had stayed at the house and taken a nap instead of coming out here to watch Brant inspect his steers.

"I thought we were having a tour," she snapped when Brant returned, "not waiting for you to check out your stock."

Brant cast a look of disgust and started the engine. "That's about as reasonable a remark as my telling you not to correct an error in a legal document because you happened to see it on your time off."

Alexis knew his argument was valid. It made her feel petty, which exasperated her even more.

Brant showed Paul the empty fields where he grew feed crops for his cows, the covered feeders containing hay for the winter, and steel-barred pens and chutes used for gathering and loading the cattle before shipping them to market, the metal water tanks, and the larger stock tanks dug into the ground. At one of the latter, they got out of the jeep and walked around, Paul examining over gopher holes, rocks, cacti, and a swarming bed of ants.

Alexis wet her dry lips, tasting the dust. "How can you stand this dust? Everything here is full of grit."

Brant ignored her and pointed out a yucca plant, its stem loaded with dry pods. "In the early summer, Paul, the yucca gets pretty little pink flowers all up the stem. Those are the seeds on it now, inside the pods." He broke off a pod and handed it to the boy. "The Panhandle is full of interesting things like this."

"Don't forget the interesting things like winds and blizzards and tornadoes," Alexis injected sarcastically, and Brant shot her a murderous look.

When Paul ran ahead of them to examine a rock, Brant gripped her arm tightly and hissed, "Would you get off it, lady? This is going to be his home, and I don't see how it'll do him any good if you run it down all the time. He'll have a hard enough time adjusting as it is."

Alexis set her jaw stubbornly. Brant was right, of course, and that made it even worse. She certainly should not encourage Paul to dislike his future home; it was selfish of her. But she was not about to admit that to Brant.

She shrugged off his hand and sauntered back to the jeep. A few moments later Brant and Paul returned also. They racketed off to a windmill so that Paul could climb it. Alexis kept her mouth firmly clamped, and Brant stared straight ahead, an occasional twitch along his jaw revealing his irritation and pent-up anger.

Alexis watched Paul climb the ladder resting against one side of the windmill, Brant right behind him in case he slipped. When they reached the top, Paul waved down to Alexis cheerfully, and she waved back.

By midafternoon they were at the ranch house again. Brant took Paul on a tour of the barn and corrals, while Alexis went upstairs and showered, washing the grit of the land off her skin and hair. She toweled her hair dry, then brushed it, letting it fall around her face in a sensual mass of gleaming red-gold curls. She pulled on a yellow turtleneck jersey that hugged her breasts and waist, and tucked it into a pair of tight-fitting jeans. Turning before the mirror, Alexis decided that she didn't look half bad, not like a lady lawyer at all. Stubbornly, she ignored the little voice within her that asked why it should matter how she looked.

Alexis found some chicken in the refrigerator and made a rice and chicken casserole for supper. When Brant and Paul came in around five, Brant glanced at the pans on the stove and at the set table with a look of amusement. Alexis drew in her breath, readying herself for a counterattack if he should offer a nasty crack about her cooking. He said nothing, however, merely herded Paul to the sink to wash his hands.

The tension between them at the table was thick enough to taste. Alexis had the same anticipatory, vaguely restless feeling that she had whenever a spring storm loomed on the horizon, the clouds thick and dark and the air heavy. But the meal passed without any eruptions.

Brant and Paul did the dishes, then retired to the cozy, book-lined den, where Brant taught his son how to play marbles. Bored, Alexis selected a novel at random and sat down to read, but the story could not hold her attention. Even though she and Brant avoided all conversation and did not look at each other, the air between them almost crackled. Their studied indifference to each other only emphasized and enlarged the uncomfortable atmosphere.

About eight o'clock Alexis took Paul up to bed. After she had finished tucking him in and telling him good night, she paused outside his door, contemplating going straight to her room instead of returning downstairs. It was terribly early, of course, but she had been tired all day. Perhaps she would be able to go to sleep. If she went downstairs, Alexis feared that the heavy emotional charge that had stretched between her and Brant all day would snap, plunging them into another raging argument. On the other hand, if she left the matter to stew tonight, tomorrow would simply be more of the same. Brant was simmering, and she supposed she might as well let him get it off his chest now and be done with it. Maybe a good fight would clear the air and enable them to get along more easily for the rest of her stay.

Alexis lifted her chin and started down the stairs. She had never run from a fight yet, and she certainly wasn't about to do so with Brant McClure. When she reached the den, Brant was pacing back and forth like a caged animal. She sat down in her chair and picked up the book as though to resume her reading.

"I want to talk to you, Alexis," Brant said shortly, and she lowered her book.

"Oh?" Her tone was disinterested, cool, and her eyebrows raised a trifle.

"When did you get Paul?"

"The first week in December."

His eyes flashed. "So you've had him almost *four* weeks . . . and you didn't see fit to tell me, his father, about it! What the hell did you think you were doing?"

"I told you we would get Paul to you, and we did!" Alexis snapped. "After almost nine years, does it really make that much difference?"

"Yes, it does!" he thundered. "Did you keep my son to make me suffer for a few more weeks, to make me dance on your string? Or was it just that you wanted to get your claws into him but good, so that he couldn't stand to leave you? Was that your revenge, Alexis, to attach Paul to you so firmly that he would be miserable without you?"

"How dare you!" Alexis cried hotly, springing to her feet. "You're loathsome, vile, and despicable to suggest such a thing! Only *you* would see something evil in the most innocent act. I was trying to help Paul—even to help you!"

"Don't make me laugh," he growled. "Good God, Alexis, must you have his heart, too?"

Blind with rage, Alexis retorted, "You're unfair! I kept him with me so that I could hire an English teacher for him. I did it because I knew you wouldn't be able to find a Vietnamese-speaking tutor here. Is that so unkind?"

"Don't pretend you were doing me a favor. I could have found someone."

"In Barrett?" Her voice dripped sarcasm.

"In Amarillo."

"Oh? And that person would have driven four hours every day, round trip?"

"He or she could have lived here. I would have gone to Dallas, Houston, anywhere until I found someone willing to come up here for a couple of months to teach him. Which you would have known if you had thought to call and give me the option!"

"I was giving *him* a little time to adjust to the new world he suddenly found himself in!" Alexis cried. "I was the only person here he knew at all. I thought it would be easier for him to get used to America while he had someone with him whom he trusted. Paul liked me, difficult as you may find that to believe. I was nice to him, and I held him when he had bad dreams. I liked him, I enjoyed being with him, I was happy. I—I love Paul. I wouldn't have done anything to hurt him."

Brant strode toward her, snarling, "You love Paul! That's a laugh! You don't know the meaning of the word. You're a female replica of Alec Stone, incapable of any heart or emotion. You don't love Paul—you only love yourself! The one thing you said just now that rang true was that you kept him because *you* enjoyed him, because *you* were happy with him. Don't pretend it was for him, or to help me. It was for yourself. You're the only person you ever think about, except for your father!"

Tears sprang into Alexis's eyes. "You are a brute!" Her hand lashed out. She wanted to hit him, hurt him as he had hurt her.

Brant caught her wrist in a cruel grip before she could reach his face. He loomed over her, his expression grim and cold with fury. "Lady, you don't know the first thing about brutality. You've lived your whole life with every advantage, every shelter. You don't know anything about the life that other people have had to lead. You've always been Daddy's little darling. I saw things in Vietnam that would turn your stomach, things that made me sick. That's brutality. Anything I ever did to you was mild in comparison."

"Just because there are people worse than you doesn't excuse you!" Alexis shot back. "You hit me, and you raped me!"

He threw back his head and laughed harshly, pulling her against him so tightly that she could feel his muscles through his clothing. A treacherous tremor shook her body at his touch.

Angry at what she felt, Alexis hissed, "I hate you! I hate you!" She tried to wrench away from him, but his arms were like a circle of steel around her. Stubbornly, she turned and twisted, pushing against his chest with her hands, arching away from him.

A golden light burst into Brant's eyes, and for a moment Alexis was transfixed by his gaze. She wanted to run from him, and yet she waited breathlessly for what he would do next. Slowly, deliberately, his head came down to meet hers. Their lips touched, at first softly, then with increasing strength and fire, until Alexis was bent backward over his arm and his mouth was devouring hers.

Alexis knew that she was drowning in his kiss, melting away in his hateful desire. He offered her nothing, no love, no kindness, but still she quivered at his touch, every nerve aflame as his searing kisses stamped his possession of her.

His grip loosened as he embraced her, one hand sliding up to cup the back of her neck, the other beginning to roam her back gently. In desperation, Alexis gathered all her strength of will and broke away from him, fleeing down the hall toward the stairs. For one shocked moment Brant hesitated, and then he moved with a sense of urgency, his heavy boots thudding ominously on the hardwood floor. With a sob, Alexis darted up the stairs, her breath rasping. He was chasing her . . . and she knew that she couldn't escape him.

Brant caught her halfway up the stairs, grabbing her arm and whirling her around to him. His eyes were bright, his face flushed with passion. For a long moment they stood looking at each other, their harsh breath the only sound, every one of their senses vibrantly alive and intensely aware of the cataclysm that swirled around them, inevitable, frightening, pulsating. Alexis glowed, her eyes deep blue pools drawing Brant to her. He kissed her, and she struggled to hold him away from her.

"No!" she cried. "Damn you, no! You won't do this to me again! Let go of me!"

"I didn't rape you, Alexis," he said, his voice low and throbbing. "You wanted it as much as I did. You wanted it, just like you want it now."

"No! I didn't want you—I didn't!"

"As I recall, you helped me take off your clothes."

"That was before— It didn't mean I wanted you to force me!"

"Oh, I see, it's okay if you tease, if you go along to a certain point, but if I want to follow through, it's rape."

"That's not the way it was at all," Alexis snapped, "and you know it! You were hateful, cruel. You humiliated me!"

"Ah, I see." Brant's voice was dangerously soft. "The perfect Miss Stone's pride was injured. Someone got the better of her, and it wounded her ego."

"You have a very convenient memory," Alexis hissed. "And are lying. I despise you completely. You're a crude, cruel, pigheaded—"

Her words were cut off by Brant's mouth fastening on hers. He kissed her deeply, his tongue a ravaging tool. Alexis struggled, but he held her head in his iron grasp, his fingers digging painfully into her neck. Leisurely, he took his pleasure of her lips, savoring the kiss with all the careless time of one who has no need to persuade, only to take. When at last he released her, Alexis felt dizzy, and she had to hold on to his arms to keep from sinking ignominiously to the floor.

"Deny it now," he demanded. "Deny that you want me. Say you didn't writhe and moan in my arms that night. Tell me you loathed my kisses in the car at Beth's, that you weren't panting to crawl into my bed."

Alexis blushed and turned her head away, mortified at how he could turn her to liquid fire so easily. Just his kiss made her knees weak and sent sparks shooting along her nerves. Damn the man—how utterly, horribly confident he was of the power he had over her!

She swallowed and forced her voice to be steady. Her pride was at stake. If she gave in to him, she would be drowned in her one-sided passion. He would own her and then toss her aside, broken, whenever it suited him. She could not let that happen.

Firmly, she said, "No matter what you think, I don't want you. I never will. You can force me, just as you did that other time, but you can't make me enjoy it, you can't make me respond. Take me, go ahead, but you'll never get anything from me freely. I'll hate you always, Brant!"

His entire body stiffened at her words, and his face contorted with fury. Suddenly he moved, sweeping her up into his arms and holding her so tight against his chest that she could not struggle. Quickly, he started up the stairs.

For a moment Alexis was too stunned even to protest, but then she began to wriggle and push, trying vainly to get away from him. He merely crushed her closer, and from the glitter in his eyes she knew that her movements aroused him further. She thought of screaming. Surely if she awakened Paul, Brant would not behave so animalistically in front of his son. But, remembering the terrors that had gripped Paul when she first met him, she could not bear the thought of waking him and having him see his father struggle with her. That would hurt Paul too much and would damage his relationship with Brant, with whom he had to live. Alexis simply could not inflict that upon the boy.

Brant entered his bedroom, kicking closed the door with one foot, walked across the floor and dumped her unceremoniously on the bed. Quick as a cat, Alexis rolled over and leaped to her feet. Immediately, he was upon her, grabbing her with one arm and pulling her back toward the bed.

Alexis struck out at him, kicking and clawing in impotent rage. Her hands and feet connected with him again and again, but Brant bore her relentlessly down on the bed and covered her with his huge body, pulling her arms up high above her head and clamping them together with one hand.

For an instant he hung above her, his amber eyes glinting with an unholy fire, his face a mask of desire. "Damn, you're beautiful," he breathed. His mouth swooped down, taking hers in a fierce, conquering kiss, as he ground his body into hers with a slow, hot yearning.

His mouth left her, and Alexis gasped for breath, closing her eyes against the sight of his face, heavy with passion. Slowly, teasingly, Brant's free hand wandered over her chest, exploring every inch of her through the tight jersey.

"Did you know what this sweater of yours would do to me?" he asked, his voice low and vibrant. "Is that why you wore it—to tease me with your breasts, to make me itch to touch you? Well, you succeeded, lady. Your being naked couldn't have made me ache for you more than when I saw your nipples pointed against this thin sweater."

Alexis melted at his words, the heat rushing up into her face and down through her lower body. Traitorously, her loins proceeded to throb. Brant wrapped his legs around her and rolled over onto his side, pulling Alexis with him. His hand curved over her bottom, squeezing, caressing, his fingers slipping between her thighs and teasing at her through her jeans. He unwound his legs and began to unfasten her zipper, expertly pushing the jeans off her hips. Alexis moved her legs, unconsciously helping him.

Brant released her hands, but Alexis did not move, all resistance gone from her mind. In one swift movement he stood and stripped off his clothes, his hot amber eyes never leaving Alexis. Alexis watched him, unable to look away from the hard masculine beauty of his form. He returned to the bed and sat beside her, pushing up her sweater to expose her creamy breasts, their rosy peaks stiff with passion. A groan sounded deep in his throat, and he cupped her breasts in his large hands, his thumbs gently circling the taut nipples. Then he bent and took one in his mouth, rolling it between his lips and caressing it with his tongue, tantalizing her until a moan broke from her lips.

His low chuckle was brimming with desire. "So you don't want me, huh, Alexis? I can't make you respond or enjoy it? Tell me again, Alexis, how much you detest my touch."

"Oh, Brant," Alexis groaned softly. "Please don't."

"Don't what?" He took her other nipple in his mouth and began to tease it while he slid one hand over her stomach and inside her panties, exploring, probing, awakening, but not fulfilling. "Don't do this? Or don't remind you of your lies?"

He pulled her flimsy panties from her, and his mouth drifted down the flat plane of her stomach. Writhing with delight, she opened her legs to his expert touch. He toyed with her, withholding until she quivered with passion.

"Do you want me now, Alexis?" he murmured.

A ragged sob escaped her throat. "Please, Brant."

"Please what?" He moved over her, his erect, hard shaft poised between her inviting legs. "Tell me, Alexis. I want to hear you say it. Say you want me."

"I want you."

A shudder ran down his long frame, and he entered

her, thrusting deep, filling her with an intense satisfaction. Alexis clung to him as he rode out his storm, and the wild longing inside her built higher and higher, until at last it exploded, shooting golden sparks of pleasure throughout her body. Brant wrapped his arms around her, groaning as he penetrated still deeper, lost in the abandoned release of his desire.

Trembling, Alexis floated down from the dizzying heights of passion. Sighing heavily, Brant rolled off her and clasped her to him. Too lazy, too fulfilled, even to think, Alexis snuggled against his chest, his arms a tight ring of security around her, and drifted easily into sleep.

Chapter 15

Alexis awoke with a start, confused until she recalled with a blush where she was. How could she have been so weak? How could she have responded so easily to him after all his boasts? She turned her head to look at Brant. He lay turned away from her, his chest rising and falling in the slow rhythm of sleep.

Cautiously, Alexis crept out of bed, gathered up her clothes, and slipped into the hall, closing the door softly behind her. She scampered to her room and grabbed a robe, then went into the bathroom for a quick shower. A shower often brought her fuzzy, early-morning mind back to a decent thought process.

However, even the shower did not help collect her scattered thoughts and emotions together. The truth was, she didn't know what to feel or do, or what she even wanted to feel or do. She felt out of touch with everything, including herself.

Alexis would never have believed that she could act as she had the night before, that she could respond to anyone with such surging passion. Even now her mind skittered away from the full reality of her lovemaking. Conflicting feelings swirled in her: hatred for herself, hatred for Brant, the impulse to run away, the duty to stay for Paul, disgust, and a wicked wish to experience Brant's lovemaking again.

Angrily, Alexis threw the towel from her and dressed in black knit slacks and a black, bulky sweater. She knew she ought to leave, but she felt too confused to do anything. Running a quick brush through her silken hair, she didn't bother with any makeup, but left the room quickly and went down the stairs. When she reached the kitchen, she found to her surprise that Paul was there before her.

"Hello, honey," she said, trying to speak in a normal tone. "What are you doing up so early?"

The boy shrugged. "Hungry," he answered simply.

Alexis smiled. "Well, I guess I'll have to whip you up some breakfast, then, won't I?"

She pulled out a skillet and set about breaking and scrambling a few eggs. "Here," she told Paul, handing him some bread and the butter dish. "Why don't you fix the toast?"

"Okay." Eagerly he popped two slices of bread into the toaster, then sat, knife in hand, waiting for them to come out.

"How did you like your first day at the ranch?" Alexis asked him while she worked.

"Oh, boy!" he responded gleefully, taking his eyes off the toaster to look at her. "It's big! I like it here. Daddy showed me all the horses yesterday. Today maybe I'll ride one."

"That would be fun." Alexis hid the irrational spurt of jealousy she felt at the boy's enthusiastic acceptance of his father. Brant was a monster, and he didn't deserve his son's love, but it was better for Paul if he loved and accepted Brant. She had to give Paul up.

Alexis dished the eggs onto two plates, and Paul proudly added the toast. "Where's Daddy? Isn't he going to eat, too?"

"I don't know," Alexis replied. "I decided we'd go ahead and eat without him. He can get his breakfast later."

Paul stuffed a forkful of eggs into his mouth. Alexis

poured two glasses of orange juice, put the coffee on to perk, then sat down to eat. She felt amazingly hungry this morning, despite the emotions boiling inside her.

There was a thud of boots, and Paul looked up excitedly. "Daddy!" He turned expectantly toward the kitchen door, and Alexis turned, too, her heart beating like a drum at seeing Brant again.

Brant appeared in the doorway, paused for a split second as his eyes flickered toward Alexis, then thrust his hands in his pockets and walked in. His expression was so arrogant that Alexis itched to slap him. How dare he look calm and superior? By all rights, he should feel embarrassed and guilty. But for some crazy reason it was Alexis who felt that way.

"Daddy!" Paul cried again, and Brant smiled at him.

"Good morning, Paul," he said, and sat down ignoring Alexis.

If she hadn't been so angry, Alexis might have noticed the hesitant curve to Brant's mouth, or the way his eyes, tinged with remorse, darted sideways at her, or the tenseness of his muscles; she might have guessed that his silence masked an awkward, eager anxiety. But she was too troubled, too confused, to see anything but Brant's indifference to her.

"Well, you are up late," she snapped. "No doubt you were tired from your exertions last night."

Brant turned toward her then, his face set in an amused look. "Yes, no doubt."

She saw that a long red scratch ran down the side of one cheek. Alexis realized with satisfaction that she had put it there in their struggle. Sternly, she repressed a desire to touch the mark with her finger. She would not feel guilty.

"Get me some breakfast," Brant commanded.

Alexis gasped at his effrontery. "What? You can get your own damn breakfast. I wouldn't lift a finger for you after what you did last night!"

"The way *you* acted last night, I would think you'd

do a good deal more for me than breakfast," he returned mockingly.

"Why, you conceited pig!" Alexis burst out, then glanced at Paul and stopped. The boy's face had become taut, and she saw a spark of fear in his eyes. It would not do to start quarreling in front of Paul. That would upset him far more than the argument was worth. She bit back her words and began to make Brant's breakfast.

Quickly, she broke two eggs in the skillet and turned on the stove, then smiled wickedly and opened the cabinet where she had found the seasonings. It didn't take her long to locate the small bottle of jalapeño peppers. She poured its juice into the eggs as she scrambled them, glancing over her shoulder to make sure Brant hadn't seen her actions, then dished the eggs onto a plate. She set the plate in front of him and stepped back.

"Pour me a cup of coffee," he said in the same domineering tone, and was surprised to see Alexis smile sweetly and go to the coffeepot to pour a cup for him. She put it down beside his plate and seated herself demurely.

Brant studied her, puzzled at her sudden passivity, then dug into his eggs. His eyes flew open in astonishment as the pepper liquid seared his mouth. He swallowed quickly and began to cough. His eyes watering, he grabbed the cup of coffee and drank from it, but the scalding brew only added to the fire in his mouth. He rushed to the sink, grabbed a glass, and filled it with water, chugging it down while Alexis burst into helpless laughter. Paul looked around, bewildered.

"Damn you!" Brant gasped, then stopped short, as Alexis had, when he saw Paul's troubled expression. His face set into grim lines, he stalked to the table, picked up his plate, and scooped the eggs into the trash.

"What's the matter?" Alexis asked innocently. "Didn't I fix them right?"

"Oh, you fixed them, all right," Brant retorted, and shoved a piece of bread into the toaster. By the time the toast was done and he had buttered it and spread jam on it, his stern mouth was beginning to lift at the corners, and a twinkle had come to his eye. Alexis sure as hell was one to go down fighting, he thought.

To hide his amusement from her, he turned to Paul and asked, "How would you like to learn to ride a horse?"

"Oh boy!" Paul exclaimed. "Will you teach me, really?"

"Sure. We'll start this morning. I'll teach you how to saddle and bridle a horse, how to mount it, how to ride —the whole works. In a few weeks you'll be a regular cowboy."

Paul bounced up and down in his chair, pretending to ride a horse, making galloping sounds with his mouth.

Brant laughed. "Tell you what. I bet if you go up to your room and look in the bottom drawer of your chest, you'll find something to wear."

"Oh, boy!" Paul repeated his favorite expression and jumped down from the chair. He stopped and looked at Alexis, his eyes seeking her approval. Alexis smiled and nodded, and he tore out of the kitchen on the run.

Brant's eyes glinted angrily. "You still have control of him, don't you?" he muttered, his voice bitter.

"What is that supposed to mean? I tried to teach him some manners, yes, such as asking to be excused from the table."

"And, of course, it is always you who has the power to excuse."

Alexis rose and began to clear the table. Her movements were quick and jerky. She felt nervous being this close to Brant, with all the raging emotions inside her and his obvious lack of any at all.

She put the plates and silverware in the sink, then came back for the glasses. Brant reached out and grasped her wrist, stopping her.

"Leave me alone," Alexis said in a low voice, standing passively. "I don't want anything to do with you."

Brant's amber eyes glittered, and he ran a finger down the scratch on his cheek. "Too late. You've already put your mark on me."

"And you marked me, too, with bruises." She pushed up one sleeve of her sweater to reveal purplish marks where his fingers had bit into her arm. "Tell me, Brant, do you enjoy it more with victims? Would you rather take an unwilling female than a willing one?"

Brant tugged at her arm, pulling her down into his lap and enfolding her in his arms. He nuzzled her neck, his lips sending shivers of delight through her, although Alexis stubbornly refused to reveal his effect on her. His hands caressed her freely, roaming over her body, sliding beneath her sweater to touch her breasts and bring her nipples to hardness. He chuckled softly at their traitorous, involuntary stiffening.

"Unwilling?" he repeated mockingly. "Even now you enjoy it. You know, last night I got some scratches on my back, too, and those didn't come when you were angry, but when you were moaning and moving and crying to me to give you your pleasure."

Tears sprang into Alexis's eyes and she looked away, afraid to say anything lest she burst out crying and admit the truth of his words. She had writhed beneath him like a demented creature; she had been swept away by passion. Even now she responded to him, wanted him, just as he said. But she could not give in to him and let him own her.

"Admit it," his soft voice insisted as his hands explored her body. "You wouldn't mind stretching out right here on this table, would you?"

"No!" Alexis choked out, and tore herself from his grasp.

They faced each other for a moment, tension stretching between them like an electric current. Then there was a clomping sound, and Paul appeared at the door. Alexis relaxed and moved away, as if some spell had been broken.

Paul paused proudly in the doorway to let them see the full effect of his costume. He was dressed in a piped Western shirt with pearlescent snaps and a pair of dark blue jeans. His feet were encased in bright red and black boots, and on top of his head sat a small, black felt cowboy hat, secured by a black cord that ran under his chin.

Alexis could not keep from smiling. "You look like a real cowboy!"

He grinned from ear to ear and stuck out his chest. "You bet."

Brant rose. "Okay, pardner, let's get going," he said, and started for the door without a backward glance at Alexis. Paul trotted happily at his heels.

Alexis looked out the kitchen window and watched them cross the yard, a funny lump in her throat. She knew that she wanted to cry, but why? She picked up the glasses and cups that remained on the table and put them in the sink, then rinsed each item and stacked it in the dishwasher.

She went back to the window and saw Brant guide a horse from the barn and swing Paul up on it. Then he led his son around the corral and out of her range of vision. Alexis sighed, then left the kitchen and wandered off into the den. Paul was getting along beautifully, and whatever she felt about Brant McClure, he was proving himself a good father. At least she knew she would be leaving Paul in good hands. Maybe he would become so used to Brant that she would be able to leave earlier than she had planned. That would be the best thing for her, but again that silly lump rose in her throat.

Her thoughts were interrupted by a firm knock on the front door. Alexis went off to answer it, and to her delight she found Beth standing on the porch.

"Beth!" she cried. "Come on in."

"Alexis!" Beth exclaimed in surprise. "I didn't know you'd still be here. This is great!" She stepped inside, shivering, and started stripping off her coat and gloves. "Brrr, it's cold out there. Sometimes I wonder why sane people continue to live in this climate. The Valley would be much nicer."

Alexis laughed. "That's true. But remember that Brownsville gets hurricanes instead."

"I know." Beth sighed and made a false grimace. "So tell me, what are you doing here? Brant said you were bringing Paul, but I figured you'd go right back."

"Don't get excited, Beth," Alexis cautioned. "Brant and I have not resolved our differences."

"I knew that would be too much to hope for."

"Would you like some coffee?"

"Sounds great."

The two women headed for the kitchen and a cozy chat.

"Well, if you haven't resolved your differences, what are you doing here?" Beth asked as she settled herself at the table.

"Paul has become rather attached to me, and he was upset when I started to leave. He carried on quite a bit, so I agreed to stay until he got a little more familiar with Brant and the ranch." Alexis poured a cup of coffee for Beth and sat down opposite her.

"I see. Well, that's good. When I saw that Mercedes out there, I thought maybe it was Libby's."

"Who?"

Beth drank some of her coffee before replying. "Libby Preston, Brant's current girlfriend," she said.

"Oh." Alexis felt a stab of jealousy dart through her. "Is she from around here?"

"Libby?" Beth laughed. "Heavens, no, she's from Amarillo. That's why I know that Brant won't ever marry her, although she's trying her best."

"Why? I don't understand."

"She wouldn't live out here on the ranch, and Brant

could never be persuaded to move into the city. Thank heavens."

"What's so awful about her?" Alexis asked, surprised at the burning curiosity that swept over her. Why should she care what Brant's girlfriend was like?

Beth shrugged. She could see that she had aroused Alexis's interest, and she wanted to keep it going. She planned to stick to her promise not to connive between Brant and Alexis, but if she could spark her friend enough so that Alexis would do a little conniving herself, everything would work out fine.

"Oh, nothing. It's not really any of my business. Besides, I know you aren't interested in talking about Libby Preston. Tell me about Paul. He's the one I came over here to see."

Alexis smiled. "Oh, Beth, he is an absolute doll. You'll love him, I guarantee. He's got beautiful hair and skin, and he's rather small. But I think he'll grow like a weed now, with decent food. He's got big facial bones, like Brant. And his eyes are dark brown and too round to be Asian; they even have gold in them like Brant."

"Where is he? I can't wait to see him."

"He's outside. Brant is teaching him to ride. Last time I saw them they were down by the corral."

"Well, I guess they'll come in pretty soon," Beth said hopefully. "I haven't any desire to walk out there in this cold."

"I don't think they'll stay out very long. Paul isn't used to the cold."

"It makes me so happy that Brant finally has him. I really appreciate what you and your father did for Brant."

Alexis squirmed uncomfortably. "Well, it wasn't entirely unselfish, Beth."

"Oh, I know that's why Brant signed the lease. That's obvious. But he would never have gotten the boy any other way, and he has wanted him so desperately for so long."

"Did Brant know about Paul when he left Vietnam?" Alexis asked.

"Yes. She was pregnant then, but Paul hadn't been born yet."

"Why didn't Brant bring him over as soon as he was born, before the Communists came into power?" Alexis burst out. "I can't understand his leaving Paul there."

"Oh, he didn't want to," Beth assured her. "But the mother wanted to keep him. I think Brant was pretty fond of her, or sorry for her, or something. Anyway, she was scared to come to America, and she refused to let her baby go. So Brant agreed. He didn't like the idea, but what could he do? After all, he could hardly take a baby from its mother. So he came back to the States and sent her money every month. But then the Communists took over. He hoped that she would escape and come here, like all those other refugees, but she never did. Then he started trying to find Paul, to get him out of Vietnam, but the only thing he ever learned was that the mother had died. She was killed by a bomb in the streets of Saigon."

"How awful." A pang of guilt touched Alexis. Brant had wanted Paul all along. She remembered the taunts she had thrown at him about abandoning his child. No wonder Brant had been so furious; no wonder he had lashed out at her. She felt ashamed of herself. "Poor Brant," she said.

Beth sighed. "It really tore him up. Brant's always been crazy about the kid. I hate to think what he must be like now that Paul's actually here."

"I think he was pretty hurt because Paul didn't want me to leave him here."

"Mmm, I bet. It will all work out now, I'm sure. You'll see."

"Oh, I know it will. Paul is already beginning to feel safe with him. What's worrying me is how *I'm* going to react. It's so wild, Beth, the way I've grown attached to that boy. I never would have believed it. I mean, I've never been around children before, and when I went to Hawaii to get him, I was afraid I wouldn't know what to do or say. But he has really stolen my heart."

The back door opened, and a moment later Paul appeared, grinning, with Brant close behind him. "Did you see me, Allie? I was riding the horse!" Paul cried, running to Alexis, then halting when he saw the woman sitting with her.

"Paul, this is your daddy's sister, Beth," Alexis said.

"Hello, Paul." Beth smiled and leaned over to him. "I have a couple of little girls about your age who I'm sure would love to play with you. They are your cousins."

"What's that?" Paul asked shyly.

"Well, see, Brant and I are brother and sister, and our children are cousins."

"Hello, Beth," Brant said, crossing the kitchen and pouring himself a cup of coffee. "How are you doing?"

"Fine," Beth replied, looking at him for the first time. "What did you do to your face?"

"What?"

"That scratch."

A fiery blush stained Alexis's cheeks, and she propped her face on her outspread palms to hide it.

Brant grinned slowly. "Oh, that. I got it in a catfight."

Beth looked a little puzzled but abandoned the subject. "Brant, Paul is just beautiful. I can't believe you have such a cute son."

"Well, thanks, Beth. That's a backhanded compliment if I ever heard one!" he laughed.

"Now listen, I came here with an invitation, so you'd better be nice to me."

"Okay." Brant sat down beside Alexis and draped one hand over the back of her chair.

Beth's eyes widened and flickered from Alexis to Brant and back. Alexis could have kicked him. Now

Beth would be convinced that there was a romance between them . . . and Alexis could never explain to her why nothing would come of it.

"I don't know if you two realize it," Beth went on, "but the day after tomorrow is Christmas. And I'm inviting you over for Christmas dinner."

Brant chuckled. "What's the news about that, Beth? You always do."

"Yes, but I mean all of you. Usually it's just you, Brant. Dinner is one o'clock, but come early. I know the girls would love to meet Paul."

"Sure, we'll be there," Brant agreed.

For the first time it really struck Alexis that she would be spending Christmas with a man she detested and his son—a cozy little family group in which she had no place at all! She had a premonition that the whole affair would be a complete disaster, at least for her.

Brant's thigh moved against hers under the table. Alexis carefully shifted her leg away.

"I don't know about you two, but I have work to do," Brant announced, rising. "Why don't you stay for lunch, Beth? Alexis, I'll see you at noon." Deliberately, he cupped her chin in his hand and bent to kiss her, a short, firm kiss, but one that left no doubt about the nature of their relationship. "Paul, you want to come with me?"

"Yeah!" Paul trotted happily after him.

Beth stared at Alexis, gaping with astonishment. As soon as Brant had gone through the door, she leaned forward eagerly. "Alexis, what did you mean by saying that you and Brant hadn't resolved your differences? What was that?"

Alexis sighed. "Oh, Beth, believe me, we haven't resolved anything. It's a worse tangle than ever."

"But obviously *something* is going on!"

"Yes, something, but— Oh, Beth, it's purely physical. Brant doesn't care about me. We don't love each other. We don't even like each other. There is just this physical attraction between us."

"That's better than some people have," Beth observed dryly.

"I suppose so, but it's nothing to get your hopes up about. I'll be leaving in a week, and that's it. The end. I'll never see Brant again."

"He's a pretty stubborn man."

"But, Beth, he doesn't want me. I mean, he doesn't have any feeling for me. I'm just handy, and he's horny."

"Don't you believe it. He's been a bear ever since you left."

Alexis laughed. "I thought that was his usual state."

"Not like this. He's been miserable, Alexis, and I know it's because he's really crazy about you. Unfortunately, he's got this weird thing about Stone Oil."

"He's miserable only because he signed that lease."

"Maybe, but I don't think so. Anyway, I'm not going to harp on it. I'm just glad to see that at least you two have something going."

Alexis frowned slightly. There was no way she could make Beth understand the truth about their relationship without telling her things that she was loath to reveal.

Beth stayed for a few more minutes, then said she had to get home to make lunch for the girls and Rusty. As she walked down the hall to the front door, she waved merrily and called out, "Don't forget to come for dinner on Christmas Day."

Alexis smiled and waved back. "Sure."

The rest of the day passed fairly smoothly. Lunch was quick, and Brant didn't go out of his way to be nasty, although Alexis still felt highly uncomfortable around him. During the afternoon she found a book that caught her interest, and also managed to take a brief nap. Paul and Brant spent their time out in the barn and corral. Before they came in for supper, Alexis took her novel upstairs. She intended to go straight to her room toinght after she put Paul to bed. She would not make the same mistake of going downstairs because she had nothing to do in her room. Tonight she would stay out of Brant's way and make sure that nothing further happened between them.

Brant grilled steaks for supper and Alexis tossed a salad.

"What a team," Brant joked.

Alexis grimaced and ignored his remark. She had no desire to be part of a jolly little family group tonight. "Shall I fix a vegetable?" she asked coolly. "Broccoli? Green peas?"

"Broccoli," Brant said decisively. "I hate peas."

"I learned how to ride," Paul announced from his perch on the kitchen stool. "Daddy taught me everything today. I know how to get on a horse and how to hold the reins. See, tight like this, not all loose."

"That's terrific," Alexis responded, putting a package of frozen broccoli into a pot of water to boil.

"I thought we'd go to the cattle auction in Amarillo sometime after Christmas. How does that sound?" Brant asked.

"Oh, boy!" Paul answered swiftly.

"I think I'll probably let you two do that by yourselves," Alexis said.

"Oh, you ought to come," Brant urged. "Have you ever been to an auction?"

"No."

"See, it will be a new experience. You know, you shouldn't turn down new experiences. Just think what you could learn."

Alexis shrugged. "Maybe."

"Besides, think how boring it'll be here by yourself all day."

"It might be a relief."

"Now, Alexis, you'll hurt my feelings."

"Why all this sudden joviality?" Alexis demanded sharply, bringing the salad and the dish of broccoli to the table.

"You like me better gloomy?" He grinned. "Sorry. I

can't help feeling good today. I, uh, got rid of a lot of tension last night."

"Terrific," Alexis snapped. "I'm glad *someone* enjoyed himself. *I* certainly didn't."

"Now, didn't your mother ever teach you that it was a sin to tell a lie?"

Alexis could think of no reply, so she dug into her food, eating as quickly as she could, then put her plate in the sink and left the kitchen.

They spent an hour or two in the den watching television with Paul. Alexis was careful to avoid the couch, where Brant sat, and she settled into a chair, even though it was difficult to see the set from that angle. Brant glanced over at her, and his amused expression conveyed that he understood very well why she had sat there. Alexis clenched her fists. If anything, she had only emphasized her weakness where he was concerned.

At eight o'clock, she rose and guided Paul upstairs. After he was washed and in his pajamas and tucked into bed, she closed the door behind her and crossed the hall to her room. She went through her nightly routine of cleaning her face and brushing her hair, then changed into a pale blue nightgown that clung to her breasts and fell loosely away beneath her bust. It was not the most conducive attire for cooling a man's lust, but then, she wasn't going to be wearing it around Brant.

She sat down on the bed, pulling the covers up to her waist and propping the pillows behind her back, then began to read. The minutes crawled by, and Alexis realized that all of her senses were alert and concentrated on the stairs and hall.

Sternly, she set herself to reading again, trying to ignore what lay beyond her closed door. About an hour later she heard his booted feet on the stairs, and her fingers gripped the novel convulsively. Keeping her eyes on the print but not really seeing it, she listened as he paused at his room, then strode toward hers.

The door opened, and Alexis forced her head up. Brant loomed in the doorway, large and powerful, and her heart began to thud in shaky leaps.

"What are you doing in here?" he asked gruffly.

"I am sleeping here," Alexis retorted with as much calm as she could muster, trying to ignore the fear and anticipation gripping her stomach.

"Oh?" Brant shrugged. "Personally, I prefer my own room, but if you'd rather—" He closed the door firmly behind him and came toward her.

Chapter 16

Brant sat down in a chair a few feet from the bed and pulled off his boots, dropping them on the floor. Alexis stared at him, stunned, until he rose and leisurely, deliberately, began to unbutton his shirt. At last her paralysis broke, and she leaped from the bed to face him.

Alexis knew that Brant acted the way he did toward her out of anger. He despised her, and this casual taking of her, this forcing her to submit to him—and even enjoy it—was his way of expressing his disgust. Perhaps if she could lessen the anger, even at the expense of her own pride, he would feel appeased and leave her alone.

"I—I feel I should apologize to you for the things I've said about your abandoning Paul," she began. He raised his eyebrows in surprise but did not stop undressing. "Beth told me today that you wanted to take him with you, but his mother wouldn't let him go. I'm sorry for the comments I made about that. I'm sure they must have hurt. I realize now that I was mistaken."

Brant looked at her for a moment, and a smile touched his face. "Why, Alexis," he said, "you give me hope. Apologizing is quite a step for you. Maybe I'll make a real woman of you after all." He shrugged off his shirt and dropped it on the floor.

"Oh!" A blaze ripped through Alexis at his taunting reply. "I might have known that you couldn't even accept an apology without being nasty about it! Let me tell you something, Brant McClure. You wouldn't know a real woman if you met one! Obviously the only kind of female you've ever associated with are sluts or empty-headed girls. Just because I don't happen to want to be barefoot and pregnant doesn't make me any less a woman! And, believe me, your forcing me into your bed doesn't make me any more of one!"

Brant chuckled as he stepped out of his jeans and padded across the floor to her. He slid his brown hands into her hair on both sides of her face, imprisoning it so that she was forced to stare up into his amber eyes. He bent and kissed her, a long, deep, melting kiss that left her trembling and weak. His mouth left hers to trace a fiery path across her cheek, ending at the lobe of her ear, working it with his lips and teeth and tongue, until finally a tiny whimper of desire rose from her throat.

Alexis clutched at his muscular arms, her only mainstay in the dizzying vortex into which Brant pulled her, as his mouth came back to claim hers in hot, breathless passion. Wrapping his arms around her, Brant backed her to the bed and bore her down onto it, his mouth never ceasing its sweet exploration. Alexis could not even find the strength to resist, could only cling to him as his lips roamed her face and throat, searching out every sensitive spot, nibbling at the tender cord of her neck, sending hot fingers of desire shooting through her.

His weight rolled from her, and he pulled her nightgown off, then lay on his side, propped on his elbow, his eyes greedily caressing her.

"Please," Alexis said weakly, "at least turn out the light."

"No. I want to look at you. You are far too beautiful to hide in the dark."

Gently, his hand moved over her flesh, exploring where his eyes looked, covering her breasts, rousing the soft pink peaks to hardness, delving between her legs, discovering all her tender, responsive places and stroking them until her veins burned and threatened to explode. Alexis writhed beneath his fiery touch, unable to combat the incredible pleasure he evoked in her. She was ashamed to reveal how much he held her in his power, and yet she knew that if he stopped, she would beg him to continue.

Brant's warm mouth assailed her, following the path of his hands, arousing her almost to a frenzy as he withdrew, then began again. Alexis moaned, digging her hands wildly into his thick hair. He slid farther down her body, his lips and tongue sending spasms of delight through her.

"Oh, no," she breathed. "Brant, please . . ."

He chuckled low in his throat. "Don't worry. You'll like it, I promise."

Alexis gasped and quivered, torn by passions she had never known. "Brant!" she cried softly as the storm he had built now burst and pounded through her. She arched her back and dug her fingernails into the sheets, writhing mindlessly in the sweet agony he gave her.

Slowly she calmed, and he stretched out beside her, his hand gently caressing her. Alexis felt liquid, lazy, but she could not resist a desire to reach out and touch his body as he had touched hers, trailing her fingers across the wiry mat of hair on his chest, following the V of hair to his taut stomach, down to the pulsing proof of his desire.

"Ahh," Brant groaned, closing his eyes. She snatched her hand away. Firmly, he replaced it. "No. Go on."

Hesitantly, Alexis stroked his bursting manhood as she leaned over him, letting her lips travel across his chest. Brant's breath was hard and rasping in his throat, and he wrapped his hands in her luxuriant hair. Finally, he rolled over, pulling Alexis under him, and plunged into her, filling her with exquisite satisfaction. Again and again he thrust, each movement reawakening her spent passion, until once more the fires flared in her, higher and higher still, exploding deliciously as he shuddered and peaked.

Brant collapsed against Alexis, his arms still around her. His skin was salty against her mouth. "Alexis. Oh, sweet, sweet Alexis."

Alexis's eyelids fluttered open; beneath her cheek was the smooth firmness of Brant's arm. With a sigh, she rolled away from him and lay for a moment staring at the ceiling. He had done it again. He seemed to take some perverse pleasure in conquering her, in proving his mastery of her. This would not be the last time.

She rose and padded into the bathroom to shower, her mind still roaming futilely over what she ought to do. She adjusted the spray and stepped in, lathering her hair with soap and rinsing it out. She picked up a washcloth and began to soap it, when suddenly the frosty glass door opened and she turned, her heart jumping in surprise. Brant stepped in beside her, enclosing them together in the tiny space.

Silently, he took the cloth from her hand and began to wash her, gliding the soapy cloth across her shoulders and breasts and down to her abdomen, even kneeling to wash her feet and legs. He rinsed her off with his bare hands, and Alexis had to close her eyes against the overpowering sensations coursing through her. Brant handed the washcloth to her.

"Now you can return the favor."

"No, I won't do it," Alexis retorted, flinging the cloth back at him and stepping out of the shower.

Brant cut off the water and followed her, gripping her arm with a steely hand and ripping away the towel Alexis had wrapped around her body. Possessively, he pulled her to him and kissed her, forcing his tongue into her mouth, running his hands over her slick, wet body.

"Why do you do this?" Alexis groaned, near tears, when at last his mouth left hers.

A thin smile touched his face, and his eyes glittered as he stared down at her. "Because you belong to me, Alexis."

"I don't! I hate you. You hate me. Why do you even bother?"

"I don't give a damn what you've done," he said huskily. "I don't even care any longer what kind of person you are. You may be a bitch. You may have a heart like a rock and may have tried every way you can to hurt me. But none of that matters. I want you, and you want me. You can't deny it. And you are mine. Whatever you do or say, you won't leave here; you won't refuse me your favors. Your body falsifies all your brave words. You are mine, for as long as I want you. Don't forget it."

Again he kissed Alexis, until the world began to rock around her, and then suddenly he released her and stepped back. Her breath was coming in quick little pants, and she leaned slightly toward him, her eyes dark with passion. Already her veins thrummed with desire, her loins aching for him. Abruptly he turned and walked out of the room, leaving Alexis standing there. She slumped against the shower door, the unspent adrenalin turning her knees weak. Brant had purposely aroused her and then left her willing and unfulfilled, just to prove his control over her.

She completely despised him, she thought, slowly toweling herself dry. Brant was egotistical and a thousand other things even worse. But Alexis could not deny that the longing in her was real, and so was the fact that she could not pack and leave. He was right. She really did not want to go.

Later that morning, when Alexis and Paul were in the den, intent on a game of Parcheesi, Brant walked in and asked, "How would you two like to go riding this morning?"

"Yeah!" Paul jumped up, the game forgotten. "Come on, Allie."

"No, I don't think I will go," Alexis responded. The less time she spent with Brant, the better.

"Oh." Paul's face fell in disappointment. "But I want you to. Don't you know how to ride?"

Brant laughed. "That is questionable, Paul."

Stung, Alexis said, "Of course I know how to ride. And now that I think about it, I believe I will come."

"Good!"

"We're going to ride over to Fred Miller's place," Brant explained. "He just called and said that two of my cows and a heifer have somehow gotten into his west pasture."

"You mean we're going to get them?" Alexis asked, astonished. "How?"

He grinned. "Why, just herd them back into their own pasture, that's how."

"Can you do it without one of your hands? I mean, I can't imagine Paul or me being much help."

"Probably not," he agreed with a devilish grin. "But I think we'll be able to manage. Don't you, Paul?"

"You bet!"

"I didn't bring any boots," Alexis confessed. "And the only coat I've got is full-length."

"That's okay," Brant told her. "I can find you something."

He disappeared upstairs, returning minutes later with a scuffed pair of women's cowboy boots and a heavy pea jacket.

"Here's something Beth left," he said, tossing the jacket on a chair. "That ought to fit you. And these are some old boots I found in the attic. See if they'll fit you."

"Are they Beth's too?" Alexis asked as she sat down to untie her sneakers. "I would have figured her feet were smaller than mine."

"I think they were my mother's," he replied, his

voice flat, and Alexis wished she could have taken back her question.

She shoved her foot firmly into the boot, and it fitted, although it was a trifle tight around the toes. "I think it will be okay."

"Good. Put the other one on, then, and let's go."

Alexis quickly finished dressing and followed Brant and a skipping Paul out to the barn. After Brant saddled their horses, they rode east toward the pale winter sun.

It was a good two hours before they passed through the gate that led into Fred Miller's property, and it took another thirty minutes to locate Brant's stock.

Brant circled the steers, yelling and whipping his hat in the air, and the cattle took off in a shambling run in the general direction of the gate. "You two keep behind them, and I'll head them off when they start to stray."

The cows herded fairly easily, but the frisky heifer kept darting off in different directions, and Brant had to race after her to keep her with the others. When at last they reached his gate, Brant leaned down and pulled it open.

"You stand on that side," he directed Alexis and Paul, spacing them, "and if any of them runs toward you instead of to the gate, scare it back. I'll do the rest."

He circled the three animals, pulling them into a small bunch, and drove them toward the gate. The heifer darted for Alexis, who stood in her stirrups, waving her arms wildly and yelling as loud as she could. The heifer stopped dead still, sprang on stiff legs, then bucked, kicking behind her, and charged back toward Brant. With a whoop, he waved her into his pasture after the other two cows, followed by Alexis and Paul. Once they were all on Brant's property, he secured the gate to the fencepost by wrapping heavy wire around both.

"Wow, that was neat!" Paul exclaimed, his eyes shining.

Alexis laughed. Even she felt excited and warm, despite the chill winter breeze. "What now?" she asked merrily, her eyes dancing, causing Brant's face to soften.

He walked his horse to hers and leaned across, cupping a hand around her neck, and touched his lips gently to hers. "You make a fantastic cowgirl." He released her and settled back into his saddle. "Now we have to locate the break where they got out."

Riding the fence was a slow, tiresome job, and Alexis's stomach began to growl hungrily. She wished that she had thought of bringing sandwiches with them. After an hour they came upon a place where the top two wires had come unfastened from a low post and hung loosely, giving the cattle enough room to jump across into the other pasture.

Brant dismounted, pulling the saddlebag from his horse. Alexis and Paul got off their horses, glad of the opportunity to stretch their aching legs. Quickly, Brant repaired the damage with a hammer and fence staples from his saddlebag.

"Okay, that does it," he declared, rising. "Now, let's go home and get something to eat."

"Great," Alexis said, not even protesting as Brant boosted her into the saddle. "I'm starving."

"Me, too!" Paul put in.

"You, my dear, are always starving," Alexis laughed.

They went home at a faster pace than they had started out, alternating between a trot and a rapid walk. The nearer they drew, the more willingly the horses clip-clopped along. When they reached the yard, Alexis slid off her mount, letting Paul and Brant tend to the animals while she went inside to prepare sandwiches and hot soup.

They had a late supper that evening, too, and stayed up longer than usual. Alexis found an old children's book in the den and read "The Night Before Christmas" to Paul, who was consumed by fascination.

Afterward, Brant asked his son if he could tuck him in. To her delight, Paul nodded. Left alone in the den, Alexis aimlessly wandered about, searching for something to occupy her, until Brant returned.

"Well, that is a step forward, isn't it? Paul let you put him to bed." Determinedly, she pushed away the thought that Paul no longer needed her and that she could probably leave any time now.

Brant smiled, the grim lines that often ran beside his mouth absent. "Yes. I don't think I frighten him any longer."

"What time are we going to Beth's tomorrow?"

"I thought we'd let Paul open his presents here, and then we could go over there about twelve or so."

"Okay." Alexis stood and stretched awkwardly. "I guess I'll go up to bed now." She paused, trembling, not sure whether she wanted him to say he would join her or would stay away.

"Is that an invitation?" His smile was frosty, but a golden light danced in his eyes.

"Of course not," Alexis snapped automatically, knowing even as she said it that it wasn't true.

"No?" His head tilted a little as he watched her carefully. "Then I suppose I should be a gentleman and say that I won't bother you." He paused, his eyes glinting mischievously. "But then, I've never been a gentleman."

He scooped her up in his arms, cradling her against his chest, and started for the stairs. Alexis did not even murmur a token resistance, simply curled her arms around his neck and buried her face in his shoulder. It was awful and weak to want him like this, but it was so warm being pressed against him that she no longer even cared.

Upstairs in his room, Brant set her down gently and cupped his hands around her face. For a moment he looked into her eyes and then bent to kiss her, at first softly, then harder, with passion. Alexis returned his kiss, molding her body to his as he slid his hands across her shoulders and down her back, his sinewy fingers lingering over her.

Brant's mouth moved over her cheek, his hot breath sending a ripple of fire through her. He nibbled at her earlobe, working the soft flesh tenderly between his teeth. His work-roughened hands beneath her blouse felt delicious against her smooth skin. As Alexis pulled away to unfasten her clothes, Brant watched, hardly breathing, his eyes bright with hunger. And when she stood naked before him, her pale body gleaming in the dim light, a soft hissing breath escaped him.

He pulled her into his arms, his lips taking her mouth greedily, his hands caressing her body urgently. Alexis felt the roughness of his jeans against her flesh; her breasts were crushed against his chest. She was filled with exhilaration.

"Lovely," Brant murmured almost incoherently, his mouth moving down over her neck. "Please. Let me."

"Brant." His name was a sigh on her lips.

A tremor shook him and he ripped at his clothing, cursing softly at the buttons that impeded him. Alexis lay back upon the bed as he undressed, a hot weakness sweeping over her at the sight of his brown body, whose power she knew so well.

Then he was beside her, his strong hands gentle upon her skin, stroking and arousing her until at last she moaned her passion. Slowly Brant entered her, filling her with his hardness, and just as slowly he moved to his peak, carefully stroking the flames of her desire until she shuddered and cried out helplessly, lost in the waves of pleasure that flooded her.

Paul was up early Christmas morning, despite his late bedtime the night before. When he rushed into Brant's room, chattering excitedly, he was completely unperturbed by the sight of Alexis and his father in bed together. Alexis smiled and assured him that they would be down very soon to have breakfast.

"But first you have to go back and put socks and shoes on. You'll freeze like that," she told him with mock sternness.

"Okay." He raced off.

"Good Lord," Brant groaned, throwing aside the covers and quickly pulling on his jeans, "I've got to put up the stocking before he gets down there!"

Alexis chuckled and said, "I'll keep him up here a little longer."

Paul's joy at the sight of his stuffed stocking hanging from the mantel in the den made Alexis and Brant smile with parental indulgence, and Brant got out his camera and started taking snapshots with all the ease of a longtime father. After the stocking was emptied, they ate breakfast, then went into the living room for Paul to open his mass of presents.

As the boy tore through them, exclaiming over the toy gun and holster, the bike, the fully equipped spaceship, Brant leaned toward Alexis and whispered, "I left his big present over at Beth's because I couldn't hide it here."

"What is it?" she whispered back.

"Can't tell," he said, shaking his head.

"Monster."

"Can I ride my bike now?" Paul asked. "Will you teach me, Daddy?"

"Not right now. We have to go to Beth's for dinner. But I promise I'll teach you when we get back this afternoon."

"Okay," Paul agreed. "Can I take some of my presents with me?"

"Sure." Brant frowned as he watched Paul search through his gifts, and he turned a trifle hesitantly to Alexis. "I—I'm afraid I don't have a present for you. I didn't know you would be here. I wish—" He broke off and glanced away.

"That's all right," Alexis said quickly. Yesterday or the day before, she would have said that she would never even think of giving Brant McClure a present, but at his words she found herself suddenly wishing that she had something for him.

"I guess we'd better go on over to Beth's," Brant said awkwardly.

Alexis nodded and went to get her coat and Paul's. They drove in silence to his sister's house.

Beth opened the door with a happy smile, her cheeks flushed and her eyes sparkling with an unusual light. Brant cast her an odd look, but hugged her and said, "Merry Christmas, Beth," without comment. The two girls came rushing into the kitchen to meet Paul, and after his initial shyness, he went off with them to their playroom until dinner. Beth wet her lips and put her arm through Brant's, shooting a meaningful glance at Alexis, which left Alexis thoroughly puzzled. Beth probably had another scheme going, but what? She seemed perfectly satisfied with the way things were between Alexis and Brant.

"Let's go into the den and see Rusty," Beth said, pulling Brant along.

Rusty was talking to a middle-aged woman. She was attractive, despite the gray that streaked her light brown hair and the wrinkles that lined her eyes. Alexis's first thought was that the woman reminded her of someone. Her attention was distracted by Brant, who had pulled up short and was staring at the woman, his face draining of color.

The woman rose. "Hello, Brant." Her voice was pleasant but shaky, as though she were afraid.

Without a word, Brant turned and strode out of the room. At that instant it all became clear to Alexis: this woman was his mother!

"Oh, dear," Beth sighed. "I was afraid he might do something like that."

Her mother sank back into the chair. "It's all right, Beth. I knew I was running that risk when you invited me here. At least I'm back in touch with you."

Alexis quickly left the den, running through the kitchen and out into the driveway. Brant stood slumped against the side of his Ford, looking blankly across the field.

When he saw her, he straightened and said, "Go get Paul. We're leaving."

"No. Not until I've had a chance to talk to you," Alexis replied. "Don't you think that was a little hasty, not to mention rude?"

"Rude! Oh, forgive my bad manners, Miss Stone. Somehow I find it a little hard to be polite to a mother who walked out on us over twenty years ago."

"My, you are a superior being," Alexis retorted sarcastically. "I wish I could attain that high level of grace you seem to think you have."

"Just what is that supposed to mean?"

"It means that you are acting like a baby, not like a grown man. That woman in there gave birth to you and raised you through your childhood. Don't you think she deserves at least a few minutes of your precious time? Don't you think she rates a little leniency and compassion?"

"Damn it, Alexis, she didn't want anything to do with us then. Why should I welcome her back with open arms now? Don't you understand? She abandoned us!"

"She left your father, she left Barrett, she left a life she couldn't stand, but that *doesn't* mean she didn't love you. And it doesn't mean that it cost her nothing to leave or that she didn't regret it later. My God, Brant, at least give her a chance!"

"Why? Just because Beth is a sentimental fool and has decided it would be wonderful for the three of us to get back together doesn't mean that *I* have to fall in with it!"

"Look, I don't know anything about your mother. I don't know how bored she was or how infatuated she was with my father or how much she loved you. But I do know that you're being unfair. What if Paul were that unfair to you? He could be, you know. You deserted him. How is he to know how hard you tried to get him back? He could have said, 'You didn't want me nine years ago and I don't want you now,' but he didn't. All I'm asking is that you act as adult and civilized as your nine-year-old son."

Brant's mouth twisted. "Alexis, don't meddle. This is none of your affair."

"Oh, isn't it? I'm supposed to share your bed like a good little concubine and never express my opinion, huh? Well, don't count on that, fella. In case you've forgotten, it was my father whom she left yours for. That gives me some interest in the matter. Besides, you've walled up all your hurt and hatred for her all these years and held it against all women, including me. I know what a kick you get out of humiliating me—"

"Alexis, don't," he said, his voice choked.

"Don't what? Don't tell the truth?"

"Damn it, that woman's got nothing to do with you. She had an affair and divorced my father in hopes of getting Alec Stone. She broke my father's heart."

"Is your father the only person who raised you until you were twelve? Did you have no love for your mother at all?"

"Of course I did."

"Did that love vanish the day she walked out? Of course not. I'll tell you what it did. You hid it inside you, buried it deep, saying she meant nothing to you any more. You cut it off unnaturally, and it festered into a bitter hatred. And the only way you'll ever get rid of that is to face up to her, talk to her, admit what you felt, and *let it go*! Don't you realize that when a man of thirty-four runs from a room, unable even to sit and talk for a few minutes to a middle-aged woman, something is wrong? If you truly had no feeling for her, if you really didn't love her, you wouldn't be so scared."

His brows drew together. "I'm not scared of her. I despise her. She's a whore."

"Oh, how high and mighty you are! It must be nice to be so far above the rest of us that you can judge us all.

I'm a whore, your mother's a whore, everyone but you is deceitful and wicked. I can't imagine anyone so exalted as you. I guess I should be honored that you grace my bed at night, even if you do use a little force sometimes. Or that you deign to talk to me, even though you do call me a lying, conniving bitch."

"Shut up, Alexis!" he barked, his face contorted.

"Or what? You'll hit me again? Or will you punish me like you do your mother, by walking away? Good heavens, Brant, can't you bend even a little? Can't you admit that other people are human, too? You were twelve years old when she left. Have you ever thought about how she felt? You condemn her for having slept with Alec, but look at yourself. You're sleeping with his daughter. Why is your mother so much worse than you?"

Alexis thought for a moment that he was going to explode with anger, but Brant merely whirled sharply, opened the car door, and got in, slamming it shut behind him and starting the engine. With a roar, the tires spitting gravel, he ground the car into gear and drove off. Alexis sighed and slumped wearily. So much for that good deed. She had only made him more furious. She turned slowly and went back into the house.

Beth met her in the kitchen, a worried look on her face. "I thought I heard a car— What happened?"

"He drove off," Alexis said in disgust. "I tried to reason with him, but no such luck. I made him even angrier."

"Oh, well, maybe he'll drive off some of it. I was afraid this might not work, but I knew he would flatly refuse if I told him I had written Mother and asked her to come for Christmas. So . . ."

"Why did you? I mean, Brant is so set against her. How come you don't feel the same?"

"Oh, I was pretty upset for a long time, and probably still am in some ways. I doubt that I'll ever feel close or comfortable with her. But I was younger than Brant when she left. I guess it wasn't such an impressionable age. Besides, I think my being a woman helps me understand her better. My father was often a hard man to deal with, so upright and honorable. Even Brant and I were never able to live up to his ideal. Eventually, I accepted the idea that I wasn't perfect, but it always hurt Brant when he disappointed Daddy. Anyway, I guess it's like those adopted children who search all over for their real parents even though they've been abandoned, even though they never knew them. There's a pull there, and it's even stronger for someone you knew for eight years and loved."

"But," Alexis mused, "the sense of abandonment must be stronger, too, at least with Brant."

"I suppose so. Well, why don't we go back into the den and make the best of it?"

They joined Rusty and Mrs. Griggs, who were making awkward conversation.

"Mother, this is Alexis Stone," Beth said, and the woman glanced at Alexis in surprise.

"Hello, how are you?" she murmured, her eyes examining Alexis's face intently.

"Alexis, this is my mother, Selena Griggs."

"How do you do, Mrs. Griggs?"

"Please call me Selena."

Alexis went to the couch and sat down beside her, determined to make conversation in order to alleviate the clumsy void that Brant's departure had brought about. Beth and Rusty moved discreetly to the door, leaving the two women alone together.

"Are you Alec Stone's daughter?" Selena asked.

"Yes, I am," Alexis replied, noting that the woman's eyes were the same amber color as her son's.

A faint smile touched Selena's mouth. "What strange twists fate plays on us."

Alexis did not know precisely how to answer that statement, so she merely nodded.

Selena continued. "I suppose you have heard from Elizabeth or Brant about my leaving."

"If you mean, do I know about you and my father, yes, I do," Alexis returned calmly.

"When I first saw Alec," Selena mused, "I thought he was the handsomest, most sophisticated man I had ever met. I guess he still is. I knew that nothing would ever come of it. I never deluded myself that Alec loved me. But after him, I knew that I could never be content with my life as it was. I wasn't meant to be a rancher's wife. I no longer even loved Judson. And I couldn't bear to live out the rest of my days being miserable for the sake of my children, as so many women did. No doubt you could say that makes me a very selfish person . . . Maybe I was."

Alexis made a deprecating gesture. "It isn't necessary for you to tell me all this."

"But I want to. I need to, I suppose. You see, I had this little speech all prepared for Brant, but he didn't stay to listen to it. I'm using you as a substitute. Do you mind?"

"You don't have to justify yourself to me. And my relaying the message to Brant won't do any good. I'm not someone he relies on."

"Brant is too much like his father. Judson was one of the most stiff-necked men—he could never forgive or let go of a hurt. Because I left him and the children, he refused to let me see them. Back then, a man could get away with things like that if his wife abandoned the children. I wrote Brant once when he was in college, hoping he would come and see me, but he sent back a withering reply and refused to see me. Oh, the bitterness in that boy . . ."

"I'm sorry."

"I can't blame him. I was aware of the risk I was taking when I left. Brant was always such a loving child, so warm and close. I knew it might break his heart and turn him against me. Sometimes in the past, I wished I hadn't done what I did, although I am happy now with my husband. But for Brant's sake, I think maybe it would have been better if I could have stuck it out a few more years, until he was old enough to understand. I'm afraid, though, that in those days I thought more with my emotions than with my mind." She sighed, tears brimming in her eyes.

Alexis looked awkwardly down at her hands. "I—I don't think you should blame yourself, Selena. After all, you gave Brant twelve years of your life. If he learned to be warm and loving then, and chose to cover up those qualities later, there is very little you can do about it now. It's been over twenty years, after all, and Brant has voluntarily decided to be cold and with-drawn. He would like to blame that on you, I'm sure, but I think he has to be responsible for what he's done as an adult."

"That's what I tell myself. But it's hard to assuage a mother's guilt." She smiled a little shakily. "I'm glad that Brant has you. You seem a remarkably reasonable girl."

Alexis laughed. "I'm glad Brant didn't hear you say that. He thinks I'm the most *un*reasonable person he's met. I don't know what Beth has told you, but—"

"Oh, she said that your relationship was tenuous," Selena put in quickly. "But as pretty and bright and nice as you are, I can't imagine Brant being silly enough to let you go."

Alexis started to say that the decision was not entirely Brant's to make, but bit back her words. After all, a mother could hardly imagine someone not wanting her son.

A few minutes later Paul came into the den to show Alexis the fantastic yo-yo skills that Beth's children had taught him. When Alexis introduced him to his grand-mother, he politely shook her hand and then proceeded to study her closely.

"You are very pretty for a grandmother," he an-nounced at last.

"Well, thank you," she chuckled. "And I am very pleased to have you as a grandson. Did you know that you are my only grandson?"

He shook his head and stood patiently beside Alexis, although his twitching fingers revealed his eagerness to get back to his cousins.

Alexis gave him a little shove. "Okay, you can go and play some more. But be sure to wash your hands. We're going to eat in a few minutes."

"Okay," Paul said, and ran off.

"He is adorable," Selena sighed, staring after him. "Such a sad story . . ."

"You all ready for dinner?" Beth asked from the doorway.

"Sure. Whenever you are."

"Well, I think it's all done. Shall we put it on the table?"

The women quickly brought out a large platter of turkey, mountainous bowls of vegetables, sweet potatoes, and stuffing, and dishes of assorted relishes. The children were summoned, and everyone sat down at the long, formal dining table.

Thirty minutes later, when they had stuffed themselves to the limit and were debating whether they had any room for the dessert of mincemeat pie, they heard the kitchen door open and heavy steps cross the floor. Before they had time to look at one another in surprise, Brant appeared in the dining-room doorway.

Alexis stared at him, speechless, her hands clenching the napkin in her lap. Please, don't let him do anything terrible, she found herself praying. Beside her, she felt Selena tense, every nerve on edge.

Brant's gaze flickered toward Alexis, then over to his mother. He looked as taut as a violin string himself, and he bit at his lip nervously before he finally spoke. "Sorry I'm so late. And I apologize for my bad temper earlier." Stiffly, he moved toward the table and placed a small picture frame beside Selena. "I went home and got this. I thought you might like to have it." He paused, then forced out through reluctant lips, "Mother."

Tears welled in Selena's eyes and poured down her

cheeks, but she did not wipe them away. "Oh, Brant, this is that wonderful picture of you and Elizabeth—you were nine and she was five—on that old horse of my daddy's! Thank you." Her words ended in a choked whisper, and she reached out and clasped her son's hand tightly.

"You're welcome," Brant said, his words coming easier now. "Did you guys leave anything for me to eat?"

Chapter 17

They did not remain long after Brant had returned. Alexis helped Beth clear the table and rinse the dishes, leaving Brant alone with Selena. An hour later Brant came into the kitchen, saying he was ready to go. Alexis did not protest. It would be crazy to expect a complete healing in one day, if, indeed, a healing could ever be possible. She called to Paul and refrained from asking Brant to tell her about his conversation with Selena.

When they were out on the driveway, Brant stopped and snapped his fingers as though suddenly remembering something. "Say, I need to get something in Rusty's barn. Hold on a minute," he said, loping off toward the barn.

Alexis shrugged and got into the car with Paul. A few moments later Brant came back, leading a black pony with a white blaze down the front of his face and white stockings on three feet. Paul leaned forward eagerly to look at the animal. Quickly, Alexis opened the door and Paul scrambled out.

Brant raised a hand and motioned to him. "Paul, come look at this pony."

"Wow! He's beautiful!" the boy exclaimed, his eyes shining. "What's his name?"

"I don't know. What do you think his name should

be?" Paul looked at Brant, wonder lighting his face. "It looks to me like Santa must have left him here for you. See this little card attached to his mane? It says 'Paul.'"

"He's mine?" Paul's eyes bulged, then he let out a yell of pure joy. "Oh, boy, can I ride him?"

"I think so. He's already trained." Brant swung Paul onto the animal's back and led the pony around the yard a few times.

Finally, with great reluctance on Paul's part, Brant lifted him and set him on the ground, then took the pony back to the barn.

"Why can't I take him home?" Paul wailed when Brant returned.

"Because I didn't bring the horse trailer with me. I didn't know Santa was going to leave a pony for you over here." Brant smiled at the excited pleasure on his son's face. "But first thing tomorrow morning, we'll come get him."

On the way home the car was filled with Paul's chatter about his horse's beauty and speed and about what name to give him.

"Why don't you name him Blackie?" Alexis suggested. "After his pretty black color. Or maybe Blaze, for the strip of white on his nose."

"Blackie," Paul repeated thoughtfully. "I like that. I'll name him Blackie."

"This horse is going to be all yours," Brant told him. "Every day you're going to have to feed him and curry him and let him out for a little exercise, like I do for the other horses."

Eagerly, Paul agreed, before launching into another discussion of his pony. Alexis smiled and looked at Brant, who gave her a surreptitious wink. When they reached the ranchhouse, Paul bounced out of the car, remembering the delights that awaited him there.

"You going to teach me how to ride my bike now, Daddy?" he reminded Brant of his earlier promise.

"Of course. In just a few minutes," Brant answered.

"Why don't you go into the den and play with some of your other toys? I'm going upstairs to talk with Alexis. I'll come down in a little while and we'll ride that bike. Okay?"

"Okay." Paul trooped merrily off toward the den.

Alexis raised her eyebrows questioningly at Brant, but he said nothing. He put his hand under her elbow and propelled her up the stairs and into his room. Once inside, he locked the door and turned around, crushing her into him in a hard, desperate hug.

"Brant," she protested breathlessly, yet excited by his embrace. "I thought you wanted to talk to me."

"I do," he said. "Like this."

Hungrily, his mouth covered hers while his hands roamed her body, clumsily tugging at her clothing. Brant came to her in need, she knew, and she responded to that need, clinging to him and returning kiss for kiss. With a hot, thirsty passion he backed her to the bed, and they fell upon it in a tangle of arms and legs and clothes, suddenly wild with the emotional overcharge of the day. Alexis didn't know if his lovemaking was a gesture of thanks or of punishment, a release of pent-up emotions or the expression of a tenderness long repressed. Frankly, she did not care. All she knew or wanted to know was the exquisite pleasure of his large, rough hands and hungry, warm mouth caressing her flesh, the wonderful torment as he carried her to newer and higher frenzies that erupted, finally, into a blissful explosion of peace and fulfillment.

"Brant," she breathed, wrapping her arms and legs about him to hold him close. "Oh, Brant."

At breakfast on Monday morning, Brant announced that they were going to Amarillo for the cattle auction.

Paul immediately began to glow with anticipation. "Oh, boy!" he cried. "When can we leave?"

"After breakfast," Brant answered with a grin. "It

opens at nine, and I figured we ought to get there about ten. The really big crowd doesn't gather until the afternoon, when the large lots of cattle are sold. This morning it'll be odd lots and small numbers, but I thought Paul would get just as much enjoyment out of it."

"Are you going to buy anything?" Alexis asked.

"Maybe. I was thinking I might buy Paul a calf of his own to raise."

"Really?" Paul exclaimed, jumping off his chair. "All my very own? What's a calf?"

Brant threw back his head and laughed. "It's a youngster, like you!"

"A baby cow? Gee, Allie, won't that be neat? I can feed him, too, just like my pony!"

Alexis smiled at him. "That will be nice."

"You coming with us?" Brant asked, rising from the table.

"I don't know. I hadn't really thought about it." Her first inclination was to say no, but the idea of spending the day by herself in the rambling house did not hold much appeal. "Would it be interesting?"

"I think so. Now, what *you* think may be a different matter. It's a big auction. They sell about six hundred thousand head of cattle a year."

"You're joking!"

"No. They sell cattle not only from this area but also from all over the country—Florida, California . . . See, this area—Oklahoma, the Texas Panhandle, Colorado, Kansas, Nebraska—provides about eighty percent of the cattle in the United States. In the old days the livestock was shipped from here to the market in Omaha or Chicago and fattened in those areas. Now they've decided it's more feasible to move the feedlots and even the packaging plants to the places where the animals are to begin with."

Brant went out to hitch the small cattle trailer to the back of his car so that he could bring back a calf if he bought one. Alexis dressed hurriedly, stacked the breakfast dishes in the dishwasher, and hustled Paul out the back door.

The drive was pleasant, and Alexis pointed out to Paul the oil wells and drilling rigs they passed. As they neared Pampa, Brant waved ahead to his right.

"Up there is one of the feedlots I was telling you about," he said.

When they came closer to the lot, Alexis leaned forward in amazement. Stretching as far as the eye could see was pen after pen of animals, each stuffed to overflowing.

"It's huge!" she exclaimed. "Look at all those cattle. I can't believe how many of them there are!"

"It's quite an operation," Brant agreed. "And it's brought a lot of business to the area. Fifteen years ago you would never have seen such a sight around here."

They entered the outskirts of Amarillo, driving past grain elevators and feed mills and a bright silver refinery.

"What's that?" Paul asked, staring at the conglomeration of oddly shaped towers and bulbs and tanks.

"A helium plant," Brant replied. "You should see that thing at night, when the lights are on all over the walkways and up and down the ladders. When I was a kid, I thought it looked like a fairyland. You could see it for miles away in the dark."

Brant turned to the right at a sign that read "Western Stockyards," then continued across a set of multiple railroad tracks. Next came the Amarillo Livestock Auction Building. Stretching behind it were wooden pens full of cattle.

They got out of the car and walked into the building. Brant went into the office to fill out the card required of every buyer, and then they approached the ring, which lay in front of the entry.

Tiered seats rose in a semicircle from the floor, and at the center of the room was a wide, curved dirt-covered alley through which the cattle paraded. A tall, sturdy fence of iron bars separated the spectators from the livestock. Two men with prods stood in the ring. Behind the walkway, at a high desk, sat the auctioneer and another man.

There were few people in the room, and Alexis, Brant, and Paul went quickly to their seats. Alexis noted with amusement that sand-filled plastic buckets were scattered throughout the auditorium, to be used as spittoons.

"This once was a real social event for ranchers," Brant told her in a low voice. "You'd see all these old men down here gossiping, maybe buying a steer now and then. That's still the way it is to some extent in the morning, when the small lots and singles are sold. In the afternoon it's more businesslike, with the professional buyers coming in."

As they watched, one of the two men standing in the sale ring opened the door on the left, and a steer was prodded inside. The animal dashed about nervously, lunging against the fence, running at one man or the other, kicking back against the railing. All the while, the auctioneer spoke so rapidly that his words sounded almost like code. Here and there a man in the audience would raise a hand or a finger, or would nod expressionlessly, and the price would go up. Eventually, the auctioneer called out that the steer had been sold, the right-hand door was opened, and the animal bolted out.

He was followed by a larger, calmer steer, which stood stolidly in the ring, swinging his head belligerently from one worker to the other. The men prodded at him to move, and he did so ponderously.

"Why do they want him to run around?" Paul asked.

"To show him off to the buyers, to let them see him from other angles," Brant replied.

"I can't understand what the auctioneer is saying," Alexis complained. "What did that one sell for?"

"Sixty-five dollars a hundred weight," Brant explained as the steer ambled through the opened door, his tail swishing. "That means sixty-five cents per pound."

"How much does he weigh?"

"I don't know exactly. The cattle are weighed after they leave the ring. I would say that one was around nine hundred pounds."

"I didn't realize they were so expensive," Alexis commented.

Enthralled, Paul watched the animals enter and leave the ring, and gasped with mingled delight and trepidation when a heavy steer leaped high against the railing, trying to butt his head through the bars. After a while, a baby calf was let into the ring, jumping on gangly legs and coming to stiff halts to stare around in fear. The bidding began, and soon Brant raised a finger negligently. The bidding continued until the price was up to seventy-eight dollars, and finally the calf went to Brant.

They remained until almost twelve o'clock, watching other cattle being sold, then got up and went into the office, where Brant paid for the calf and received his loading slip.

"That's it?" Alexis asked.

"That's it. Of course, if I were from out of state, I'd have to do more. I'd have to give them the proper papers for the state where I was going to take the cattle, and they'd do the vaccinating or whatever had to be done. They keep a vet out here full time."

Paul and Alexis were awed by the massiveness of the pens, in which young men and women moved on horseback, directing cattle toward the auction ring.

Alexis turned to Brant in surprise. "You mean they use girls in this masculine stronghold?"

Brant grinned. "Yeah. They found out that teen-age girls are more responsible and hard-working than teen-age boys. I'd say that now they have about six girl horsebackers."

"What do they do?"

"When the weighmaster calls to them for a certain

pen of cattle, they're supposed to move the animals in here. The procedure has to go smoothly for the auction to run efficiently." He handed his loading slip to one of the workers and then went out to back his car and trailer into position. Once the calf was loaded, he pulled away, parked the car, and unhitched the trailer.

"I think I'll leave the trailer here. It'd be rather cumbersome to lug it around Amarillo and the canyon. We can pick it up tonight before we leave. Well, what do you say to getting a hamburger, then going down to Palo Duro Canyon?"

"Sounds fine," Alexis agreed, and Paul, of course, cheered for the hamburger.

Alexis gasped her surprise as they drove down the steep, winding road into Palo Duro Canyon. "I didn't realize it was so big!" she cried, craning to look at the bluffs and outcroppings. "It's like a small Grand Canyon. I thought it was just some river breaks."

"It is pretty large," Brant agreed. "The Comanches used to winter here. In fact, the cavalry broke the Comanche resistance here in the late 1800s. They drove the Indian ponies over the cliffs into the canyon, effectively wiping out the one thing the Comanches absolutely had to have to exist. The buffalo, of course, were already gone, and without ponies, there was nothing for the Indians to do except go meekly to the reservation in Oklahoma."

"Oh, no!" Alexis exclaimed. "How horrible! How could they kill all those horses?"

"They looked at things differently then, I guess. The white men did so much out here that seems barbaric to us now."

Alexis pointed to the ruffled-looking base of the cliffs, striped in yellow, red, and dusty mauve. "Look at the colors on those cliffs."

"Those are called Spanish skirts."

"I can see why," Alexis said with a laugh. "It's amazing that dirt could bring out such colors."

They drove through the canyon, Brant pointing out the sights and telling them the names given to the strange outcroppings that adorned the canyon walls: Sad Monkey, Lighthouse, Devil's Slide. They crossed several streams that flowed thinly across the road itself; there were no bridges over these shallow stretches of water.

"These are water crossings," Brant explained. "Usually the water's so low that there's no problem getting through. But sometimes it'll flood, and then the crossings are impassable."

"Flood?" Alexis repeated in disbelief. "I thought it never rained enough here to cause a flood."

"Rarely," Brant agreed with a grin. "But every once in a while there'll be a real gully-washer. The rain will come down so hard and so fast, the ground can't absorb it, and then these dry creeks will really swell. A couple of years ago there was a big flood down here, and the people in the canyon were stranded. They couldn't cross any of the streams, and they had to be helicoptered out. That was quite a storm."

"Does the water really go as high as those markers show?" Alexis asked, pointing to the white posts with black marks indicated at foot levels, all the way up to six feet.

"I've never seen it," Brant admitted, "but I know that at times it'll go several feet over the road."

At the end of the canyon, they stopped at a shady little park dotted with picnic tables and got out to walk around. Soon they were climbing one of the bluffs that was less steep. Panting, but full of enthusiasm, Alexis kept up with Brant and Paul until they reached a large outcropping of rock above which the cliff rose sheerly. When he had clambered to the top, Brant reached down to pull Paul up and help Alexis. Holding tightly to his hand, she struggled upward and found herself standing on the ledge, Brant's arms tight around her.

The chilly winter breeze touched her face and tugged at the escaping tendrils of hair. For a moment she was lost in his arms, aware of nothing but the cool air, the warmth of his chest, the golden glint of his eyes as they looked down into hers. He reached out and began to pull the pins from her upswept hair, digging his fingers into its luxuriance.

"You belong here," he said huskily, his hands holding her head still as he looked at her. His eyes swept her face hungrily, as though soaking up the picture of her. "You're beautiful and dangerous and tough, just like this land."

Alexis could not tear her gaze away from him. She was mesmerized by his words and eyes, conscious only of a longing that this moment would last forever. Then Paul spoke, and the magic was gone. Brant released her and turned to his son, and Alexis was aware of a sharp pang of loss.

They returned to the bottom of the canyon and drove back the way they had come, stopping to ride the Sad Monkey Railroad, which ran up and around a small portion of the canyon. As they left it, Brant showed them the outdoor amphitheater where a musical drama, *Texas*, was performed each summer.

"It's something to see," he said. "They use the land behind the stage for part of the action, so the characters can ride in and out on horses. A railroad engine comes through at the end, and they even have an amazingly realistic summer storm with thunder and lightning."

By the time they left the canyon, it was growing late enough for an early supper. Brant drove through Amarillo to a steak and prime-rib restaurant that he particularly liked. Alexis had to agree, when she bit into her thick, juicy steak, that it was one of the best she had ever tasted. They ate hungrily, in a companionable silence, and Alexis realized with amazement that this was the only day she had spent with Brant that had passed in such unadulterated pleasure. There had been no sarcastic interplay between them, none of the usual struggle.

"Why, Brant!" a cool, feminine voice drawled

behind Alexis, slicing into the friendly calm that presided at the table.

Brant looked up, and his face went stiff and blank. "Hello, Libby."

Libby! The food suddenly tasted like ashes in Alexis's mouth. Libby was the name of Brant's girlfriend from Amarillo. Deliberately, Alexis did not swivel her head to look at the woman, but waited with seeming indifference until Libby walked around the table to stand beside Brant.

At her first glimpse of the woman, Alexis's heart sank. Libby was stunningly attractive, with a statuesque figure that any man would have fallen for. Her hair was thick and black, and she wore it in a smooth coil on the nape of her neck, the severity of the style only emphasizing the lush sensuality of her lips and down-turned eyes. Her complexion was smooth and white, with just the right touch of color in her cheeks. It made Alexis think regretfully of her own redhead's skin, which tended to freckle deplorably and flushed at the faintest emotion.

Libby swept Alexis with silver-gray eyes, then turned them on Brant, clearly dismissing Alexis as inconsequential. She placed a long, slender, perfectly manicured hand on Brant's shoulder in a familiar way.

"Brant, darling, where have you been? It's been ages since you've been in Amarillo!"

"I've been working, Libby," Brant answered flatly. "You know how it is. We came to Amarillo today to show Paul the auction."

"Oh, is this your darling little boy?" Libby gushed, turning to Paul. "What a handsome little thing you are," she told him, reaching down to envelop Paul in a hug. Alexis observed Paul's lack of response with amusement.

"Libby, this is Alexis Stone, a guest at the ranch. Alexis, this is Libby Preston."

The two women nodded, tight, false-smiles on their faces as they measured each other. The icy warning in

Libby Preston's eyes was obvious. In no uncertain terms, she was telling Alexis to stay away from Brant.

Libby sat down on an extra seat and began to talk smoothly of things that had been going on in Amarillo since Brant had been there, her hand resting possessively on his arm. The low intimacy of her voice and the way she sat turned toward Brant clearly excluded Alexis and Paul from the conversation. Alexis continued to eat her steak, barely tasting the delicious meat as she concentrated on appearing unconcerned, while her insides jangled with anger. It was horrible to be exposed like this to Brant's mistress, to have to face the other woman whom he slept with, the one who had first claim on him. Alexis knew that she was the outsider, the woman who was handy and whom Brant used to satisfy himself when Libby was not around. The thought made Alexis burn with rage and embarrassment.

Finally, Brant broke into Libby's monologue. "Don't you suppose the people you're with are beginning to wonder what happened to you?" he inquired with quiet firmness.

Libby paused for a fraction of a second, then smiled and said, "Yes, I imagine so. They probably think I couldn't find my way back. Well, bye, honey, I'll see you." She stood up, leaned over, and kissed Brant fully on the lips.

As she walked away, her hips swayed with a provocativeness that had every man in the room staring after her. Alexis looked at Libby's retreating form, her fingers gripping her fork tightly, and she was aware of a primitive urge to jab the instrument into the other woman's back.

The earlier, pleasant mood between Brant and Alexis was shattered, and they quickly finished their meal. Brant drove across town to the stockyards to pick up the calf, Alexis sitting beside him in huffy silence. Paul was oblivious to the change in the atmosphere.

When he had hitched the small trailer to his car,

Brant drove to I-40 and headed east on the smooth, wide road. Paul fell asleep between them, his head in Alexis's lap. Alexis looked out at the darkness, determined not to start a conversation to ease the tension.

She had been acting like an idiot today, she thought, relaxing and enjoying herself with Brant just as though everything were normal. But, of course, nothing was normal. He had a mistress. Alexis told herself sternly that she must not forget that. She really disliked the man. Today had been just a momentary lapse on both their parts.

Brant stared moodily before him, as grimly silent as Alexis. His face was unreadable as he watched the miles pass beneath his wheels. Alexis wondered what he was thinking, whether he was wishing he were with Libby.

The monotonous swish of the tires on the highway lulled Alexis to sleep, despite her roiling thoughts, and she did not awaken until they had pulled into the driveway of the ranch house. Sleepily, she struggled to sit up and collect her thoughts. Brant pulled to a stop by the barn and got out to unhitch the trailer and put the calf up. Groggily, Paul sat up and stretched, and Alexis eased him from the car. With Paul leaning against her, still half asleep, she walked down the drive to the back door and propelled Paul through the kitchen and up the stairs to his room. He tumbled onto the bed, and she didn't even bother to try to get him to change into pajamas. She merely took off his shoes, socks, and jeans, then drew the covers over him.

After he was snugly tucked in, Alexis crossed the hall to her own room, stripped, and crawled into bed. Surely Brant would not bother her tonight, not when he had just seen Libby.

However, a few moments later she heard the familiar sound of his steps outside her door, and Brant entered the room as casually as if nothing unusual had happened this evening. Alexis sat up, preparing herself for a fight. He would have to say something about Libby, and then she would tell him exactly what she thought of him. Arms folded, she watched him pull off his boots and jeans and place his watch on the dresser.

Brant came to the bed and got in, and Alexis braced herself for whatever he would say. But he said nothing, merely reached out and embraced her, kissing her thoroughly, competently. For a moment Alexis held herself rigid in his arms, enraged that he would dare to take her like this, without even the slightest apology or explanation about Libby Preston. Then, as always, her defenses folded, under his expert caress, and she began to relax. Almost against her will, her arms crept up around his neck, and she returned his kisses eagerly, the last shred of her resistance melting away as he engulfed her in the swirling pleasure of his lovemaking.

Chapter 18

Alexis chafed under Brant's dominance. She despised herself for allowing him to control her, for quivering beneath his touch while he remained indifferent to her. Brant was fully in command, and she bent like a willow to his demands. And now, added to her frustration was the resentment she felt as soon as she had met Libby.

Alexis told herself that it couldn't matter less to her if Brant had a girlfriend. After all, she already knew how casual his relationship with herself was. It should not surprise her at all that he had someone who held his love. Certainly, love had nothing to do with what he did to *her*. However, Alexis could not reason away the rage she felt every time she thought of Libby.

She flung herself down on her bed and stared up at the ceiling. She should be getting ready to go to Beth's tonight for a good-bye supper for Selena. They would be leaving in another hour, and she hadn't even run her bath water yet. But her mind sullenly refused to think of anything but Brant.

Damn the man! Why did he have to be so uncaring about the passion he created? Suddenly Alexis sat up, her mind whirring. Was he really so insensitive? Oh, certainly he maintained a mask of calm control, but she had been making the mistake of taking him at face value. Look at the way he had held her and made love to her Christmas evening—that had been anything but calm. Perhaps his actions then had only been a result of his emotional meeting with his mother, but even so, they were clearly a rip in the cloak he wore.

Thoughtfully, she went back over their relationship. From the very beginning, Brant had wanted her. But because he always initiated the lovemaking, he had the advantage; he forced her to respond without his revealing anything he felt for her.

The way to wrest control from him, to prove that she could pull the strings and Brant could dance, would be to take the initiative away from him. Stir his passions, set him on fire, make him long for her—*that* would give her the upper hand! A smile touched her lips. What better time would she have than tonight, when they would be at Beth's party, surrounded by people? She could tease and entice him, and he would be unable to do a thing about it.

Alexis bounced out of bed and went to the closet, removing a soft blue dress whose narrow skirt outlined her hips and derrière, and whose V-necked bodice exposed part of her creamy breasts and hinted at a great deal more. If this dress didn't set his blood pumping, she thought, nothing would.

She bathed quickly and splashed herself with a delicate perfume, then made up her eyes carefully and touched her mouth with lipstick. A few quick dabs of foundation and rouge, and her face was as lovely as it could be. Next, she wound her hair up into a severe knot, leaving a few tendrils trailing wispily down her neck, which gave her hair the sensuous look of just having been mussed by a man's hand. Zipping up the low-cut garment, she revolved slowly before the mirror and smiled. She was, she decided, absolutely sizzling.

Brant waited for her at the bottom of the stairs, casually handsome in tan slacks and a shirt. A brown and tan sweater vest and a soft tan suede jacket completed his attire. A light glittered in his eyes when he saw her, and he straightened involuntarily, proving to Alexis that she had achieved the right effect.

All through cocktails, as Alexis moved among the crowd, talking to Beth, Selena, Rusty, or one of the other few guests, she could feel Brant's eyes on her. Finally she approached him, smiling, and slipped her arm through his.

"How are you doing?" she asked demurely.

"Fine. I'm enjoying your performance," Brant replied in a sardonic tone.

"Are you?" Alexis returned. "I'm glad. It's just for you, you know."

He looked down into her purple-blue eyes and drew in a funny half breath. "You seem to be pulling out all the stops tonight. Why?"

"Must I have a reason?" Alexis lowered her eyelids secretively, seductively.

"I can't imagine you without one."

As Alexis tilted her head back to look at him, she trailed a forefinger down the front of his shirt, her touch as light as a butterfly's, pausing slightly at every button. "And what do you think my reason is?"

"I don't know." His eyes took on a faint glitter. "You tell me."

"Maybe I just want you to notice me."

"I think you've succeeded."

Alexis laughed, a throaty, low laugh that stirred Brant's blood and made him itch to grab her. She swayed toward him tentatively, her breasts grazing his arm and sending a stab of desire through his groin. Standing on tiptoe, Alexis kissed his ear, nipping lightly at the lobe with her teeth, then quickly stepped out of reach.

"I think Beth wants us to sit down and eat," she said, noting with satisfaction the flush that had mounted to his face and the golden sparkle in his eyes.

"Alexis," he breathed huskily, and pulled her to him, one hand cupping her breast.

For an instant she leaned into him, then twirled away. "Really, Brant—in public?"

Muttering a curse beneath his breath, Brant followed her into the dining room. However, he found that his delicious torment was not to cease there. He and Alexis were seated side by side at the table, their chairs close together. As soon as they sat down, Alexis brushed her thigh against him. The first time it happened, Brant thought it was accidental, but when she pressed her leg to his again, he knew that she had done it on purpose, and that thought made it doubly exciting.

"Witch," he whispered into her ear. "What do you think you're doing?"

She smiled. "Can't you tell?"

"Well, Brant," O. L. Raines boomed from across the table, "how are you doing with those new pens?"

"Just fine, Mr. Raines," Brant replied. "I think they'll hold up real well." He barely suppressed a gasp as he felt Alexis's hand slide smoothly up his thigh and dig into his flesh.

"Peas?" Alexis offered, holding out a bowl, her blue eyes dancing wickedly.

With a glare, he took the bowl from her and spooned peas onto his plate, then realized with irritation that he hated peas.

"We've had a nice winter so far," Mr. Raines continued sociably.

"Yes, sir, no snow."

Alexis began to stroke his leg rhythmically beneath the table. Brant managed, with great difficulty, to keep his voice even as he spoke to Raines. He could not disguise, however, the quiver that ran through his leg at her touch.

All through dinner, while Brant struggled to maintain a normal appearance, Alexis teased at his leg with her fingers, gently stroking, or running one nail swiftly up the inside of his thigh, or making slow, circling figures upon the cloth of his trousers.

When the meal was over and everyone rose to retire to the living room, Brant grasped Alexis's wrist in an iron grasp and dragged her into the kitchen.

"What the hell do you think you're doing?" he snapped, backing her against the wall and pressing his body into hers, imprinting his swollen desire on her.

Alexis did not answer, merely smiled. He groaned deep in his throat and kissed her, grinding his lips into hers just as he ground his throbbing manhood against her. Alexis kissed him back, slipping her tongue into his mouth teasingly.

His lips moved to her throat, trailing fiery kisses down the white column of her neck and across her chest, tracing the neckline of her dress to where it met over her breasts. "Alexis," he mumbled, his breath hot against her skin. "God, I want you." His hand came up to fondle the soft orb of her breast. "You love to torment me, don't you? To tease me till I'm bursting with wanting you." Suddenly he straightened, the flame in his eyes mesmerizing her. "We're leaving. Get your coat and find Paul. I'll tell Beth."

Within minutes they were on their way to the ranch. Paul, his lids drooping, soon fell asleep in the back seat of the Ford. Brant, taut as a coil of wire beside Alexis, said nothing, did not even look at her. With a quick glance at the sleeping boy, Alexis shrugged out of her warm coat. Then, sitting forward, she unzipped her dress inch by inch. Brant swallowed, barely able to keep his eyes on the road as Alexis tantalizingly drew down the bodice of her dress, slipped it over her hips, and pulled it off. Involuntarily, he reached out to touch the smooth, rose-peaked breasts that swayed enticingly free, but Alexis swiftly slid across the seat, out of his reach. There, she continued to strip, maintaining an agonizingly slow pace as she eased out of her hose and half slip, and finally her sheer panties.

The blood pounded in his head, and it was only with the firmest of efforts that he kept his hands on the wheel and the car on the road. "Damn you, Alexis," he muttered huskily. "When we get home, you're going to pay for this."

She laughed throatily. "Oh? How?" She ran a bare toe down his leg.

Thickly, in a few short words, he told her of his lustful intentions, and again her low laughter rippled. "Is that a threat or a promise? Well, if it disturbs you so, I guess I'll just have to cover up." She drew her coat on over her bare skin, buttoning it with slow precision.

They pulled off the highway at a fast pace and onto the unpaved road that led to the McClure House. Soon the looming bulk appeared. Brant stopped in front and instantly cut off the engine. Opening the rear car door, he lifted Paul out and swiftly carried the sleeping boy into the house. Gathering up her clothes, Alexis followed them more leisurely.

By the time she was halfway up the stairs, Brant had reappeared at the top, hands on hips, feet apart, waiting for her. Alexis did not increase her pace, and stopped two steps below him. He waited silently, watching her, as she lazily began to unbutton her coat.

"Tell me something, Brant," she said, pausing above the last button and seeing his eyes glittering ferally at her through the darkness. "Do you want me?"

His laugh was short and shaky. "You have to ask? Yes, Alexis, you know I want you."

"How much?"

"More than I've ever wanted anybody in my life. Now take off that damn coat and come here."

The coat slid smoothly off her skin and folded around her feet. Alexis went up one step, and Brant's arms caught her, pulling her up the final step to him. He kissed her wildly, with passionate abandon, holding her as if he would never let her go. Mumbling unintelligible words, he moved his lips over her naked body, caressing, adoring, nipping, devouring, until Alexis was a pillar of flame. He swept her up and carried her the last few feet into his room, laying her gently on the bed.

Quickly, his eyes never leaving her, Brant peeled off his clothes and stretched out beside her. For a moment they looked at each other with a last, tantalizing restraint, then came together, their hands and mouths touching, tasting, loving. Locked together in a wild frenzy, they rolled across the bed, and Alexis felt the furious tumult build in her under his ardent embrace. She cried out his name, sobbing with desire, and he thrust his pulsing manhood inside her, driving her ever onward to the beautiful shattering that caught them both and swirled them high into a blissful oneness.

Alexis stretched languorously, remembering the night before, a small smile playing upon her lips. Nothing had ever been as glorious, and Brant had been as lost in desire as she. She swiveled her head to look at him. He lay on his stomach, his face turned toward her, relaxed in sleep. Tenderly, she trailed a finger along his outflung arm. It was hard to imagine that his face had been blazing with such passion only a few hours before. Again she smiled, feeling strangely liquid inside.

Brant's eyelids fluttered open and he gazed at her in confusion for a moment; then his expression changed and he smiled slowly. "Hello, Alexis." His voice was soft, and he reached out a hand to stroke her cheek.

"Hello, Brant," she returned a bit shyly.

"You are one beautiful lady," he said, and pulled her into his arms, rolling onto his side to hold her. "What got into you last night?"

Alexis giggled and shook her head. "I don't know. Did you mind?"

"Mind!" he repeated in astonishment. "Listen, any time you get the urge, you just go ahead."

"I—I wanted to see if you felt anything for me. If you wanted me, too."

Brant laughed delightedly. "You wanted to find out if I wanted you? Lord, woman, you must take a lot of convincing!" He kissed her thoroughly. "Tell you what. I'll prove it again right now if you want."

"Wicked," Alexis teased, melting against him deliciously.

Later, after they had reached the dizzying heights again, Alexis and Brant had a leisurely shower together and took their time dressing. Once downstairs, Brant discovered that he had a ravenous appetite.

"Alexis," he said gravely as she moved about the kitchen, slapping a pat of butter in the skillet and breaking eggs into a bowl, "do you—that is, would you consider staying a little longer?"

Alexis whirled to face him, the color high in her cheeks. "What? Are you serious, Brant?"

"Of course I'm serious. Couldn't you take off a little more time for your vacation?"

She couldn't, of course. There would be work piled sky-high on her desk when she got back, and Alec would be ranting and raving for that lease. It was impossible to stay any longer, even a day. The sudden realization of how little time she had left here was like an icy grip on her stomach.

"Yes, I can stay a little longer," she said shakily, hardly believing what she heard herself say. "I don't know how long . . ."

He grinned. "We'll worry about that when the time comes. Right now, the butter sounds like it's about to burn."

With a horrified gasp, she whirled back to the stove, lowered the flame under the skillet, beat the eggs quickly, and poured them into the pan. All the while she was doing this, her insides were quivering madly. Brant wanted her to stay, and she was staying . . . Her mind lingered over the thought but could not quite accept it. Whatever was happening to her?

Alexis was almost shy as she sat down with Brant and Paul. Her emotions were so confused, so topsy-turvy, that she hardly seemed like herself. She found that she wanted to grin idiotically at nothing.

After breakfast, Alexis cleaned up the kitchen and straightened things around the house while Brant went out with Paul to do a few chores in the yard. About ten o'clock, Brant and Paul returned with logs, which they stacked by the fireplace in the den. Alexis watched Brant build a fire, feeling cozy and peaceful as the flames flickered and grew. Brant smiled and flopped down on the couch beside her, one arm resting familiarly around her shoulder.

As they watched the leap and crackle of the flames in a contented drowsy state, a knock sounded at the front door. Brant sighed and got up to answer it, Alexis and Paul trailing after him into the hall.

When he opened the door, a feminine voice cried, "Brant, I thought I'd come over and keep you company! Aren't you glad to see me?"

Brant stepped back slightly, revealing the lush figure of Libby Preston. She was dressed in a form-hugging wool dress, her coal-black hair perfectly in place, her face elegantly made up. A red-hot blade stabbed through Alexis's vitals. Until this moment she had been swept away by a silly flood of feeling for Brant, forgetting that he had a girlfriend in Amarillo. After all, Alexis told herself, she was only filling in temporarily, since Libby lived out of town. No doubt now that Libby was here, Alexis's services would no longer be required.

Libby came inside, flinging her arms around Brant's neck and kissing him resoundingly. Alexis's eyes flashed. She turned abruptly and stalked toward the kitchen. Brant broke away from Libby and followed her, catching hold of her just inside the kitchen.

"Alexis, please, wait a minute. Listen to me, will you? I didn't know that Libby was coming here. I didn't—"

"Please, don't bother! It is perfectly clear!"

"Alexis, don't fly off the handle. Let me explain."

"You'd better get back to your guest," Alexis sneered, her tone dripping with sarcasm. "She'll wonder why you left her so abruptly."

"I didn't ask her down here!" Brant snapped.

"Well, then, it must be a nice surprise. Really, Brant, I couldn't care less. What concern is it of mine if Libby Preston chooses to visit you?"

Her cool indifference stung him, and Brant retorted bitterly, "I guess you're right. What difference does it make to you? Of course your feelings are not involved. And I don't have any obligation to explain a thing to you!"

Brant stormed down the hall, slamming the front door behind him as he went out. Alexis followed more slowly and saw that Libby remained by the entrance, where he had left her. She looked at Alexis, her gray eyes pale and dangerous.

"Did you make him mad with a jealous little scene?" she asked with amusement. "Tsk, tsk. That's always a bad move with Brant. He doesn't like possessiveness."

Alexis glared at the other woman, her eyes dark purple with unspent anger. "Don't worry," she responded glacially. "I have no interest in trying to keep Brant McClure pleased. In fact, I detest the man. Believe me, he is all yours."

Libby raised her eyebrows in disbelief, then swung the door open and followed Brant out. Alexis stood staring after her for a moment, fuming. Paul, who had retreated into the den at the first sign of discord, now peeked around the doorway.

"Allie?" he said, his eyes round.

Alexis forced her voice to be normal. "It's okay, sweetheart. Someone whom I don't particularly like has come to visit your father. That's all."

"I don't like her, either," Paul stated loyally. "She's the lady we met the other day, isn't she? She kept squeezing and kissing me."

Alexis hid a grin. Obviously Libby had not made points with Paul with her excessive display of sweetness and light, even though Brant might have been taken in by it.

"I tell you what," Alexis said to the boy. "Why don't we go into town today, maybe do some shopping and visit Beth and the girls? Would you like that? I think the girls' Christmas vacation is still going on."

"Yeah!" Paul cried enthusiastically. "They're fun!"

"Good. Run and get your coat, and we'll go."

Alexis went out to warm up her car. It had been several days since she had driven it, and she wasn't sure how it would respond to the freezing Panhandle weather. She had to get away; she simply could not bear to spend the rest of the day watching Libby paw over Brant. Brant, of course, would probably lap it up. Men seemed to lose what little good sense they had around a woman like Libby.

Alexis's silver-green Mercedes created something of a stir in Barrett, since the wealthy people in the area favored Continentals and Cadillacs. She parked the elegant car, and she and Paul got out to explore the downtown area.

There was little to see in any direction. Like most small Panhandle and west Texas towns, Barrett was built around a square, the center of which was an imposing pink granite county courthouse set on a grass-covered lawn. Spreading elm trees had been planted many years ago to border the outer sidewalk. Stone benches were dotted here and there, and in the warmer months would be occupied by old men.

The streets around the courthouse square comprised the financial and business district of the small community. The stores were built up from the ground, and the cement sidewalk was likewise several feet above it. She and Paul had to climb three or four steps to reach the walk. Alexis was positive that, not too many years in the past, the sidewalks had been the original wooden-plank walkways of Western towns.

The first block they explored contained a dilapidated movie theater that was still in operation and showing a Western, a furniture store, a drugstore with a marble soda fountain and old green stools, and a dress shop. Crossing the street, they found a bank, several empty buildings, and the library. On the third side stood a

vacant lot where a building had been torn down, a
five-and-dime store, and an abandoned cafe. At either
end of the block, cater-cornered to the courthouse, was
a much newer-looking filling station. On the final lap of
the square were some office buildings that primarily
housed real estate agents, lawyers, and land surveyors.

"It isn't very busy," Paul remarked aptly, and Alexis
nodded her head.

"I'm afraid that it's dying, like most small towns,"
she explained.

"How can it die?"

"Well, what I mean is that people don't do as much
business here as they used to. Lots of the children go off
to bigger cities when they grow up, and the population
keeps shrinking. Those who do remain here more and
more frequently drive to a larger town a few miles away
to buy most of the things they need. These small places
just don't have as good a selection, so their business
falls off."

"I see. Is there any place else to go?"

"Well, down that street there's an old church I think
they've turned into a museum. Would you like to
see it?"

The museum was tiny and consisted mostly of spurs,
barbed wire, and gun collections that had been donated
by local residents. It scarcely did a thriving business, as
Paul and Alexis were the only visitors, and they soon
saw everything in it.

Afterward, Alexis took the highway to Beth's, stopping off first at Nora's for hamburgers. At Beth's,
Stephanie, Jennifer, and Paul retired immediately to
the back of the house to play.

"It's nice," Beth said, "for Jenny and Stephie to have
a cousin to play with. Playmates are so few and far
between out here. There aren't that many younger
people with children to begin with, and the kids they
know at school are scattered all over."

"I guess the original settlers were so far apart that

the children didn't really have friends," Alexis commented. "They must have depended on their brothers and sisters."

"Yes. Good thing for them that they had large families." Beth paused, then asked, "What are you two doing out? I mean, I'm glad you came, don't get me wrong—I was dying for some company besides Jenny and Steph—but where is Brant? Why isn't Paul out investigating the ranch with him?"

Alexis grimaced. "He's busy with other things today."

"Oh?" Beth's eyebrows rose at her friend's tone. "What do you mean? What's going on?"

"Nothing. Brant just had a visitor today—Libby Preston."

"So *that's* why you left. I don't blame you. I would have, too. That woman is so saccharine that the government should declare her hazardous to one's health."

Alexis laughed at Beth's witticism. "I don't think that's what Brant thinks about her, though."

"He doesn't love her, I can assure you of that."

"It really doesn't matter, Beth. I've told you that nothing is going to come of me and Brant."

"Not with Libby poking her nose into everything." Beth's irritation was obvious. "I can't imagine what Brant sees in her!"

Alexis shot her a meaningful glance, and they both dissolved into laughter.

"Aside from an oversized bust, that is," Beth amended when she could catch her breath again.

"I met her the other day when we went to Amarillo," Alexis continued. "She must have decided that she'd better come up here and defend her property."

"Well, don't let her frighten you off," Beth said stoutly. "Believe me, you've already got her beat all hollow."

Alexis smiled stiffly. "Thanks, Beth, but as I said, it

doesn't really matter. I've always known that Brant had another girlfriend. I've never expected any lifelong devotion from him."

"Tell me, where did you learn to lie so well? Law school?"

Alexis laughed grudgingly. "Oh, Beth. I have to admit that it pricked my pride some, her showing up and throwing herself all over Brant. But that is all it is, a little wounded pride, nothing more."

"Okay, if you say so," Beth conceded, holding her hands up. "Now, could we get off the subject of Libby Preston?"

It was almost five o'clock when Paul and Alexis returned to the McClure ranch house. They walked in the door to find Libby sitting in the living room and Brant pacing up and down in front of her, his face thunderous.

"Where the hell have you been?" he snapped at Alexis.

At his angry tone, Paul slid his hand into Alexis's and moved a little closer to her. Alexis quirked her eyebrows and said coolly, "Must you shout so? It frightens Paul."

"I am not shouting," Brant answered through clenched teeth. "And my question was directed to you, not to him."

"We toured the town," Alexis told him lightly, "and then we dropped by Beth's for a while."

"If you want to go running off, that's one thing," Brant snarled, "but there was no reason for you to take Paul. What right did you have to drag him out of this house? Libby wanted to see him again and get to know him better."

"Did she, now?" Alexis said, and glanced at Libby, her mouth curling up sardonically.

"Of course I did." Libby rose and came toward Paul, hands outstretched. Her voice was as stickily sweet as sugar water. "I just love children, especially this dear little boy."

Paul stood stiffly as she wrapped him in a cloying embrace and planted a lipsticked kiss on his cheek. He turned his head toward Alexis, an agonized look of pleading on his face.

"I can't breathe," he said bluntly. "You smell funny."

Libby let go of him as quickly as if he had changed into a writhing reptile. "Why, you little—" She broke off and put a smile on her face. "That's very expensive imported French perfume, young man. Someday you'll learn to appreciate it."

Paul stuck his chin out stubbornly. "I don't like it. It makes my nose itch."

Libby let out a short, brittle laugh. "Children are so blunt, aren't they? Paul, dear, someone really should teach you better manners."

"Like forcing a hug and a kiss on a stranger who obviously doesn't want them?" Alexis suggested, her voice falsely congenial.

Libby swung on her. "It doesn't surprise me that the boy is so rude, when he had you for a teacher!"

"No doubt you could do a better job of raising him."

"I certainly could! If I were in charge of him, he would at least know his place."

"Which is where, Libby?" Alexis returned slyly. "At the bottom of the heap?"

Her cheeks flaming, Libby glared at Alexis with venom but could think of nothing sufficiently scathing to say. So she pointedly resumed her seat.

Alexis turned to Brant, who looked about ready to explode, and declared icily, "Brant, you may want Libby to turn your son into a houseboy, but I, for one, refuse to be either her servant or yours. I am not cooking dinner tonight for the lot of you."

"I didn't expect you to," Brant replied tightly. "We'll go to Nora's."

"Oh, boy!" Paul exclaimed, and clapped his hands. "Can I get another hamburger?"

Brant had to laugh. "Yes, I guess so. You'd better watch it, kid, or one of these days you're going to turn into a hamburger yourself."

Alexis glanced at the sophisticated woman sitting like a mannequin on the sofa. Libby would stick out like a sore thumb at Nora's, she thought maliciously.

"Sure," Alexis agreed. "That ought to provide the town with enough entertainment for a week at least."

Brant glared at her and stalked to the door. Libby followed him quickly, climbing into his car and claiming the seat next to Brant. She scooted across the upholstery and patted the vacant place beside her with a pasted-on smile. "Here, Paul, you can sit next to me."

"No, thanks," Paul said politely, tumbling into the rear seat with Alexis.

Alexis had to choke back laughter at the sight of Libby's face, frozen with chagrin. Yes, this evening should certainly give everyone a store of gossip. If only, she thought with a spasm of misery, she did not have to witness it.

Chapter 19

At the restaurant, things went from bad to worse. Everyone turned to stare at them when they walked in, and avid curiosity gleamed on Nora's face.

Libby glanced around the cafe with surprise. "This is where we are going to eat?" she asked incredulously.

Alexis smothered a giggle and received a quick glare from Brant before he said, "Yes, Libby. We aren't in Amarillo, you know."

"And I thought Amarillo was the height of boredom," Libby commented. "Really, Brant, is this a joke, or do you actually intend to eat here?"

"Yes, I actually intend to eat here!" Brant snapped, and strode across to his favorite booth.

They sat awkwardly at the table while Nora brought menus and handed them out, casting a blank, cool look at the woman who so patently did not like her restaurant, and bestowing a big, warm smile on the other three occupants of the booth.

"How you doing, Alexis, Brant? Say, kid, you get cuter every time I see you," Nora rattled cheerfully. "Is it going to be the usual all around for you all?"

"No," Alexis said. "I think for once I'm not going to have a hamburger. I'll try Brant's chicken-fried steak. But I imagine Paul will stick to his old favorite."

"I want a hamburger," Paul piped, to make sure his desires were accurately understood.

"You know me, Nora," Brant chuckled. "Chicken-fried steak. What about you, Libby?"

Libby stared in consternation at the menu. "Are the steaks here any good?"

Nora bristled at the criticism in Libby's voice, but Paul flew to Nora's defense before she could speak. "Of course they are," he said with unmitigated scorn. "Everything here is good, most especially the hamburgers."

"I am quite aware of your preference for hamburgers," Libby replied. "But not everyone shares it." The condescending look she threw at Alexis implied that only common types such as Alexis actually liked hamburgers.

"Well, you would if you knew what was good," Paul returned rebelliously.

"Paul, that's enough," Brant said. "Don't be rude to our guest."

"She's not my guest," Paul protested. "I don't like her. She's nasty to me and Allie and Nora, and I wish she would go away."

"Paul! I said that was enough. Miss Preston is my guest, and you had better learn to be polite."

At his father's harsh tone, Paul's lower lip began to tremble, and he slouched lower in the booth, beginning a silent sulk that would last throughout their stay at the restaurant.

"He's only being honest, Brant," Alexis murmured. "Besides, I imagine he finds it a little difficult to understand why it's all right for Miss Preston to be as rude as she pleases to Nora, but it's wrong for him."

"I think I'm capable of disciplining my own son, thank you, without any interference from you."

Alexis merely rolled her eyes up and settled into a silence of her own. Libby provided more than enough conversation for everyone, however, as she babbled on about clothes and parties and gossip until their orders arrived. Alexis, who had been bored stiff except for the laughable incongruity of Libby's chatter with their surroundings, devoured her food eagerly. The sooner they got out of here, the better, she told herself, and once they were back at Brant's, she would retire to the privacy of her room as quickly as possible.

On the ride home Libby snuggled up against Brant, completely ignoring Paul and Alexis in the back seat and speaking to Brant in a whispering voice. Alexis, seething, would have very much liked to reach out and give Libby's smoothly coiffed hair a healthy tug. Brant deserved a cold-faced bitch like that, she decided.

When they reached the house, Paul made a beeline for the stairs, with Alexis not far behind him. They played together in his room for a while, and then Alexis put him to bed.

As she opened the door to leave, Paul asked, "Allie, is she going to stay?"

"I don't know, Paul. She will, probably."

"How long?"

"I guess as long as your daddy wants her to."

"She's not going to move in, is she?" His small voice was worried.

"I don't think so," Alexis reassured him.

"Why does Daddy like her?"

"Now, that I don't know," Alexis said with a laugh. "She is very pretty."

"But she's got mean eyes. I don't like her eyes."

"I'll tell you something. Neither do I."

"Allie, couldn't you stay? Couldn't you marry Daddy?"

A pain slashed through her heart. "No, honey. Your daddy wouldn't want to marry me. He and I— Well, most of the time we don't get along together very well."

"Why not?"

"I don't know. It's all too complicated. You wouldn't understand. As a matter of fact, I don't think *I* understand."

He looked puzzled, but seemed to accept her statement. Alexis gave him a final, wavering smile and stepped into the hall, flicking off the light switch behind her. Poor Paul, she thought as she closed the door, it was so hard for him, loving them both.

Alexis went to her room, intending to stay there for the rest of the evening. However, she found that she had left the book she was reading in the den. With a sigh, she wandered about, looking for something else to do. After examining every picture and photograph on the wall and the dresser, she slumped onto the bed. There's no point, she said to herself, in sitting up here boring myself to death just to avoid Libby Preston. I can go down and get the book and come straight back up. There's no need even to speak to her. And there's certainly no reason to let that woman force me into spending the evening up here, hiding like a scared animal.

Firmly, Alexis got to her feet and went down to the den. Libby and Brant were sitting there, Libby on the couch and Brant in an easy chair, neither saying a word. Alexis walked in and crossed to the table where her novel lay.

"Oh, are you going to spend the evening alone with a book?" Libby asked, her voice syrupy.

"I prefer it to the company around here," Alexis snapped back.

"Of course, I guess you're used to spending the evening alone," Libby went on, her voice sharpening.

Alexis looked at her deliberately, raising her eyebrows and letting an amused smile float across her lips. "Do you think so? You must be more naive than you look."

With that parting shot, Alexis turned on her heel and walked out without a glance at Brant. Her back straight, she went up the stairs and shut herself in her room. Quickly, she got ready for bed and settled down to read the rest of the evening away.

But she found it hard to concentrate on the words before her. Her mind kept straying to the den. It was none of her business, she told herself, who Brant saw or how he spent his time. There was no feeling between him and herself; she should know that better than anyone. No matter what Paul or Beth wanted, Alexis and Brant did not share the same idea. There was a sexual attraction between them, nothing more, and it shouldn't bother her that Brant had a mistress besides. It was just being relegated to second best that upset her.

Alexis slammed the book closed and stared moodily at the wall. Again she started to read, and again she stopped, and at last flung the book onto the night stand. Obviously nothing was going to help tonight.

She pulled down the covers and climbed into bed, staring for a long time at the ceiling. Sleep simply would not come to ease her thoughts. Finally, after another hour or two had passed, she heard the tap of two sets of footsteps on the stairs. She held her breath as the sounds traveled down the hall and stopped at Brant's room. Then she heard the opening and closing of the door, followed by silence.

Alexis turned onto her stomach and pulled the pillow over her head, choking back the hot tears that welled in her throat. Damn him! He had taken Libby to bed! Suddenly the tears flooded from her, gushing forth in torrential sobs until she had cried herself to sleep.

After Alexis had left, Libby smiled sweetly at Brant and said, "You know, honey, I think that poor girl's jealous of me."

"Jealous!" Brant repeated, and laughed. "Why should she be jealous, Libby? She is intelligent, pretty, and an oil heiress, besides."

"I mean, I think she rather has a thing for you." Libby looked at him, her eyes narrowing involuntarily. She wished she could see through the impenetrable mask that Brant wore, wished that she knew what he thought about Alexis Stone. Just how far had things gone between them?

Everything seemed to be falling apart. Libby had always had to battle Brant's insane attachment to his ranch, but she had been confident that once she had caught him, she would be able to wean him away. Then the child had come along to complicate matters. And as if that weren't enough, now there was this strawberry blonde who was living here with Brant. It didn't take much intelligence to realize that Alexis was after Brant, and the cunning, blue-eyed witch was no doubt scheming to get at him through the boy. As soon as Libby had seen her in the restaurant in Amarillo, she had known that Alexis spelled trouble.

Alexis was the real reason why Libby had hurried out to the McClure ranch, even though she hated the desolation of the place. She had to find out where things stood between Alexis and Brant and how far their relationship had gone. Most of all, she had to do her best to get rid of the woman. Libby did not trust any woman, especially where a prize like Brant McClure was concerned. And even less would she trust someone as attractive as Alexis Stone.

The only problem was that, so far, Brant had been less than enthusiastic to see her. In fact, he had been downright surly all day. Nor had she had any success in wooing his obnoxious little boy. Then they had gone to that awful little cafe. To top it all off, despite their snappish words to each other, Brant couldn't keep his eyes off Alexis. It was clear that he wanted her; the only question was whether they were already sleeping together.

"Alexis doesn't even like me," Brant replied. "I doubt very much that she is jealous. More than likely, she's relieved."

"Relieved?" Libby repeated puzzledly. "What do you mean?"

"Nothing. It doesn't make any difference." He firmly

changed the direction the conversation was taking. "Libby, why did you come up here?"

"Why did I come?" Libby gave a half laugh. "Why, that's pretty obvious, isn't it? To see you."

"You don't usually come here."

"Well, when I ran into you the other night, I realized what a long time it had been since we'd seen each other last, and I just decided to drive over and surprise you. Besides, I wanted to get to know your darling son better."

"Come off it, Libby. You don't care about kids."

"What a mean thing to say." She pouted prettily. "That's not true, Brant. I'm not one of those women who slobbers all over a child, but that doesn't mean I couldn't be fond of one."

Libby moved uncomfortably under Brant's flat, uncompromising gaze and reached up to smooth her jet-black hair into place. It was always so difficult to lie to Brant; he seemed to be able to see straight through her. She understood now that if she married Brant, she would have to take the boy, too. That wouldn't be too bad, of course, for there were always sitters and maids, and then, when he was a little older, they could send him away to school. But it wouldn't do for Brant to believe that she didn't love Paul.

"How did you get Paul?" Libby asked, to break the uncomfortable silence and Brant's unswerving gaze.

"Alexis's father managed to get him out of 'Nam."

"That certainly doesn't sound like an oil magnate to me."

"It was not out of the kindness of his heart, believe me," Brant answered, his voice low and dry.

"Oh, I see. A bribe, huh? And was the lovely Alexis the one who held the sword over your head . . . or is it the carrot before the donkey?"

"It was a business deal, nothing more," Brant said firmly.

Libby laughed throatily, arching her neck in a deliberately alluring gesture. "I bet. She seems like a tough one to me. Did she soften you up with sex before she brought out the heavy artillery of getting Paul for you?"

"No!" Brant scowled fiercely, his voice gruff. "It was nothing like that. You don't have any idea what you're talking about, Libby. You don't even know the woman."

"I don't have to. She's a conniver. I could see that at a distance. And now she's using that child to get her hooks into you."

Brant glared at her, itching to grab her by the arm and hustle her out the front door. He had never had any illusions about Libby. She was a schemer, and her eye had been on his pocketbook from the start. He had had no qualms about using her, just as she had hoped to use him.

But now, as he compared her lush form with Alexis's slender loveliness, Libby seemed overblown, too ripe. And the jealousy that stamped her features whenever she looked at Alexis destroyed the pretty lines of her face. Brant wondered what he had ever seen in her.

He had no interest in her, and would have asked her to leave as soon as she had arrived, if it hadn't been for the stupid way Alexis had acted, turning cold and reminding him that she was indifferent to him or whatever he did. He had endured Libby all day simply to spite Alexis, but his endurance was beginning to wear rather thin.

"Libby, I think it's time that we ended this conversation," he said, and stood up. "I'm going to bed."

Libby bit her lip and rose with him; it had been silly to let him glimpse her jealousy. Her attacking Alexis only served to make him go to the other woman's defense. She put on a sweet smile and took his arm in hers.

"You're right. I shouldn't say things like that. I just hate to think of anyone taking advantage of you, that's all. Let's forget it."

They slowly mounted the stairs, and Brant opened

the door to his room. Turning to Libby, he said, "I put your bag in the room across the hall."

A cold shiver darted through Libby, but she continued to smile. "Oh, now, Brant, don't be so prudish. I'm sure that Miss Stone is a sophisticated woman. We don't have to put on a little charade for her."

"It's not a charade," Brant began, but Libby slipped into the room before him. With a sigh, he closed the door. "Okay, Libby, I guess we'll have to have a talk."

"A talk?" She stepped closer to him and ran one long, red nail down the buttons of his shirt. "That wasn't quite what I had in mind."

Firmly, he lifted her hand from his shirt and moved away. "No, Libby, that's what we need to talk about."

"Whatever do you mean, Brant?"

"I mean that it's over between us. I don't want to sleep with you any more. Tomorrow I want you to go back to Amarillo."

Libby's face drained of all color. "Brant, you can't mean this . . ."

"I do."

Tears welled in Libby's eyes. "Brant, how can you hurt me like this? After all the time we've been together, all that we've meant to each other!"

"We haven't meant anything to each other, and you know it," he replied harshly. "If you thought any differently, you were deluding yourself. I never deceived you, Libby. I told you from the very beginning that I wasn't interested in love or marriage."

"It's because of that bitch, isn't it?" Libby snarled viciously, her eyes becoming silver-gray slits. "You have a big yen for that leggy, intellectual type, don't you? Well, let me tell you something. I know her kind, and she can't give you half the enjoyment that I do. She doesn't know how to please you like I can. After a month in her bed, you'll be crawling back to me!"

"Don't count on it." Brant's eyes were as hard as marbles. "And if I were you, I'd be more careful how I spoke about Alexis."

"Oh, the white knight coming to his lady's defense!" Libby's voice dripped with sarcasm. "Boy, has she ever done a job on you! Are you in love with her, Brant? Has she hooked you that well?"

Brant stared at her for a moment, his immediate words of denial dying on his lips. Softly, almost wonderingly, he said, "Yes, perhaps I am in love with her. Maybe that's my whole problem, that I love her."

Libby felt the world rocking beneath her feet. Everything she said only made the situation worse. She had been a fool to come here. If she had stayed at home, Brant might have tired of Alexis in a month or two and come back to her. But now the breach was irrevocable. For almost a year she had been working on catching Brant McClure, certain that eventually he would completely succumb to her charms, and now all her efforts had suddenly crumbled to dust.

"I'm sorry, Libby. I don't mean to be brutal. It has all happened very quickly, but that's the way it is. There's no point in stringing this out."

"Well, I wish you well with her," Libby retorted bitterly. "You poor, dumb country boy. She's gotten what she wanted out of you, whatever that business deal was. Now she'll get bored with you, and you'll be the one who's left here crying. She's a city girl, honey, and she's run through more men than you could count. Surely you don't really believe she could stay interested in you!"

Brant's face darkened. "I think that's enough, Libby. I suggest you go to your room now."

"Thanks," Libby sneered, and pushed past him. "I don't need your *hospitality*. I'm leaving right now."

She wrenched open the door, grabbed her small bag from the other room, then clicked down the stairs on quick, angry heels and ran out to her car. Brant heard the distant rumble of her engine and the squeal of tires on the drive.

He sagged against the bed. He could hardly deny what Libby had said. He had known from the beginning that Alexis had no interest in him, other than a brief physical attraction. Piercing cold stabbed him as he remembered her words this morning: "Really, Brant, I couldn't care less."

But neither could Brant deny what he had said to Libby. He loved Alexis. Despite all the things that had happened, despite what she had done or how she felt about him, he loved her and wanted her. Even now, thinking of her lying in bed down the hall sent a red-hot quiver through his loins. He loved her, and he couldn't let her go. No matter what, he would not let that happen.

Brant straightened up and started out the door.

Alexis was asleep when Brant entered her dark room. She awoke hazily at the sound of his undressing and blinked her eyes. "Brant?"

"Yes, it's me." He moved toward her, his tanned body glinting palely in the moonlight streaming through the window.

Alexis sat up straighter, memory flooding in on her. He had just been making love to Libby while Alexis slept. And now he was standing by her bed, naked, coming to her fresh from another woman's arms!

Anger surged through her, and she hissed, "What the hell do you think you're doing? Get out of here! Go back to your precious Libby!"

"No, I don't want to," Brant said, looking down at her. How beautiful she was in the moonlight, her fiery hair tumbling carelessly around her shoulders, her gauzy nightgown slipping down one arm, revealing the top of one creamy breast.

"I want you," he whispered huskily, his eyes roaming greedily over her.

"Well, that's too bad!" she snapped.

Brant sat down on the bed, sliding his hands up her arms, pulling her gently to him and enveloping her in a long, sweet kiss. Alexis pushed against his chest, struggling ineffectively, hating him, hating herself because even as she fought, she found delicious pleasure in the touch of his lips.

"Get out!" Alexis wrenched away from him, fighting for control over herself.

"No way." Brant's voice was harsh, raw with desire. "I told you, Alexis, you're mine."

"No!" She tried to pull away, but his arms were around her like iron and his mouth fastened on hers, claiming and subjugating. His hands slipped inside her nightgown, arousing her flesh, until at last a whimper of surrender rose in her throat. Alexis relaxed against him, giving in to the swirling, pounding ecstasy he evoked in her and despising herself all the while.

Alexis went slowly down the stairs the next morning, dreading facing Brant again. How he enjoyed degrading her as he had done last night! He loved to prove his mastery of her, his complete sexual dominance.

She felt painfully debased, and she didn't think she could bear to look at Libby, knowing what had happened the night before. She wondered if Libby realized how little pride or will Alexis had where Brant was concerned, how she had submitted to taking another woman's leavings. The thought made her throat choke with tears. And if Libby touched Brant's arm possessively, or if he put his arm around her or kissed her in front of Alexis, Alexis thought she would fly into a screaming rage and claw at the other woman's perfect face.

Fortunately, Libby was not in the kitchen when Alexis entered. Paul and Brant were there, busily making breakfast. Brant glanced at her, his expression surly, then swung back to the stove without saying a word.

"Where's Libby?" Alexis forced her voice to sound bright and unconcerned.

"She's gone already," Brant said shortly, not turning around.

"Good!" Paul exclaimed unabashedly, and clapped his hands.

So that explained Brant's mood this morning, Alexis thought. Libby must have awakened during the night and found him missing from bed, then stormed out of the house in a rage when she discovered that he had slept with Alexis as well. Which proved, Alexis thought wryly, that Libby Preston had more pride and self-respect than she.

"Look, Alexis!" Paul cried, taking her by the hand and pulling her to the window. "Snow!"

Alexis looked out. Sure enough, fat flakes were drifting down, becoming thicker even as she watched. The ground already had a covering.

"How beautiful," she said, looking around at the corral and outbuildings now frosted whitely.

"Yes, it looks to be a big one. Blizzard warnings are out. Before long, I imagine the roads will be closed." Brant set the dish of eggs on the table. "Come on, let's eat. I have to get out and feed the horses before it gets so bad I can't see my hand in front of my face."

They ate rapidly, silently, Alexis avoiding Brant's gaze. When he had finished, he stood up and began to put on his sheepskin jacket and thick gloves.

"Can I go, too?" Paul asked, jumping from his chair.

"I guess so. Just bundle up real good."

"I will," Paul promised, abandoning his plate to dash upstairs. He reappeared a few moments later in his warm coat, struggling simultaneously with his galoshes and gloves.

Alexis watched as Brant knelt and helped the child fasten his garments. He was so kind with Paul, so loving. Why did the man possess none of that kindness with her?

Paul and Brant disappeared into the swirling snow, heading for the barn. Alexis put the plates and glasses in the dishwasher, then wandered back to the window. The snow was falling more heavily, the flakes splashing against the window. The wind swirled the flakes around, filling the air with whiteness. Brant had said that soon the roads would be closed. They would be snowed in, stranded by one of those blanketing Panhandle blizzards that Alexis had read about in the newspapers for years.

She thought of being imprisoned in this house for several days with Brant, and the idea was stifling. Every time, in every way, she gave in to him. Whatever he wanted, whatever he forced on her, she ultimately accepted. It seemed as though, with Brant, she had no willpower at all.

What had happened to the independent, free woman she had once been? No man had ever controlled her. She had charted her own destiny, her own life. She alone had exercised power over herself . . . until Brant.

She had to get away! Before she lost all self-respect, she had to leave him. At home in Dallas, she could get rid of these bizarre feelings, could be herself again. If only she could escape . . .

Alexis glanced at the clock and wondered when the snow had started. If she could reach the highway before it got deep, maybe she could outrun the storm and be south of it before it became really treacherous. But even if she couldn't escape the weather, she could get as far as Beth's, where she could stay until the storm lightened.

Spurred by the yawning fear that had suddenly opened before her, Alexis darted up the stairs and began to pack in a flurry of haste. Fingers shaking, she glanced around the room to see if she had everything, buttoned herself into the parka Morgan had loaned her for skiing, pulled the hood over her head, and shoved her hands into a warm pair of gloves. Then she hurried down the stairs and out the front door and quickly threw her luggage into the back seat. The Mercedes was cold, and it took several tries to start it. She let the engine warm up while she got out and brushed the snow from the windows.

The snow fell faster than Alexis could scrape it off. She turned on the wipers and the defroster to combat it, then put the car into reverse and started slowly forward down the driveway. The road should not be too bad yet, but having been raised in Dallas, she was not used to driving in the snow. Dallas had recently had two snowy winters, and driving had been very hazardous for the poorly equipped drivers. Her experiences then had made Alexis very cautious about navigating in the snow.

The flakes were so rapid and thick that Alexis could hardly see past the car hood, and she inched along, searching for the gate that signaled the turn onto the section-line road. She had not realized how poor the visibility would be, and she breathed a sigh of relief when at last she saw the gateposts and felt the bump of the cattle guard under her wheels. Cautiously, she turned right and set off down the road at a snail's pace. It didn't take her long to decide that the safest course would be to seek the shelter of Beth's house. She wouldn't be able to drive many miles under this sort of strain.

Her fingers were wrapped tightly around the steering wheel, and she leaned forward, trying to peer through the cloud of whiteness. The wind was now whipping the fallen snow back up into the air, sending it in sickening undulations across the road. The effect was hypnotizing. Alexis decided that she was going too fast, and stepped lightly on the brake.

Suddenly the rear end of the car turned almost sideways. When it began to slide, Alexis panicked and stepped firmly on the brake. The Mercedes whipped around, and the rear wheels sunk terrifyingly down. She was halfway in a ditch. For a moment Alexis sat shaking with fear. Why had she done such a stupid thing? She should not have braked on the slick, wet caliche; that had sent her into a spin. Now what was she to do?

Alexis stepped on the gas and heard the futile whine of her wheels. She opened the door and stuck her head out, looking back at the rear tires. They were firmly embedded in the wet soil. She was stuck. Stuck and alone in a Panhandle blizzard.

Chapter 20

For the moment, Alexis could only sit there numbly, an icy terror sweeping over her. She remembered the stories she had read about people being trapped in their cars during blizzards and freezing to death. Or dying of asphyxiation because they had run the engine to keep the heater going and the snow had blocked up the exhaust pipe, sending the fumes back into the car. Instantly, Alexis reached over and switched off the ignition.

Clasping her hands together tightly, she forced herself to be calm. She could not panic; she had to think clearly. Alexis knew that she was in a potentially very dangerous situation and that she had to act with all her wits about her, not go running off in all directions. She took a deep breath and closed her eyes, compelling her muscles to relax and her brain to get back on the track.

She was still very near the house. At the speed she was traveling, she could not have gotten far. Dressed as warmly as she was, in sweater and parka, she ought to be able to walk back to the house without freezing. There was certainly no question now of her getting back on the road and driving to Beth's. Gone was her fear of being consumed by Brant; it had been replaced by the more elemental desire to survive.

Quickly, Alexis got out of the car and opened her trunk to remove the heavy ski boots, then sat back down in the car to pull them on. She tucked her hood around her face as far as it would go, drew the drawstring tight, and checked her boots and gloves to make sure they were tight also. Satisfied, she opened the door and stepped out into the driving snow.

The gale nearly knocked her off her feet, and Alexis clung to the door for a moment to right herself. The wind flung snow into her face, blinding her. She had to lean hard into the wind to propel herself forward. For every few steps she took, she staggered back two.

Alexis kept her eyes on the road, her head ducked to avoid the sting of the snow, as she scraped the drifts to the side with her foot now and then, to ensure that she remained on the caliche. Crabwise, she moved forward at a slant to cut down on the resistance her body offered to the wind.

Her progress was slow, but at least she stayed on the road. After a while, however, it occurred to her that, as thick as the snow was, she would probably not be able to see the gate to the ranch and could walk right by it. At that thought, she inched cautiously to her left, edging off the road into the deeper piled snow of the ditch. The wet stuff came up over her boots and crept inside, chilling her further, but she grasped the wire of the fence and pushed on, running her hand carefully along the wire to avoid the sharp barbs that stuck out irregularly.

For a long time she slogged through the snow by the fence, though her feet were becoming numb. At last she came upon a post, followed by emptiness. The gate! Alexis felt about with her foot and was reassured by the steel bars of the cattle guard. She plowed through the gate, now heading crosswise to the wind, so that it blew at her from the side and almost shoved her off the driveway. Alexis continued to check beneath her feet every few steps to make sure that she was still on the dirt ruts of the road, not on the ground beside it.

On and on she plodded, mechanically. It seemed as though it had been hours since she had started out. Had Brant come back inside yet? Had he noticed she was gone? And if he had, would he come after her, or would he think that she could take care of herself, and good riddance to her?

Not that, she prayed silently. Oh, please, don't let him think that. Please, Brant, come looking for me, because I don't know how much longer I can walk.

Alexis was chilled to the core and deeply tired from battling the weather. She felt that if she could just lie down and take a nap, everything would be all right. Sternly, she jerked her head upright and slapped at her cheeks with her gloved hands. That was another thing she had read about the cold. It made you want to drift off to sleep, a sleep from which you would never awaken. Alexis dragged one foot in front of the other. One came down upon a rock, throwing her off balance, and she stumbled, then fell, soaking herself in the snow. Tears of exhaustion rolled down her cheeks. She would freeze now. Dear God, why had she been so crazy as to leave in the first place?

Wearily, she staggered on, and then suddenly, looming up in front of her was a snow-covered shape. Alexis almost ran to it, reaching out to touch the cold metal beneath the snow. A car! She had somehow stumbled around and wound up back where she had started, at her Mercedes!

The tears came freely now, as she leaned against the car in despair. All that effort, all that numbing cold, for nothing. She was worse off than she had been to begin with. Well, there was nothing to do now but get in and wait and hope that Brant would find her. She did not have the energy to start back to the house again.

Alexis groped her way to the driver's door, opened it, and crawled in, feeling for the keys in the ignition. To hell with asphyxiation. She had to have some warmth. But her gloved hand did not come into contact with the keys on the steering column. She bent to search for them. The keys were not there. She straightened, that information slowly penetrating her brain, then twisted her head around to look at the interior of the car. What an idiot she was, she thought excitedly. This was Brant's car, which sat by the garage, not a hundred feet behind the house.

Quickly, she twisted the door handle and stepped out. All around her was the pure white of the swirling snow. She couldn't even see the outline of the house or the barn. Closing her eyes, she tried to remember the exact way Brant parked his car. Did its nose point toward the garage, the house, or the corral?

A distant sound pierced her concentration. "Sis!" She turned her head, listening, and again a male voice drifted through the air to her. "Aleexxiiis!" It was Brant, calling to her, stretching her name out in the wind.

"Brant!" she cried, but the wind tore the words from her lips. Again and again she called, but she knew that her voice was not reaching him.

"Alexis, where are you? Aleexiis!" Again his voice sounded, a little closer this time, but she could not determine the direction in this blanketed, whistling wasteland.

Again Alexis screamed his name, terrified that he would move away from her and never find her. Then an idea came to her, and she whipped open the car door and leaned in to blow the horn. She kept up a steady tattoo of beeps, some long, some short, but never stopping.

And then, above the sound of the wind and the horn, she heard his voice. "Alexis!" In the next instant he was there, looming out of the whiteness, a huge, shapeless figure in his army parka, the hood pulled forward to cover his face.

With a sobbing cry, Alexis released the horn and stumbled toward him. His arms went around her, pulling her hard against him, pressing her face into his snowy jacket as he squeezed her so tight she thought he would crush her bones.

"Alexis. Jesus, I thought you were gone! You scared the living hell out of me. What were you doing out in weather like this?"

Too cold to speak, Alexis could only shake her head mutely and lean against him, feeling his strength seep through to her.

"Come on, let's get you inside." Brant slammed the car door shut and led her through the blizzard's fury until at last her feet touched the blessed security of the back steps.

Once inside the kitchen, Brant wasted no time or words, merely pulled Alexis's clothing from her quickly, leaving it in a sodden heap on the floor. Shrugging off his jacket and gloves, he picked her up, and cradling her in his arms, carried her into the den. He deposited her on the rug in front of the fireplace, where a roaring blaze was burning, and went to a closet to pull down a blanket, which he wrapped securely around her.

"God, Alexis," he exclaimed, holding her close, "you gave me the fright of my life! Don't ever do a crazy thing like that again! Did you want to get away from me that badly?" His voice broke, and he hugged her to him even tighter, burying his face in her damp hair. "You don't have to do that. You're free to go whenever you want. But please, don't ever, ever do anything like that again. Do you realize you could have been killed?"

"I'm sorry, Brant," Alexis mumbled, feeling incredibly drowsy.

"I'm the one who's sorry," he said, kissing her temple gently. "I didn't mean to scold. I was just so scared. You sit right here, and let me get you a brandy. That'll warm you up real fast."

When he released her, Alexis stretched out on the rug, thankful for the lovely warmth of the fire that was creeping through her skin. She felt chilled to the bone, as if she would never be completely warm again.

In a moment Brant was beside her, forcing a strong liquid into her mouth. Alexis coughed, then drank sip after sip of the brandy, which rolled like fire down her throat to her stomach. Then Brant pulled the sofa closer to the flames and lifted Alexis, with her blanket, onto it.

"There, now, you just relax while I go tell Paul that I've found you and you're all right."

"Paul—" For a moment Alexis came out of her dazed state. "He's not . . . outside looking for me, is he?"

"Heavens, no. I wasn't about to let him get lost, too. He's upstairs in his room, where he went on my orders in quite a huff. He wanted to find you himself, I'm afraid."

"Oh, I'm so sorry, Brant. I was such an idiot."

He bent and planted a light kiss on the tip of her nose. "Well, that is something, at least. I never thought I would hear you admit that."

With a faint smile, Alexis closed her eyes and drifted off to sleep. She slept for a couple of hours, and when she awakened, she found Brant sitting in a nearby chair, watching her.

"Hi," she said, a little weakly.

"Hi yourself," he replied. "How are you feeling?"

"Okay, I think."

Brant moved from the chair to kneel beside the sofa. His face was concerned, his eyes dark with worry. At the look on his face, a shudder ran through Alexis, and she threw her arms around his neck.

"Oh, Brant, thank you," she breathed, her voice choked with emotion. "I was so scared. I was afraid you wouldn't look for me, that you would figure I could take care of myself. For a while there I really thought I was going to die. Thank you for coming after me. You saved my life."

His arms tightened convulsively around her. "As if I'd let you go without trying to stop you! I didn't know why you'd left or what had happened to you. I was so worried . . . Please don't ever do something like that again."

"I won't," Alexis replied earnestly. "Believe me, I won't."

"Oh, Alexis, I don't know what I would have done if anything had happened to you." He gently kissed her forehead and then her ear, his lips sliding across to her cheeks and finally to her mouth.

Eagerly, Alexis's lips met his, her mouth clinging to him as her hands ran across his chest and back. Suddenly he broke from her, his face tortured.

"Why did you leave, Alexis? Do you hate me that much? Fear me so much you would risk your life?"

"No—oh, no. I'm not frightened of you. I think . . . I'm more frightened of myself. I didn't realize how bad the weather was, or I wouldn't have gone. But suddenly, looking at the snow, I felt trapped, hemmed in. I was scared because of the way I've been acting." She stopped, not wanting to reveal how completely her soul had succumbed to him, how great his power over her was. She was already too dominated by him to let him know that; at least she could retain some shred of self-pride.

"I don't understand." His eyes searched her face tenderly, and Alexis felt as though she would melt under this kindness.

"Don't," she choked out. "Please . . . I have no control with you. I want you so badly that I—"

His mouth stopped her words, seizing her lips in a long, probing kiss. "Alexis," he breathed, pushing back the blanket and feasting his eyes on her smooth, naked body. "God, you're lovely."

Worshipfully, his mouth trailed over her flesh, seeking out every quivering, longing part of it. Alexis moaned beneath his kisses and caresses. She yearned to feel his fullness within her, filling and satisfying her as nothing else could.

"Please," she whispered. "Love me, Brant. Love me."

With a groan, he tore off his clothing and pulled her down onto the rug. The hot flicker of the flames played across their bodies as they lay before the fireplace, lost in the wonder of their passion. Teasingly, they stroked and kissed each other, holding back until their desire burst its bounds, and then came together eagerly, riding the crest of their rapture to new and still greater heights, melding in the white heat into a heart-stopping oneness.

The storm continued throughout the day, wrapping the house in a blanket of whiteness, shutting the inhabitants inside their own small world. They played subdued games, ate hearty bowls of chili for supper, and lazily stretched out before the fireplace afterward. Alexis, following her great emotional upheavals of the day, hardly dared utter a word that might break the fragile peace that existed between her and Brant. Now and then she would shyly glance at him and smile, or he would reach out a hand and touch her. For a time that afternoon, such wonder had passed between them that they feared to say anything that would spoil its glow.

They did not make love that night, but slept wrapped in each other's arms, secure against the howling wind. The next morning they awoke to a clear, sparkling white world. Even the wind was at its normal velocity.

Alexis rose, and shivering, went to look out the window. The snow lay deep over the ground, piled on the rails of the corral, and blown into drifts against the barn and house.

"Wow," she said with wonder. "I've never seen anything like this!"

Brant came to stand behind her, putting his arms around her. "Quite a sight, isn't it?"

"It's beautiful—so wild and yet so fragile. I can't believe this is the same place as it was yesterday."

"Yes, it's pretty. Too bad the snow causes such destruction."

Alexis frowned. "What does it do to your cattle?"

"Kills a lot of them," Brant answered succinctly.

"Oh, no."

"Yes, and a storm like this quite often kills a few people, too. Today they'll have the helicopters out, searching the road for stranded motorists. Then the pilots will relay the motorists' positions to the rescue crews on the ground. I'll probably try to get out this afternoon in my jeep to help. Usually, some people get stranded along the road to Amarillo. A blizzard's so sudden and fierce that it's pretty easy to get caught in it."

"I know," Alexis said wryly, and Brant chuckled. "What do you do about your cattle? What happens to them?"

"Hopefully by tomorrow the pilots will be able to start helicoptering feed to them. Then, when I can get out in my jeep without getting stuck in a drift, I'll drive around the ranch and see if I can rescue any of the strays. The ones that stick together in fair-sized herds won't do so badly. They clump together and keep each other warm, and they're easier to spot and drop feed to. But the ones that stray are more likely to freeze. If they stumble into a gully and break a leg, they're goners. They can freeze, or smother in the snow, or starve to death. During the years when we have a really bad blizzard or a couple of bad snows in a row, this area and northern New Mexico can lose millions of cattle."

"How dreadful!"

He shrugged slightly. "It's one of the risks of ranching. But that's enough of all this gloom. This morning I think we ought to take Paul out for his first romp in the snow."

Alexis turned around, smiling. "Great!"

After breakfast, all three of them bundled up and went outside to explore. Paul was fascinated by the thick, cold, white snow and ran from place to place, falling, rolling in the drifts, and laughing with sheer joy. Alexis followed more slowly, looking in amazement at the six-foot-high mounds piled against the house and the barn, and at the huge, gleaming icicles that hung down from the roof, some of them three or four feet long and as thick as an arm.

They built a snowman close to the house by making three graduated balls and sticking an old straw cowboy hat on the top.

"A Texas snowman!" Alexis chortled.

Brant picked up a clump of snow and threw a soft ball at her. Alexis retaliated in kind, and soon the three of them were engaged in an all-out snowball fight. Finally, with snow caked on them from head to toe, laughing and exhausted, they declared a truce and trooped back into the house.

They dumped their wet outer clothing on the floor of the kitchen and settled down to steaming bowls of leftover chili. After lunch, while Alexis dozed and read in front of the fire, Brant went out to the garage and took off carefully in his jeep to join the rescue teams in Barrett. It was late in the afternoon when he returned, tired and red from the cold.

That evening, after Alexis put an exhausted and happy Paul to bed, she and Brant sat in front of the fireplace, sipping hot buttered rum. Alexis could not remember ever feeling such peace and contentment, especially around Brant McClure.

"Tell me about Paul's mother," Alexis said, certain that he would answer her now without constraint.

"Lea?" Brant cast her a surprised look. "What about her?"

"What was she like? Did you love her?"

"Love her? No, I didn't love her any more than I've loved any other woman in my life. But she was there for me at a bad time, when I was scared and sick and wishing I were home and out of that treacherous jungle. 'Nam was a nightmare, Alexis, and Lea was about the only comfort I had. I'd go into Saigon to see her every time I got the chance. She was a sweet, pretty girl, very small, with fragile wrists and a waist that looked as if it would snap. There wasn't any spirit to her; she was very submissive. I remember getting angry with her once because she would never stand up for herself if I got too demanding."

He paused and looked into the fire. "The one exception was that she wanted to keep the baby when she had it, and I foolishly agreed. I always wanted a child, but I couldn't take Paul away from his mother. Hell, he wasn't even born yet. Lea wouldn't move to the States, either. She was scared to death of going to a foreign country. So I agreed to let her stay and to send her support money each month. And then the Communists took over, and, well, you probably know that story as well as I do."

"What is it that you have against women, Brant?"

He threw her a dark glance and then laughed. "You sure have a way with words, lady."

Alexis smiled. "I'm an American woman, remember, not Vietnamese."

"Not all American women use questions to attack."

Alexis sighed. "Oh, I guess I do. I've been trying too hard for too long to intimidate male lawyers."

"I bet you succeed real well."

"Sometimes I do." Alexis thrust her chin up somewhat belligerently. "That's the way the game is played, but a woman starts out with two strikes against her."

"Why?"

"Because men come in expecting a woman to be weak, to give in to them. They're more confident. They'll stick it out longer than is rational simply because they can't quite believe a woman is giving them legal arguments. So I have to be tough from the word go and win at all costs, or next time I'll get nowhere with them. I have to build a reputation."

"And what is your reputation?"

A shadow touched Alexis's face. "What you think of me—a chip off the old block."

Lightly, his hand touched her hair. "And is that what you are, Alexis?"

Tears sprang into her eyes, and she swallowed,

finding it hard to speak without watering up. "No. Actually, I'm not like Alec at all. Well, that's not quite true. I am like him in some ways. I'm not like my mother. She is very feminine."

He laughed. "And you're not?"

"Not very."

"Who convinced you of that?"

Alexis shrugged. "Nobody. It's something I've always known. I'm not interested in clothes and decorating and all that. I'm not emotional. I'm ambitious and hard-working and I live up here, in my head." She tapped her temple. "That's how I'm like Alec. But the other ways—the things you talk about, the deceit, the using of people, the selfishness—truly, I'm not like that. Or at least I never thought I was."

"Until when?"

"Until recently, when I started doubting myself. I've been looking at my life, my work, the things I do to people. Sometimes I'm not sure any more who I am."

Sadness settled on Alexis's face as she stared broodingly into the flames. Gently, Brant brushed her cheek with his fingertips, and his voice was soft and light, almost teasing when he spoke.

"Well, let me assure you of one thing. You are feminine, whatever you think. Women's lib would line you up and shoot you, from what you just characterized as feminine."

Tears rolled down her cheeks, surprising Alexis as much as Brant. "Daddy always wanted a boy, you see, and I tried so hard to live up to that, to be what he wanted. I've always thought of womanliness as being bad."

Brant pulled Alexis against him, cradling her head on his shoulder. "What in hell does it matter what your father wanted? You aren't here on this earth to be what Alec Stone wants. You're here to be you. And what you are is more than enough for anyone. You are a lovely, intelligent woman. I can personally testify to your femininity. After all, I'm the one who's been sleeping with you, aren't I? Who should know better whether or not you're feminine? I, for one, am very glad that Alec Stone didn't have a son."

Alexis laughed a little tearfully. "Oh, Brant."

"Trust me. I'm qualified to judge. I've been around enough to know what makes a woman beautiful or sexy or charming. And you have it all."

Alexis dashed the tears from her eyes with her hands and smiled up at him. "Enough about me. Tell me something about you. Please."

"Well, let me see. Shall we go back to the question you asked a long time ago? What do I have against women? Truthfully, I've never really thought of myself as being 'against women.' I've simply never fallen in love. Have you?"

Alexis shook her head. No one had ever touched her heart, at least not until now. But she was not about to reveal that.

"So it's possible, isn't it? You don't necessarily have anything against men, do you?"

"No, but I'm twenty-six, not thirty-four. It seems a little more likely at my age."

He grinned. "Touché. Okay, maybe I've had a wall around me because of my mother. I loved her very much, you know. I could always talk to her about anything, whereas Dad sometimes didn't understand mistakes or feelings of uncertainty. When she left, I felt horribly betrayed. It was as if she had left me, not Dad. After that, I guess I always had my guard up against women. I was determined not to let any of them get to me, hurt me." He looked down at Alexis, thinking, *And none of them had the strength or determination to batter it down, until you.*

He leaned over and kissed her lips, barely brushing them with his own. "I think that's enough soul-searching for one night. Let's go up to bed."

Alexis smiled at him and lifted her face to kiss him again. Their lips clung, their embrace deepening.

"Now I'm positive I want to go to bed," Brant teased, helping her to her feet.

They walked slowly up the stairs to Brant's room, Alexis leaning dreamily against his side. No longer did she want to go to her own room and close him out. Somehow, somewhere, she had lost all the remnants of her hatred and fear. She floated along now, living only in the present, ignoring the past and the looming future. Perhaps this idyll would end soon; perhaps Brant would shatter her life. But she preferred not to think about that. Right now, it was enough merely to feel and not to analyze. Tonight, it was enough to lose herself in the joy of his arms.

Chapter 21

The temperature had plummeted during the crystal-clear night, freezing solid what little snow had melted the day before. It was treacherously slippery outside, and Brant and Alexis stayed snug indoors, keeping Paul entertained. Brant made several phone calls and reported to Alexis that the hay drop for the cattle would begin in the afternoon.

About midmorning, while Alexis was absorbed in a game of checkers with Paul, the phone rang. Brant answered it, then turned to her with a carefully blank expression and held out the receiver. "It's for you," he said.

Alexis gaped. Who knew that she was here?

"Hello?" she breathed into the phone.

Her father's voice came rolling over the line. "Alexis! What in the blue blazes is going on? What are you doing up there?"

"If you didn't know I was here, why did you call?" Alexis returned imperturbably.

She could picture his face suffusing with anger as he bellowed, "Because I checked every place else first! I called that damn ski resort, and they said you never showed up. So then I checked with the highway patrol in three states to see if you'd had an accident. This call

351

was an outside chance. I was beginning to think you'd been kidnapped!"

"I'm sorry," Alexis said contritely. "I should have called Betty and let her know where I was."

"Well, now that I do know, would you have the goodness to explain what you're up to there? Why aren't you here in Dallas, where you're supposed to be?"

"I took another week of vacation."

"I know that . . . although I had to call your secretary to find even that out! But your vacation ended on Monday. That's two days ago, and you're still in Barrett. Why?"

"There was a blizzard up here, Daddy," Alexis explained, trying to sidestep the issue. "It's been impossible to travel."

"You should have left before, then," Alec growled. "What are you doing there so long, anyway? Are you having trouble getting the lease?"

Alexis sighed. Her father would never understand the situation she was in now. Even she did not understand it.

"Yes, a little. But I'm getting it all straightened out, and I'll be home as soon as the roads are clear."

"Okay. But next time let me know what's going on."

"I will, Daddy."

She hung up the phone and turned back to the others. Brant was gone. She didn't know if he had left the room out of courtesy or anger. Alexis resumed the game with Paul, but she could not concentrate on what they were doing. For the first time in days, it struck Alexis that she had to leave. She had a job and a life in Dallas that she must return to. She could not simply while away her days in Barrett. Paul was fine now with Brant; there were no reasons to keep her here—except one: Alexis did not wish to leave. Tears filled her eyes at the idea of returning to her condominium to sleep once more in her lonely bed. No more masculine warmth beside her at night, no strong arms about her or heated moments of passion. No sight of Brant at the breakfast table, smelling of soap and aftershave, his face in its familiar hard lines, his eyes gold as he looked at her, telling her that he was remembering the night before.

She swallowed and pushed her thoughts away. She could stay until the roads were clear, at least. There was no point in upsetting herself before that time.

The days passed all too quickly for her, and despite the chill weather, the snow melted under the glare of the sun. Brant took the jeep out to investigate his loss and to toss hay to the hungry cattle he found. Alexis tried to busy herself with Paul and with some work around the house, fighting determinedly to keep her mind off her upcoming departure.

One day she went exploring in the attic, which yielded all sorts of quaint treasures, from chests full of old dresses to some marvelous antique furniture to photo albums from Brant's childhood. With an eager cry, she sat down to pore over the photographs, a smile curving her lips as she looked at Brant as a child. There was a picture of him and a baby Beth seated on a small paint pony, Beth obviously crying at the top of her lungs. In another, he squatted beside his father, proudly showing off a fish he had caught. The last pictures in the album had been taken at Christmas, when Brant looked to be about twelve, opening presents and displaying his prizes, and in one he stood beside the tree with Beth on one side and his mother on the other. Alexis bent over the photo, searching for signs of discontent in Selena's smiling, pretty face.

She sighed and set the album down. How sad; it was as though Brant's father had stopped taking an interest in his children when Selena left. In the same box, Alexis found Brant's high-school album and several trophies for football and track, and she giggled over his fierce adolescent football pictures.

Toward the end of the day she came upon a real find, a trunk that contained leather-bound books containing ledgers from the early days of the ranch, order slips, bills of sale, and even a diary of a McClure ancestor, a country minister who had fought in the Civil War. Delighted, Alexis hauled the books downstairs and occupied herself in the succeeding days by delving into the old records.

One evening Brant came in and suggested cheerfully, "How about our getting out tonight? Aren't you two going stir-crazy?"

"Yes!" Alexis exclaimed. "But where can we go?"

"Well, they're showing a western at the theater downtown. I thought we might drive in and see it."

"Are the roads okay?"

"Fine. Even the section road is navigable. It's easy in the jeep. Oh, by the way, I pulled your car out today and drove it back into the yard. It seems to be okay. I guess you'll be glad to have your suitcases back."

"Will I! I'm getting pretty tired of wearing Beth's old jeans and shirts. In fact, I'm going to get all dressed up in honor of the movie tonight."

Alexis chose a soft brown wool dress that set off her hair and was slit alluringly halfway up one thigh. She primped before the mirror, realizing that she was hoping to achieve a look of admiration in Brant's face. When the hoped-for expression appeared as she descended the stairs, joy suffused her and she smiled brightly. Brant stepped forward to slide his arms around her and kiss her. "You look good enough to eat," he murmured against her hair, and she leaned into him.

"Is that a promise?" she asked huskily, and was gratified to feel the muscle in his arm jump.

"Lady, that's a promise."

The movie was a good old-fashioned western, with plenty of shooting and much riding of horses, although occasionally it displayed the gritty realism that today's directors found necessary to insert. Despite Alexis's initial nervousness that some of the blood and gore unfolding on the screen might awaken Paul's bad memories, he sat on the edge of his seat, enthralled by the action. Alexis, however, closed her eyes when the blood became too thick. Brant's arm around her shoulder sent a wave of warmth through her, and she snuggled cozily up to him, enjoying the rest of the movie.

Afterward, they ate hot apple pie at Nora's and drove home through the cold, the moonlight sparkling over the snowy landscape. They put Paul to bed, and then, in the privacy of Brant's bedroom, he made hard, sweet love to her, his hands and tongue lifting her to the brink of ecstasy again and again, until at last they reached the peak of blissful union.

With his arm curled around her shoulders and her head resting on his chest, Brant fell into an easy sleep. But sleep did not come that quickly for Alexis. Listening to the even sound of his breathing, tears welled in her eyes. She could not stop the flood of thoughts that had been pushing at the back of her mind ever since Alec had called.

It was time to leave. But she could not! Just the thought of leaving made her want to burst into tears. Rolling away from Brant, Alexis lay staring at the ceiling, deciding to confront the bubbling emotions within her. She was in love.

Instinctively, her mind skittered away from that idea. She could not be in love with Brant McClure! Not the man she had fought against for months. Firmly, Alexis cut through her resistance. She had been pretending to herself and the world for too long. It was time she faced facts, time she came to terms with herself.

Alexis looked across at the man who slept beside her, a flood of feeling surging through her. She wanted him desperately; she could not bear to leave him; the time she spent with him was precious. She loved him. She might as well admit that she loved Brant McClure. Something around her heart moved and eased as she at last accepted the irrevocable truth. Despite everything that had happened between them—the bitterness, the anger, the furious accusations—Alexis loved him.

A smile played across her lips as she thought of all the wonderful little things she loved about him, and for a moment she was lost in a dreamy world in which Brant loved her back and everything was right between them.

Before long, however, reality intervened, and her thoughts returned to her immediate problem. What was she to do about leaving? She did not want to go; she thought it would be almost impossible to break away.

And Brant . . . Surely she could not be mistaken about his desire for her. He enjoyed their nights together as much as she. He had been worried and anxious the day she had been lost in the snowstorm. And before Libby had showed up that morning, hadn't he asked her to stay longer? That had to be some indication that he cared for her. It didn't prove that he loved her, of course, but maybe if she stayed of her own volition, Brant would be pleased.

But if she stayed, what was she to do about her job, her father, her life in Dallas? She could well imagine Alec Stone's reaction if she called and said she had no idea when she was coming back. He was frothing at the mouth as it was to get that lease.

The lease! Alexis bolted up in bed, her brain racing. She could not do that to Brant, not now. She loved him too much to make him follow through with the deal. It had always grated on her conscience that she had used Paul to get Brant to sign the lease, but now, loving him as she did, it tore at her heart. Alexis simply could not turn the lease over to her father and let him drill on the land Brant loved. No matter how wrong she thought Brant was about his hatred for oil and her father, she knew how much he would be hurt, and she could not bear that.

Silently, Alexis slipped out of bed and padded down

the hall to her room. She closed the door and turned on the light, then picked up her briefcase and swung it onto the bed. She flicked open the locks, opened the case, and pulled out the two blue-backed copies of the lease that Brant had signed. Decisively, she tore each one in half, then in quarters.

Looking at the pieces of paper in her hands, Alexis wondered what she should do with them now. Brant should be told that he was no longer obligated to Stone Oil, but somehow she could not summon the courage to do that face to face. He would probably ask her why, and then what would she say? It would be far better to leave the torn pieces someplace where Brant would see them. Then he would know about the lease, and, moreover, he would be able to guess something of her feeling for him. His actions at that point would give Alexis an idea of what he truly felt about her.

Alexis turned and walked back to Brant's bedroom. It took a moment for her eyes to adjust to the darkness, and then she went to the dresser and laid the shredded documents on top of it. There. She had cast her die, and what happened from here on in would depend on Brant.

The winter sun was streaming in the window when Alexis awoke the next morning. She sat up slowly, blinking and looking around her, still slightly confused. What time was it? It seemed so late. Brant was already gone. She glanced toward the dresser and saw that the pieces of paper were gone as well. Her heart began to thud in great, pounding leaps.

Alexis threw back the covers and got out of bed. After a hasty shower, she threw on slacks and a sweater, ran a brush through her hair, and hurried downstairs, feeling both scared and excited at the prospect of facing Brant.

There was no one in the kitchen, and Alexis came to a disappointed halt. She looked at the large clock on the wall, which read ten-thirty, and knew that she could not reasonably expect Brant to be inside waiting for her. He had many chores to do. Still, she could not keep her spirits from drooping as she mechanically went about making coffee.

Alexis was on her second cup, staring moodily into space, when the back door sprang open and Paul catapulted into the room.

"Hi!" he called cheerfully when he saw Alexis. "I've been down at the barn taking care of Blackie. Daddy told me that I had to feed and water and curry him myself, and I haven't forgotten yet."

"That's terrific." Alexis grinned at the boy's enthusiasm. Trying to keep her voice casual, she asked, "Is Brant still down there?"

"No, he isn't there," Paul said, his voice faintly scornful that she should know so little. "He left real early, right after breakfast."

"Oh? To inspect his losses?"

"What's that?"

"To ride around the ranch and look at his cattle, you know, like he did yesterday."

"Oh, no, he went to Amarillo."

"Amarillo!" Alexis exclaimed, her heart dropping to her feet. Why, with all the work he had to do, would Brant suddenly take off for Amarillo? She could think of no reason except one: to see Libby. "Did he say why he was going there?" Alexis wet her lips nervously in anticipation of Paul's reply.

"No." Regretfully, Paul shook his head. "I asked, and he said that he couldn't tell me, 'cause I would tell you."

Alexis felt as if she had just received a blow to the stomach. That statement made it even more obvious to her that Brant had gone off to see his girlfriend. If he had driven to Amarillo on business, there would have been no reason to hide it from Alexis.

Brant had seen the lease, had guessed that only love for him could have prompted her to tear it up, and then he had high-tailed it to Amarillo to see his mistress! It was clearly a slap in the face to Alexis. He obviously wanted to show her that no matter what she might feel about him, he felt nothing for her and would not be tied down by any woman.

Alexis rose from her chair, her fists clenched and her eyes flashing fire. Paul stepped back a pace or two at the expression on her face. Slamming the chair seat under the table, she marched out of the kitchen and up the stairs to her room. Once there, she closed the door and began to pace angrily.

The gall of that man, the nerve! To go to Libby after Alexis's revelation of her love. He had no feeling for her at all. He just wanted to use her, as he had used all the other women in his life, and when he was finished with her, he would toss her aside like a withered leaf.

Tears streamed down her face as she walked back and forth, remembering the degradation she had suffered during Libby's visit. If she remained here, the pattern would be the same for the rest of her life with Brant.

She could not accept that! Alexis came to a halt, dashing away the tears from her face with impatient fingers. She had been an idiot to have let Brant make her love him. He had won. If she stayed here, her spirit would be totally crushed before long. For her self-preservation, she had to get out.

She sank down on the bed. That prospect struck her as almost as bad as remaining. Life without him seemed suddenly bleak and arid.

Shakily, Alexis began to pack. Within an hour, she was ready to go, although her stomach was churning sickly.

Going downstairs with her bags, she found Paul playing in the den. Swallowing, she said, "Paul, I have something to talk to you about."

He turned toward her expectantly.

"I'm afraid it's time for me to leave here."

"What!" His face contracted and he scrambled to his feet. "No, you can't leave! You were going to stay."

"I can't, Paul. Remember that I said I would stay only a week. It's already longer than that now. I must get back."

"But I don't want you to go!" he cried, his eyes clouding with tears.

"I know. I shall miss you dreadfully, too. But you must stay here with your father. You know him now and like him, don't you?"

"Yeah. I want to live here, but I want you to be here, too."

"I'm afraid that's impossible, Paul," she said, fighting to keep the tremor from her voice.

"Why?"

"Because my life is in Dallas. I have to get back to work. I have to return to my house. I don't live here, I live in Dallas."

"But you could live here. You could move here."

"No, I can't, Paul. Your daddy doesn't love me, and both of us will be better off apart. Believe me, I have to go back, Paul. I will miss you very much, but I have to go back."

The boy seemed about to protest again, but then looked down at his feet, apparently giving it up as useless. "Okay," he said in a tiny voice.

Alexis took a deep breath. "Now, I want you to come with me to Beth's. I'll write Brant a note and tell him that you're with her. Then I'll drop you off there and continue on to Dallas."

Paul shrugged as if to say he had no power to change her mind, but was certainly not in agreement with her. Alexis breathed a little sigh and picked up her luggage. It was dreadful to see Paul react in that withdrawn, silent way, but she hoped he would come out of it before too long. At first he would miss her, but surely he had come to love and trust Brant enough to be happy here without her.

They maintained an unbroken silence on the ride to Beth's house. With a stab of guilt, Alexis felt that she ought to cheer him up somehow, but she couldn't even summon the energy to think of a way. Tired and gloomy now that she had acted on her decision, she wanted only to put as much space between her and Barrett as possible, and quickly.

Beth answered their knock with a smile, which vanished as soon as she saw the two glum faces before her. "Whatever is the matter? Come on in and tell me what's going on. Is something wrong with Brant?"

"No, as far as I know, he's all right," Alexis answered tonelessly. "I brought Paul over here for you to keep an eye on until Brant gets back. I'm driving to Dallas."

Beth's mouth dropped, but she recovered quickly and turned to Paul. "Honey, why don't you go find the girls? I want to talk to Alexis."

"It won't do you any good," Alexis warned as Paul went off obediently. "I'm not going to change my mind."

"But why are you going back?" Beth wailed. "What happened? Did you have a fight? You know Brant's temper, Alexis. He'll be over it by the end of the day. Please, don't storm out in a huff."

"No, we didn't have a fight. Brant went to Amarillo to see Libby."

"Are you sure? Did he tell you that?"

"No, he didn't tell me. He sneaked away before I got up. But from what he told Paul, I'm sure that's where he was going."

"At least stay until he gets back, Alexis. He might have some good explanation. Maybe he went there to tell her it was over between them. Give him a chance. Don't run away like this."

"Beth, I've made up my mind, and nothing you say can change it. I have to leave. I have to get back to my job—"

"Forget your job!" Beth snapped. "My God, Alexis, you don't have to work, and you know it. Besides, you could get a job anywhere. You don't have to rush back to save your job at Stone Oil!"

"Beth, I have to! For the sake of my own self-esteem!"

"What in the world does *that* mean?"

"It means that I can't live with a man who doesn't love me, who doesn't care about me at all! If I did, I wouldn't have any self-respect left."

"Oh, no, Alexis, you're wrong about Brant. I'm sure that he loves you."

"Beth, you have been overly optimistic about the two of us ever since we met. Brant and I just don't work! That's all there is to it. Please, I don't want to get in an argument with you."

"I don't want to argue, either, but I can't bear to stand by and watch you and Brant louse up this relationship."

"There isn't any 'relationship,'" Alexis sighed. "Please, Beth, can't we drop it? I'm going in to tell Paul good-bye."

Beth's look was disapproving, but she clamped her lips tightly together and said nothing. Alexis walked down the hall to the playroom, where Paul was sitting morosely, watching the girls play. The sight of him tugged at Alexis's heart, but she steeled herself to fold him in her arms.

"Good-bye, Paul," she whispered, tousling his jet-black hair. "I love you."

He threw his arms about her neck and clung to her. "I love you, too, Allie. Please don't go."

Tears spilled from Alexis's eyes as she gave him a kiss and firmly released herself from his grasp. After squeezing his hand one more time, she turned and walked away, tears pouring down her face. Once out of Paul's sight, she stopped and leaned against the wall to draw a shaky breath and dab at her wet cheeks. Finally, she straightened and moved toward the den.

Beth did not try again to dissuade her friend from leaving. She simply hugged Alexis and wished her the best, tears sparkling in her own eyes. Then she accompanied Alexis to the front door and stepped out to watch her depart.

As Alexis started toward her car, a glint of sunlight reflecting off metal caught her eye. Brant's car was turning into the driveway. Alexis stood in surprised immobility as the Ford spun to a stop before her and Brant jumped out, a wide grin on his face.

"Well, I didn't expect to see you here, Alexis," he remarked cheerfully.

Anger bubbled inside Alexis at his nonchalant attitude. One would never guess that he had just come from visiting another woman. She wondered with a sudden ache if this was the way her mother had felt whenever Alec returned from one of his trips.

"Don't worry, you won't see me for long," she retorted in a tight voice. "I was just about to leave."

"For where? The house?"

"No, for Dallas."

"Dallas!" he echoed in astonishment.

"Yes. That's where I live, you know. I have a job I have to get back to."

A slow, confident grin spread across his face, and Alexis itched to slap the smugness from his smile. "Wait a minute," he said, holding out one hand with a jewelry box in it.

So he thought he could buy her off with presents after he visited another woman! Furious, Alexis swept the box onto the muddy ground. "No matter what you think, I am not a whore!" she flared.

Brant straightened, his cheerfulness instantly wiped away and replaced by the familiar cold stiffness. "What are you waiting for?" he snapped, his voice icy with rage. "I thought you were leaving."

"I am!" Alexis whirled and got into her car, slamming the door shut with a thud that matched the sound of her heartbeat. She started the Mercedes and shot down the driveway without a backward glance.

Brant bent and picked up the jewelry box. Wiping

the mud from it, he put it carefully in his pocket, then turned to Beth, his face drawn and old beyond its years. With a cry, Beth started to go to him, but his stern look held her off.

"Where's Paul?" he demanded. "I'm taking him home."

Chapter 22

Alexis drove to Dallas, her fury and hurt speeding her on. By the time she had reached her condominium, she felt exhausted and drained. She carried in her baggage and the unused ski gear, then searched her kitchen for something to eat. She could find nothing except a can of tuna, but since she didn't want to go to the store, she sat down listlessly and ate the tuna, along with a glass of water. It was not a very interesting diet, Alexis reflected, but frankly, she didn't care about what she ate.

She watched television for an hour or so, then stumbled wearily up to bed. Sleep did not come quickly, however, for she found that as soon as she closed her eyes, she was haunted by visions of Brant McClure. Before long, Alexis had dissolved into tears. She sobbed helplessly, clinging to her pillow, crying for her love and her lost opportunities, crying as though she would never stop.

The next day Alexis remained in her apartment, going out only to restock her refrigerator. She didn't even call her secretary. Nothing interested her, and everything seemed appallingly gloomy. She found herself crying over nothing, watching the soap operas and empathizing with the characters, bringing out her favorite sad books to read.

This, she thought, wryly, was called wallowing in your grief. But again, she really didn't care. Somehow the strength and the repose that had once been her hallmarks no longer seemed important.

Late in the afternoon Alexis was seized with a longing to see her mother. It was the first time in years that she could remember feeling like this, and she told herself not to be foolish. Nevertheless, she still drove to Walnut Hill. There was no point in denying herself her mother's comfort.

Ginny looked surprised when she answered the door and saw her eldest daughter standing there, but she held out her arms to Alexis.

"Hello, honey," she said. "What's the matter?"

"Is it so obvious?"

"To me it is. What's happened?" She led the way into the living room and sat down on the couch, patting the seat beside her.

Alexis followed her. "It finally happened to me, Ma—Ginny."

"That's okay, honey. Call me Mama if you want."

Alexis's eyes teared slightly. "I fell in love, Mama—finally—cool, indifferent me."

"But what's the problem?"

"He doesn't love me back. He has another girlfriend, and he divides his time between us."

"Oh, baby." Ginny's face fell sympathetically. "I'm so sorry."

The whole story poured out of Alexis, while Ginny patted her hand and murmured words of encouragement. At the end, Alexis leaned back and smiled weakly at her mother. "Quite a tale, huh?"

Ginny sighed, her green eyes brimming with tears. "Yes. Oh, I'm so sorry that something like this should happen to you. You've always been so crazy about your father. I was afraid you would fall for—" She broke off abruptly, looking guilty.

For a moment Alexis was puzzled by her mother's

,expression. "It's okay, Mama. You don't need to hide Alec's faults from me. I know all about the way he cheated on you. So you thought I might fall for a faithless man like him?"

"Well, yes. All those years with your father . . . I loved him so, but I always knew, or at least suspected, that he was having an affair with this woman or that, or with somebody I didn't know. It's a miserable thing to love a man and yet be jealous and angry and humiliated by him. I'd go to parties and wonder which of the women there he had slept with. If I hadn't loved him so, it wouldn't have hurt as much. Maybe I could have behaved like some women did, and stayed with him and enjoyed the kind of life I had, let him go his way and me go mine. But that wasn't the way I was, or how I felt about him."

"I'm sorry, Mama." Alexis clasped her mother's hand. "I never knew. I didn't realize."

"I understand. You were so blinded by your father that you could never see his faults. You always had your head in a book and didn't know what was going on in the family."

"That's the sad truth."

"I always dreaded that someday you'd meet a man like Alec, with the same kind of power and charm and good looks . . . and the same philandering nature." Ginny sighed and ran a hand through her hair. "Divorcing your father was the hardest thing I ever did, and I always hoped you'd be spared that kind of pain—loving a man and not being able to bear his nature. It's so awful to reach the point where you know that if you remain, if you submit to him and his ways, you'll lose every shred of pride, and become, in effect, a nonentity. I couldn't let myself be trampled on any more, Alexis, and yet it broke my heart to leave Alec. I still loved him after all that."

Alexis studied her mother with troubled eyes. "Are you still unhappy, Ginny?"

The other woman brightened and shook her head. "Oh, no, not now. For several years I was, but I finally got rid of all those feelings for him. I think now that I could see Alec and talk to him and feel nothing more than a little sadness and fond remembrance. But my feelings aren't what's important—it's *you* we're talking about. I think you did the right thing, Alexis, although I know how very hard it must have been for you."

"I feel empty, lost without Brant," Alexis said. "It's so painful that sometimes I feel like going straight back to Barrett and telling him that it doesn't matter, that I'll stay whatever he does. Yet if I did, it would be madness."

Ginny nodded decisively. "I agree."

"He really isn't like Daddy at all. He's very honest and upright and high-principled. He's just very cold where women are concerned, and he despises me for being Alec's daughter."

"But he has that same attraction, that power."

Alexis thought for a moment, then agreed. "Yes, I guess he does, in a way. He's just as stubborn as Daddy, as strong and determined. I was very drawn to him like everyone is to Alec."

"All the time you were growing up, I was aware of your fascination with Alec, and I didn't think it was good. You idolized him. Everything he said was law, and you worked constantly to get his approval. 'That isn't right,' I would say to myself. 'Ginny, you ought to do something.' But I never knew what to do about it. I didn't want you to stop loving him, and I couldn't see how I could make you do *that* even if I wanted to. But it wasn't healthy. It cut you off from relationships with other men and left you open to something like this."

"Oh, Mama, sometimes I look at my life and wonder what I did everything for! I built my life around Daddy, but I was only a small part of his. I was always running after something, trying to achieve for him, not for myself. And no one can ever succeed at that. I can't make Daddy happy by changing my life. I can't make him be satisfied with us girls or not wish he'd had a boy. Those are things only he can do."

"I know." Ginny squeezed her daughter's hand tightly. "But don't feel so blue, Alexis. You've accomplished a lot of things for yourself. You have a career, looks, intelligence, money. The whole world is open to you. And you can change all the things you want to change."

"Change now?"

"Why, sure. I've changed in the past few years, and I'm forty-eight years old. It's never too late to try to improve yourself. You can learn from this and go on to better men and better relationships. I have."

"Oh?" Alexis said with a smile. "Does that mean you and your senator are still a hot item?"

"Congressman," Ginny corrected, her face glowing. "Yes, it does. In fact, Alexis, he has asked me to marry him."

"Oh, Mama!" Alexis cried. "How exciting! Did you say yes?"

"I told him I would have to think very carefully about it."

"That hardly sounds like you!"

"I've told you, I've changed. I don't enjoy leaping into the dark any more. There are a lot of things to consider, including living in Washington for long stretches. Not to mention Cara, who still comes home from school on her vacations. And leaving you and Morgan."

"Oh, we would visit you, and you could come back here. It doesn't take long to fly to D.C."

"But the most important thing I had to consider was, whether that would make me happy. And after much thought, I have decided it would."

"Terrific!" Alexis leaned over and gave her mother a hug. "I think you are doing exactly the right thing. I only hope I come out as well."

Their conversation was interrupted by the slamming of the front door, and in a few moments Cara entered the room. She was slender and tall, healthily tanned even in winter, and her eyes were a clear blue-green. Of all the Stone girls, Cara resembled their father the most. Her long, thick hair was the same raven-black, and her square face and jutting chin were diminutives of his. She was not a plain girl, but neither was she pretty. Rather, there was something arresting about her that made people want to take a second look at her.

"Alexis!" she exclaimed, smiling happily. "I thought that was your car in the driveway. How are you?"

"Okay." Alexis rose to hug her younger sister. "It's been ages since I saw you. What are you doing home?"

"I'm between semesters. I came home before Christmas, but you had already left to go skiing."

"So sit down and tell me what you've been doing." Alexis felt, as always, a little uncomfortable, around the girl. It had been so many years since she had lived at home with Cara. "What are you majoring in?"

Cara laughed and threw a sideways glance at her mother. "Don't mention that in front of Ginny, or she'll start up again."

Alexis smiled. "Why? What's the matter?"

"She's thinking about becoming a nurse, of all things," Ginny answered for her daughter. "With all the opportunities that are open to a girl now, it seems criminal to me to be a nurse. She could do anything."

"Why not be a doctor?" Alexis suggested.

"Always the professional," Cara said in a bantering tone. "What's wrong with being a nurse? I don't want to wait all those years to become a doctor. I'll be old by then. I want to get involved now. I want to help people, make them well, be at the heart of things. Ginny wants me to major in something useless, like Morgan did— French or English or something, but I don't want that. And I don't want to go into Daddy's business, or law, or accounting, or anything else that's dry and boring."

Ginny sighed. "Really, Cara, I—"

"Besides," Cara continued with a mischievous gleam

in her eye, "I haven't definitely decided on nursing. I thought I might go to A and M and become a veterinarian."

"A and M!" Ginny and Alexis chorused, staring at Cara as though she had taken leave of her senses.

Laughter bubbled up in Alexis's throat. "Cara, you can't be serious! Daddy would absolutely die!"

Cara smirked, tossing back her long black hair. "Wouldn't he, though?"

"Well, if you're going to talk so foolishly, I'm not going to sit here another minute," Ginny declared, rising. "I have a date tonight, and I have to get ready. Bye, Alexis." She leaned down and kissed Alexis. "I'm really glad you came over to talk."

Alexis watched her mother leave the room and then turned to Cara. "You're teasing, aren't you? About being a vet? Honestly, Cara, Daddy would have apoplexy."

"I know. He'd say, 'Your mother's father, Judge Benton, would turn over in his grave if he heard a grandchild of his had gone to A and M, and a girl at that!'" Cara imitated their father's voice and expression so cleverly that Alexis had to giggle. "No, I don't guess I'll do that. I just said it to get a rise out of you all. You'd have thought I'd said I was planning to go to a whorehouse."

"Do you really want to be a nurse?" Alexis asked.

"Yes, I do," Cara replied, her face resuming serious lines. "I've always wanted to help people, to make them feel better, to fix things so that they're right. You know what I mean?"

"I think so." Alexis paused. "I tell you what, Cara. If that was what I wanted, I'd go ahead and do it. I know Mama can accept your not being a society girl; she did with me. And I think it's about time Alec learned that not everyone marches to his tune."

"You always have."

Alexis smiled faintly. "Well, it hasn't done me any

good. I let the desire to please Daddy warp my life. And I don't think—I don't think I'll ever get my life straight again unless I break the cords that bind me to him."

Alexis spent a turbulent night, her mind trudging over her problems, but the next morning she arose early, white-faced and grimly determined. Today she was going to begin her new, independent life.

She drove to the office, as she had so many times in the past, barely noticing the buildings that slid by. When she reached the Stone Building, she parked her Mercedes and rode the elevator directly to the top floor.

"I have to speak with my father," she told Mrs. Jenkins.

"Oh, dear, I'm afraid he's got a meeting this morning."

"Is he in it already?"

"No, but it starts in ten minutes."

"Then I'll talk to him first," Alexis said firmly, and walked through his door.

"Alexis! Thank goodness you finally got here!" Alec exclaimed, rising from his desk. "You have the lease with you?"

"No, I don't." Alexis looked him straight in the eye, steeling herself against his wrath and, more difficult for her, his disapproval.

"Why? What happened? Did that bastard back out of the deal? I'll make him regret it if it's the last thing I ever do."

"No, Daddy, it isn't like that. Brant signed the lease."

"Then what's the problem?"

Taking a deep breath, Alexis replied, "I tore it up."

Her father stared at her, speechless with astonishment for several minutes. Then, in almost a whisper, he said, "You did what?"

"I tore it up."

"Are you serious? Alexis, is this some kind of joke? You can't mean that! You tore it up!"

"Yes, I did. It's no joke, Daddy. I couldn't feel less like joking."

"Why in God's name did you do something idiotic like that?"

"Because I couldn't stomach it!" Alexis retorted. "From the very first, I didn't want to do it. I thought it was low and contemptible to use Brant's son as a weapon. It was wrong, and finally, when it got down to the nitty-gritty, I didn't want any part of it. So I tore up all the copies."

Alec shook his head in disbelief and sank heavily into his chair. "Alexis, that is the most irresponsible thing I've ever heard. I would never have believed it of you—of all people! You've always been such a hard worker, so industrious and ambitious, like me."

"No, Daddy, I'm not entirely like you. I can't use people the way you do. I can't lie and cheat and twist things to my own advantage."

His expression turned cold. "Alexis, even though you are my daughter, you are also an employee here, and you have certain duties which you have failed to carry out."

"I know that. I realize I'm not cut out to work for a company where I have to do such things. That's why I'm resigning."

"Resigning!" Alec looked thunderstruck. "Alexis, what in the world—"

"I haven't lost my mind, Daddy. You might say I've just come to my senses. I no longer enjoy what I've been doing. You know as well as I that I don't need the job here."

"Of course, you've got plenty of money from the trust funds I set up for you girls," Alec said quickly. "But how in hell are you going to sit around just being a lady of leisure? You've worked all your life . . ."

"Oh, I'm not going to stop. I could work for another company or try to get a job with a law firm. I don't think it should be too difficult. I have excellent credentials as well as experience. Maybe I'll even go into practice by myself."

"You're serious!"

"Very much so. I think it's time I stopped living in your shadow, Daddy."

"And what about Stone Oil? I was grooming you to run it when I die."

"I thought so. But I'm not an oil man, I'm a lawyer. I would never really qualify for that. Anyway, the company's already gone public, and Cara and Morgan and I would own only half of it. You need to build up a nonfamily management, the way other companies do."

"You actually mean it." Alec said this as a statement, not as a question. He leaned back in his swivel chair and studied her. His face was blank, but there lurked in his dark blue eyes something close to respect. "Independent cuss, aren't you?"

"I guess I am. I want to be, anyway. All my life I've tried to be what you wanted me to be. I've finally realized I can't do that and be a person in and of myself."

"I see." He was quiet for a moment, then asked, "Does this mean that I'm on your blacklist? Or will you still come and see Laraine and me?"

"I'd like to," Alexis replied evenly, fighting the tears that clogged her throat. "I'd like you to be my father. I've always wanted that."

He nodded slightly. "I'd like that, too. Now, I have a conference that I'm already late for."

"Sure." Alexis smiled and backed out of his office.

On her way down the hall to the elevators, she felt her chest swell with a burst of emotions she had never experienced all at the same time: love, freedom, excitement, regret, and fear. For the first time in her life she was embarking on an uncharted path.

Arriving at the tenth floor, she walked quickly to her office and rang for her secretary. When Betty appeared in the doorway, full of messages and questions, Alexis waved her in to silence.

"Just a minute. I'll get to all that later. I want to dictate a letter now."

Betty nodded and sat down, flipping open her steno pad and holding her pencil poised. Alexis began, "This is a memo to Lawrence Davis from me, dated today. 'I herewith present my resignation from the legal department of Stone Oil Company. My years here have been happy ones, and I sincerely regret leaving. However, I have decided to seek opportunities outside the field of oil and gas.'"

At Alexis's opening remarks, Betty had stared at her open-mouthed, then hastily scribbled down her words. When Alexis stopped, Betty closed her note pad and stood up.

"Are you really leaving?" she asked.

"Yes. I think I'm going to go into private practice."

"Miss Stone! I can't believe it. Why?"

"I got tired of it. I thought I'd see if I could make it on my own, someplace where I wasn't the owner's daughter."

"Oh, Miss Stone, you would be good anywhere. I know you can do whatever you want."

"Thank you for that vote of confidence, Betty. Now, dump all your messages on me. I've got to get things cleared up in a hurry."

It took Alexis over two weeks to move out of her office. She worked late every evening, just as in the old days, trying to finish as many of her cases as she could and filling her colleagues in on those that remained. It was really good to have so much work to do that she fell into bed exhausted almost as soon as she got home every night. This way, she could keep Brant McClure out of her mind most of the time.

Sometimes, of course, Alexis cried herself to sleep,

or woke up in the middle of the night from a too-vivid dream of him and lay aching for the touch of his flesh, the scent and warmth and feel of him. But at least she was too busy at work to constantly miss his companionship.

After she had cleaned out her desk, said her last good-byes, and driven out of the underground garage, the true loneliness set in. She had nothing to do except type up her résumé and read the *Bar Journal*'s classified ads and ponder whether to join a firm or go out on her own. Now her memories set in good and hard. She thought of Brant almost always, seeing him again in her mind's eye in all the scenes she had gone through with him. Sometimes it was all Alexis could do to keep her fingers from dialing his number in Barrett and asking him to take her back. Only the thought of the worse pain that would follow if she returned to him prevented her from doing it.

One evening, in the throes of despair, she called Morgan. "Hello, sister," Alexis began, trying to keep her voice light. "You doing anything tonight?"

"I was going out to a party, but it isn't important. You want to do something?"

"Oh, no. I just thought we might get together and talk."

"Well, sure. I'll call and tell them I can't make it."

"I wouldn't want you to do that."

"No problem. I go to so many like this one, it's hard to tell them apart. I just go to keep from getting bored. Why don't you come over here? I'll whip up some crepes and a salad, and we can have a little white wine. How does that sound?"

"Like heaven," Alexis admitted.

Morgan laughed. "Then come on over."

It took Alexis only a few minutes to reach Morgan's plush apartment on Turtle Creek. Morgan greeted her at the door, dressed in jeans and a T-shirt, holding a glass of wine.

"I've decided what this dinner can be," she announced to Alexis.

"What?" Alexis took the proffered glass of wine and sipped at it. "Mmmm, that's good."

"It will be a celebration of your leaving our esteemed father."

"Now, Morgan, that's not quite what happened."

"Leave Stone Oil, leave Alec Stone," Morgan quipped. "What did happen, and why didn't you tell me about it? I heard about it third-hand, I'll have you know. Jeff Stein told me at a party that he heard it from Robert somebody-or-other, over at your office. I was caught flat-footed. At first I thought he was trying to make a joke!"

"Well, it wasn't any big fight, Morgan. I didn't renounce him forever."

Morgan grimaced and laughed. "I knew it couldn't be anything so dramatic. Worse luck. What *did* happen, then?"

"I decided that I was stifling myself. I had a long talk with Mother the other night. Can you imagine that? We talked about a lot of things, among them Daddy and the way I've tried to please him all my life. I think it's a decision I've been coming to for a long time, but that talk seemed to bring it to a head. So I quit. I'm giving up my father complex, so to speak."

Again Morgan laughed. "I wish it were so easy."

Alexis smiled. "So do I. Tell me something, Morgan. How do you really feel about Daddy?"

"The straight-out truth?"

"Yes."

"Okay. Hold on a sec. Let me get the crepes on the table, and I'll tell you." She went into the kitchen, deftly folded the crab-filled crepes in the pan, and dished them up, carrying the plates into her small dining room.

Morgan and Alexis sat down at the table, both of them glancing automatically out the window at the sparkling lights of Dallas below. Morgan tasted her food thoughtfully, her gaze fixed on the window, before turning to Alexis to speak.

"How do I really feel about Daddy? Well, I love him. He's charming, he's my father, and I've always been his 'princess,' his little replica of Ginny with none of the entanglements attached. I can't help but love him. However, I also think that he's a faithless, heartless bastard who loves power more than anything else in the world and who will use almost any means to achieve it. I have sworn to myself, ever since I got old enough to reason, that I'd stay out of the way of men like him. None of those charismatic, powerful, domineering men for me, no, sir. That's how I feel about Alec Stone."

"Then I guess you won't fall into the same trap I did," Alexis said wryly.

"What trap?" Morgan cast her an interested glance.

"I fell in love with someone like Daddy."

"Oh, no, Alexis, who? What are you talking about? Not that rancher out in the boonies somewhere!"

"The same. He doesn't really seem like Alec. He doesn't have that hunger for power over money and lots of people. He's a loner who loves the land, and he's far too honest and not nearly tricky enough. But that same drive is there, that inner strength. Stubbornness, determination, whatever you want to call it. He's the kind who doesn't lose. And he also likes to keep more than one mistress."

Morgan sighed. "Oh, Alexis, I'm sorry. I had no idea it had gotten that serious between you two. I thought it was all over when you came back here in November."

"So did I. Only it started up again. I finally decided that I had to leave. If I'd stayed, I would've been crushed by him."

Morgan nodded, swallowing a piece of crab meat. "That's probably the smartest decision you've made all year, aside from leaving Daddy."

"Only—" Tears came unbidden to Alexis's eyes. "It's so hard, Morgan. I miss him so. Sometimes I feel like going to Barrett and asking him to take me back, on whatever terms."

"Don't you do it," Morgan said fiercely, spearing another bite of crepe with her fork.

"Have you ever been in love, Morgan?"

"Me?" Morgan laughed. "Haven't you heard? I'm the 'ice queen' of the social set. Half the men I date think I'm a lesbian. The other half think I'm frigid. I've never met a man I could admire or feel more than a liking for."

Alexis allowed herself a small smile. "Maybe it's because you stay away from all the strong ones, and the rest are too dull."

Morgan shrugged prettily and joined in her laughter. "I think it's more likely because most of the men who pursue me are fortune hunters."

Alexis took another long sip of wine and pushed seafood around on her plate. She hadn't been hungry since she returned from Barrett.

"You'd better eat something, Alexis," Morgan advised, watching her toy with the food on her plate. "I know it isn't my cooking, because I make the best crepes this side of the Trinity. That lean and hungry look is fine up to a point, but hollow cheeks and circles under your eyes can become rather unattractive, you know."

"Morgan, I simply can't work up any feelings about anything any more!" Alexis exclaimed in frustration. "I've never felt this way before. All of a sudden everything seems totally uninteresting. I can only think about Brant and how much I miss him."

"You want a little advice from your sister?" Morgan asked, and continued without waiting for a reply. "They say the cure is the same as the one for a hangover: the hair of the dog that bit you."

"What does that mean?"

"An affair—with the right man, of course."

"Why do I have this feeling in the pit of my stomach that I know the name you're about to suggest?"

Morgan laughed, showing her perfect white teeth. "Because he's the perfect solution, that's why. Nick Fletcher is handsome and charming, and I'm sure he can seduce you with the utmost mastery. Best of all, he loves you. You can step right into a perfect love affair that will wipe that cowboy out of your mind."

"What is this thing you and Mama have about Nick? If he's so wonderful, why don't you try for him yourself?"

Morgan shook her head. "Don't you remember? You're talking to the woman without feelings. Besides, he's been taken for years. I'm not fool enough to get myself into that kind of situation. Although I do think that Cara had a little crush on him when she was an adolescent."

"Talk about pressure," Alexis said ruefully. "I tell you what, Morgan—I'll think about it."

"It seems to me I've heard that before," Morgan teased, tilting her head to one side.

"No, I mean it. I'll really think about it. If I thought it would work, believe me, I would try it. But I can't bear to hurt Nick."

"It won't hurt Nick. He'll get what he's been after for so many years."

"What good is love on the rebound?"

Morgan shrugged. "Better than no love at all, I guess."

Alexis did think about her sister's idea. In fact, it rotated in her mind with pictures of Brant McClure on a pretty regular basis. Could it be that Nick was the answer to her heartbreak? It seemed unlikely, and yet . . . She remembered what her mother had said about falling for someone like Alec, and how that painful habit could be broken eventually. It took effort, Ginny had said, and perhaps that effort meant trying to fall in love with someone like Nick Fletcher, who didn't resemble her father at all.

Everything Morgan had said about Nick was true.

Alexis believed he would be a considerate and skillful lover, although, considering his past, she doubted if he had the capability to remain faithful any more than Brant did. At least Nick liked women and loved her. That was certainly more than she could say for Mc-Clure.

The next evening, as Alexis sat watching a silly television show that only half caught her interest, the phone rang. When she answered it, there was a slight pause at the other end. Then a low masculine voice said, "Hello, Alexis."

For one stunned moment Alexis could only stand there, her hand gripping the receiver tightly. It was Brant!

When she did not reply, he went on. "Alexis, I—I think we should talk."

A treacherous trembling began in her limbs, and Alexis thought she was going to break down and pour out her feelings. But no, she couldn't do that to herself. What if he asked her to come back? Told her he wanted her, or lied about Libby, or merely offered Alexis the same degrading situation? What would she do then?

Forcing a steadiness into her voice, she replied, "No, Brant. We have nothing to talk about. It's over, and I'm not going to listen to you."

That's the only way, she told herself. Cut him off before he has a chance to get to you. Don't allow yourself even to listen to him, or you'll be lost.

"But, Alexis—" he started to protest, his voice rumbling with the familiar anger.

"No! I mean it. Good-bye, Brant." Quickly, she slammed the receiver down.

Alexis leaned against the wall, her breath coming in brief, shallow bursts, her heart pounding wildly. The shrill ringing of the telephone beside her head made her jump and sent her heart to pumping even more fiercely. She turned resolutely away from the phone, folded her arms around herself and went back into the other room.

Shakily, she sat down in her chair, listening to the persistent rings until at last they died away. In all its dire finality, the feeling again washed over her that she was scarred for life, hurting and doomed; hopelessly, helplessly, in love. For a long time she sat there, holding herself as if against an assault, her expression set and withdrawn.

Eventually, Alexis rose and climbed the stairs to her bedroom. She undressed and took a scented bath, brushed her hair until it shone, and brightened her face with a little makeup and lipstick. She slipped into jeans and a clinging lavender sweater, then went downstairs and out to the garage. After turning on the car's ignition, she pushed the electric door-opener and backed out into the street, driving quickly, mechanically, toward Walnut Hill Lane and Nick Fletcher's apartment.

Chapter 23

Nick's townhouse apartment was constructed of cedar, with a modern, slanting roof and tall windows. When he answered the door and saw Alexis standing there, surprise flitted across his features.

"Alexis!" he cried, reaching out to draw her inside. "I didn't expect to see you tonight. Can I get you something? Scotch and water? A Coke? Coffee?"

"No, I'm fine, thank you." Alexis hung back awkwardly. It had suddenly occurred to her that a woman might be here with Nick, that she might have disturbed an intimate scene. Why hadn't she thought to call first? "Uh, listen, Nick, I'm not interrupting anything, am I? I mean, I could come back some other time."

Amused understanding lit his dark eyes. "No, Alexis, there isn't a nude woman reclining in my bed, growing impatient. I don't go in for all the debauchery I'm credited with, you know."

Alexis smiled. "How was I to know? I didn't want to be sitting around while you waited for me to leave."

"Never," Nick said. "I'd just sneak in and tell her I had more important company and to slip out the back door."

He led her into the large living area that centered around a circular metal fireplace in which a few large logs were artistically stacked. They sat down on a dark

print couch, and Alexis looked around with interest.
She had rarely been in Nick's apartment, and then only
for a few moments while he changed or picked up
something. It seemed odd to have been his friend for so
long and to know so little about where he lived . . . or
about him, for that matter.

For all his flirtatious teasing, Nick had never attempted a seduction scene with her. Alexis remembered
thinking once, with slight pique, that she must be the
only woman in Dallas in whom Nick Fletcher had no
sexual interest. Having finally accepted that Nick had
loved her for years, she could understand his reluctance. There was a protective aspect to love that
wouldn't allow him to trick her into doing something
she didn't actually want to do. Nor could he expose
himself to the pain of knowing that persuasion, not
love, had brought her to his bed.

Alexis felt shy now, uncertain of the correctness of
her visit, embarrassed to admit her motives. For want
of anything to say, she nodded at the drafting table that
stood before the bank of windows. "What's that?"

"My drafting table."

"I know that. I mean, what do you use it for?"

"Well, contrary to your opinion, I don't spend *all* my
time in complete idleness," Nick teased. "I bought a
house in Munger Place and I'm restoring it, so that's
where I work out my renovation plans."

"Really?" Alexis said, surprised. "Do you mind if I
look at them?"

"No, of course not. I'll show you." They moved to
the worktable and Nick spread out a large blueprint.
"This is the bottom floor," he told her, pointing. "The
house was turned into four apartments after it became
run down. These divisions in the living room and the
dining room weren't in the original house. I'm going to
remove them, and also this partition that used to be a
pair of sliding doors between the front room and the
sitting room behind it. I'm also taking out the other
kitchen that was put in downstairs, and since the

plumbing's there, I'm converting it into a bathroom. Now this is the top floor. Again, two kitchens that I'm turning into bathrooms. All the original bathrooms are too small. Fortunately, they adjoin the kitchens, so I can make them into one big bathroom. And this partition in the hall will have to go. The place was divided in an interesting way. The old house had a central staircase, and beside it, separated by a rail, a smaller servants' staircase. The former owners divided the upper story down the middle of the two stairways."

"I can't believe this, Nick," Alexis said, studying the blueprint intently. "I had no idea you were interested in such things."

"I told you I wasn't quite the wastrel you thought I was," he laughed, and showed her a photograph of the house. "And this," he added proudly, holding out a large colored pencil sketch, "is how it's going to look when I'm finished with it."

"Nick, it doesn't even look like the same house! That's extraordinary! Did you draw this sketch?" He nodded, and she murmured thoughtfully, "That's right, you were always pretty good at art. I can remember you drawing cars and girls when we were teen-agers."

His dark eyes gleamed wickedly. "Ah, yes, my early works of genius."

"Do you still paint? Or draw—whatever?"

"Yes, I still work at it, mostly pen-and-ink sketches or prints."

"Why do you hide all these wonderful qualities, Nick?"

He grinned. "I don't think most people would be impressed by my industriousness in drawing. That's considered a hobby, at least in the world we grew up in. But who knows? Maybe one day I'll come out of the closet and be a professional artist."

"What are you going to do with the house, Nick? Are you going to move into it?"

"No, it isn't exactly what I'd want. Besides, a house would be too big for me, and I don't like being tied down by all the responsibility for it. When I'm through renovating, I'll sell it, hopefully at a profit."

"A capitalistic enterprise, no less," Alexis teased.

"Yes, can you believe it? Like father, like son, they say. You can see that I've followed him into real estate . . . though in a somewhat lesser fashion."

They returned to the sofa, Alexis feeling more at ease, though somewhat overwhelmed by what she had learned about her friend. Perhaps she really had been blocking out Nick's good qualities all these years; she might not even know him at all.

"So what have you been up to?" Nick asked, curious about the reason for her unusual visit.

"Oh, not much. I've been changing my life around, that's all."

"What do you mean?"

"I quit my job."

"With Stone Oil?" His handsome face went slack with amazement. "Alexis, this is a far greater surprise than my dabbling with a livelihood! What on earth is going on?"

"I guess I decided to grow up," Alexis replied. She didn't want to go into the whole thing about Brant again, especially not with Nick. "I'm cutting the umbilical cord. And I'm trying to change . . . the way I am with men."

He eyed her narrowly. "The way you are with men? What way is that? I'm getting some strange vibes that tell me this is the purpose of your being here."

Alexis sighed and turned away, unable to meet his gaze. "Oh, Nick, maybe I shouldn't have come. I was feeling desperate, and I thought that this might be a way out for me. I wanted to put myself in your hands and let you lead me to some kind of sweet, nicer love."

Nick stared at her solemnly, not asking with what "nicer" love was being compared. He had reached a moment that he had thought would never come and he was not about to spoil it by asking a lot of pertinent but foolish questions.

"Alexis," he began slowly, "are you saying that you came here because you wanted me to make love to you?" She nodded, and he let his breath out in a long, controlled escape. "I have to admit, you've really caught me off guard."

"I've gone about this all wrong," Alexis said, embarrassed.

"Well, it *is* unusual," Nick allowed, faint laughter in his voice. "But that's not to say it's wrong."

"I shouldn't have come."

"Are you getting cold feet?"

Alexis flicked a glance at him, her eyes huge and purple with indecision. "I feel stupid and clumsy. I don't know what I'm doing. Or even if it's the right thing."

"I have a suggestion. Let's give it a chance and see how it works out. Okay?"

"Okay."

Nick took her hand. "Come on, loosen up. This is just me, old Nick, not some ravenous monster. I'm not going to rape you, or anything."

"I know." Alexis tried forcibly to relax, settling back into the comfortable couch. If only she didn't feel so numb, so out of place and confused.

Quietly, Nick began to talk of other things, until at last Alexis was soothed by the sound of his voice. He put his arm around her shoulder and she leaned against him, seeking comfort. Gently, Nick tilted her face up with his hand and kissed her just as gently. Gradually, his kiss deepened, and Alexis could feel the heat of his breath against her face. He embraced her tightly, his mouth moving expertly, tantalizingly, to her throat and ears.

Alexis lay in his arms, quiescent, her eyes closed, but her emotions were not caught. No fires sizzled through her as they had when Brant had touched her. She recognized Nick's mastery of the art of lovemaking and willed herself to respond, but still she felt nothing. I can't expect a cure the first time out, Alexis told herself. It'll probably take several tries for me to forget Brant and feel the same delicious thrill with Nick. But her heart sank within her at this thought.

Nick's hand cupped her breast and then slowly began to roam her body while his mouth came back to claim hers again. Abruptly, he dropped his hand and pulled away from her.

Alexis opened her eyes and looked at him in bewilderment. "What's wrong?"

"What's wrong!" he repeated hoarsely. "I feel like I'm kissing a corpse."

"Thank you very much," she said stiffly.

"Look, Alexis, I love you, and I've wanted to make love to you for a long time, not force myself on a passive body."

"What do you want me to do?"

"I want you to feel something!" he snapped.

"I want to, Nick! I really want to!" Alexis cried in anguish, tears welling in her eyes.

Nick sighed and stood up, running a hand through his hair. "Alexis, there's no point in going on with this. Obviously you want to force something that just isn't there. Is it another man?"

Alexis nodded miserably.

"Then what are you doing here with me? How do you expect me to awaken any feeling in you when you've already given your heart to someone else?"

Alexis began to cry quietly, crystal tears streaming down her cheeks. "Oh, Nick, I'm sorry. I'm so sorry. I don't know what I'm doing any more!"

He resumed his seat and took her in his arms, cradling her against his chest. "Listen, Alexis, it's all right. I'm not mad at you. You don't want to be in love with this guy, and you were hoping that somehow I could steal your heart away. Right?"

Alexis nodded.

"Sweetheart, I wish I could. But I'm not a miracle worker, you know. How can I make you switch your affections from the one you love to me? I've been trying to do that for myself for years, with no luck."

She gave a tearful chuckle. "Oh, Nick, I am sorry. I wish I loved you."

"I know. But that's hardly enough, is it?" His eyelids closed over the deep pain behind them, and he bent his head to brush his lips against her hair. "Ah, Alexis, I wish I could make you love me. But it looks like it wasn't meant to fall out that way. I guess we'll both have to do our best with what we've got. Now, tell Uncle Nick all about it. What's the matter with this guy whom you wish you didn't love? Who is he?"

Alexis sighed and dabbed at her eyes. "His name is Brant McClure, and the thing that's wrong with him is that at this very moment he's probably enjoying himself with one Libby Preston!"

"What an idiot!" Nick replied with feeling. "Does he have brain damage, or what?"

Alexis chuckled again. "Nick, you're a dear. Listen, that's enough of my troubles. I've been bending everyone's ear about it until I'm tired of hearing myself." She wiped the tears from her cheeks, and Nick offered her a handkerchief. She blew her nose, dried her eyes, and stood up. "I think I'd better go now. I've messed up enough of your evening as it is."

"Are you sure you're all right?" Nick asked, also rising. "I want you to talk to me if you need to."

"That's very sweet of you, and thanks, but I don't need to talk. I just need to figure out how I'm going to live."

His mouth twisted slightly. "Alexis, believe me, I wish I could help."

"You've been a great help already. At least now I know that this method isn't going to work. Just be my friend, Nick, that's all I ask."

"You know I'll always be that, Alexis."

"I know." She squeezed his hand and he responded in kind. Then she turned and walked toward the door and out of the apartment, not seeing the sadness in his eyes as they followed her departure.

Brant McClure awakened in the chill black dawn of winter, blinking away the sleep from his eyes. The loneliness that always hovered in the background settled upon him now, and he knew that it would remain with him forever. Since Alexis had left, every day had been like that. He had almost, but not quite, become accustomed to it. The first searing pain had lessened into a constant dull ache.

Mechanically, he rose and went into the bathroom, shaved, showered, and returned to his room to dress. Brant had found that the best way to escape his feelings was to think of nothing at all, to try to focus entirely on the tasks he was performing at the moment and to keep the rest of his mind a blank. He pulled on his jeans and a heavy turtleneck sweater and thrust his cold feet into socks and boots, concentrating on what he was doing, oblivious to the memories that clamored in the recesses of his brain.

He left the room and checked on Paul to make sure he was awake, then clattered down the stairs into the silent kitchen. Brant prepared hot water for his instant coffee, hoping that the teacher who was coming next week would be a coffee drinker so that he could use the percolator again. He broke three eggs into a bowl, added milk and seasoning, and whipped the mixture until it was a creamy yellow froth.

As Brant put the butter into the skillet to melt, Paul came into the kitchen and went over to the counter to take up his duties as toastmaker. In companionable silence, they finished making breakfast and sat down at the table to eat. Thank heavens for Paul. Brant didn't think he could have made it through the last few weeks without the boy.

"Are you excited about Major Kendall coming to teach you next week?" Brant asked, to make conversation. He had been fortunate enough to receive a quick response to the advertisement he had placed in papers around the state. A retired army major who had been an interpreter and who spoke Vietnamese was interested in the job. His children had grown up and moved away, and he could easily transplant himself from San Antonio to Barrett for a few months. Moreover, he had a fondness for children and was looking forward to teaching Paul his school subjects.

"I guess so," Paul replied without much enthusiasm. "I'd rather work on the ranch with you."

"You will . . . later. But right now, the thing you need to do the most is to catch up with the other children your age so that you can begin school next year."

Paul frowned a little. School sounded dull in comparison with staying at the ranch. Of course, there would be other kids to play with, like Jenny and Stephie, and that would be nice.

Brant looked at his son's glum expression. "Paul, do you miss Alexis?"

The child nodded, a lump forming in his throat. "Don't you?"

"Yes, I miss her a lot, too."

Paul leaned forward earnestly. "Couldn't you— Don't you think you could call her and ask her to come back? Maybe she would if you asked her."

Brant shook his head. "No, I don't think so, Paul. I think she left to get away from me; it had nothing to do with you. So my calling wouldn't be likely to change her mind."

"Don't you want her to come back?"

Brant's face was etched with longing. "Yes, I want her to come back. But that's enough of that. Finish your breakfast, and we'll go out to the barn. Maybe this afternoon I'll take you over to Beth's and you can play with the girls. Would you like that?"

"Yeah."

Brant worked steadily throughout the morning. It was easier to keep his mind off Alexis outside. In the house, he could hardly look at anything without being reminded of her. So he sought every job he could to keep him outdoors, even in the cold winter weather.

He stopped only for lunch, going back out to ride the fence, searching for damage caused by the heavy snow. The snow had long since melted, leaving the usual bleak January landscape, which Brant decided suited his mood perfectly. As always, the question came back to him with piercing uncertainty: *why had Alexis left?*

Later in the afternoon he took Paul to Beth's. So far, his sister had been good about keeping quiet on the subject of Alexis. One look at his closed, hard face, and she had not asked him a single question.

Today, however, Brant was the one who brought up Alexis's name. It was like a sore tooth that one's tongue felt out again and again despite the pain. He couldn't let go of the thought of Alexis, and suddenly he felt the desperate need to talk about her.

"Beth," he began tentatively, "did Alexis say anything that day she was over here? The day she left, I mean."

Beth looked at him in surprise. She had been itching to question Brant about what had happened, but had held herself in check before the pain in his eyes. "What do you mean?"

"I mean, you know, about why she was leaving," Brant mumbled, keeping his eyes fixed on his hands.

"Well, yes, she did say something. She said that she couldn't stand your seeing Libby."

"Libby?" Brant looked up, astonished. "What does Libby Preston have to do with anything?"

"Didn't you go to see her the morning that Alexis left?"

"Good Lord, no! Is that what she thought?"

"That's what she said to me. She was certain you had gone to see Libby because of something Paul said. I told her to wait and hear out your explanation first, but—"

"What Paul said!" Brant repeated, cutting in on her

words. "What could he have said? I didn't tell him anything about what I was going to do. I wanted to surprise Alexis, and I was afraid he'd tell her if he knew what it was."

"Maybe she interpreted that to mean you were doing something underhanded."

Brant groaned and rose from his chair. "What an idiotic thing to think! I haven't seen Libby since the time she came to visit. I broke up with her that night."

Beth got up eagerly and followed her brother around the kitchen. "Brant, if that's all it was—just a mis-understanding—don't you think you ought to call Alexis and explain, try to get her to come back? I just know that if you told her, she would—"

"I did call her!" Brant interrupted savagely. "She wouldn't listen to me. I couldn't even ask her why she left. She hung up as soon as I opened my mouth."

"Well, go to Dallas to see her, then," Beth insisted, undaunted.

"If she could hang up on me, she'd simply slam the door in my face," Brant predicted darkly. "She's dead set against me, Beth. Besides, if she has so little faith in me that she'd assume the worst about me, what hope is there for us? She even refused to stay long enough to tell me why she was mad and get my version of what happened. The instant she had the slightest suspicion, she took off."

"Well, maybe she was a little touchy, but then, your relationship was never exactly steady. You have quite a temper, too, if you'll recall. And after all the things you've been through, all the mutual suspicion and anger, it doesn't seem unreasonable that the slightest thing would spark her off." Beth paused, looking helplessly at his stiff back. "Brant, don't you care? Don't you want her?"

The face Brant turned toward his sister was tortured. "Of course I do, Beth. What do you think I've been going through for the past couple of weeks? I love Alexis more than anything in the world. But what kind of relationship could we have if she distrusts everything I do? How can I convince that suspicious mind of hers that I'm telling the truth?"

"You'll find a way," Beth declared firmly, "if you love her enough. Be fair, Brant. You weren't especially trusting, either. Did you ever tell Alexis that you broke up with Libby?" At his negative shake of the head, she went on triumphantly. "See? How was Alexis to know? She's smart, but she's hardly a mind reader."

"I don't know, Beth," he sighed as he sank down into his chair. "Things have never been right between Alexis and me."

"Then you must start making them right. You have to try, Brant . . . or are you scared of getting rejected again?"

"What the hell does that mean?"

"It means that I wonder if you're scared of her hurting you—like Mother did—if you let her know how much she means to you, if you admit how deeply you love her. That would give her an awful lot of power to wound you."

Brant glared at his sister. "You don't know what you're talking about," he said gruffly, then looked away, the stabbing in his guts telling him that she had hit too close to home. "Let's talk about something else."

However, for the rest of the afternoon, Brant could not get what Beth had said out of his head, even though she had immediately changed the subject to something innocuous. When he left to drive home with Paul, he was still brooding over her words. Had she been right? Was he a fool not to try everything he could to patch things up? Was he really afraid to admit to Alexis how much she meant to him?

Brant had never thought of himself as a person who feared risks, yet . . . why else hadn't he done something more than make a phone call to get Alexis back, when it cost him so much for her to be gone from his life?

"I think I've been lying to myself," he said aloud.

Paul looked at him bewilderedly. "What?"

"Just thinking out loud. I did call Alexis, but I don't think that was trying hard enough to get her back. Do you?"

Paul shook his head. "Why don't you go see her?"

Brant chewed thoughtfully on his lower lip. "No, I don't think that would work, either. What I need is to get past all her stubbornness and distrust so she'll listen to me. Then I could convince her she's wrong. The only problem is, what will make her come back here?"

Paul frowned, puzzling over the problem with his father. As they pulled into the driveway of the ranch, a sudden light touched Brant's face, and he sat still for a few minutes after he had shut off the engine, thinking.

"Do you know a way?" his son asked eagerly, watching the shadows that shifted across Brant's face.

"I just might, son. Let's go inside and see. I have to give somebody a call."

They went into the house, Paul skipping excitedly beside him. Brant headed straight for the phone and dialed long-distance information, asking for the number for Stone Oil.

"You going to call Allie again?" Paul asked.

"No," Brant said as he dialed a string of numbers. "This time I'm going over her head." He paused, waiting for his call to be answered, then spoke into the receiver. "I would like to talk to Mr. Alec Stone, please. Tell him Brant McClure is calling."

Chapter 24

Alexis sat at the desk in her study, her forehead knitted in concentration as she wrote down her educational achievements for the résumé she would send to law firms. On the table beside her were a cup of strong coffee and a folded newspaper, its ads for available office space circled in red. She was still undecided which of her options to pursue.

The phone rang in her bedroom and she grimaced with irritation, then walked down the hall to answer it. Much to her amazement, she heard her father's voice on the other end of the line, his excitement barely repressed.

"Hello, Daddy," she said cautiously, uncertain about Alec's motives.

"You'll never guess who I just got a call from," he went on, sounding almost jocular and arousing her suspicions even more.

"Who?"

"Brant McClure."

"Brant McClure!" Alexis exclaimed. "What on earth—"

"It seems he wants to sign the lease again."

"What! You've got to be joking! Daddy, did you pull something with him?"

"Alexis, please, have a little respect for me. *He* called me and asked to sign the lease. Apparently he feels that he made a solemn promise and is obligated to go through with the deal no matter what you did to the copies he signed."

"I can't believe that." Alexis sat down on the side of her bed, stunned. Brant lease his land voluntarily to Alec? The idea was absurd!

"He obviously has a deep sense of honor, one that I must say is frankly beyond me, but I'm not going to gripe about it. Anyway, your secretary is typing new copies of the lease, and they should be ready tomorrow morning. I want you to come by the office and get them, then take them to McClure for his signature."

"Hold on a minute, there. You seem to be forgetting something. I don't work for Stone Oil any more."

"Alexis, this is a job you were working on when you quit. It was your baby. No one else knows anything about it. You have to finish what you started. Especially since it was something *you* did that makes it necessary to do the whole thing over again."

"Daddy, you know as well as I that any moron could take the papers up there. Send one of your assistants."

"It just so happens that I don't want any 'moron' to handle this, Alexis. It's your responsibility."

"No. I am simply not going to do it. I have had enough of Brant McClure. Get somebody else to do it."

"Alexis, I can't. When McClure called me this afternoon, he was very specific about your being the one to bring him the lease."

"What?" Alexis's stomach gave a leap. "He asked for me?"

"Yes. He told me that he was willing to go ahead with the deal, but only if you'd deliver the documents to him in Barrett. Now, it's a peculiar stipulation, I agree, but a fairly simple one. You just pick up the copies tomorrow morning, get in your plane, and fly up there. You can be home tomorrow evening."

Alexis was suddenly afraid and excited at the same time. She could think of nothing to say. What did this mean? Did Brant want her back? Or did he want to humiliate her further?

She should not go. She knew that. It would be all too easy for her to give in to him, to believe whatever stories he told her. She would have two enemies to fight if she went—herself and Brant. No, no, it would definitely not be a wise move.

"Okay, Daddy. I'll do it for you, then," she heard herself say.

"That's my girl. Your secretary said she'd have the lease ready by ten o'clock."

Alexis hung up, still stunned by what she had agreed to do. She would be walking straight into the lion's den! Why had she been so foolish as to accept Brant's demand?

"Because I want to see him again," she whispered aloud, and knew that she could not deny it.

The next morning Alexis rose and dressed carefully in a tan, businesslike pants suit, one that she considered suitably crisp and unrevealing of her figure. A knot of fear gnawed at her stomach, and in the clear light of day she regretted her rash agreement of yesterday. She had been caught off guard and stupidly pleased by Brant's insistence that she come to Barrett. Today she was more coolheaded, more aware of the danger that lay before her.

She drove to the Stone Building a little after ten and went up to Betty's office. It felt strange to walk down the familiar hall and know that she no longer worked there. Already the surroundings seemed to belong in her distant past.

Betty greeted her with a smile and held out a manila folder. "Whew!" she exclaimed. "I tell you, I did those in a hurry, but they're perfect. When your father called *me* yesterday and asked me to type up the copies, I nearly fell apart. I sat right down and typed away, then reread them about a million times to make sure they were perfect."

Alexis laughed. "Don't let him overawe you. I've found out that's the worst thing you can do with him. Pretend he doesn't scare you at all, and he'll respect you for it."

"Easy for you to say," the other woman scoffed with a friendly smile. "What happened to the first batch I typed, anyway?"

"I had a momentary dysfunction of the brain— nothing serious."

"What?" Betty said in confusion, but Alexis merely waved and left.

She drove quickly along the Central and across Mockingbird to Addison Airport. There she filed her flight plan, obtained clearance, and was soon on her way to Barrett.

An hour and a half later Alexis smoothly set her Cessna down on the Thompson landing strip and approached the blue Chevy that sat at the end of the runway. She thought of stopping off to see Beth before her confrontation with Brant, but she quickly brushed the idea aside. She was impatient to get the thing over with. Or was it that she was impatient to see Brant? a tiny inner voice inquired.

Covering the rutted land at a much more sedate pace than Beth had done, she reached the highway and headed for the McClure ranch, her palms on the steering wheel growing sweatier by the moment. She wondered nervously what Brant would say when he saw her again. What would he do? What would she do, for that matter?

Her heart gave a sickening lurch as she turned down the long driveway and saw the house ahead. Alexis realized with amazement that she had actually been homesick for this old place. With the same new awareness, she looked around at the landscape and found it strangely beautiful.

When her car stopped in front of the house, the door

burst open and Paul catapulted down the steps, yelling, "Allie! Allie!"

A sweet anguish tore at her chest at the sight of the boy, and Alexis flung open the door and ran out to meet him. Paul threw his arms around her, clinging tightly, shouting incomprehensible things. Alexis hugged him close; she had forgotten how good it felt to hold him in her arms.

Finally he released her enough to stand back and begin to jabber. "Allie, did you come to stay? Daddy said you might come, but he didn't know. Oh, I'm so glad you came!"

"Me, too," Alexis said, then hastily amended that. "I'm glad to see you again."

"Daddy's in the barn. You want me to go call him?"

"No, not right now," Alexis replied quickly. "Why don't you and I sit down and talk a little first?"

"Okay. Did you know that Daddy got me a teacher?" Paul asked as they walked into the living room and sat down.

"No, really?"

"Yeah. He used to be in the army, and he even speaks the same language I do. Daddy said he's going to teach me how to read and write and add and subtract and multiply and everything! Then I can go to school, but I'd rather stay here and help on the ranch."

"Well, when you go to school, you'll learn a lot, and someday you'll be able to do more and better things here because of what you've learned."

"Honest?"

"Honest. Now, tell me, how are you doing? Are you enjoying yourself?"

"Yeah, most of the time. But, I miss you. I wish you'd come back and live with us. Daddy misses you, too. He told me so. Why don't you want to live here?"

"It isn't quite that simple, Paul."

"Then what is it?"

Alexis sighed. "It's very hard to explain, Paul. I don't think you would understand."

"Neither do I, apparently," a low, masculine voice said from the doorway, and Alexis jumped.

Seeing Brant looking lean and handsome in his jeans and rancher's jacket, Alexis felt a familiar tingling pulsate through her body. She knew instantly that she should not have come. She could never hold up against him, not with the power he still exercised over her.

She rose shakily. "Hello, Brant. You surprised me."

"Not as much as you've surprised me," he remarked. His eyes were blazing, and for a moment she feared that he might stride cross the room and take her in his arms.

"Get the lease," he said abruptly, "and bring it into my office. I want to talk to you. Paul, why don't you find something to play with while Alexis and I talk?"

Alexis bristled, as always, at his domineering manner, but she reminded herself that soon she would no longer have to put up with it. There was no point in getting angry about it now. She started toward the door to get the folder from the front seat of the car, where she had left it, but Brant did not move out of her way, and she had to sidle past him, so close that she could feel the warmth of his body and smell the clean male scent of him. His nearness scared her.

When Alexis returned to the house with the copies of the lease, she went down the hall to the small room that served as Brant's office. Brant sat nonchalantly on the corner of the large desk, and his presence was overpowering in the tiny space.

Alexis thrust the documents at him, almost as a defense. Brant took them, flipped through them idly, and leaned over his desk to sign both copies. He handed the papers back to her, and Alexis clutched them to her chest. An awkward silence hung between them.

Finally she asked, "Why did you agree to sign again? After I tore up the originals, you were free of obligation to us!"

He shrugged. "I felt I ought to stick to my deal."

"The Code of the West?" Alexis sneered.

"No, just mine," he replied evenly. "Besides, I suddenly realized that I didn't hate your father so much any more. It no longer ripped out my guts to think of him drilling on my land. Somewhere along the way I lost a lot of my old bitterness."

"I see."

"There was one other reason—the main one."

"Oh?"

"I did it so that you'd have to come here again."

"Why?" Alexis persisted.

"Paul misses you," he answered quietly, looking away from her.

"You dragged me up here so that Paul could see me?"

"No, so that I could see you. I—I miss you, too. And I had a very important question I wanted to ask you."

Alexis's breath caught in her throat. "What?"

For a moment he looked at the floor, avoiding her eyes, then asked, as though the words were torn from him, "Why did you tear up that lease, Alexis?"

She stared at him. "Why! Surely you can't be that stupid!" Her voice turned brittle, and unshed tears sparkled suddenly in her eyes. "I couldn't stand to do it to you, that's why. I simply couldn't hurt you that way. I loved you!"

A hushed silence followed her words, and then she spoke in a sarcastic tone. "It must give you a lot of pleasure to have conquered me so. How satisfying it must be for you to get back at the Stone family this way!"

"No, Alexis, it didn't give me any satisfaction. I've had no pleasure at all since the day you left this house. Good God, woman, if you felt that way, why did you leave me?"

"Because I wasn't going to stay here and take the humiliation you love to heap on me," Alexis retorted.

"I handed you back your land, exposed my feeling for you, and what did you do? You ran off to Amarillo to visit your girlfriend!"

"Beth told me you had some crazy idea about my going to see Libby, but I could hardly believe it. Why didn't you stay for at least a while and let me explain? Why did you have so little trust in me, so little faith?"

"Faith! Trust! Don't make me laugh! Why should I have trusted you? I knew she'd been your mistress even after you started sleeping with me."

"That's not true!"

"You slept with her the night she visited here! First you made love to her, and then you came crawling into my bed!"

"I didn't sleep with Libby that night, or at any other time since I met you—even before you brought Paul here."

"Don't lie to me, Brant. I heard you come up the stairs and the two of you go into your bedroom together."

"Then if you have such keen hearing, you should have heard the argument Libby and I had there. And you must have heard her slam out of the house a few minutes later."

Alexis stared at him, her eyes wide with amazement and disbelief. "But you went to Amarillo. Paul said that you wouldn't tell him why because he might tell me. Why else—"

Brant snorted. "I thought lawyers weren't supposed to jump to conclusions! I'll tell you what I went there for. I went to get that present you didn't want. Remember? The one you knocked out of my hand and into the mud." He reached across the desk in a swift, fluid movement, grasped the square jewelry box that sat there, and extended it to her. "Here, take this and look at it. Tell me why, if I didn't love you, if I was sneaking around with Libby while I was there, I bought this for you!"

Hesitantly, Alexis reached out to take the box, and

with trembling fingers opened it. On the blue velvet cushion inside lay a set of rings, one a solid gold band, the other a brilliant diamond solitaire. An engagement ring . . . a wedding band. A cold hand clutched at her lungs, squeezing the air out, and Alexis stared at the rings, hardly able to speak.

"But—but this—this wasn't the box," she stammered.

"No. Like an idiot, I was trying to surprise you and had the salesman put the ring box inside a watch box." He paused and then continued, his voice husky with emotion, "Alexis, please, I ache for you. I want you to come back. I feel empty without you. Do you want me to humble myself before you? I will. I'm begging you, Alexis. Marry me."

Alexis gazed at him with wide eyes. He loved her; he wanted to marry her. She could not deal with her sudden, swirling emotions. With all her heart she wanted to cry out that she would marry him, but another part of her held back in shock and skepticism.

"Brant, I—what about all our differences? About my family, your land, the oil? That's all still there. How could we get married?"

"I want to marry you, not your family. I told you before, all my hurt and bitterness have disappeared. I found love with you. And I found that I no longer hate your father. I've signed the lease, I agreed to let them drill, and I won't regret it. There have been a lot of misunderstandings between us, a lot of twisted feelings. But despite all that, I love you. I know you're not the deceptive bitch I said you were. I've seen you since, with me and Paul and Beth, and I know that my very first instinct was right. It was my brain that messed everything up. I love you, Alexis. I want us to start over, to forget all the bad things between us."

"Can we?"

"Yes!" he declared vehemently. "I know we can. I'm sure of it."

"Oh, Brant, I don't know." Alexis sat down shakily

in his leather chair. "What about my career? I—I couldn't just spend my life in Barrett being a housewife."

"Who said anything about that?" Brant demanded. "I'm not the chauvinist you claim I am. I'm not asking you to give up your career. There are lawyers in Barrett and in the towns around here . . . and the biggest specialty is oil and gas, which I believe you have some expertise in. Oh, no, Alexis, you can't use that as an excuse."

He turned angrily away from her and hurled himself across the room, slamming his hand against the wall. "Damn it, Alexis, face up to it! It's not your career, or Libby, or anything else. What's bothering you now is what made you scamper out of here like a scared rabbit—you're frightened of your own feelings. You're too tied to your father."

"That's not true!" Alexis flared.

"No? Then you tell me what the problem is. Why do you say you love me but refuse to marry me?"

Alexis stared at him, the words sticking in her throat. Emitting an inarticulate sound, Brant closed his eyes briefly, as if to wipe away some painful vision, then strode out of his office.

For a moment Alexis stood as if paralyzed, listening to the retreating thud of his boots and the slam of the back door. Suddenly she raced after him, her heart thudding violently. Over and over in her head beat the dire warning that he was out of her life for good, simply because she had been so idiotically indecisive.

"Brant!" she screamed, tumbling out the kitchen door and running toward the garage. "Brant, wait, don't go! Please." Tears were streaming down her face, but she ignored them and hurtled into the dark garage, only to find he wasn't there. Quickly, she darted back outside and glanced anxiously around her. She spotted him leaning against the fence, staring moodily into the corral. "Brant!" she shouted again, and sped toward him.

At the sound of her approach he turned, his face suddenly eager with hope. "Alexis!" He began to walk toward her, then broke into a run, his arms outstretched.

"I love you," she cried as she flung herself against his broad chest. "Oh, Brant, I've been such a fool. I love you, and I want to marry you. There's nothing else in the world I want to do. I'm miserable without you."

"Oh, Alexis, Alexis," he breathed, wrapping his arms around her and burying his face in her hair. At last he felt a supreme peace. At last he had come home. "I love you," he said simply.

Alexis raised her head, and Brant gave her a long, searching look before he lowered his lips to hers in a clinging kiss.

41